DORIAN GRAY:
DARKER SHADES

Micah S. Harris

Peter Rawlik

Kevin Heim

David MacDowell Blue

T. Casey Brennan

Robert E. Wronski, Jr.

Christofer Nigro

Cover design: David MacDowell Blue with
embellishments by Elden Ardiente
(https://ldnrdnt.com/ & rdnt.arts@yahoo.com.au)

Preface art: Joshua Torrito
(Brokenrocketart@gmail.com)

Special thanks to Wild Hunt editing staff Matt
Hickman and Gordon Long for their important

contributions, and to James Bojaciuk, CEO of 18thWall Productions, for his invaluable contributions to this anthology's Timeline!

DEDICATIONS

This book is dedicated to my grandmother, Gertrude "Trudie" Nigro, who has always been my best friend and the greatest person in my life, and to the memory of my grandfather, Thomas James Nigro and my beloved aunt, Concetta "Connie" Denisco. Much love also to the memories of my Aunt Marie and Uncle Pete, who always supported me and believed I would someday achieve success.

Many thanks to the great creative mind of Chuck Loridans for not only bringing the world MONSTAAH and his theories regarding the Dracula soul-clones and Frankenstein lineage & copycat monsters but also for suggesting this very anthology. Equal thanks go to the work of creative mythographers Win Scott Eckert and Sean Lee Levin for their respective work on expanding Philip José Farmer's Wold Newton Universe into the Crossover Universe. The work these three did in building MONSTAAH and the Crossover Universe did much to inspire me creatively and set the standard and foundation of the Wild Hunt Universe I am now constructing, beginning officially with this very publication.

Beyond the above, I dedicate this tome to anyone whom the various contributors may have wanted to dedicate it to; as well as to the memory of Oscar Wilde for daring to be different – and the numerous fans of his greatest literary creation, Dorian Gray, particularly those who have always wanted to see a publication devoted entirely to new tales of this amazing character's multi-shaded exploits.

Table of Contents

PREFACE

From the Mansion of the Macabre...

Greetings, Pundits of the Profane and the Paranormal! (How was that for alliteration? Thankfully, I am someplace where I won't have to see your eyes roll or listen to your jeers! Ha!) This is Mike Nero, also known as Beowolf, admitted werewolf and monster hunter extraordinaire! You may not have heard of me yet, but that's okay, because eventually you will. I hope. Unless I'm killed first, or exiled to some Hell dimension, or you simply do not bother to buy any books recording my exploits. Hey, all that can happen, especially to me.

Anyhoo, enough of my belaboring the point -- which I have an annoying habit of doing, by the way. I am coming to you from the Mansion of the Macabre and its stored records of the dark and the mysterious to say a few things about the contents of the volume you are now reading. Whether it's in digital form or one of the gloriously old-fashioned printed tomes containing ink rather than pixels, it really doesn't matter. The point is you're *reading* this! And that means you're clearly a fan of Dorian Gray's sinister but incredible saga.

Okay, maybe you're not that much of a fan, and you're only reading this because someone gave you the book as a gift and you do not want to feel guilty by simply using it as a coaster for your drinks, or as a door stop, etc., et al., blah blah blah, you get the gist. In any case, you're reading this, so you're stuck seeing these words! Or hearing them, if you activated the audio selection on your tablet. But, yanno what I mean; there's no need to get technical here!

Alright, where was I? And how the Hel did I get here in the first place? And why am I talking to people who likely live in a whole other universe? And why in regard to some tome about Dorian Gray? I dunno, I just am, so maybe I should get back to doing that before the people reading this get even more annoyed with my tangents than usual and skip over the whole damn thing!

So… Dorian Gray. Yes, Dorian. I haven't run into him yet, but it would be interesting if I did. Because I have personally yearned for what he managed to achieve: eternal youth without having to worry about all the nasty things that happen to your body when you age; or catching one of the plethora of nasty illnesses that mortals are prone to be afflicted with even when they're young. I have some measure of resistance to these things thanks to my being a lycanthrope, but nothing like the level enjoyed by Dorian!

Whether you're willing to admit it or not, you have likely yearned for these attributes too, even if just a *little* bit. If not, then you're sort of weird; but at any rate, I am betting my entire arsenal of monster-fighting paraphernalia that you have sometimes been just a trite curious about what it must be like to have an endless number of years and youth ahead of you. And to have the potential to grace the world with your presence and royal ass-holiness forever.

Since such thoughts have likely crossed your mind at one time or another – especially after you notice your first wrinkles or gray hairs; or you or someone in your fam has a serious cancer scare; or you feel that first pain in your shoulder when trying to lift a box you've lifted with no problem for years prior to that; or some other reminder that you're not going to be here forever, and you're not going to be able to ignore the inglorious setbacks of advancing age forever, blah blah blah -- you may have wondered what price you may be willing to pay for such an amazing and precious gift.

What if such a price is more than just a few dollars and the secrets of your awesome pizza-making recipe? What if the price is nothing less than your soul, possibly in more than one sense of the word?

What might such a gift do to your personal ethics if you had far less consequences for your actions to be concerned about than the typical asshole you may live with, work with, or regularly guzzle down a couple of brews with? Will you end up becoming not only the biggest asshole in a world that already has far too many of those already? And, worst of all, one who never dies or at least suffers unduly for getting kicked in the groin?

How would the numerous people you met throughout the unending decades be affected by you? Would you even care? And even if you did, in what *way* would you care?

What might happen when you crossed paths with the handful of others in the world who managed to achieve the same thing you did? What types of friends, enemies, and frenemies (that is a word now, right?) would you make over such a lengthy span of years? I mean, just think about the number of enemies, both blatant and covert, *you* managed to make in just *twenty* years of living! Considering how bad *they* were to deal with, now try to imagine the type of enemies you would make when operating within the milieu that Dorian does. Not only would some rather powerful good people be pissed with the very idea of you, but so would other powerful assholes like yourself.

And what if your immortality wasn't exactly secure, and you had to constantly protect and periodically perform some form of costly upkeeping of a certain object your eternal life depended upon? What if something happened to that object? What if someone stole it? What if you accidentally slipped one day while carrying it and smashed it like the clumsy oaf you are?

So yea, even though you may have a potentially never-ending life with no worries about aging or disease, it wouldn't exactly be an eternal life free of some rather serious concerns.

Those questions and situations are a constant part of Dorian's life as it progresses through an endless succession of years. But they aren't the only questions that pertain specifically to Mr. Gray. All of which are also directly confronted within the stories contained herein.

For instance…

What happens if someone like Dorian knocks heads with the likes of Becky Sharp, Dracula, Prof. Septimus Pretorius, and other perilously powerful personages (ha! More alliteration!), and Lovecraftian forces beyond even his reckoning? How interesting might it be if he shares a drink with none other than Carmilla Karnstein in all her blood-sucking beauty and glory?

And what may happen as a result of Dorian's story inspiring a creative dude like author T. Casey Brennan in a whole other universe where Dorian is *actually* nothing more than a fictional character in a novel… yanno, just like the general public in *my* universe incorrectly believe him to be? (At least as far as I know! I'm not fully informed on those weird-ass mundane universes with such rigid laws of physics like the one *you* probably live in!).

What consequences may Dorian have incurred for his brutal murder of Basil Hallward, the ill-fated young painter who first created that damn portrait of another young man he made the mistake of admiring?

After all, poor Basil has no way of getting back at Dorian now that he's dead, amirite? I mean, whoever manages to exact retribution from beyond the grave? It just can't happen! Killing someone has always been a totally reliable means of dealing with a person you need out of the way permanently, is that not the truth? Well, maybe you should read "The Hallward Restorations" in this very volume before you become too comfortable with that assumption. And that's all I'm gonna say on that!

Then we get to what may be the ultimate questions. What, exactly, is the source of the mysterious supernatural forces young Hallward tapped into when creating the portrait that conferred immortality upon Dorian, thus allowing him to continue his debauchery and bizarre adventures indefinitely? And is Dorian the only beneficiary of such a cursed work of art?

The answers to all the above are provided in the tales found within this collection, so read on! See what it's like to be Dorian Gray throughout his over 150 years of life, and all that can happen to a never-dying asshole and the various people he meets throughout that span of years. And in places as diverse as 1919 New England, 1970s Chicago, and modern day Providence.

Okay, I said all that. Can I go now? Or, wake up now? Or... how exactly am I here in the first place...?

Silence...

INTRODUCTION: DORIAN GRAY – WHO HE IS, HOW HE CAME TO BE

Micah S. Harris

"A case of nature imitating art" – the British Press's description of Oscar Wilde after he had gained so much weight that he began to resemble his fictional precursor "Reginald Bunthorne" from Gilbert and Sullivan's *Patience, or the Wedding of Reginald Bunthorne*.

"Caricature is the tribute which mediocrity pays to genius" – Oscar Wilde, who was a spectator in the audience on the opening night of *Patience, or the Wedding of Reginald Bunthorne*.

"It is the spectator, not life, that art really mirrors" – Oscar Wilde, Preface to *The Picture of Dorian Gray*.

The Picture of... Reginald Bunthorne?

More than one scholar has noted that, for a man who held the Aesthetic principle that there was no relationship between art and life, Oscar Wilde's own life was one where the line was crossed more than once. Like his character Dorian Gray, Wilde would also both gain and lose because of this transgression. And the losses, when they came, would be immeasurable.

15

Despite his retort to Gilbert and Sullivan's fictional Reginald Bunthorne's association with his true self, the fact is Oscar Wilde's initial notoriety *was* as a caricature, not a writer. Historians differ on whether Wilde was a model for Reginald Bunthorne, or if after the fact, Wilde simply became a living canvas on which to paint the portrait of the character to promote the D'Oyly Carte Opera Company's stateside tour of *Patience*.

In either scenario, it was part of D'Oyly Carte's publicity stunt that Wilde would make a tour of America lecturing on the proper appreciation of beauty for its own sake. This was the basic doctrine of the Aesthetic movement of which Wilde was a part, and Reginald Bunthorne was a parody.

The intersection of art and life that had led to this opportunity could not have come at a better time for Oscar Wilde. The prodigious lad from Ireland, whose extravagant aesthetic and sensual tastes did not make him a particularly good fit for parochial Dublin, had gotten his ticket out when he won a scholarship to Oxford. But he had tripped going out the door with the hoped for subsequent literary career. And his personal life was on wobbly feet as well.

His initial publication, a book of poetry, sold out its 750 print run. However, it managed to be both ruled plagiarism by the Oxford Union *and* also be panned elsewhere as Wilde's original verse ("The poet is Wilde but his poetry's tame," said *Punch* magazine in a very Wilde-like quip).

Wilde's book's publication also ended his relationship with society painter Frank Miles. He had already lost his suit for the lovely Florence Balcombe (who would marry the next guy, one with much better prospects -- a gentleman named Bram Stoker). Wilde had been, in fact, conducting a homosexual affair with Miles behind Florence's back.

Though he and Miles' relationship had, at this point, long ceased to be sexual (Oscar could not abide kissing a man with a moustache), Frank's father read Wilde's poems and realized his son's live-in buddy liked men *that* way and wanted Frank *out*. But it was Wilde who left – stormily.

That same year of 1881, Gilbert and Sullivan produced a play called *Patience, or the Wedding of Reginald Bunthorne*. The character of Bunthorne was a parody of the then new Victorian Aesthete, but initially owed more to painter James Whistler as a model than Wilde. It was Wilde, though, who would become, as it has been put, "the poster boy of Aestheticism:" the picture of Reginald Bunthorne.

Indeed, the outfits he wore on his lecture tour were fashioned after those designed for the Bunthorne character in *Patience* (though Wilde had his own hand in his lecture wardrobe as well).

As described by *New York World*, "He wore patent leather shoes, a smoking cap or turban, and his shirt might be termed ultra-Byronic... a sky blue cravat of the sailor style hung well down upon his chest. His hair flowed over his shoulders in dark brown waves, curling slightly upwards at the end."

Like his later character Dorian Gray, Wilde had turned art into life. And, like Gray, at first the transgression of his own Aesthetic principle was working out pretty well for him.

The Fantastic Variations

Although the tour was a success, Wilde's subsequent attempts to revive his literary career were not. Abandoning poetry for potentially more lucrative forms of writing, he became a playwright. Editing for *Woman's Day* and continuing to lecture paid the bills. But his New York play bombed and a planned production in France was aborted when the actress supporting it abandoned the project. Wilde turned from scripts to prose and began publishing his original fairy tales. Among these were "The Selfish Giant," the poignant story of the eponymous giant who encounters unawares the Christ Child twice, the second time at the giant's death.

In 1889, Wilde, along with Sir Arthur Conan Doyle and fellow author T.P. Gill, met over dinner with J.M. Stoddart, an editor for *Lippincott's Monthly Magazine*. Stoddart was soliciting novellas for the magazine. Out of this one meal came two Victorian classics: Arthur Conan Doyles' Sherlock Holmes tale *The Sign of Four* and, of course, *The Picture of Dorian Gray*.

Wilde's original offering to *Lippincott's*, however, was one of his fairy tales, "The Fisherman and His Soul," which *Lippincott's* turned down because it wasn't the novella length tale Stoddart had solicited, and because they found it "more suitable for children."

Really? Did any of the editorial staff at *Lippincott's* actually *read* it?

Of course, they did. The fact is, adults were as hot for original fairy tales in the nineteenth century as they are for *Wicked* and *Frozen* in the twenty-first. More likely, the story was rejected for being found *not* suitable for children – or *Lippincott's* adult readership for that matter.

My thought is that Wilde wrote "The Fisherman and His Soul" in the contemporary Symbolist style of painting, invoking fantastic images outside of nature to address concepts that cannot be approached directly. The irony is that "The Fisherman and His Soul" manages to address alternative sexuality *more* directly than even *The Picture of Dorian Gray* (which *Lippincott's* published only after Wilde had muted the homosexual content).

But the world can thank the editor for that rejection, my friends, because now Wilde had a paying gig but no story. And so, he had to come up with *The Picture of Dorian Gray,* a popular classic that "The Fisherman and His Soul" never became, and which probably would have never been written otherwise, given the turn of Wilde's career, as we shall see.

As Wilde searched for a new idea for a story to replace the rejected one, his thoughts went back to his honeymoon reading while in France. Oscar had married the former Constance Lloyd in an apparent attempt to conform sexually and socially. He *did* find her physically appealing – at least initially – and was able to get enthused about the situation enough to father two sons with her.

Constance herself is a sad figure who had been madly in love with Wilde and had wanted nothing more than to marry him. She was probably, as a Victorian woman, oblivious to the fact that sexual attraction between men was in the realm of reality.

So, while honeymooning with a blissfully ignorant Constance, Wilde picked up a French book called *A Rebours* (*Against the Grain*) by Joris Karl Huysmans – no doubt attracted to it because it was scandalous, cutting edge decadent literature.

Alternative sexual experience is present in the text, but that doesn't seem to be what particularly inspired Wilde – I don't think he needed any encouragement along those lines. Instead, it gave him the idea for what he later called a "fantastic variation" on the novel which he felt compelled to write down someday. That someday would come with the rejection by *Lippincott's* of "The Fisherman and His Soul" and Wilde suddenly needing a new story. And that story, of course, became *The Picture of Dorian Gray*.

My theory is the central conceit on which Wilde would do his variation came from one particular and outstandingly bizarre episode in an overall bizarre novel.

The protagonist of *A Rebours* is a hedonist – no, make that *debauchee* – who indulges himself in a series of decadent and surreal episodes to acquire new sensations outside the regular pleasures offered in nature. In one sequence, he embeds gems into a live tortoise's shell, an attempt to make art out of life. But the creature cannot bear the weight of the stones – nor real life, the unbearable ideal of being art – and it kills him.

And there we have the "moral" of *The Picture of Dorian Gray* in a tortoise shell.

For, the protagonist of *A Rebours* does here something very similar to what Dorian Gray will do later. Dr. Donald Lawler, former editor of *The Victorian Journal* and the editor of the first Norton Critical Edition of *The Picture of Dorian Gray*, expresses it succinctly in one of his textual notes: "…his error was to try to realize an aesthetic ideal in his life and thus to make life into an art form of self-gratification."

Wilde's transformative use of the idea (like Chaucer and Shakespeare, he superseded his source material) was for his protagonist to turn, not another living creature, but *himself* into art. Thus, he receives upon his own person the penalty for presuming to seize for his own advantage the properties and privileges unique to the aesthetic realm.

Dorian as the subject of the portrait is a captured transitory moment of masculine beauty in nature that should have remained transitory in the proper flux of material things. But Dorian as a human being exchanges places with his image in an attempt to defy the natural order and extend his sensual existence forever (the same motif is present in the character of Lord Henry Wotton's tobacco addiction: he is trying to maintain a moment of pleasure indefinitely by repeating it).

According to Lawler, Dorian sees his portrait as "...self-absolving (him) from the effects of a life of self-indulgence." The irony, of course, is that the portrait, instead of absolving him, puts his sinful soul on display, and becomes an externalization of the failure of self-absolution.

There were other literary antecedents besides *A Rebours*. Most significantly, and oddly enough, Dorian's last name seems to originate with Prime Minister Benjamin Disraeli's anonymously published *Vivian Gray* (1826). The last name of the eponymous character is particularly suspicious because *Vivian Gray* features a fantastical portrait which reveals a mystic link with its subject, when, at the death of said subject, who is described as "a beautiful being," the portrait's eyes begin to move!

Dorian's first name comes not from literature, but ancient Greek culture and history, of which Wilde had long been an enthusiast. The Dorians were the last tribe to migrate to Greece, and, according to some historians, the ones who brought pederasty with them. This was a homosexual relationship in which an older man sexually dominated an adolescent male. Once the young man had a beard, society would hold him in contemptuous ridicule if he continued to be the passive partner during sex. That relationship, no longer recognizable as pederasty, was expected to come to an end.

Wilde's *"Dorian" Gray*, then, would appear not to be about the character's wish for mere eternal youth but wish fulfillment for a particular *fetishized* eternal youth. Freezing the natural biological process at the moment when adolescence is at its most boyish would allow the older man who practices pederasty perpetual dominance of the object of his desire.

In fact, this type of dominance describes the Lord Henry Wotton/Dorian Gray relationship in the novel. Wotton, the older man, does take control over the ever-dewy fresh Dorian through his pernicious influence. And, in one version of Wilde's story (there are at least three), the two men spent time together at a get-away that was a known vacation spot specifically favored by homosexuals as a retreat in the Victorian era.

Small wonder that Wilde's original manuscript submitted to *Lippincott's* was toned down before publication. Even so, enough homoerotic content came through that *The Picture of Dorian Gray*'s initial reception, was, shall we say, less than warm. With such accolades as "unclean," "contaminating," and "grubbing" is it any wonder *The Picture of Dorian Gray* was Wilde's last work of prose fiction?

Wilde then turned his talents back to the theater and this go 'round he was a phenomenal success. He eventually had three plays running simultaneously in London's West End. How big was that? My fellow writers, how would you like to have three hit plays running on Broadway at the same time? Yeah – THAT big!

But around the period of his greatest success, Wilde once again broke his own Aesthetic principle and tried to turn art into life. This time the results would not be as advantageous as his assumption of the identity of Reginald Bunthorne. This time the results would be a disaster.

As with his titular character in his only novel, Oscar fell in love with a person who seemed indeed to be the embodiment of an Aesthetic ideal. Unfortunately, Lord Alfred Douglas was no Sybil Vane. And, in a wicked inverse of the novel, this time it would be the lover, not the beloved, who was destroyed by the object of his affection's inability to live up to the perfect image.

The NEW Reginald Bunthorne – Dorian Gray Team!

This was what happened when the image of Reginald Bunthorne met the very picture of Dorian Gray.

Lord Alfred "Bosie" Douglas claimed to be the biggest *Dorian Gray* fan ever. He could even quote long passages from memory to Wilde. Perhaps he would have presented Wilde with his own Dorian Gray fan fiction if the concept had existed at the time. But then, why write about it? Bosie was *living* the life of Dorian Gray: he possessed both Gray's blond handsomeness and some of the *mal vivant*'s better attributes: "spoiled, reckless, and insolent."

Pictures of him and Wilde together have survived, and one particular photo of Lord Alfred "Bosie" Douglas is indeed "the picture of Dorian Gray" – at least, with the expression it would have been sporting after it had been locked upstairs in the schoolroom long enough for Dorian to have become mean-spirited and dissipated.

Anyone looking into those eyes and that face from the distance of over a century can see this boy is obviously trouble. Wilde, at a distance of less than an inch, appears oblivious. Here, Oscar is the epitome of "love is blind." And deaf. And *dumb*. Of course, he knew that flaunting his homosexual lifestyle in general and doing it with Bosie in particular, was courting self-destruction; he called it "feasting with panthers." And he was about to be raked, bitten, and nigh-eviscerated.

At this point in his career, a new Wilde play was such an event that even the Prince of Wales attended the premiere of what will become Oscar's most well-remembered piece for the theater, *The Importance of Being Earnest*. It will also be his swan song for old Thespis. For not everyone was wild about Wilde: enter Bosie's father, John Douglas, the 9th Marquess of Queensbury.

Wilde's relationship with Bosie was probably especially personally humiliating for The Marquess because he was a noted "manly" sports enthusiast who sponsored the regulation of the testosterone charged competition of two people violently pummeling and pounding each other. For Bosie's sire was none other than the Marquess of Queensbury of "Marquess of Queensbury Rules" of boxing fame (though actually written by John Graham Chambers).

25

He was, then, the most stereotypically manliest of manly Victorian era men that had produced a son who was… not so much.

In retaliation against Wilde, the Marquess planned to ruin a performance of *The Importance of Being Earnest* by presenting Wilde with a bouquet of rotten vegetables. Wilde was tipped off and the scheme came a cropper. But Bosie's father was resilient. And he had it in for Oscar Wilde, whom he apparently blamed for ruining Bosie's character.

To be fair, the Marquess had just lost another son in a "hunting accident" that was rumored to actually have been a suicide due to his being involved in a secret homosexual relationship with the British Prime Minister. The Marquess was desperate to save his younger son from a relationship with Wilde, which he foresaw bringing Bosie to a similar fate.

The truth was that Bosie was the bad influence on Wilde. It was Bosie who introduced Oscar into the Victorian underworld of gay prostitution, and consequently Wilde began indulging himself from time to time in liaisons with young working class men who sold themselves as "rough trade." But due to Wilde's popularity in the Victorian "entertainment industry," he was the one who was "high profile," the older man, and thus an easy scapegoat for young "impressionable" Bosie.

And at least part of the Marquess' problem with his son had nothing to do with Bosie's sexuality – or Wilde's. Quite frankly, Lord Alfred Douglas was just a wretched example of a human being, a spoiled Narcissus. His dad was paying for his Oxford education and Bosie could have cared less. He was flunking out and running around in disreputable circles with Oscar when he should have been studying. And he just enjoyed p.o.-ing his father.

Wilde, the poor sap, was in love with Bosie, despite a tempestuous relationship in which Oscar typically ended up being used. As with any of Dorian Gray's fictional admirers, whether man or woman, Wilde's erotic fascination with Bosie would be a ruinous and ultimately fatal one.

After the failure of the rotten vegetable gambit, the Marquess left a note in plain view at Wilde's club where the members picked up their mail. It was addressed to: "For Oscar Wilde Posing (?) Sodomite." Wilde was obviously very displeased, but Bosie was all a-glee, at least secretly. For now, he had a way to get back at his father. He egged Oscar on to sue the Marquess for libel. Oscar was willing to let it go, but, oh no, that didn't suit Bosie.

So, Wilde sued. The short of it was, the Marquess came out smelling like a rose. More, he seized the opportunity to countersue Wilde and succeeded in having him arrested for gross indecency.

By the time of the guilty verdict, both England *and* America were already thoroughly revolted by Oscar Wilde and his lifestyle as put on public display in the courtroom by the Marquess of Queensbury. Now his name was taken off the marquee of theaters that continued to perform his plays – but refused to pay Wilde one farthing of a royalty for the privilege. Thus, they managed to both repudiate the man while profiting off his reputation.

Oxford blacked his name off his honorary plaque. His wife, Constance, changed her last name and those of their two boys, whom he was forbidden to see. To be fair, if this was the last straw for her, it was understandable. She had been desperately in love with him and had been rewarded with wrong -- make that *atrocious* -- treatment by Wilde at times during their marriage. And now she was an innocent suffering unspeakable public humiliation, all of it his fault.

(To her credit, when Wilde was imprisoned, Constance showed him the compassion of visiting him in jail to be certain he was personally and privately informed of the news of his beloved mother's death. Constance actually proceeded Oscar in death from a botched operation on her spine after a fall down the stairs. She was only 38).

The judge sentenced Wilde to two years of breaking rocks with a pick (he was lucky; just a few decades earlier, the sentence for his behavior in England would have been execution). Fortunately, his obvious lack of physical condition to wield a pick allowed some sensible show of compassion, and he was put in charge of the prison library and gardening instead. He was given the special privilege of being allowed to read in his cell but shorn of his long hair of which he was so proud (he cried as it was cut).

While in prison he fell, hurt his ear, and developed an infection that exacerbated into the illness that took his life a few years later.

Upon his release, Wilde went right back to Bosie (twice), but the two did not stay together long. Wilde became an alcoholic and was reduced to begging. After the Marquess of Queensbury died and left Bosie a fortune, the instigator of Wilde's ruin only ever grudgingly sent his former idol and lover mere monetary tokens, and only then at the urgings of Wilde's friends.

When Wilde himself wrote Bosie for money, begging an advance, he only received this response: "You are wheedling me like an old whore, Oscar. Quit bothering me about money."

One Final Relationship Between Art and Life

In 1895, Wilde had been at the pinnacle of his career: three plays running concurrently in London's West End, all of them hits.

Just five years later, he was dead, publicly disgraced, and disowned by his family. He had been financially ruined and lived his last years practically in exile. The firsthand account of his dying in an ugly Paris hotel room is painful to read.

Wilde died in a catatonic state, alone, except for two faithful friends and the hotel proprietor, at 2:00 p.m. November 30, 1900.

But Oscar had long made it known that he desired to receive a priest at dying, and one of those true friends with him at the end, a former lover named Robert Ross, saw to it that the request was honored.

In the last correlation between Wilde's art and his life, he became, not Dorian Gray, still seeking self-absolution at the end by stabbing the portrait of his wretched soul, but the repentant selfish giant of Wilde's fairy tale, who accepted "the wounds of love" on his behalf and was taken into the garden of God. For a man who loved beautiful things, could there be a better heaven?

A Popular Culture Legacy but A Paucity of Pro Prose for Dorian Gray

Although Wilde found, in his own day, his greatest success as a playwright, it has been his initially reviled *The Picture of Dorian Gray* that became his greatest literary legacy, both in academia and popular culture.

As of this writing, Dorian Gray's most recent pop culture incarnation in mainstream entertainment was on the *Penny Dreadful* television series and prequel comic book series follow-up by Titan Comics. He had first made his continued presence known in the 21st century in the film adaptation of *The League Extraordinary Gentlemen* (he is a filmic addition to the original comic book series). This, however, as *Dorian Gray: Darker Shades* editor and publisher Christofer Nigro has noted, isn't exactly Wilde's Dorian Gray, as he is given an immortal existence in the distant past -- long before the events of Wilde's novel, long enough to have seen "empires rise and fall." What the heck that's all about, or why that's supposed to be better, I have no idea.

Oddly enough, given Wilde's theatrical associations, no one seems to have been in a rush to mount a stage production of *The Picture of Dorian Gray*. According to Wikipedia's listing, that did not happen until the 1970s. The first movie adaptation, however, appeared ten years after Wilde's death, in a 1910 Danish silent film (the same year as the Thomas Edison *Frankenstein,* but beating out the first Dracula inspired movie by a decade!). Other silent versions followed. But the sound era brought us a classic with 1945's MGM production. The prop portrait here was painted by two men who specialized in forensic renderings of corpses, and its Technicolor reveal in a black and white film is still a flinch-inducing moment today.

George Saunders is the perfect Lord Henry. Unfortunately, Hurd Hatfield is a weak lead. His bland screen persona is serviceable enough in Dorian's early, naïve stage, but "dark" and "decadent" are beyond his acting range, which, to borrow a line from Dorothy Parker, runs the gamut from A to B.

Nevertheless, on the whole it is a wonderful production, and was the last attempt to put a picture of Dorian Gray on film until the sixties. At that point, Dorian became a denizen of the still relatively new medium of television with a handful of adaptations, one version featuring make-up by the great Dick Smith, who would later go on to realize the wretched countenance of Linda Blair in *The Exorcist*.

Unfortunately, TV also gave us a Dorian that is, I suppose, a feminist revisionist version of the classic about immortality that probably actually knocked a few years *off* Gloria Steinem's life if she was anywhere near a television when it aired. The movie is 1983's *The Sins of Dorian Gray*, and Dorian is now a female model whose image on her movie audition footage ages instead of her.

This exercise in girl power is from none other than Rankin and Bass, the same guys who bring you the animated *Rudolph the Red*

Nosed Reindeer every Christmas, not to mention classic monster kid movie matinee stuff like *King Kong Escapes* and *Mad Monster Party?* (both 1967). After having immersed themselves for years in kiddie fare, these two guys apparently decided it was time to announce to the rest of the world that they were, after all, conversant with how kids got here in the first place and gifted us all with the Rankin/Bass brand of bringing sexy back.

Thus, the guys who had previously only gotten as bawdy in their ballads as "Oh, ho, the mistletoe / Hung where you can see / Somebody waits for you / Kiss her once for me!" now aim for more piquant erotic verse in these lyrics from *The Sins of Dorian Gray*: "Someone who will fight with me / and spend the night with me – WHOA-WHOA!"

Cut to Dorian with a "I can't believe you went there – you are so *naughty*" smile on her face as she is inexplicably turned on by this lounge lizard at the piano. This, by the way, is the gender swapped version of Sybil Vane belting out this song. This is followed by a "sex scene" between the two. Trust me. There's more heat going on under the mistletoe in *Rudolph the Red Nosed Reindeer*.

So, given eternal youth via her audition footage, what does our female Dorian do with all the time in the world before her? Does she invest in the opportunities the modern feminist movement is opening up for women in the second half of the twentieth century with an eye ahead on the twenty-first?

Of course not. Feminism *schminism*; this is a *woman* we're talking about here. She decides it's all about looks, after all, and she'll spend her immortal life in an endless narcistic indulgence of vogueing as a living display for clothes, heels, hair, and make up.

(Let's be honest though: even with no eternal cover girl aspirations, how many women today can honestly say that they *wouldn't* want a selfie that keeps their boobs from sagging and absorbs all their cellulite? Matter of fact, I wouldn't mind one myself!).

Apparently, *The Sins of Dorian Gray* was enough of an artistic transgression to make an Aesthete like Dorian want to hide his true face like never before, because the character doesn't show it in public for another twenty years with *The League of Extraordinary Gentlemen* in 2003.

And suddenly, Dorian Gray was a hot property like never before. Seemingly anybody with just a camera on his phone wanted to do something with the character. *The League of Extraordinary Gentlemen* was immediately followed the next year by *three* cinematic resurrections in 2004! Before the first decade of the new millennium was done, there would be no less than *eight* new movies in total featuring Dorian Gray.

Dorian's new popularity extended into comics at this point as well. Although there had been graphic story adaptations of Wilde's original novel before (and continued to be), until the 2000s, no one seems to have ever used comics as a medium to convey further adventures of the character. Even the late Al "Horror Mood" Hewetson's script for "Dorian Gray, 2001" isn't an extrapolation of Dorian's misadventures in the sci-fi far future – which is what 2001 was when Hewetson wrote the story for a 1972 issue of *Creepy*. No, it's yet another retelling of the original, this one making Dorian a vampire! Trust me: it made for an edgy reversal for kids in the early '70s.

In the '70s and '80s, other comics' characters were finding Dorian "inspiring." Both occult investigators at Warren magazines (Barbara Vashi in *Vampirella*) and Sergio Bonelli Editore (Martin Mystery in *Operation Dorian Gray*) probed cases involving Dorian wannabes.

Movie version aside, writer/co-creator Alan Moore has never made Dorian Gray a member of *The League of Extraordinary Gentlemen* in the comics (Dorian's portrait in their headquarters could simply have been appropriated by the group as part of their collection of intertextual artifacts and doesn't demand he was ever a member of the group).

However, Moore *did* write Dorian – and Basil – into his *other* turn-of-the-millennium metafictional comics series, *Lost Girls*, but as *fictional* characters. That is, they appear in a faux "cut chapter" from Wilde's *Dorian Gray* and have no interaction with the rest of the mash-up cast.

Still, Dorian's participation in the *League* movie seems to have made him the comics crossover anti-hero of choice over at Dynamite Comics, where he seems especially popular with the sexy ladies: Witchblade, Vampirella, Red Sonya, and Pantha are among his costars. Even given his propensity to swing, I seriously doubt Dorian was as enthused about sharing the close confines of a comics panel with Herbert West, Dracula, or his old pal from the *League* movie, Alan Quatermain, as he was with these often scantily clad heroines.

Also available only in comics shops, Dorian *and* Oscar Wilde met the still-occult investigating Martin Mystery in a 2005 adventure. Amazingly, around this time, the Dorian themed '80s *Martin Mystery* comics album, *Operation Dorian Gray*, was adapted into a video game.

(Now that the way is clear, I, for one, cannot wait for the inevitable Dorian Gray/Sonic the Hedgehog/Mario Brothers/Pac-Man/Dirk the Daring and Daphne/Legend of Zelda digital smack down to ensue. How many points earned for successfully completing Dorian's digital seduction of Ms. Pac-Man with intent to caddishly toss her aside afterward?)

Perhaps the ultimate absorption of Dorian Gray into the milieu of comics occurred when Marvel Comics anti-hero Deadpool dispatched the decadent one by firing bullets into his portrait, leaving Sherlock Holmes and Doctor Watson to mop things up as it were in *Deadpool Killustrated* issue four.

I'm not much of a Deadpool fan, but I find this particular scenario kind of cool. Plus, I know the writer Cullen Bunn who is a super nice guy. Didn't know it at the time, but when he was a kid, Cullen used to frequent the recently passed *Heroes Are Here* comics shop in Goldsboro, N.C. as I did. (To all *Heroes* proprietors over its three decades, "Little" Ed, Adam, Bradley, and its founders, the late "Big Ed" Sutton and his late wife Pat… thanks so much, guys. It became like family.)

Our main interest here, though, is prose, not comics, movies, or TV, and, surprisingly, very few mainstream writers have picked up Wilde's pen to chronicle further Dorian Gray adventures. It was nearly a century after Wilde's original, in 1985, that horror writer Graham Masterton continued the story of the portrait in *Picture of Evil* (a.k.a., *Family Portrait*) and extended its longevity powers to an entire family.

That's right: it's been almost a hundred years and the *portrait* gets a sequel, not Dorian.

Kim Newman's amazing alternative universe of *Anno Dracula* (1992) gives Basil Hallward a close-up, but Dorian doesn't get to show his dissipated face. To be fair, even Sherlock Holmes is only a referenced mash-up, having been banished by Queen Victoria's Consort Prince Vlad to an out of country penal colony!

Also in the nineties, Neil Gaiman in his short story "The Wedding Present" did a postmodern, revisionist take on Wilde's original, which Gaiman's characters are meta-textually familiar with and its parallels with their own situation. But it doesn't seem this is actually a new Dorian Gray adventure, either.

Will Self's *Dorian, an Imitation* in 2002, once again dodges actually extending Wilde's continuity, but updates a retelling of the original novel to 1981 Britain.

Finally, in 2013, *The Wilde Passions of Dorian Gray* (get it?) actually takes Dorian's story further. Author Mitzi-Szereto reveals that Dorian faked his death (stab your portrait and leave a hideously disfigured and aged beyond recognition corpse lying in front of it wearing your ring. Who could ever have questioned it wasn't anything *but* a suicide?). The text reportedly depicts our immortal's fornicating in detail. It's *Dorian Gray* reduced to "a good beach read," a.k.a., "respectable" lady porn.

As of this writing, *The Picture of Dorian Gray* got its latest shout-out from the mainstream press, in, of all places, a 2014 Disney juvenile novel titled *The Beast Within*, a prose prequel/adaptation of the studio's version of *Beauty and the Beast*! Of course, the original *Beauty and the Beast* story's appearance in 1740, and Disney's animated movie being set in the same century, precludes any actual crossovers with Wilde's cast of characters. Or even the portrait.

What *The Beast Within does* have is an eccentric, egocentric, and temperamental mysterious artist known only as "the Maestro," who has managed to anachronistically channel the Aesthetic principles as expressed by Wilde's mentor Walter Pater in his *The Renaissance: Studies in Art and Poetry,* which will not be published until 1888 (perhaps he received an advance copy).

In this authorized retelling by Serena Valentino of Disney's beloved take on the classic, the effects of the Prince's curse are not immediate. He is proceeding with his plans to marry a lovely princess, and the Maestro is commissioned to paint a portrait of the future royal couple.

In the Maestro's portrait, however, the not-yet transformed Prince begins to reveal beastly facial attributes. These are subtle, and it may be that only the Prince can see his portrait's externalization of his already monstrous inner self. Nevertheless, he is offended enough to ask his best bud Gaston to arrange an "accident" for the Maestro, who himself seems to have acted without intent and is completely unaware of what his portrait has revealed.

In short, Valentino's Maestro storyline in *The Beast Within* foreshadows the fate of Basil Hallward while recapitulating Wilde's original. Even one of the Maestro's lines, "It seems every portrait that is painted with any real feeling is a portrait of the artist, and not of the sitter," is a close paraphrase of what Basil says about his painting of Dorian.

Ms. Valentino's employment of Wilde's novel makes for one of the most original and subtle mash-ups ever. Still, though the influence of *The Picture of Dorian Gray* in particular and the Aesthetic movement in general are present here, this is not an actual Dorian Gray story.

Most mainstream writers of fantastic fiction, more interested in the paranormal than debauchery, have apparently felt that Dorian was best left dead, that he was a character with a one note schtick: immortality through a portrait. And Wilde had worked that concept out pretty much the first time.

In a May 2017 interview, novelist M.L. Rio (*If We Were Villains*) light-heartedly talks about writing Dorian Gray fan fiction. Her comment is illuminating as to why there is a shortage of Dorian Gray mainstream prose in the wake of the original:

"I just feel that there would be something inherently hilarious about that particular character in a modern context. It's almost too easy; you transpose Dorian Gray and Henry Wotton into a twenty-first century setting and it turns into a classic collegiate May-December romance, only they're gay and May's immortal..."

"It's almost too easy..."

Yes, it is, because it's extremely unimaginative. From her brief exemplary passage of her idea of what a Dorian Gray story should be, you can tell that Ms. Rio is a talented and witty writer. Even so, she can only see the concepts of *The Picture of Dorian Gray* as material for a paranormal romance, one bordering on a situation comedy.

I have to wonder how soon before *The Golden Boys* leaves Wilde's (and Ms. Rio's) wit behind and sinks to prime-time sitcom level joke set-ups; say, like maybe this one about how the unlikely pair of Gray and Wotton got together:

"So, how did you two meet?" their nosey next door neighbor, acoustic guitar strumming singer Sibyl Vane, asks while checking her phone to see how many hits her YouTube channel is getting.

"I was *antiquing...*" Dorian answers, his eyes and caustic tone aimed at the sixty-something Lord Henry Wotton.

Wotton regards the young-appearing but over-a-century old-Dorian before drolly retorting, "... And so was *I*."

Sibyl doesn't get it.

End scene!

So, is the immortal Dorian Gray at a dead end, creatively speaking? Or are mainstream writers missing something, Wilde's homosexuality having overshadowed his creation-- not to mention Oscar Wilde himself?

Fortunately, the millennial rise of independent and self-publishers has allowed for more creative explorations of Wilde's characters in ways which mainstream publishing has shown little to no interest. For instance, Brian Ference's *The Wolf of Dorian Gray* trilogy (2016-2017) is a reinterpretation involving lycanthropy as well as gender swapping some of the novel's established cast.

At the end of 2017, Britain's Swan River Press released *The Scarlet Soul*, an anthology of tales described on the publisher's website as written "*for* Dorian Gray" (emphasis added). Indeed, there would seem to be a notable tendency among these stories to only have been *inspired* by Wilde's novel. They are, in fact, described as "bold reimagining(s)" of various "key element(s)" of the original by editor Mark Valentine. Thus, Wilde's anti-hero's active participation in any particular work therein was not considered essential to the goals of the Swan River Press collection.

But now, with the publication of *Doran Gray: Darker Shades*, Wild Hunt Press publisher Christofer Nigro has produced the first anthology whose primary focus is on collecting new adventures of the character of Dorian Gray himself.

If there is an overarching theme herein, it is, appropriately enough, immortality. This theme is as deep in human literary expression as death is in human experience. Both are, in fact, the springs of the *Gilgamesh* epic compiled as far back as 1200 B.C.E.

But once you've achieved immortality, how easy is it to keep it? And might you discover there are different paths to the same eternal end you might have taken if you had but known? And that those paths, in fact, have already been actualized by others?

In this crossover-centric group of mash-up tales, Dorian will encounter some of those "others," fictional characters of extraordinary longevity who took alternative inroads into forever, such as vampirism, mad science, flaming fountains of youth...

Does the nigh-immortal Dorian Gray indeed have a future in prose? Delve now into his secret history and read of his heretofore untold adventures and learn...

-Micah S. Harris

Closing in on the end of yet another year in Eastern North Carolina... and still no portrait.

Marking the 117th anniversary of Oscar Wilde's death, (November 30, 2017).

Micah S. Harris teaches British literature and film on the collegiate level in North Carolina. As a graduate student, he studied The Picture of Dorian Gray *with Oscar Wilde authority Dr. Donald Lawler (who, in his Norton Critical Edition, first put the original* Lippincott's *novella version of Wilde's classic back in print, making it possible to compare the two texts for the first time in almost a century).*

Harris's Ravenwood, the Stepson of Mystery: Return of the Dugpa, *from Airship 27 Publications, won the 2016 PulpArk award for best novel. His big break, however, came in 2004, at the tender age of 42, with the publication by Image Comics of his graphic novel,* Heaven's War, *drawn by Michael Gaydos, artist of Marvel Comics* Alias *(now known as* Jessica Jones *after the Netflix original series it inspired).* Heaven's War *pits the Oxford Inklings, including J.R.R. Tolkien and C.S. Lewis, against Aleister Crowley and is still available in its second printing from Image.*

His monthly column Just Like In the Movies *on the 18th Wall Productions website traces the history of screenwriting from the beginning. He is also an authority on Schlitze the Pinhead.*

In his spare time, he daydreams of writing his own contribution to Frozen *fanfiction: "Elsa, Bride of the Wyrm."*

PORTRAIT OF A LADY

Micah S. Harris

I

"Who is that fascinating woman beside Lyndon Thackery? And *please* do not identify her as either his wife or mistress. Especially if either is the case."

"Where?"

"There." The elderly man pointed across the floor of the spacious art gallery, over the individuals still in the gala attire that they had worn earlier that day at the commencement exercises of Queen Victoria's Golden Jubilee. Some couples milled about the exhibits while other patrons were chatting in little groups. A collective, gentle rumble from demurely delivered small talk made the aural background of the event.

But one woman was anything but demure. She was the object of the elderly man's interest. Her laughter occasionally pealed into the air like a happy shriek, prompting both slight inclines of the head in her direction and a rolling of the eyes from the other women present.

Their initial annoyance had turned into vexation at these sporadic disturbances, for with each eruption it had become more difficult to reengage the attentions of their young men once drawn to this petite, shapely, slender-limbed beauty with marmalade hair. They became increasingly fascinated with this youthful woman who, refreshingly, seemed she could care less what anyone thought of her.

47

How uninhibited her natural self could be had yet to be realized by most of the men in the room. But most of their ladies had, and they had been careful to direct their escorts, without the latter realizing it, from a certain alcove of the gallery.

That alcove was directly behind the questioning man who was now stabbing his finger in the vivacious woman's direction to guide the still seeking eyes of his friend. "*There*," he repeated, and then the other saw her. He smiled under his walrus moustache.

"The woman with whom you are smitten, Eustace, is the dignitary from Kor, Miss Rebecca Sharp."

"Did you say… *Rebecca Sharp*?" Lord Eustace Durrance immediately leaned forward for a better look, forgetting himself to the degree that he was oblivious to the crease he had made in his suit with the action, thereby compromising the crispness in his attire that he had been so careful to maintain since entering the art gallery that afternoon.

"No," he said under his breath. "It isn't possible."

"If you wish a better view," his friend said, "you need not strain your eyes. A much more *intimate* one is nearby."

"Whatever do you mean, Edwin?" Eustace said, straightening as he tugged at his waist coat, for he could feel that crease now.

"Turn around." Edwin made a stirring motion with his index finger pointing down.

Durrance turned. And gasped.

There she was. In clay. Every inch of her replicated. She had been Lyndon Thackery's model for this sculpture… the nude model. Which meant Thackery had had knowledge of her. The *real* her.

He whipped back around to look at the young woman across the room, ignoring the smile on Edwin's face.

Durrance frowned, turned back to the sculpture and approached it, comparing the likeness, but this time not directly to that of the woman present. He produced from his coat pocket a small portrait he always carried on his person, a miniature reproduction of a painting of a young woman with the same face as the clay statue's. She had been eighteen in 1811 when the original had been painted. Over seventy-five years ago. Impossible, of course, that Thackery's model at this moment on the gallery floor with him had posed for both.

But the girl's father had been the painter. And his last name had been "Sharp." First name…? He had signed his full name on the back of the canvas, but Durrance could not remember it now. And she had written hers under his: "Becky." There was an inscription from the painter. To her. His handwriting.

Durrance remembered well what it had said: *A ma fille, t'aime au étage du paradis.* It was what he had always purposed to say should he meet her. He was certain that special knowledge would forge an immediate, favorable bond between them. But that had been long ago, a boyish fancy, and the meeting had never happened. He had not been born until 1821 and it was ten years later when he first saw the portrait... saw *her*.

He looked back at the young woman who currently possessed that same beauty in her youthful, mortal flesh.

She must be some descendent of the Becky Sharp in the portrait he had possessed for decades. It was impossible *that* woman would still be modeling, still "muse-ing" seventy-six years later with face and body untouched by age! It was not natural. Worse, for Durrance, it denied the principles of Aestheticism.

She was fiddling with her hair now before two blond male admirers, recreating how she had put it up for her modeling session.

49

Lyndon, the only one of a darker aspect in the group with his black hair and beard, was holding her fan for her as in the role of her attendant.

Widening even further her doe's eyes and slightly tucking her head, she asked the two young men, the constant murmur parting just enough to let her words cross the room that Durrance might hear, "How do you like me?"

This inquiry prompted both men to turn and take a look (doubtful their first) across the room at the nude sculpture of her. Their look quickly became full on stares. Durrance saw her triumphant smile behind their backs. Without looking at Lyndon, she held out her hand for the return of her fan. He gave it to her, and she snapped the fan back into full spread to cover her lower face. When the men turned around, they found her batting her lashes over it at them.

And she owned them.

Durrance reddened. "She's behaving like a little minx!"

"Where do you think you're going, Eustace?" Edwin said, grabbing at his friend's arm only to be shaken off. "Remember that 'minx' is Her Majesty's governess of one of her African colonies – not your granddaughter!" he called after him.

Granddaughter. Lord Durrance winced at Edwin's choice of words as he strode toward Rebecca Sharp's group. Besides Thackery, these two blond Adonises appeared to make up her entourage. One was tall and muscular as well as having a handsome face; his puppyish fawning over Becky turned Durrance's stomach.

And then there was the always nattily attired Gray. Slighter of build than the other, to be sure, but possessing a sophisticated worldliness beyond his bland rival's capacity. This put Gray on equal footing in the race for the prize: while not as physically exciting as his strapping rival, his lust for life, Durrance suspected, was more suited to Miss Sharp's own.

Of course, Dorian Gray would have set his mark on this beautiful young woman, a refreshingly novel face in the regular crowd. No doubt he hoped to find a new companion, having tired of whomever his latest had been. And Miss Sharp's worldliness and sense of self-possession, combined with a willingness to shed inhibition as she had shed her clothing, made her a prime candidate.

Tainted and spoiled, he thought. *Coarsened*! *Why did it have to be this way?*

And, even given my own age… why does there seem to be so much youth *radiating from this particular group? Moreso than any of the other of the gatherings of young people in the gallery? And how is it that Lyndon Thackery fits right in?*

"Ah, look who it is," Gray said. "Old 'Useless' Durrance himself."

"That's 'Eustace,' Gray," Durrance said. "And how *is* London's most renowned *mal vivant*?" he asked Dorian. He then nodded at Thackery. "Doctor Lyndon."

"Durrance, hello," Thackery said, extending his hand to shake Durrance's. Durrance made no effort to take it. Instead, he continued to eye Gray with contempt.

None of this sudden tension was lost on Becky Sharp, who watched it all with detached bemusement.

"Well, Lord Durrance," Thackery was asking. "Have you seen my latest sculpture? Please, if so, do not hesitate to let me know your opinion of it. I assure you that I can take it. I have been criticized by experts, after all."

Durrance turned from Dorian and looked at Thackery. "By far, it is your best work, Lyndon," he said. "But, then again," he turned and smiled down at the petite Becky, "you had most charming inspiration."

Thackery humphed. "Ah, I see you desire an introduction," he said. "Lord Durrance, Miss Rebecca Sharp, governor over her Majesty's African colony of Kor; Rebecca Sharp, may I present London's premiere art critic, 'Useless' Eustace Durrance."

"By your usage of playground level insults, I see you have stooped to pick up the child's rattle that Dorian dropped, Lyndon," Durrance said.

Becky curtsied. "My Lord Durrance: greetings from Kor. Have you ever been?"

She even possesses a trace of the French accent of her predecessor, he thought.

"No, Miss Sharp, I am afraid I cannot say that I have had the privilege."

"Our Lake Superior is without match," the blond Adonis whose name was Leo Vincey said with a smile. "You must drop in some time." Grinning at having achieved a pun, he looked from face to face in his circle for affirmation of the desired effect. And received none.

"Do I know you, sir?" Durrance said. "I am certain if we had ever met, I would recall your rapier wit."

Becky pressed her fan to her lips and giggled. Leo looked at her, then back at Lord Durrance, then Dorian, and finally Thackery. The corners of his mouth drooped. "Well, everyone else was being a wag," he said.

Becky snapped her fan closed and touched Leo's muscular bicep with its tip. "And your bulldog-like efforts are appreciated, darling," she said. "Now, my Lord Durrance: Lyndy has shown me some of your reviews of his work. 'Dilettante,' I believe, is the recurring term."

"The man is a surgeon by profession, Miss Sharp. His 'art' is a sideline. You cannot find fault with me for merely stating the facts."

"Hmmm. Yes. You are correct, of course. And I do suppose the damning with faint praise you just lavished upon him represents a step up in your estimation of his endeavors."

Durrance flustered and could feel himself turning red. *Is that why she seems determined not to like me? I have offended her friend and thus her, too? I meant what I said to praise her beauty. Can she not see that?*

Then a new thought occurred to him, one that made his heart sink into his stomach.

"We have not been introduced," he said, looking at Leo. "Is this gentleman your fiance, Miss Sharp?"

Leo beamed at this, but for Becky it was her time to blush. "Leo came to Kor looking for love, it is true," she said. "But, unfortunately, all he found was me."

Leo's face sagged. Then he took a deep breath and straightened, tugging at the wrists of his gloves. "You *are* in love with me, Rebecca. Your memory is still occluded by centuries of amnesia is all."

"Wait – *hundreds* of years?" Durrance asked. Unprompted, Leo had attributed extreme longevity to this Rebecca Sharp, if not immortality. Durrance felt his heart quicken as he looked at her.

Becky frowned and gnawed her lower lip at Leo, then Durrance, and then back again at Leo. Then she smiled, snapped open her fan and began working it. "Leo is a romantic, Lord Durrance, who believes in the transference of souls. He thinks to woo me with this prattle."

Seeing Leo's disconcertion begin to appear in his face, Becky quickly reached out and made a stroke of his jaw with the velvet touch of her gloved fingers. "But it is adorable prattle."

Leo's perturbed features were immediately smoothed by bliss.

"My darling!" he said, grasping at her glove before she had completely withdrawn it. He was simultaneously moving to kiss her hand when Becky managed to pull free, leaving Leo's lips to touch only air.

Durrance looked at Leo. "A romantic. So was I in my youth. But now I have found a form of idealism in Aestheticism that fulfills the old longings, though in a bracing, ascetic manner that eschews the old sensuality that inevitably accompanies and drags into the mud 'romance.'"

"How so?" Thackery asked.

"The ideal sought in the physical form of the beloved can only truly exist in a realm untouchable by the drift, not only of nature itself, but our human perceptions, which, achieved as they are via faculties that are subject to dissolution by that same nature, must themselves fade away until they are only capable of vaguer and vaguer impressions.

"The way out, the way of rapture from this flux of elements and into that over realm of Zen-like stillness, where we may pick up and examine frozen gems of flame that are so startling sharp that we jolt at their contact as from a prick, and for a moment, we are truly alive again-- the way of rapture, I say, gentlemen and Miss Sharp, is through Art. Particularly the visual arts."

"My dear Lord Durrance," Rebecca said with a feigned concern in her voice and expression, "How you go on. You must really find a mistress. And soon."

"I had one, mademoiselle. But I was able to, as Doctor Johnson said, 'quit my tyrant.' And, paradoxically, possess her at the same time. I believed her to have become completely and totally mine. But I was wrong. It would appear she has betrayed me. She has slipped free of me and that high place where I kept her."

"'Kept her?' The way you look at me when you say that," Becky said and began to flutter her fan between her and the staring Durrance, "makes it seem as if you intend to recapture the poor girl at your earliest convenience and lock her up. I should warn her of your intentions, should I ever meet her, I assure you."

"You misunderstand. I only ever knew her through her portrait."

Though he was intently focused on Becky, Durrance could not help but notice Dorian Gray lean in.

"You were so smitten by a two-dimensional image of someone you did not even know was real?" Becky asked.

"But there was indeed a model. I have a copy of the original upon my person at all times. May I show her to you? As she was painted in 1811?"

Becky nodded, and the men all leaned in as he took the cased miniature from his pocket and opened it. Becky gasped, and the others startled.

"That is me!" Becky said.

"That *is* you?" Dorian said and began to look Becky over with a full reappraisal.

55

"What? Of course not; it can't be," Becky said, beginning to fan herself rapidly. "Not if the original was painted in 1811! Really, Dorian. Why, I wasn't even a gleam in my grandfather's eye when this portrait was painted."

"The original's subject wrote her own name on the back of the canvas," Durrance said, "and it was 'Becky.' The painter was her father, and he signed his work 'Sharp.' So, you must understand my fascination with you, Miss Sharp."

Seeing her entourage were now all staring at her as though they expected an explanation, Becky could only stand there, mouth open but silent, her eyes shifting.

"It *is* a most extraordinary resemblance that would seem to defy mere coincidence," Thackery said. "And to a woman who just happens to have the same name at that."

Dorian spoke up. "I know. Rebecca, why not simply write down your name as a sample of your handwriting and have Durrance compare it to the signature of the woman who wrote 'Becky' on the painting's back?"

"Yes, Rebecca. Why not?" Thackery asked.

Becky's jaw dropped at this suggestion, and she glared at both Dorian and Thackery. "Have you both lost your minds? Do you actually require proofs that I am not the woman in that picture?"

Dorian narrowed his eyes at her and shook his head. "Of course not." He pointed at Durrance. "I meant a handwriting comparison would disabuse *him* of this outrageous notion *he* is obviously harboring."

She now turned to Durrance and frowned.

"So, *you* describe these incredible details of a portrait that none of us here but you have seen – if it even exists. But even if there is a portrait – *this* miniature *isn't* the original. It is but a copy. What is a rational explanation, one that lies within the realm of sanity, is that the miniature's image was altered from the original in the reproduction… and I suspect intentionally so to resemble me!"

"Wha--? No, no, my dear. How could that possibly be? We've only just met."

"Perhaps you have been watching me. And who knows for how long?"

"I have never seen you in the flesh before today. I swear!"

"Oh no? I sensed otherwise from the way you looked at me as you talked of how the girl in this portrait had slipped free of you; and did I not state then that you seemed intent on taking possession of her?"

Leo thrust his chest out at the elderly man. "Shall I thrash him for you, Rebecca?" he asked.

Thackery imposed himself between Leo and Durrance.

"No one is thrashing anyone, Leo," he said. "While Rebecca's surmise is an understandable one, this could all be nothing but a big coincidence after all. We should all reserve judgement concerning Durrance's motivations until we have seen the original, compared it with the miniature, and then determine if there has been any tampering with the reproduction to make the girl appear as our Becky. Is that possible, Lord Durrance?"

"Indeed! I can offer you a viewing of the original, which I keep in the large attic of my flat at the Hesparus Hotel. I can show you; *all* of you. Miss Sharp, your friends here can be your chaperones. And I will show you… *you*."

Becky began to frown as she considered, then, with an expulsion of breath, she shook her head. "Show me what I can see in my own looking glass whenever I wish? I think it not worth the effort to extend myself for what you propose. However, I am willing to concede that my judgement of you may have been overwrought and hasty. We may part as friends, sir. That is my best offer to you."

"Please, Miss Sharp. Won't you reconsider?"

"I have told you 'no,' sir, and I do not retract it." She waved her hand over the crowd. "Remove myself from the unveiling of my form? That does not happen every night; at least, not publicly." The corners of her mouth rose, and her lips parted to show the tips of her even, white teeth. Her circle of men laughed.

Must you present yourself as the coarsest of trollops? Durrance thought, his hands clinched into fists at his sides.

He took a breath and relaxed his hands.

"Well, then, would you do me this favor, my lady? The woman in the painting possesses a complexion of perfect peach. But art is perfection, the ideal, not life. Having seen you, your appearance shall haunt me and rob me of certainty for the rest of my days that she is not you, unless you would deign to show me some imperfection of your own?"

"*What?*" Becky frowned, looking from man to man in her entourage, all of whom, other than Dorian, were politely trying to restrain giggles. Gray appeared distracted, staring into space, stroking his chin.

"A freckle?"

"*Really*, sir!" Becky said and reddened.

"A mole, then? The more irregular the better!"

Durrance snatched out and grasped both her wrists together raising them so that his hands seemed to be folded about hers in prayer. "You *must* grant me this, dearest Miss Sharp!"

Becky found she could not tug free. She was surprised to find the elderly man capable of a grip so unrelenting. "'Must?' And 'dearest?'" she said. "I do not even know you, sir! How dare you make such a demand with such... familiarity. Release me!"

Thackery stepped forward. "Durrance! Have you lost your mind, man? Release her!"

Leo stepped up. "Shall I thrash him for you *now*, Rebecca?" he asked.

"No, you shall 'thrash' no one, Leo. He is only an *old* man. Lord Durrance, I said 'release me.'"

Durrance looked around at the glaring men – all upset with him except for Dorian, who remained strangely detached from what was happening, preoccupied with his own thoughts. His face turning red, Durrance's hands fell away from Becky's own and he withdrew, head bowing.

"Thank you," she said primly. "Lord Durrance, I do not begin to understand you. I have never laid eyes on you until this evening, yet your behavior toward me is that of a pining lover. It is completely inappropriate. Now, sir, the sculpture on display here *is* me, as I am bodily. Your friend Thackery can testify to that. Search it for imperfections if you will, but do not ever approach my actual person again."

"So, we do not part even as friends, then, as you said we might?" Durrance said, head still bowed.

"I gave you that option and you tossed it away when you laid hands on my person," Becky said.

She looked around as she readjusted her gloves, first at Thackery and then Leo. "Thank you, my gallants." She looked at Dorian, who had made neither move nor offer of aid during the altercation, but had been staring away, as he continued to do. "You, too, Dorian," she said.

He looked at her. "Hmm? Oh, yes, yes. No problem, Rebecca."

She shook her head, huffed, and walked away, Leo and Thackery following. Durrance continued to stand there; he had yet to lift his head.

Then he looked up, eyes wide, and shouted after her: *"T'aime au étagedu paradis!"*

Becky went suddenly stock still at this. Then she slowly turned, and, her back to both Thackery and Leo, who had turned around with her, silently but emphatically mouthed these words at Durrance:

"Leave. Me. Alone."

She turned her back on him once more and proceeded on her way.

Without acknowledging the still-remaining Gray, Durrance, slowly shook his head and moved to leave. Dorian stepped in his way.

"What was that about, Durrance? Where did that come from, what you just said to her?"

"It is also inscribed on the back of the actual portrait of the young woman. It also was written by the subject's painter, her father. Now, if you will kindly remove your dissipated self out of my path, Dorian …"

Dorian stepped aside, staring after Rebecca. "She understood you, Durrance," Dorian said to himself. "Add that to how adamant she was that she would provide no handwriting sample, and her refusal of the opportunity for us all to see the actual painting… I've been turning it over and over in my head since seeing that miniature, wondering if it could be, and if so, how *but*…." He smiled broadly. "It *is* you, Rebecca. And I shall soon have incontrovertible proof with which to confront you – without ever needing to see that portrait."

II

More than a half hour passed. During this time, Thackery set up a portable podium before his sculpture of Becky and held forth on his artistic method to the group that gathered there. Then he introduced his model, Rebecca Sharp.

"Stay," Becky said to Leo who had remained by her side throughout Thackery's speech, arm interlocked with hers, grinning like a fool in paradise. Now she slipped free of him and stepped forward to join Thackery in front of his representation of her in clay.

The men of the press received her gladly, but quickly moved on after their questions were answered. The audience for Thackery's lecture had already departed. Then Becky and Thackery heard clapping: Dorian Gray, slapping the wrist of his other hand that held a glass of chardonnay.

"Fame is fleeting, eh, Rebecca?" Dorian said. "Fame -- or is it *fama?* -- the desire for immortality. You know what I mean, I am sure."

"Why are you here, Dorian?" she sniffed. "I have not yet forgiven you for your indifference to my plight earlier when I was being manhandled by Father Christmas. In fact, I do not know if I shall ever forgive you at all."

"I am here, now, Rebecca," Gray said, advancing with the drink. "To make amends. See?" He held up the chardonnay. "I remembered your favorite and sent out for it, or I would have been here sooner."

"And where is my alcoholic beverage of choice?" Thackery asked.

"I did not recall offending you, Thackery," Dorian said. "But since you asked: the barley beer is at the local tavern, same as always."

"Yes, do not continue to deny yourself on my account, Lyndon," Becky said, smiling into the crystal glass as she took it from Dorian. "I am certain that your speech left you dry."

Thackery sighed. He had been dismissed. And there was no point arguing it. This was par for the course in a courtship with Rebecca. She had had her fill of him, and she would have it of Dorian soon enough. Poor Leo was already out, though he refused to realize it.

"I'll slake my thirst," he said.

"And Leo?"

He stepped up. "Yes, Becky?"

"The flower in your button nook is starting to droop. Don't embarrass me. We passed a street vender of carnations coming into the gallery. Be a dear and go fetch a fresh green one from her, won't you?"

"At once, my love."

Becky looked after him until he was out of earshot, then looked at Dorian and shrugged. "He does everything I tell him," she said and smiled. "It is the funniest thing."

Then she sipped her beverage. "Ummm, thank you, Dorian. I'm glad to see that you have not forgotten entirely what it means to be a gentleman."

"Not until you wish me to."

She looked up and smiled as she took another sip. "Ha! Oh, Dorian. I am glad you came after me. I have always sensed a kindred spirit in you."

"And I you, Rebecca. You are so refreshingly audacious! You throw aside all propriety – while visiting the Queen herself on her birthday, in your official capacity of colonial dignitary, and you abandon your dignity in the most public way imaginable. You are fearless in your impunity! However are you getting away with it? Why isn't Victoria 'much displeased' with you, and publicly so?"

Becky smiled and girlishly twisted back and forth at the waist as she took another sip. "Let us just say that Her Majesty and I have a special relationship."

"And so could we, Rebecca," Dorian said, leaning into her and stopping her glass en route to her mouth. "Never before have I met a woman with a spirt commensurate with my own in its capacity for sweet wickedness." His hand now made a fist around hers and the glass. "Let us be wicked together! Let us 'feast with panthers!'"

The irises of Becky Sharp's eyes were a wet jade, but the jadedness they typically expressed now evidenced desire. Her moist lips parted and with a coy smile she said, "Mister Gray. Dear, dear Dorian, I –"

Her sentence broke off in a shriek. Gray released her hand and Becky dropped what was now the broken chardonnay glass. She regarded her palm, the torn material of the glove and the dark blood welling there.

"You clumsy booby! What have you done?" she said.

"Rebecca! Forgive me. In my excited ardor, I forgot I grasped the hand that grasped the glass. Please, let me see."

"No," Becky said, turning at the waist from him and raising her arm so that the palm was now shielded from Dorian's view by the back of her hand. "It will be fine."

He leaned in. "But there may be glass in…"

She turned further away, hand still raised, as Dorian continued to snatch after it. "It will *be* all right. I don't want your bumbling fingers picking through my wound."

But he seized her wrist, pulled her hand palm down, and began struggling to pry open her clinched fingers.

"Get off!" Becky shouted.

Now he opened the hand. Among the shreds of her glove, there was no longer an open wound.

"But – you were bleeding…"

"I told you it would be all right," she said, eyes simmering.

"How--?"

"How did *you* escape being cut yourself?" Becky asked, nodding toward his palm.

Dorian smiled. "I told you we are a perfect pair, Rebecca."

Becky raised her chin and sniffed. "I am happy that your manly loveliness is unmarred. Despite your continual, apparently irrepressible caddish behavior, I am not sure that I am through with you yet, Mr. Gray. But at the *moment* I…"

"Rebecca?" Dorian asked. She was suddenly staring at a man in the distance, a man in a bowler hat and checkered pants and coat. Dorian could not discern his identity either from face or figure. "Who is that? Do you… do *I* have another rival, Becky?" He winced. "A man in *checkers*? Please, Rebecca, say it isn't so."

"Anything but," she said. "You must go now, Dorian. And quickly. Before Leo returns. He is always asking my leave to thrash someone, and, as I am yet cross with you, I am afraid this time I might indulge him. Go!"

"Until we meet again, then, my love, and know that the moment cannot come too soon," Dorian said.

Once his back was turned, Gray looked into his palm and smiled.

Rebecca watched after Dorian until she saw him exit the building. She looked back to see if the checkered man in the derby was still there. He was, of course. Becky sighed and quickly made her way to him, motioning for him to meet her in a side alcove.

"Why are you here and in that tastelessly loud outfit?" she asked. "Do you have no conception of what it means to blend in? What are they teaching you in agent school? Apparently not a fashion sense!"

The man looked down and inspected his checks, as though to make certain they were all in place. "This is all the rage at Oxford," he said.

"Yes, but *this* is a Chelsea gallery showing!"

The man sniffed. "I am of the League of Zervan Arkarana. My race has had all the time since your atmosphere became breathable for mammals until your sun went black to perfect our technique. 'Blending in' is our specialty. This is method number 3: 'hide in plain sight.'"

"One does not hide in plain sight by sporting a sartorial disturbance so loud that you are drowning out Parliament three kilometers away! Now, what do you want?"

"Merely to shadow you for your own safety. You know how dangerous these men..."

"I *know* how to deal with the dangers of men," Becky said. "I assure you, as a woman who has dealt with them for going on a century of adult life! You are making yourself a complication I do not need for this mission."

"I have my orders, Miss Sharp."

"To see the mission fail? Your grandiose group who go by that mouthful of nomenclature that would choke an elephant —"

66

"'Diogenes Club, Meonia Division, Yithian Branch, Special Unit Zervan Arkarana.' Yes, ma'am."

"Yes! *Them*! *They* evidenced great faith in my abilities when they went to such lengths to set me up as a puppet ruler of Kor for Her Majesty's interests. And I have demonstrated that faith was rightly placed. I have endured much in their cause– the fear when I was tossed into that pillar of flame almost killed me before it could endow me with nigh-eternal life. And toppling 'She-Who-Must-Be-Obeyed' was no easy task even after that, I can assure you. So, I *believe* I have shown myself of sufficient resolve and capability to bring about the demise of the most formidable of schemes that may oppose Her Majesty!"

"Neither your capabilities nor your resolve are in question, Miss Sharp. However, you must concede you did not conquer Kor alone. Therefore, we have found it prudent to send for assistance for you on this mission."

"More cooks to spoil the broth, then? *Who*?"

"Well, besides myself… we have already sent a summons to Benchurch…"

"Ben Church? 'The Judge?' Not that, surely!"

"Do not call me 'Shirley.' And the Black Madonna is on the way as well."

"If you will but stay in the shadows where you belong and leave me alone, I shall have this matter resolved before they arrive. There is no need to bring in those heavy weights you just mentioned. They are just needless complications. Now, leave me alone, 'Checkers!' I can take care of myself."

Oh, the male of the species, Becky thought as she stormed off. *It doesn't matter whether they are of the human or extraterrestrial variety. Sometimes a woman just has to take them in hand –*

At which point, masculine hands reached out, powerful ones, one grasping tightly Becky's mouth, the other arm wrapping about her waist, and yanked her aside. The hand over the mouth held a cloth with a bitter scent that made Becky wince, just once, before she lost consciousness.

III

Becky Sharp came to in a well-lit room, opulent and fragrant from burning odorous gums of the East. How had she come here? She remembered having the rare moment with no eager male's accompaniment, and she had taken the opportunity to approach the dandy in the bowler hat. Her 'handler.' At the gallery. But after that, she could remember nothing.

She was looking up at a ceiling of vermilion and gold, and her eyes lowered along olive-green lacquered walls of a room loaded with *objects d'art*: blue china vases; a mounted bejeweled Catholic monstrance with a vacant nimbus; a life-size, carved-from-jade tortoise whose shell was set with a ruby the size of a cricket ball; a shrouded, five-foot in length wooden tube trumpet of the Rio Negro Indians, forbidden to the sight of women and the young, named the *juruparis*, "the demon." Beside it, with enough instrumental intricacies to rival a Cathedral organ's stops, set an Indian sitar; a stuffed panther in the corner, its eyes emeralds, pinned to the floor an equally taxidermied gazelle.

Becky lay bound on a divan over whose back was spread a tapestry depicting the Ragnarok and the swallowing of the sun by the great wolf Sköll. By the door directly across from her, a furry frog green coat and a ducal hat with pear-shaped pearls and studded with diamonds, hung from the coat rack. Above an active fire place perched a mantle carved with peacocks, unicorns, basilisks, and Medusa faces. Peacock feathers protruded from a corner vase painted with sunflowers.

On a silk scrim room divider were etched, in Japanese brush fashion, birds frozen in flight. Rendered in watered down ink, the birds appeared to be melting, as though the silk might otherwise be easily rent like rice paper by the weight of a beauty the drawings themselves could hardly bear.

Becky sighed. The décor made it apparent to whose rooms she had been taken.

"Dorian," she called.

To her left, a black velvet curtain with three hundred golden bee ingots, in the fashion of the burial shroud of the Frankish king, was drawn aside, and Gray stepped out, carrying a draped canvas on an easel.

"Ah, dear Rebecca. You are awake," he said as he placed the easel before her.

"You have a keen grasp of the obvious, Dorian. Untie me immediately! And where is Bertie?"

"Who is 'Bertie?'"

"Bertrand Moran! 'M.!'"

"'Him?'"

"*M.*! Moran!"

"I am sure I do not know who you are talking about."

69

"As if *you* could forget a fashion offense like that bowler hat and Dandy checkered coat and trousers!"

"*Him?*"

"M.!"

"I never saw the man before tonight."

"Don't play coy with me, Dorian."

Dorian looked at her sidelong. "'Bertie Moran?' I know a Colonel Moran…."

"Of course, *you* do; you're a scoundrel! Bertie is his brother. He went the other way than the Colonel. Or so I thought… until he lured me aside to help you kidnap me! His own mind must have found a way to co-exist with the alien one in his head – giving new meaning to 'double agent,' I must say."

"Rebecca, *your* mind is obviously not quite lucid, yet. Do like this – take some deep breaths -"

"I am *not* breathing the same air after you, you snake!"

"Not much choice there…. Listen to me, Becky. No one named Bertie 'M.' Moran helped me kidnap you. I was perfectly capable of that myself. Do you really think I would risk being captured as a criminal alongside such a fashion malefactor? Risk having my photograph taken alongside a man in…

Dorian shuddered. "… a man in a *bowler* hat and… and… *dandy* checks. For all London to see? Really, Rebecca. It isn't done. Not by me, anyway."

She strained against her bonds. "Untie me."

"I do not think I shall. Not yet."

"There is no need for this!"

"But there is. I do not wish you to be harmed," Dorian said, as a switch blade seemed to twirl into being in his hand with a gleam and rattle.

Becky screamed.

"Calm down, Becky. I bound you to forego a struggle in which you might be hurt. I have no desire to harm you, especially since I broke that glass in your hand. I had to see that your body handled a wound in the same preternatural manner as mine, and that it was not just eternal youth you have been granted. Now, you are more precious to me than before."

"Then what is the knife for?"

With a smirk, he snatched away the cloth that covered the picture of Dorian Gray.

Becky Sharp's was a toughened soul, but even she was compelled to shriek, startled as she was at the sight of Dorian's true face revealed. The flesh of youth showed random, gangrene splotches, as though someone had tried to ruin the portrait by flicking a palm full of turpentine on it. The jaws were sunken as were the jaundiced, bloodshot eyes; the hair was too long and unkempt and showing here and there graying tips. What could be seen of the gums were pale and puffy, the teeth yellowing, with one tooth apparently already fallen out from the pyorrhea.

"Dorian! Who painted this wretched image of your wrecked beauty and *why* are you showing it to me? I have seen the same visage on the most dissipated hash addicts and the syphilis-stricken abandoned to the streets! It is an abomination that it was done to you!"

"'Done to me,' Rebecca? It was done *for* me."

"Surely you did not sit for this thing?"

71

Gray smiled, and Becky would have sworn at the same moment, the corners of the face's mouth on the painting had downturned. She blinked and stared, yet the change remained. But it could not have *changed*; it had to have been that way when he unveiled it. In the initial shock of its revelation, she simply had not noticed.

"Ah, my dear Rebecca," the still-smiling Dorian said. The tone of his voice, however, matched the downturned mouth on the canvas, "I continue to sit for it, every day of my life. It is a work in progress, you might say."

"Why ever would you – what kink makes you indulge in this disfigurement by proxy?" Becky said while she tugged at her bonds again. "And am I to understand that I am 'sitting' now for you to have me rendered the same?"

"Oh, no, dearest Becky. I have not brought you here to model. Look at the one hand that is held open on my portrait, Rebecca. Remember our accident today?"

Becky leaned her head forward and started. There was the nasty wound Dorian's actual flesh had avoided. "What compelled you, having escaped that pain, to come to your portrait and render it there?"

"'Twas rendered the moment the glass shard did cut my flesh. The canvas absorbed the effect."

Becky shook her head and worked gently but firmly at her bonds. "That is madness."

"Is it?" Dorian brandished the knife, prompting Becky to scream again for fear she had provoked an attack upon her.

Instead, Dorian turned the end of the blade upon himself and again Becky shrieked in fascinated, wide-eyed horror as Gray gashed his own cheek, a deep cut that should have resulted in a peel-back flap of skin exposing the inner mouth.

But Dorian's fair complexion remained unmolested. The portrait, however, immediately manifested the gash, revealing part of his tongue and a row of lower teeth. And there was sudden anguish in the expression of the Dorian of the portrait that had not been there a moment before.

Becky's eyes flew open wide. "This isn't possible," she said.

Dorian began to clap. "Bravo, Becky, bravo! Ellen Terry could not have delivered so convincing a performance. You act so startled, but this business with my portrait is not entirely unknown to you, is it?

Becky's facial features contracted into a scowl, the only expression capable of conveying the violent denial this false accusation prompted.

"Your palm was gashed as well as mine, enough to shred your glove. I saw blood there, Rebecca. And then it was gone. You were so adamant that I not see, for you knew the flesh had mended and that quickly, just as mine did. You, too, have a portrait, Rebecca, one that absorbs your wounds without, I wager, depicting the scars you should bear.

"To judge from Durrance's duplicate, your portrait also absorbs the ravaging of your flesh by time yet shows it no more than you do in your actual face and figure! There is an entirely different metaphysics at work with you than with me. How did your father pull it off? Can the technique be taught?"

"Dorian, I know nothing of any such 'technique,' let alone any 'metaphysics' involved in that portrait of whomever that young woman was who resembles me."

73

Dorian clucked his tongue, smiled and shook his head. "Who *is* you. Stop lying and tell me your secret. How is it that the power of your portrait supersedes my own? You need not fear a canvas you dare not destroy falling into an enemy's hands because of what it reveals about you!

"*How*? What *was* your father's occult technique by which he secured this gift for his daughter?"

"Must I keep repeating myself? There is *no* such technique in regard to me, Dorian," she said, squirming more intently against her bonds.

"You *will* tell me, Rebecca," he said. "You may not register the marks of pain, but I saw today that you certainly can still feel it."

"Oh, no, no…," Becky said, shrinking into the cushions of the couch, her eyes wide and her face suddenly so pale that even her lips had gone waxen. "Dorian, *don't*! I can tell you nothing about that portrait Durrance says he possesses except that it is *not* the source of any supernatural resilience or lifeforce for me! Your torturing of me will be for *nothing*. Dorian! I thought you liked me -- I saw it in your eyes; that same desire which was in my *own*! How could you have been plotting to do this to me all along?"

"Rebecca, now you wound *me*. If you did not constrain me to force what I want to know out of you I would have never dreamed of cutting you unless it was your own masochistic desire. Then it would be my pleasure to accommodate you.

"I have never assaulted a woman who did not first wish it, Rebecca. So, again, I implore you: don't force my hand. Tell me your secret! Then I shall call Basil –"

"Who is that?" Becky said. "Not another sadist to join in?"

Dorian threw back his head and laughed. "Basil Hallward would not pull the wings off a fly! No, my dear. Basil has discovered his own … 'technique'… that keeps the subjects of his portraits immortal."

"Through a *painting*? Immortality? I do not know what kind of magic trick you just performed with your own portrait just now, but…"

Dorian raised his forefinger. "Basil – or 'Frank Hollyward,' as was his birth name – became an acolyte of the cat goddess Ubasti during his grand tour of Egypt upon finishing his studies at the *Ecole Belle Arts*. In the ritual of Osiris, he took the name 'Bast' in honor of his new goddess. But his surname also had to be changed. Christianity, you see, had baptized 'holly,' so much that it became 'holy,' thus 'holly' is a 'ward' against evil. Hence, 'holly ward.'

"For the pagan goddess Ubasti to receive him, 'Hollyward' had to be erased on every level, for a name has long had the potential to form a mystic barrier between man and the demonic, and it was especially so in this case.

"Upon his return to France, the former 'Frank Hollyward,' with some Europeanizing, had become 'Bastille Hallward,' still incorporating his patron goddess in his first name. Then, when he came back to England, he began to prefer the anglicizing diminutive 'Basil.'

"He set up an idol of his goddess in his studio and made it a shrine, giving the ancient entity a stronghold and locus of power in the heart of the most up-to-date empire on the Earth. And, yes, sacrifice was made there –"

Becky flinched. "Of humans? How horrid!"

"-- of his manly potency."

"How more horrid!"

"At least 'potency' in the normal fashion. But *we* are his children now. And *hers*, I suppose."

"'We?' I don't know the man!"

"I meant the others Basil has chosen to paint and grant immortality. Freedom from age, freedom from disease, freedom from the due recompense from fleshly indulgences...

"This very moment, there are portraits locked up all over England, my dear; in attics, bricked up in basement walls, locked away in safety deposit boxes requiring two keys in synchronization to open... These are 'the beautiful people,' of course, and we are legion: The Cult of Fama!"

"Then I am glad I cannot tell you what you want to know, Dorian. How many of those people deserve eternal life? Whose only merits are having been born rich? Decadent, in-bred, spoiled cows who only offer the world an insulated, dead end existence. Oh, I have long despised their ilk."

"But they have already 'put forth their hands and live forever --!' Now, will you not speak? What is the secret of your greater magic?"

"I *have* no 'greater magic.'"

"Very well, then, Rebecca..."

Dorian fell upon her, and immediately the point of his knife pricked her throat's skin. Becky wailed. Dorian tried to silence her shrieks, but she turned her head from side to side, caterwauling the whole time, until he finally pressed his palm firmly over her mouth. Now the hand with the other knife was poised to come down...

And Gray stopped, stared into space, then turned to look toward the outer door.

Now Becky heard the beating of hastening feet up the steps and across the flat landing. Fists now pummeled the door with harsh shouts accompanying them – Thackerey's: "Open the door, Dorian! Release Miss Sharp and cease whatever wicked thing you are inflicting on her, or, I swear, Dorian…"

And, another, younger voice: "Do you wish me to thrash him for you, Becky?"

Becky managed to jerk away from Dorian's hand and shout: "Leo! Leo, oh my darling! *Help me!*"

"Leo!" Dorian mumbled, eyes widening. He looked down into Becky's face, smiled, and with a final, scratching flick of his knife's point over her cheek, he kissed her on the forehead. "*Au revoir, mon amour,*" he said and leapt up, snatched his portrait from its easel, and dashed with it for a nearby window.

In response to Becky's screams at Dorian's superficially cutting her in the passing –a cut which had vanished almost as soon as it was inflicted --, Leo's shoulder was now battering the door harder. Then it was pushing the door into the room with Leo following through.

In a moment, he was at Becky's side, grabbing her up in his arms and lifting her from the divan. "Are you hurt, Rebecca? My dear Ayesha?"

He lifted me as though I were a babe, she thought. *And with my arms and feet still bound, leaving me completely helpless in his strong grasp – I must confess I do find it all very exciting. And dear Leo would never actually harm me.*

Becky looked up into Leo's face, the dazzling eyes of azure, the cleft chin, the lantern jaw, the flawless golden skin and neatly groomed blond hair… he *was* rather cute, after all.

"I am fine, dearest," she said, looking into his eyes, her bosom heaving.

"Good," Leo said, and dropped her back onto the divan.

"Leo!"

He looked down at her. "I know how you make fun of me behind my back. Dr. Thackery told me."

"And you believe him? He wants me for himself! Why do you trust your rival?"

"I am *not* an idiot, Rebecca. He told me nothing that your blatant contempt in my presence did not confirm. And, frankly, I don't have to take that from a woman. I can always find another incarnation of you in the future, Ayesha, a much kinder one. You see, Rebecca, *you* are not really so important as you think you are. And now that I see you are well, I bid you adieu – until we live again."

And then he was gone.

"Leo," Becky said softly. Then she shouted: "Leo, come back! I see now that you deserved so much better! Leo --!"

She turned her face to look at Thackery who had entered behind Leo.

Thackery nodded toward the now open window. "Well, Dorian has made good his escape it seems." He looked down at her. "And how are you doing down there, Rebecca?"

"You despicable…. how dare you poison Leo against me by telling him –"

"The truth? Oh, the boy wasn't *that* thick. He had already pretty much figured you out on his own. He told you so."

"Untie me!"

Thackery smiled. He bent over her, but only to chuck her chin. "Fortunate we came looking for you when we did, eh? Leo was much concerned when he could not find you at the gallery upon his return. Since you were last seen alone with Gray, locating him was the logical thing, but Leo did not know his residence.

"After first confirming Gray had not escorted you back to the Kor embassy, well, he did know where to find me, and *I* knew Gray's residence."

Becky sneered at him. "Thank you for your timely efforts on my behalf." Then she began frantically yanking at her bonds again. "Now, untie me!"

"The way I left you both flirting, of course, I assumed the two of you wished to be alone. But I instantly saw here a way to separate you from both Gray and Leo and take you away."

"Leo!" Becky shouted out. "Leo, help –!"

Thackery clamped an unyielding hand over her mouth as Becky writhed under it on the divan.

"I stoked his jealous fears that Gray was enjoying your affections at that very moment, while, at the same time, disabusing him of any notion of you having *any* affection for him." He shrugged. "Well, perhaps that of a sister…

"Oh, I got him all worked up to give Dorian a thrashing, so he 'compelled me' to bring him here. Although he did not render Gray senseless, as I hoped, he did send him running, and then quit you in contempt, as I was sure he would eventually once his blood had cooled. But he wasted no time in abandoning you, I must say."

Becky had stopped struggling now and was glaring up at him, breathing heavily through her nostrils.

"Leo's good and gone by now," Thackery said. "So, no screaming? And I will allow you to breathe easier."

Becky nodded. He immediately removed his hand. She took a few quick deep breaths, and said:

"Well. You may think you have me now, because the competition has all been eliminated, but I will never–"

"Well, see, there is where you are wrong, Rebecca. As long as you are bound, I *do* have you. Right where I want you. Nice of Gray to have left you all wrapped up in a convenient little bundle for me."

"*Untie me!*"

Thackery straightened and produced a small bottle and handkerchief from a coat pocket. "You owe me one more session, Rebecca. And my greatest critic, the great Eustace Durrance, finally convinced me of something. Well, he and seeing how dodgy and bothered you became when he brought up that portrait. *Your* portrait, Rebecca."

Becky opened her mouth to cry out again for Leo...

And the stringently fumed handkerchief descended and stopped her mouth and nostrils, and all quickly became dark.

IV

Cold.

An unconscious Becky's shivers became so incessant and violent that they shook her awake.

She sat up with a sharp, deep intake of breath, eyes bulging.

Naked.

Thackery took me back to his...

--she turned on her side – and nearly fell off the side of a narrow stainless steel table –

-- *his operating theater?*

Then she saw the instrument tray.

With its mean looking instruments …

…with the blood gelling over their edges …

Hers?

Becky instinctively began searching her body for wounds. But, of course, there would be none.

She slid her bare rear toward the end of the operating table, then eased herself to the floor, careful to see if there were any residual effects from her drugging.

Now she had taken enough stock of her surroundings to know that she was, indeed, back in Thackery's home. She saw the cloth that should have been covering her piled beside the table. She snatched it up and wrapped it around her. Then she selected the sharpest looking scalpel.

And then she was on the prowl.

She made her way to the bedroom that they he had always wanted to share with her. But she would never grant that shift of power in their relationship, nor his being able to hold his conquest over her other 'suitors.' It was a lesson she'd taken from old Queen Bess, though in Becky's case, it was too late to actually maintain her virginity.

Yes, that ship had already sailed long ago – in fact, it had probably reached Pago Pago by now. But she knew that they all – Thackery, Dorian, and even Leo -- had to think they had a chance with her, that she had not been possessed. It was a contest of masculine ego, and the right to brag had always been the prize as much as she.

Leo was never meant to be a contestant. He had been an annoying prat ever since he had showed up to surprise her on the embassy doorstep after she had given him the slip back in Kor. Perhaps… she should not have been so annoyed with that devotion. He was at least a man, who, as it turned out, was something more than just sweet talk -- always ready to thrash someone for her at her whim…he really *was* quite sweet. She sighed. She could certainly use him now.

At the time, though, he had been but a complication in a contest that was only meant to be between Thackery and Gray.

"It is good to see you looking so well, Rebecca Sharp," the man with the sunken cheek face under the judge's wig said.

The two were on a floor of the Diogenes Club that did not officially exist. This was the base of the Meonia, an unacknowledged branch of the Club which dealt in both international and trans-temporal secret activities in the service of the crown and the British people. It also maintained a branch office in Australia circa sixty-six million years in the past, manned by the extraterrestrial race from the lost planet of Yith.

"Serving as a puppet ruler agrees with me, I admit, Magus. And the occasional jaunt out of Africa on holiday is nice, though it is a bit spoiled by knowing that wherever I go, your agents' various and sundry eyes will be upon me. I catch their stares on occasion. They make my flesh creep."

"I would think you would be used to drawing interested stares, Miss Sharp."

"The normal interest, yes."

"Ah," the Magus said, and, behind his large wooden desk, leaned back and templed his fingers. "That of the admiring male of your species. Of course. Your attractiveness, after all, is why we have called you in on this, Rebecca. And because you like no other know how to utilize your looks to achieve an end."

"Yes, but under cover of attending the Queen's jubilee? Could my being high profile as a visiting governor somehow not increase the risk of my exposure?"

"Ha!" the Magus clapped his hands, then cupped his mouth with them both and giggled, mirthful eyes regarding Becky over his fingertips.

"Why are you acting like a silly school girl?" she said. "Stop it! What is so funny?"

"Your choice of words shall prove unwittingly prophetic, I think. Your mark —"

"Dorian Gray?"

"Your second mark."

"I am to have another, then? Is he also part of this secret society of immortals of whom you suspect Gray to be a member, who threaten the throne's monopoly on immortality?"

"No, this is not a member of the Cult of Fama. He is a rogue immortal. In fact, being a rogue has been his modus operandi on general principle since he first came to our attention two centuries ago. His current identity is that of one Doctor Lyndon Thackery..."

Becky raised her chin. "'Thackery?' Why does that name sound so familiar?'"

"He's the doctor who saved the life of Flavia Rassendyll, Lady Burlesdon by an experimental operation."

"Yes, of course. Princess Flavia who managed to abdicate before taking the throne as queen of ...?"

"'Ruritania,' my dear."

"Yes. That's right. News of that intrigue even reached us in Kor. Quite a scandal. Of course, the king only had his own dalliance to blame... and the mistress blackmailing him. I found her efforts heavy

handed, but it is hard to argue with success, n'est-ce pas? Who was the author of the roman de clef *that made it all an open secret?"*

"John Watson, Ph.D. – a talented amateur – wrote A Scandal in Graustark.*"*

"So, this Doctor Thackery's lifesaving intercession for Lady Flavia is the source of his own fame."

"Famous as a surgeon. But he is a frustrated artist who wishes to achieve celebrity through his hobby. It is this second would-be-career, his amateurish one, that concerns you, Miss Sharp. He is a sculptor. And, as such, will always be in search of a new model. As you have kept your girlish figure so admirably, I am sure he will find that you will do nicely."

"Oh, ho! I am to doff my knickers for Queen and Country, then? Grit my teeth against the chill and think of England? Oh – now I understand my 'prophecy" how I am to risk exposure as an agent. What will be my entre into the man's company?"

"Why, we understand he is interested in learning French…"

She looked around the bedroom, then dashed to his bureau, began yanking the resisting, creaking drawer open. Succeeding, she began plundering… and there she found his traveling papers. Passports with different names:

"Henry Esmond," "Arthur Pendennis," "Philip Firman," "Dennis Duval," "Samuel Titmarsh*?"* Tit*marsh? Lord! Is the man that desperate for a pseudonym? He must have already used every other surname in the English language. Twice!*

Whoever he had originally been had come walking out of the African jungle in the mid-seventeenth century, a white man in a loin cloth. The natives about the British colony in which he had shown up in a fever-madness had shunned him and refused to attend him in his illness. Those who had been baptized crossed themselves if he was even so much as mentioned.

In his fever he spoke of himself as a deposed high priest of a lost civilization; when he regained lucidity, he claimed to know nothing about what he had said. Upon full recovery, he had murdered and stolen the identity of the scion of a wealthy Irish family of Bally Barry. A few years after his ascendency to family head at the ancestral seat, the murders of the women had begun.

That was when he became known as Redman Lyndon, for his ritual bloodshed was an open secret. The family wealth in the coffers to which he now held the keys had kept him free, but eventually it was all gone. His lack of aging, coupled with the stories of how he purchased eternal youth, however, had long made the people fear him as a warlock; so, he continued to live like a king and kill when he desired, even when lacking money with which to bribe.

That was until a holy man and swordsman named Brom Cromwell, protector of the secret of Saint Patrick, and seemingly ageless himself – but wholesomely so – and a Buccaneer named Kane, who had first opposed Redman Lyndon when he had sat on his throne over that lost, depraved civilization in Africa, had put him to the sword.

But he had not died, at least not past his powers to revive. In the past century he had returned to the ancestral home at Bally Barry, where the family still dwelled in the poverty in which he had left it in the previous century, passing himself off as his own descendent, Redmond Barry Lyndon. His actual descendent Nora, whose cousin he claimed to be and to whom he had made overtures of romance, turned up murdered, her body bearing the ritual markings still remembered as those on the women killed by Redman Lyndon.

Having subsequently fled Ireland, he embarked on a rakish lifestyle in England, still managing to gain a seat in Parliament as "Barry Lyndon." But the Meonia Division of the Diogenes Club, Yithian Branch, Special Unit Zervan Arkarana, which had been on his trail for some time, finally caught up with him. He was locked up in Fleet Prison, but he faked his death and fled to the States where he had disappeared again.

According to his papers, Becky could see that he had since become a surgeon for the Union during the Civil War. When he returned to Britain in the mid-nineteenth century, he was still a practicing physician but now calling himself "Lyndon Thackery." It was then that his peculiarly bloody endeavors, no longer hidden amidst the general gore of the battlefield, alerted the Diogenes Club to his emergence.

Here, now, Becky held in her hand the papers for his next identity, and his next escape hatch: France. That was why he had wanted the French lessons that had been the excuse for her meeting him initially. He would become 'Jordi Bonet' on the continent.

That information would be useful… if she could disengage herself from her present sticky wicket. She looked over her shoulder to confirm she was still alone, then returned all the papers back to the drawer as best as she remembered their placement and shut it.

Now she focused on a smoking jacket on a standing coat hanger. Putting it on would still leave little to the imagination, but her only option was to go completely *au naturel* or run through the streets clinging to a sheet.

She was just letting that sheet slip as she reached out for the jacket, when she heard the floor creak under another's foot.

She grabbed up the sheet before it fell, holding it tightly against her as she turned. There he stood in a waistcoat and sleeves.

"Lyndon! How could you bring me here with the intent of the surgical invasion of my person? Never would I have suspected you, in all our time together, capable of -- of... violating me!"

"And have you any evidence your person has been 'invaded,' Rebecca?"

She raised her chin and held out the scalpel. "This is not a tool for shaping clay, Lyndon. And it has blood on it. *And*, as I awoke naked and on an operating table beside it, I cannot help but conclude that it is mine."

"Can't you? Are you wounded, Rebecca?" he asked and stepped forward.

She jabbed forward with the blade and he leapt back. "Do *you* wish to be? Because I have no compunctions about stabbing you if you try to put your hands on me."

Thackery shrugged and smiled. "I am amazingly resilient, but not so amazingly as you." He sighed. "After all our sessions together as artist and model, I would have sworn your body held no secrets from me, but it seems I have been very much mistaken."

"What do you mean?"

"Oh, come, Becky! You know that is your blood and you also know why, regardless, there is no cut on your body. What is your secret, Rebecca? Scalpel in your hand or not, I *will* have it from you if you ever wish to leave my house."

At that, Becky lunged at him, swinging the scalpel before her in a wide arc, yet not getting so close that he might grab her arm and wrest it from her with his superior strength. Thackery stumbled backward, almost falling over a footrest before righting himself and turning the tumble into a plunge out of his bedroom. He slammed the door on Becky before she could follow.

She ran to it, grasped the door knob even as she recognized the sound of a key turning on the other side. Her eyes widened, and she turned and tugged at the knob to no avail. Then she dropped the scalpel and her sheet and pulled with both hands. The door refused to give.

"Lyndon! Let me out!" She began beating on the door with the heel of one hand.

"I told you that you were not leaving, Rebecca. Not until you give up your secret. I know that you can tire. Eventually. Despite your ability to stay up all night and maintain a pose for extremely extended amounts of time, which impressed me so much – well, that was part of your body's extraordinary resilience."

She heard him snap his fingers. "Of course! I should have realized that would apply to your reaction to the fumes with which I drugged you. That is how you recovered so quickly, isn't it? If I had suspected, I would have certainly placed you in restraints before my visit to the water closet."

Becky began beating the door again, then returned to yanking on its knob, but it was heavy oak, firmly set in its frame.

"Lyndon, if you do not let me out, I shall scream!"

"Oh, please do. I should like to hear it. I suspect you are an excellent soprano."

Becky squinted her eyes tight, clinched her fists, took a deep breath and then belted one out, long and wild and high with the intent that her scream would rattle the windows of Buckingham Palace, wherever she was on the isle of Britain in relation to it.

"Ah, thank you for obliging," he said. "I was correct! You are a fine mezzo, my dear. You have missed your calling, it appears."

The effort left her spent. And doubled over. That had hurt! She had literally screamed her throat raw in that one effort.

"But listen, listen…," he said, "…*and…* wait for it… *and…* There! There you are! You are hearing absolutely nothing in response. Did you forget where you are, Rebecca? Where, on the East End? Across the street is that opulent flagellation parlor that is so popular with what passes for a Victorian gentleman these days. No one pays special attention to a woman shrieking in these parts."

Becky rolled her eyes, dropped to her knees on the floor, and smacked her forehead with her palm.

"What do you want from me, Lyndon?"

"I told you --your secret! Whenever I made an incision, your flesh immediately healed up. You have taken rejuvenation to a point that is beyond preternatural. You must share this ability with me."

"I have *nothing* to share with you."

"You will find it within you somehow. You are most resilient, Becky, but you do tire. I have seen it. And you do genuinely hunger, for I have heard your stomach's growl. I have seen you fall upon a plate of food ravenously. Do you remember that, Rebecca? We had a session that was twenty-four hours straight. I ordered from the brothel across the street's excellent kitchen."

"I am not interested in a walk down memory lane, Lyndon, for I would surely encounter *you* there."

"Oh, you shall be ready for that stroll, my dear, after twenty-four hours in that room with nothing to eat."

Becky leapt to her feet. "Lyndon! Let me out!" She began beating the door with her fists.

"I shall… in twenty-four hours. When I invite you to enjoy a repast on the other side of the door."

"But I will be expected to sing for my supper, eh?"

"You *are* an excellent mezzo soprano, after all. You can sing…or you can continue to refuse to share your secret and just stay in there and smell the aroma, Becky."

"Ha! 'Twenty-four hours?' Is that all? And you expect me to talk? I will hunger, yes, but not enough to give you satisfaction!'

"Forty-eight hours, then."

Becky screwed up her face and shook her head from side to side. *"Je suis trope bête! Petite imbécile!*

"Rebecca, think before you speak next. I can just as easily make it seventy-two, or even a week. I won't be going hungry."

"You sadist! You are worse than Dorian Gray!"

"Not at all. I will be all too willing to accommodate the breaking of your involuntary fast. Once you are willing to share with me your secret. To free me from this recurring need to murder so that I might continue my own longevity! I have never grown used to it, Becky. I had to harden myself to cut into you."

"I only have your word on that."

"'Only my word?' After all the time we have spent together, you cannot find it possible to believe that I have genuine regard – even affection – for you? Rebecca, you wound me!"

"You wounded me first – with a scalpel! Perhaps if your first instinct in approaching me on this matter had not been true-to-form predatorial, I might believe you. But you only seek to *parle* now because you could not get what you wish by killing me."

Silence.

"Lyndon?"

Silence.

"Lyndon, is that you having a reflective moment out there?"

Silence.

"*Lyndon!*"

"There, now, is the note of desperation in your voice that I have been wanting to hear. I hope to find you have fine-tuned it when I return in forty-eight hours."

"*Let me out!*"

"Oh – you might have noticed there is no WC in there. Something else to… reflect upon. When the moment comes. Until then…"

"*Lyndon! Let me go!*"

"… I will not say 'good-bye' but, as you yourself have schooled me, Rebecca …"

"*Don't! Don't…!*"

"*Au revoir!*"

"*… don't leave me here! Lyndon! Lyndon! Please!*"

She heard the key turn, although there was no need to do it again and loudly this time except to make a point.

She did *not* hear it being withdrawn for equal effect.

Then she heard his steps retreating and the door beyond opening and shutting.

And she was alone.

Or so he wanted her to think.

He had focused on her hunger, trying to steer her thoughts away from his own words about her need to sleep. He knew she could stay awake for over twenty-four hours, but he also knew how quickly she had fallen asleep after that.

He would not wait two days. He would be back as soon as he expected to find her deep in sleep and vulnerable to him. She looked at the scalpel again. Starving her was too passive. He might not be able to dissect her, but he would think that he could still excise the answer to her secret from her through repeated, painful cuts.

He might very well still be in the house at this moment, whetting his knives.

She shivered, felt herself pale. *Leo…* she thought. She hugged herself, feeling her nakedness, the utter vulnerability of her flesh to what Lyndon would do to it…

She clinched her fists until she drove her nails into the soft skin of her palms, bit into her lower lip until it bled, and tightened her eyes, refusing to yield to paroxysms of rage and fear.

No. With a quick snap back and forth of the head, she regained her grip. She needed no savior. She had fended for herself – admittedly, far from admirably – when she had climbed up from nothing to obtain her former position of wealth and position. She since had led a coup against a queen so fierce, so cunning, so capable of unrelenting, implacable wrath. And she had come out on top, even at the end, when the two of them were toe-to-toe, tooth and nail, struggling at the edge of that fountain of flame that took life as readily as it gave it.

She had grown soft as the Crown's puppet ruler. Galling as it was to admit, old Bertie Moran, a.k.a. 'Checkers,' the Yithian, had been right: she had needed someone to watch over her. And now they had had her playing the coquette for them? No more. Not now.

Henceforth, I play the coquette for no one but myself.

She picked up the scalpel from the floor, grasped it up in her fist, and started to stab it into the door…

... he wanted me to know the key is still in the lock...

... then thought better of it. She looked at the scalpel in her hand, then, at the half-inch of space under the door. She lowered the scalpel back to the floor.

She went to his desk, slid open the drawer, quietly, and looked inside for a piece of stationery. Only prescription pads, and the paper there was not large enough to guarantee that it would catch the key so that she could slide it back under the door to her, *if* she could first successfully dislodge it with the tip of the scalpel. Nor was the paper the length needed to increase the odds that it would not slide out from under the key. Better to use the sheet with which she had covered herself. It made for her best chance to get the key, draw it in, free herself and flee.

She looked at the door and smiled. *At least that will be the plan apparent.*

She spread out the sheet, smoothing and flattening it, then began sliding it under the door, inching it as far as the length would allow her for the maximum chance to catch the key, especially if it bounced, and then pull it back to her.

That done, she went back to the scalpel, took it over to the lock, and, wedging its point in, began to poke, working it. *The blade's tip is too large for precision*, she thought.

Pin.

She put the scalpel aside again and began searching her hair.

Yes, she thought, claiming one, *this pinch-nez will do nicely.* Feeling the hair drop and brush against her hand, she shook her head so that her reddish-gold locks fell to the small of her back.

She straightened the pinch-nez pin, extending its length. Then she slid it into the key hole and began to probe, turn the wire this way and that, and listen, holding her breath. She heard the thud as the key landed on the sheet. She smiled.

Now, big fish, let me reel you in.

Dropping to her knees, she began to draw the sheet, inching it carefully lest her prize weigh down on its place and cause the sheet to slide out from under it. She paused, looked through the crack between the door and the floor–yes! She could see it!

Then the sheet darted from her hands, withdrawing like quick surf back under the door.

"*Lyndon!*"

"Really, Rebecca, such a predictable, melodramatic ploy right off the gas lit stage. Did you truly think I did not know you would try it? I only suffered it so that you might feel the full futility of your situation: you are mine, Becky. It is only a matter of time until I get what I wish. Now, I am taking the key with me this time. Save your strength, mon petit imbécile!

Of course, I knew you wanted me to try it, you idiot! You telegraphed it loudly enough. I have played out your plan; now I shall play my own!

Again, she heard the door of the room outside the study open and close.

Becky walked over to where Lyndon's smoking jacket hung. She took it, slipped it on. Just below the waist length on him, it came down to the knee on her petite body. Her breasts were loose under it, of course, but the open front, thankfully, was not *too* open.

Now, if she had indeed successfully provoked Lyndon into exiting the room in triumph after removing the key, there should be no obstacle to her picking the lock now with her hair pin.

There was not. She slid the elongated hair pin into the right pocket of the smoking jacket and held the scalpel with her right hand. With her left, she turned the knob slowly, then pushed the door inward even *more* slowly, hoping for no betraying creak.

Then she shoved the door forward, thrusting her body through the doorway, swinging her blade out and about, turning this way and that.

The room was empty.

Was he truly gone, then? She might have time to snatch a suit of clothes from his bureau, all the better to move through the streets.

A creak of the floor, and before she could turn, Thackery was upon her from behind, exerting a grip like a steel vise on her extended forearm of the hand that held the scalpel. He tightened until she felt he was near breaking the bone. Then, as she screeched in pain, her hand flew open, fingers splayed, and the scalpel fell to the floor.

Now he picked her up by the waist, lifting her as she screamed, "No! No! No!," bare legs kicking and arms flailing.

"Oh, ho! You are so adorable when you try to fight back! Try to match wits with me? It's back to the operating table with you, dear Rebecca," he chortled. "You are most certainly a much better playmate with your physical chest than you are playing mental chess, my dear! You have been checked…"

Becky fell limp in his arms.

Lyndon's brows arched at the sudden swoon. But it pleased him. He turned her now, a fainted damsel in distress, to eye her as her head, tilted back, lolled from side to side…

"Well, Rebecca, it seems you finally acknowledged a master and accepted that you have been out played. 'Check,' my dear!"

Becky's eyes sprang open as she dipped her hand into the smoking jacket's pocket, simultaneously bringing her head up, blowing a raspberry with sputtering lips in Lyndon's face, and in his wide-eyed, jaw dropping momentary response of complete surprise –

--she brought the elongated hairpin into his eye, stabbing it in as far as where the pinch-nez had originally bent.

"Checkmate!" she shouted, before he dropped her as he staggered backwards, bellowing, one hand grabbing, then yanking the pin free, prompting a new belting out in agony. "You are a fine soprano yourself, Lyndon!" Becky said, already back on her feet and fleeing the room –

--and straight into Lord Durrance, who was entering Thackery's home, pistol in hand. He was accompanied by a bearded, stocky man in a sculptor's smock flecked with dried clay. He wielded a long knife.

"Ho! Now, what is this?" Durrance said, grabbing her by the forearms.

Becky winced, then her eyes widened as she could not pull free of the elderly man, and she recalled the unsuspected strength with which he had grasped her hands at the gallery.

"Durrance! Why are you here?" she cried out.

"You know why I came here – looking for you, to snatch you away for my own! I heard sounds of a struggle and we broke in to save you. But…" he looked over her, obviously naked under the brief smoking jacket. "Trollop!" he shouted into her face. "I had hoped that you were just a flirt after all, but…"

"No, my lord," she said, still trying to yank herself loose of him. "It isn't what you think. Lyndon and I never, not before, not now…"

"Iorga! Now!"

She looked over her shoulder to see his associate coming at her with the long knife. She screamed, now frantically writhing to free herself from Durrance's unyielding grasp, then saw that it was the butt of the handle of the knife his man had raised back, ready to strike her head.

She looked at Durrance, immediately ceased struggling, and stamped her foot. "No! I have been rendered unconscious and carried off *two times* today already! Now, *that's* the limit! At least let me put on some proper clothes fir—"

Her sentence cut off in a shrill yelp and a wine-colored veil seemed to unfurl over her eyes. Durrance caught her as her knees buckled and hefted her over his shoulder.

The last thing she felt before all consciousness left her was his hand stroking her hair gently as she heard in a whisper, as though he spoke from far away:

"There, there. I still retain some degree of tender regard for you. We are together now and soon shall be forever, one way or the other. Whatever *your* choice, you shall remain mine at last."

V

The bite of smelling salts provoked the sharp intake of breath and wrenched her awake. Eyes flying open, Becky immediately saw above her the toothily grinning, painted face of Lord Durrance. This sudden revelation tore an involuntary shriek from her.

Standing beside her portrait perched on its easel, Durrance wore a black robe. Under its dark cowl, his creased forehead revealed in its folds a blue upside down crescent moon. On his chin was a similarly hued sun disc crossed by a bar. Azure, concentric circles sagged along the drooping cheeks, rutted with age. The withered canvas of his face was broken by the yellow grin of his teeth.

Once more, Becky found herself having awakened in an inconvenient state of undress. At least this go 'round she retained Lyndon's brief smoking jacket. For the second time, she awoke in restraints. Her wrists were secured by clamps at her sides in the long wooden trough in which she lay. She felt the roughness of the wood against the backs of her bare legs, and, along with it, a layer of a cuticular substance also under her fingers.

She found that she could not move her feet. They were clasped together so that her ankles touched under a third clamp fastening them to the trough.

She immediately began pulling against her bonds but found herself held fast.

Durrance observed her efforts, then shrugged and quoted the inscription on the back of her portrait. "*T'aime au étage du paradis!* What does it mean, Rebecca?"

Becky strained her wrists and ankles against her restraints one more time, then, with an expulsion of breath, she ceased her struggling. From her clinched-shut eyes, tears began to wet her cheeks.

"'Papa...'" she said softly and began to tremble with emotion.

"I mean, I know what it *says*..."

"'I love...'" she began and choked.

"I *said* I know what it says..."

"'...I love you to... to heaven's floor.'"

"But whatever does that *mean*?"

"It *means*..." Becky said, opening her eyes on him and regarding him with an austere gaze, "that his love for me was of such height as to reach that of heaven. It *means* only God, who is above even heaven, could love me more."

"Sentimental tripe," Durrance said and clucked his tongue. "I am quite sorry I asked, as it almost ruins the entire portrait for me now."

"Now that it actually means something?"

"Now that it means something related to *life*! When it was Art… when you were the ideal… you had deep meaning for me, Rebecca."

She squalled, "*That wasn't real!*"

"Not as real as your relationship with your father?"

"No!"

"And how did that relationship end?"

Becky was silent.

"I am asking you a question."

Becky tightened her eyes and turned her head from him. In a whisper, she said, "He drank himself to death and left me with no one."

"And *that* is the life you find preferable to Art?"

She turned her head toward him. "And is *this* –" she squirmed against her bonds again "— this *Grand Guignol* production in which you have trapped me, your idea of *Art*? How does this *end*, Durrance?"

"It… we… *could* still end as Art."

"What is *that* supposed to mean? What are you going to do to me, Durrance?"

"Perhaps you should be asking yourself what it is that you have you done to *me*, Rebecca."

"Done to you? Man, I did not even know you until a few hours ago!"

"But I have known you! That cursed image of you! That enchanting, alluring image that has left me wretched. You have driven me to do dark things, Rebecca."

"You kidnapped me of your own volition!"

"I speak of long before tonight! Madame, *you* have compromised me!"

Becky furrowed her brow at him. "Sir! As I have said, I never knew you until a few hours ago – and *never* in the Biblical sense!"

"Sex!" Durrance shouted down at her, spit flying from his lip. Becky winced as it struck her own mouth. "Must you turn everything into a matter of the flesh? Yes, you have even turned *me* into such a thing! You compromised my principles before they were formed; you made it so that I could never live up to them!"

"I am sure I *don't* know what you are talking about!"

"You did this to me!"

Durrance's fingers were in paroxysms at the clasps and buttons of his enveloping cloak. He threw it open to expose his chest.

Durrance's withered torso was carved with various degrees of finesse with Celtic-Pictish body art symbols. His chest was marked by four parallel, vertical slashes. His drooping, tiny man's breasts sagged with concentric circles that had stretched into ovals about his equally stretched raspberry dugs.

But it was his paunch that bore the tattooed face: Nodens of the Abyss, he who was bound in the upper atmosphere until That Day; Nodens, the Outer One, "He Who Snares," "Wielder of the Net," "God of Fortresses." A Satyr's face was his; Durrance's ruptured navel bulged like a Cathedral gargoyle's tongue from the leering mouth tattooed around it.

Durrance leaned his paunch toward Becky, so that the tumor-like rupture of his navel came near brushing her face. She cried out in disgust, turned her head, but he quickly ran to the other side of the trench to thrust his paunch into her face again. Again, she turned away.

"You *must* look, Rebecca," he said, ignoring her protestations. "Be glad that you only have to see the symbol, that you did not behold *him* face-to-face. I sought the Zen-like state of the perfectly still abyss through Art – through the contemplation of *your* face on that canvas – to unite with the feminine ideal. Instead, I found *him* waiting. He compelled me seek to make Art of myself! To make Art out of Life!

"Know, then, my shame, Rebecca Sharp: look on the Chief Transgressor! Look upon the hypocrite!"

"I had nothing to do with your self-mutilation," Becky said, flinching as the tumor-tongue of Nodens again came near touching her face. "That was your madness!"

"Madness for *you*! To join you whom I loved, who *was* Art, I had to become Art myself, don't you see? But I was tricked! In so doing, I was cast out and barred myself from that exalted realm forever for my transgression!

"All this I did for love of that portrait! All this I did for love of Art! All this did I for love of *you*! And now that you are incarnate, you *will* love me back! You must!"

He dropped his face to hers and began to wet her forehead and cheeks with kisses. Becky grimaced and flinched against his breath as stale and offensive as the odor of mothballs, straining her wrists and ankles against her unyielding bonds.

"Give yourself to me!"

Then Durrance hungrily pressed his thin lips into her plush mouth. Becky could not twist her head away. She could not breathe, and that meant she would have to open her mouth, and his tongue would fill it. –She bit down hard on his lower lip, and, as he tried to withdraw, held her pinch as long as she could, causing him to tear the flesh as he jerked free.

Durrance sprang away, pressing his palm against his bleeding mouth. He withdrew his hand with a flip of the wrist, flicking blood. "Is this an example of your whorish ways? Is this how Lyndon craved you behave toward him? *Impure*! I gave you one last chance that we might join together on a canvas of a fleshly life! But you have destroyed that chance with this act.

"You have transgressed exceedingly in your own presumption to retain in life the moment of perfection captured in your portrait! But you shall no longer make life into Art. We shall make something else of you, Rebecca Sharp, a fit punishment! We shall make you *kitsch*! Iorga! Fire up the wax cauldron!"

Becky remembered the paraffin on which her fingers were pressed. "What are you going to do?" she said as Durrance began to roll the trough she was surprised to discover was on wheels. "Durrance, *what* are you doing?"

"You are going to become a wax statue, my dear. Iorga here is quite the artist, or *was* …"

Becky was now staring up at a series of glass tubes. She could see they connected to a large cauldron above her, heated by gas jets Iorga was lighting even now.

"Durrance, perhaps I was hasty to dismiss such… such great a love as yours."

"Too late, Rebecca! You shall be lathered with hot paraffin – and then I shall join you."

"*What?*"

"I am as guilty as you, my dear. Your love might have redeemed us both. But now, I, too, shall suffer the eternal fate of becoming kitsch! To be exhibited in a wax museum's Chamber of Horrors as Bluebeard, with you my latest wife-become-victim!

"To become a sensationalistic display in the sideshow, designed to be gawked at by the unwashed masses – if there is a Hell, could it possibly make for a worse fate for the art critic? I – and you – deserve no less. Has the wax heated to the proper degree, Iorga?"

"Nearly there, my lord!"

"Durrance!" Becky shouted. "*Don't!*"

"'Don't?' Deny myself absolute and eternal possession of you? Oh, no! I have lived for such a moment as this…"

"I am *begging* you –!"

"…when I shall cut away that smoking jacket from your body, and, with the full glory of your perfection filling my vision, the deluge of liquid wax will cover us together, wedding us forever. It is a type of consummation."

"It is *death*! For us *both*!"

"Be at ease, my love. You shall not be alone in your eternal shame for long."

He began to completely disrobe.…

But Becky was not looking. Becky was *bellowing*, loud and long and hard to be heard, for the least possible chance of rescue. Enduring the pain in her throat, she screamed over and over –

A strong shoulder jolted the door from the other side. Another joined it, and the door went down flat. Leo and Dorian ran over it, followed by the Yithian possessed Bertrand "M" Moran in his checkers and accompanied by armed men sent by the Magus from the Diogenes Club.

They were headed for Becky. Durrance ran forward to intercept them but succeeded in running only into Leo's swinging fist to the temple. Durrance staggered back, and Leo, at last, had someone to thrash.

"Help me!" Becky shouted. She saw the tubes above her were quickly filling to their openings, about to overrun...

But Dorian threw himself into the mobile trough, rolling it out from under the tubes and screaming as the boiling wax of the last tube he passed under struck his shoulder and steamily streamed along his back.

Durrance, bent double to shield himself against Leo's pounding, looked up and saw how things were shaping up – or down, as it were – for him. Level with Leo's crotch, he punched him between the legs, making it Leo's time to double over. Grabbing up the portrait of Becky Sharp, Durrance threw himself into the steaming shower of streaming hot paraffin.

He shrieked as both he and the canvas were ruined forever, the searing wax plastering itself to him. He collapsed onto his stomach as it continued to coat him with its clinging, dripping wet heat. He whooped shrilly in his convulsions.

"Is no one going to pull him out?" Bertrand shouted at his men.

"Do *you* want to get a blistering from that stuff – for *his* benefit?" one of his men asked him.

Bertrand looked at the yelping, jerking Durrance, the smoking liquid paraffin piling on him. "Well... no. I guess not," he said. "Wait for the shower to be over and him to cool down. No rush."

"Oh, let him *baste!*"

Bertrand raised a forefinger. "That would be Miss Sharp. Right. Excuse me, men."

Dorian was over her, mopping her brow beaded with perspiration from the furnace-like heat that had swathed her before she had been rolled from beneath the boiling wax.

"Dorian! You were *singed!*" she said. "You took that for *me?*"

"The pain was excruciating – for a moment. But, no need to be concerned. It won't even show in my portrait since my back took the burn."

"But *why?* I recall you had no problem torturing me while I was helpless only hours ago."

"Ah, Rebecca, you know I would never wish any harm to come to you. At least, any *real* harm. I certainly do not wish you dead. I have found that I can no longer conceive of a world without you."

"Such sweet talk – coming from the Grand Inquisitor!"

"But it's true. After all, you brought all *that* on yourself by not talking."

"How did you ever find me?"

"You should thank 'Checkers' there for not listening to you. Having lost your trail, he began rounding up such scorned paramours of yours as he could find, keeping each of us in his custody as we were collected. Naturally, his search brought him to Thackery's studio."

"But… I am not there."

He smiled and stroked back a troublesome strand of marmalade hair from her face. "So we discovered. No one was at home. Then we heard a woman screaming next door."

"We are at the flagellation parlor?"

105

"No. We mistook the doxy taking a lashing for you, of course. Fortunately, a young, uhm, 'lady' having a cigarette break outside the brothel saw you being carried off earlier. She was able to give us a direction – for a fee, of course. She would only take payment in *sterling* – from my own purse – so," he gave her body an appreciative look-over, "every *pound* of you now belongs to me. A fair exchange, wouldn't you say?"

"Are you going to remove my restraints or not?"

He again brushed away that obstinate strand of marmalade hair which had crept back over her forehead. "Just a little longer. I find you adorable this way.

"Anyway, as we moved in the prescribed direction given us by the trollop, your own screams directed us to this wax museum. You know the rest. And now I shall release you."

"Thank you," Becky said as he began removing her restraints. She sat up, caressing her bruised wrists. Then she reached out and cradled Dorian's face in her hand. "Thank you for everything you have done for me."

He buried his face in her palm, nuzzled then kissed it. He brought his face up and flashed her the grin of an adorable, adolescent scamp. Becky cocked her head at him, smiled, then reached out with her other hand to touch his cheek – and drug her raking nails over his face.

"Owww!" Dorian shouted, jolting back and slapping his hand over his scratched cheek. "What was *that* for?"

"*Because* – you had no problem torturing me while I was helpless only hours ago! You bastard! Stop whining. You know that's going straight to your portrait. Move your hand. *Move* it. Let me see…"

Grinning again, Dorian dropped his hand to reveal an unmarred complexion.

"There. You're all right." She clucked her tongue and shook her head at him. "You big baby. Ah, there you are... 'Checks.'"

"And how are you... 'Becks?'"

"I suspect I will be sore in the morning, but... would you two gallants help me out of this trough, please? I am loath to spend another unnecessary moment here."

"When exactly *was* it necessary?" Checkers asked as Becky stood, and she glared down at him as he and Dorian took an arm each and helped her out and over the side. Then she saw Leo, still partially bent at the waist from Durrance's punch to the crotch.

"Leo!" Becky squealed and ran to him. "Oh, my darling, are you wounded by that – that *beast*? Did he hurt you, Leo?"

"Only my pride. Though even he did not do that nearly as badly as you have," he said and frowned at her as he rose to full height.

"Oh, Leo..."

"I am glad they were able to round me up as part of this rescue party, and to have helped save you, once again. But to be quite frank, Rebecca, you are a most tiresome woman to keep up with. Perhaps in another life, I will find you have gotten it out of your system and slowed down a bit. Until then, once again, I shall wish you adieu, my dear Ayesha."

"But – *Leo*!" Becky stomped her little foot and looked after him as he walked away.

"Trouble in paradise, Miss Sharp?" Bertrand asked.

"Ha. Ha. Tell me, are the Meonia boys still interested in getting going what that astral-projecting Yank Darrell Standing suggested to the Diogenes Club, that division of what Standing called 'Karma Cops?' 'Making consecutive life sentences a reality,' and all that?"

"Indeed."

She nodded after the departed Leo. "Then, there is a partner for Standing, an excellent bloodhound, I'd wager. And I happen to know he is in need of a job. One in which he won't be reminded of me on a daily basis. Or, who he thinks I am. 'Checks?'"

"Yes 'Becks?'"

"Do you think he would be upset with me to know that I killed the true love he thinks I am and set him back a lifetime?"

"I am going to go out on a limb here and say 'yes.'"

"Hmmm," Becky said, nodding, still staring in the direction in which Leo had departed. "Then let us allow him to keep such fond memories as he has."

The Diogenes officers, Iorga in tow with hands cuffed behind him, walked up to get Bertrand's permission to leave. With a scowl, Becky stepped over and slapped Iorga-- cracking his face.

With a slight shriek, she leaped back. Bertrand furrowed his brow.

"That was a bit much, don't you think?" Iorga said as the lower half of what had been a mask fell off, revealing a terribly scarred and scabrous visage with no lips.

"Your face – was *wax*!" Becky grasped her abdomen with both hands, leaned back and squirmed. "You *fiend*!"

"And *that's* a rather shallow value judgement based on my unfortunate appearance, wouldn't you agree?"

"You were going to broil me to death under a blistering coat of hot wax, so, no, I do *not* think I am being one bit harsher than you deserve... *fiend*!"

Iorga looked away, raised his chin, scarred from old burns, and sniffed. "Fair enough, I suppose."

Then Becky tentatively stepped forward and bent down to get a better look at the lower half of his face protruding from the broken mask: "Good lord, man! Are you hiding the Elephant Man under there?" Becky said.

"You really *are* going the extra mile to hurt my feelings, now, aren't you?" Iorga said.

Becky grinned. "I admit that I was. *You* have to admit, though, that you *are* quite hideous."

"You know, I never wanted to make you a wax sculpture of a bride of Bluebeard."

"No?"

"No. That was *his* idea." He smiled. "I always saw you as Marie Antoinette."

Becky looked at Bertrand and slashed her finger across her throat. "Off with his head!" she said.

Iorga was still beaming that eerie half-smile upon her as they led him off, and Becky's flesh crept with the uncomfortable feeling that he was committing her appearance to memory.

"Everything all right?" Dorian said as he stepped up.

"Umm-hmm," Becky said. "Now that you are here."

"Always, dearest," Dorian said. "And, you do understand me – I do mean 'always.'"

"Umm-hmm. Got it. 'Checks?' I can confirm that Dorian Gray is indeed part of the secret immortality cult that the Diogenes Club has been looking for. You should arrest him."

"Wha --?" Dorian startled. "But I just *saved* you."

"For yourself! To begin again at your earliest convenience torturing this supposed secret of immortality out of me you remain convinced I possess. Do you think me such a fool as to ever trust you again, Dorian?"

Bertrand pointed at two of his men and then Dorian. Immediately they were one at each side of him, cuffing his hands. Dorian shook his head at Rebecca, scowling.

"Why, you ungrateful…"

"Take him straight to the Judge, men."

Becky's eyes widened at this. As Dorian was led off, she touched Bertrand's arm. "You don't mean Ben Church?"

"I mean the Judge *from* Benchurch."

"You mean that painting!"

"Mr. Gray will be locked in a room with it, and his preternatural life will be cut short when the Judge steps out of the painting to strangle him to death – leaving, no doubt, the Judge with his 'happy face' when he returns to the canvas. And Mr. Gray no longer a complication in our schemes. And not a moment too soon, if I might venture forth an opinion."

"Oh, no! Bertrand… *Bertie*, no!" Becky said, squeezing his bicep and looking at him doe-eyed.

"Really, Miss Sharp. This show of familiarity!" He looked at her hand on his arm. She withdrew it and then waved him off.

"Oh, bosh, 'Checkers.' Shall we speak of 'familiarity?'" she indicated her barely-there smoking jacket. "You have been looking at my legs since you got here."

He arched a brow. "Miss Sharp, I have been looking at almost *all* of you since I got here. I haven't had much of a choice."

"And I have not heard you complain once. *No* one offered me the use of his coat, because they all were enjoying what they saw, and that includes you. In fact, I think you *like* me, 'Checks'…"

He cleared his throat, looked at his jacket cuff, and began brushing an imaginary piece of lint from it. "Miss Sharp, you are not without your appeal…"

Becky leaned in and nudged him with her shoulder. "So – straight to the sweet talk, eh, 'Checks?' I have obviously made a new conquest."

Bertrand looked up from his cuff as though she had dealt him a bracing slap. "You have made no such thing!"

"Oh, Checks, stop playing hard to get. It's all quite useless. Men *like* me. Even, you know…" she pointed at his head and made a circular motion with her finger, "… you extraterrestrial types who are only men on the outside. And that means I usually get what I want from the fellows."

"Yes, now see, that is what I do not begin to understand." He pointed in the direction of the departed Dorian. "He had nothing but ill designs on you! You said it yourself – and yet you plead for his life?"

"He saved mine! Whatever his motivations, I am not a blistering mass of flesh at this moment because of Dorian Gray! I happen to think that deserves some mitigating of his particularly stringent sentence."

Bertrand gave a heavy sigh, still staring toward the door through which his men had just led Dorian Gray. He said nothing.

"Listen to me, Checks: if you let that hanging judge get out of that painting and strangle Dorian, you will be making a huge mistake."

"How so?"

"Dorian Gray can be a very useful man to you in your endeavors. An inside man. I suggest you have him assassinate one of his intimates, one Basil Hallward, and your problem of rogue immortals popping up unchecked will be solved."

"How so?"

"Take my word for it: Basil Hallward is the one bestowing preternatural longevity on his clients. Well, he and some Egyptian kitty-cat goddess. I believe this Cult of Fama is her intended revival of her cult in the modern world. Hers is the inspiration, but Basil is her hands, as it were. Cut them off, obtain a list of his clients, stick the idol of Ubasti that you'll find in his studio in a museum, and the present monarchy's monopoly on immortality remains unchallenged – in perpetuity."

"Mr. Gray will have no scruples about performing… wet works?"

"Ha!"

"Even taking the life of someone he knows, and with whom he may have formed an attachment?"

"He had no problem torturing *me*, and I daresay he was far fonder of my person than that of Mr. Hallward."

"But, you barely knew each other."

Becky made a dismissive wave of her hand. "That is of no consequence. The moment a man experiences sexual attraction to a woman with whom he thinks he has a chance, those who have theretofore made up his masculine society are immediately regulated to the back of the queue."

"Really?"

"It is an empirically established fact of human life."

"Hmmm. Well, as a member of an alien race whose origins lie lost beyond recall in an infinite cosmos, and whose true body exists in a past so distant that it will never encounter human life when it appears on the planet, I realize I am speaking as something of an outsider here, but…"

"'But?'"

"…what you've just described sounds completely self-centered and a shameful abandonment of proven camaraderie to insure one's physical gratification."

"Actually, that is as accurate a definition of romance as any. Good call, 'Checks.'"

"So, if I understand you, because of his sexual attraction to you, if you so impress it upon him as your wish, Gray would willingly throw a man who has shown him nothing but unrelenting devotion and loyalty – a man who has granted him *immortality,* mind you – under the omnibus?"

"Oh, he'll throw him anywhere I tell him to."

"And, for services rendered, you wish that we give Gray his life?"

"And his freedom."

"Perhaps."

He motioned to one of his remaining Diogenes Club men. "Overtake the men transporting Mr. Gray. Have them put him in a holding cell. Alone. No Judge. Understand?"

The man saluted and darted out.

"'Checks,' I suppose Thackery got away?"

"For the moment. We have some idea where he's heading, of course. France."

"Because of my French lessons? That *was* his plan. I saw his passport. But he may suspect that I did. And French is not just spoken in France."

"No, but it will most likely be his first harbor in the storm due to its proximity."

"Well, look for a man with an eyepatch. Although… I was a bit rushed. I stabbed him there, but that doesn't mean I put his eye out. He might not be so easily visually marked for long. Also, I got a look at his faux identity papers. Look for a man named 'Jordi Bonet,' or some variant thereof."

"The Black Madonna has arrived. She will be disappointed that he got away."

"Let it give her something new to cry about."

Bertrand looked at her. "Miss Sharp, you *do* know that when that idol of the Knights Templar begins to weep tears of blood that someone must die?"

Becky shrugged. "Is she still crated up? Yes? Then forward her to France, addressed to 'Jordi Bonet.' Let him be her next victim as planned."

"You have all the answers, don't you? And, I must say, you dispense death with the coolest of heads, *mademoiselle*."

Becky waved him off. "Don't look at me as though you're appalled at how detached *I* am."

"'Appalled?' I must apologize. These new human facial muscles, you will please to understand. I am still getting used to them. That was supposed to be frank admiration."

"Why, 'Checks,' I do believe you are making love to me."

"Don't get sentimental. Well, Miss Sharp, we will get you in appropriate street wear and out of here soon for a proper debriefing with the Magus. Oh – and Her Majesty wants you to know that she is grateful for your continued service, including the extra duties you have taken on in her interest during this Golden Jubilee."

"Thank Her Majesty for me."

"And she looks forward to your attendance of her Diamond Jubilee…"

"Her Majesty is too kind."

"And her Sapphire…"

"It will be my honor."

"And her Platinum…"

"I will be there."

"… and, of course, any and all various and sundry precious minerals that may follow…"

END

NOTES FOR *PORTRAIT OF A LADY*

Micah S. Harris

I met Chris Nigro during one of my always enjoyable interviews on Robert E. Wronski, Jr.'s Television Crossover Universe podcast. At this writing, these interviews are still available, by the way, like the one at https://www.buzzsprout.com/52660/403894-tvcu-34-micah-s-harris-and-the-return-of-becky-sharp.

Anyway, one go 'round the topic was my 2008 novel *The Eldritch New Adventures of Becky Sharp*. In that story, the villainess of William Makepeace Thackeray's Victorian classic *Vanity Fair* became, against her will, an agent of H.P. Lovecraft's time traveling-through-serial- possession Great Race of Yith. It's a mash-up affair with Becky meeting and sharing adventures with other fictional characters from both classic and pop literature and film.

Chris contacted me after the interview and asked if I would crossover my version of Becky with Oscar Wilde's Dorian Grey for an anthology he was putting together for his Wild Hunt Press. I hadn't written a new Becky Sharp story in years, since the novella *Slouching Toward Camulodunum* (initially serialized in Black Coat Press's *Tales of the Shadowmen*). I loved writing my version of Becky, and I was pleased that fans of my take on the character tended to be intellectual, well-read, and sometimes exceptionally creative individuals.

In fact, I could have hardly asked for a better compliment than when talents of the caliber of writer Matthew Baugh (who has chronicled tales of classic adventure heroes like the Phantom and the Avenger) and writer/artist Mark Schultz (*Xenoxoic Tales*, a.k.a.

116

Cadillacs and Dinosaurs, Prince Valiant, The Adventures of Superman, and *The Coming of Conan*) were enthused enough to volunteer their own ideas for further Becky adventures.

(Matt's idea became our collaboration "The Scorpion and the Fox," also in *Tales of the Shadowmen.* Mark's suggestion became the basis of *Slouching Toward Camulodunum* – see Robert E. Wronski, Jr.'s Dorian Gray timeline in this volume for plot details).

Yes, the fans of Becky's career as an agent of the Yithians were a flattering group of followers for a small-time writer like me. The problem was there were not that many of them. So, in search of a larger readership in which to invest my writing time (I seem to never have enough and I'm slow, too), I abandoned Becky for other characters and stories.

Then Chris was nice enough to invite me to write a new Becky story for the first ever anthology to focus on new Dorian Gray adventures. I was a longtime fan of *The Picture of Dorian Gray,* having studied the novel in graduate school, and taught it in my British Lit. classes. As it turned out, Dorian was already immortal, and I had endowed Becky Sharp with preternatural longevity in my *Eldritch New Adventures of Becky Sharp.* So, I had the basic set-up for the novella I would write going in.

Here, however, Becky's adventures take a turn into an alternative universe – the Wild Hunt Universe (WHU). In *Eldritch New Adventures,* Becky became Ayesha's (She-Who-Must-Be-Obeyed) agent as well as the Great Race's. But in the WHU, the coup of which Becky was a part was a success; she killed Ayesha, and was installed as Queen Victoria's puppet queen on the throne of Kor

Along the way, I came up with "The Cult of Fama," and an additional reason for Dorian to kill Basil Hallward: in service of the

Queen. That all began with my college professor noting how the 1940s' MGM adaptation of *The Picture of Dorian Grey* suggested an actual trigger for the answer to Dorian's wish for eternal youth. It's indirect, but it's there if you're watching closely enough, and it's more than Wilde ever gave – which was nuthin'.

It occurred to me that the version of the novel in this particular cinematic adaptation did not contradict the original as much as complement it, providing extra details such as Basil Hallward's niece who loves Dorian as a small child and grows up to love him as a woman. And her jealous, jilted suitor.

And that statue of the Egyptian cat goddess Bast.

Somewhere along the way I came across the idea that had been put out there by more than one writer: Barré Lyndon's *The Man in Half Moon Str*eet was a mad scientist variation on Wilde's *The Picture of Dorian Gray*. Although Lyndon was also a screenwriter (he did the screenplay for the George Pal classic of '50s sci-fi, *The War of the Worlds*), he wrote his story initially as a play, the first movie version suspiciously appearing from a rival studio the same year as MGM's 1945 *The Picture of Dorian Gray*.

I was familiar with the Hammer remake of *The Man in Half Moon Street*, entitled *The Man Who Could Cheat Death,* which transposes the story to France in the 19thcentury and is one of those rare Hammer movies where Christopher Lee is the good guy. I haven't been able to actually see *The Man in Half Moon Street* and the stills make it hard to tell if it's meant to be set in the 1940s or a previous century. But no matter: The Hammer version had made Doctor Georges Bonnet, the renamed mad doctor of Lyndon's original, a contemporary of Dorian Gray.

And from there... I was reminded of the second villain in the rogues' gallery of my childhood hero Carl Kolchak-the titular antagonist of *The Night Strangler* (1973), written by genre great Richard Matheson *(I Am Legend; The Incredible Shrinking Man;* and select episodes of the original version of *The Twilight Zone,* among so much more). Just as *The Picture of Dorian Gray* looms as a suspicious precursor to *The Man in Half Moon Street,* so *The Man in Half Moon Street* appears to be an even more direct ancestor of Matheson's Dr. Richard Malcom, who also has obtained extraordinary longevity through organs taken from unwilling donors.

So, *Portrait of a Lady* references all three immortals, Wilde's original, of course, and then a riff and the riff of the riff. My story is intended in part as a metatextual parody of the literary connections between these different immortal characters and the apparent literary fruit borne from the pollination of Wilde's concept into other notable creative minds.

And hopefully it was an enjoyable read to boot.

(And if you'd like to know what happened to the *other* Becky Sharp, the one who took a different path at Kor and had a much wilder fate with even more crossovers than in *Portrait of a Lady, The Eldritch New Adventures of Becky Sharp* is still available as a Kindle book on Amazon for only $2.95.).

THE HALLWARD RESTORATIONS

Peter Rawlik

Don't look at me like that, Herbert, you arrogant misanthrope. If I choose to take a circuitous route through the cemeteries and alleyways of Boston, rather than using the main streets, that is my business. You wouldn't laugh if you had seen what I had seen. There is a kind of safety in the disused byways and forgotten avenues, and yes, even in the boneyards of our past. I take comfort in the things that haunt these places, restless and hungry. They are an honest kind of horror, as they do not hide their monstrosity, but rather revel in it.

I prefer that to other horrors, those which don the masks of humanity and ape our customs and courtesies. I have seen things that would chill you, Herbert; monsters of the most perverse kind, supping as if they were men and women like any other. I've no proof, of course, but that doesn't make what I saw any less real. Wipe that smirk off your face, damn you. I'll tell you my tale if that is what it takes. I've never told anyone else, not even that whining sycophant Thurber.

It was in the winter of 1919 that the missive from Lord Kelso arrived. One of his agents had been touring the Americas and had seen some of my work hanging in the Boston Art Club. This was most ironic as my exhibition had been part of Charles Hovey Pepper's so-called New England Artists' Series, which had been met with cheers from critics, but jeers from the public. From what I heard, Pepper had been threatened with bodily harm for his selection of Cubist paintings, which some considered obscene.

Lord Kelso's note was a simple inquiry into my interests in studying abroad. He had established an atelier – an artist's workshop – in London, and there was a place for me if I so desired. All my expenses; including my travel, lodging, and board, would be paid for by the benefactors of the workshop. We would work for a few weeks, and then display our pieces at a local private gallery.

This was the first I had ever heard of the Elpis Academy, but honestly, I didn't care about whether they were notable, famous, or even infamous. At last, someone had noticed my artistic endeavors and found them worthy enough to extend a kind of patronage, even if it was only for a few weeks. Eager to accept, I contacted his man in Manhattan, and within a week I began to prepare for my journey.

I had been ordered to travel light, and so it was that I arrived in early April and found myself in the streets outside Grosvenor Square with just a second-hand steamer trunk at my side. The house used by the Elpis Academy to board students had once been a luxuriant, multistory townhome, but sometime in the last few decades it had been divided up into small apartments. My rooms occupied the uppermost level, an attic with a large fireplace and a few small windows that overlooked the square outside. The room held a few pieces of furniture -- relics, really -- that would have been out of style seventy-five years earlier, but still serviceable. It was not fancy, but my needs were simple. My only complaint was that the weak light that leaked through the windows was inadequate, at least from an artistic perspective; but then again, this was not meant to be my studio.

There were ten of us: myself, seven Brits, and two Scots, and we spent our first few days ranging out first to the Wallace Collection, and then the National Gallery, followed by the British Museum, and

121

of course the Victoria and Albert. Afternoons were spent in Hyde Park promenading round the Serpentine, where young men walked with their ladies and old women fed birds, while gentlemen of leisure strolled with canes and top hats taking in the air and the sights.

Our guide in all of this was a greybeard New Yorker by the name of Jack Scott. It was a name I knew, for he was considered a minor master in the field, and the last disciple of the late ultra-realist Boris Yvain. While in France, Scott had used Yvain's name and legacy to establish a small school of his own, but he had fled to London when the winds of war had blown into Paris. With the help of Lord Kelso and his charitable Pheme Society, Scott had re-established himself and his school as the Elpis Academy. This was just the third year of their operation, and I was their first American student.

Assisting Scott in guiding us around London was a young man by the name of Jules Pickering. He was a friendly sort, who had a habit of bursting into song. He seemed to always have a story or two to tell about nearly every landmark or building that we encountered. Also, everywhere we went he seemed to encounter someone he knew, and these encounters ranged from lowly chimney sweeps to the directors or curators of the various museums we visited. On more than one occasion his connections allowed us to gain entry to exhibits or locations that were usually off limits to the public. He was the most astounding of men, though it annoyed me to no end that he never once removed the ragged cap he wore, not even in the presence of a lady.

After those first few days we settled into painting under Scott's tutelage, using very attractive models. There was one girl whose beauty was so natural, so alluring, that we all seemed to fall under her spell. All of us, that is, except for Jules, who said he preferred his women more voluptuous.

Not that it mattered, as despite all our attempts to capture her attentions she barely ever said a word to any of us. She refused all invitations, saying she preferred to spend her evenings in music halls, which hosted the most avant-garde of performers. Her favorite of these was a most flamboyant organist who was often accompanied by his wife, a rather accomplished ingénue. Scott frowned on carousing, but recognized it as a necessary evil, particularly amongst artists, but being the only American, and with limited spending money, I rarely joined them. Instead, I spent my evenings in the studio obsessing over my oils.

My studies were going well, at least Scott implied such, but I had my doubts. Which was one of the reasons I so diligently sequestered myself at the studio, even into hours well after midnight. Some nights I was so paralyzed by my insecurities that I took to pawing through Scott's collection of canvases, some of which dated back almost a century. There was a small piece by Seurat, a sketch by Manet, several Klimts, a grotesque Schiele, and even a triptych by Kirchner.

Despite all these works, the piece that drew my attention – that captivated me like no other – was a full-figure study, a masterpiece by Scott's departed colleague Boris Yvain, in a kind of abstract style that seemed an early precursor to cubism. As interesting as the painting was, so was the frame, which echoed the style of its contents. Even the small brass tag that named the piece and identified its subject was magnificent.

I had, of course, heard of Basil Hallward, the realist painter who had been so in vogue three-quarters of a century ago, and I even knew that he had known Yvain. It had been on a trip to visit Yvain that Hallward had vanished, and based on the date in the tag, the painting had been finished not long afterwards. One could see that it had once been something to marvel at, but time and poor curatorship had taken their toll. The canvas was terribly dirty, which muted the colors. In some areas, the paint had cracked. Worst of all, was the fact that the canvas was separating from its stretcher, relaxing the tension in some places while maintaining it in others. This warped the piece and threatened to cause some thicker areas of paint to fall off completely.

Saddened by the state of the thing I began a plan to restore the piece to its former glory. I had for many years studied the repair of paintings under those commissioned to do such things for the great auction houses of Boston. I had the skills, and I recognized the issues that presented themselves, and I believed it wouldn't be that difficult to affect the required repairs. I had all the tools I needed right there in the studio. My only fear was that Scott might disapprove, thinking me too arrogant. Who was I to think myself worthy of restoring a Yvain masterpiece?

So, I undertook the task in secret, working on it only after Scott and the others had left, and always making sure that it was properly hidden away in an unused storeroom behind some old easels and tarpaulins. My secret project thrilled me to no end and having this purely mechanical piece seemed to help me focus my own creative drives. My artistic studies of Vulnavia and the other models we employed suddenly began to take on an amazingly subtleness of style. Scott was particularly pleased with my portraits and suggested that I had captured my subject's features in an almost photographic manner.

I did once slip up, however. So inspired had I become by my nightly activities, that Yvain's abstract style began to contaminate into my own more natural work. Scott noticed this and reprimanded me for letting the cubists influence me. I could pursue such decadent studies if I wished, but not under his tutelage.

Four weeks after we had begun our work Scott announced that we were ready for our first show. We balked, of course; well, most of us did, but he calmed our fears by informing us that the exhibition would be a private one reserved for members of the Pheme Society, and then only for one night. Each of us would display three paintings of our choosing, albeit with advice from Scott. The exhibition would be at a gallery run by Jack Laird, which was infamous for catering to artists and patrons who preferred their subject matter of a grotesque and morbid sort. None of us really knew what to choose for such a display, and so we surreptitiously inquired about the nature of the Pheme Society in hopes of gleaming some hint of how to garner their favor.

Old Scott would say little, only that the group had been formed in the previous century by members of London's high society. It was not a social organization, though its members did tend to mingle with each other. Nor was it any sort of arts club, though it did sponsor the Elpis Academy and maintain what was rumored to be an extensive private collection of statuary and paintings. At its core, the Pheme Society was a kind of investment club, buying and selling not dry goods like common merchants, but rather estates, farms, and great houses throughout the British Isles.

Rumor had it that the society owned as much property as the Royal Family itself, and used the holdings to fund their lifestyles, which were not so much extravagant, as extended. That was the word Scott had used, "extended," which seemed odd to me at the time.

It was on the First of June that we opened the doors to the Night Gallery and welcomed in our patrons. Based on what Scott had said, I expected the crowd to be older than they were, but instead of aging patricians and dowagers, the arriving guests were my own age or even younger. And they came in style, arriving in gilded carriages and the most ostentatious motorcars. They came wearing the most extravagant top hats and overcoats in their repertoire of finery. The woman came clad in vast petticoats and silk gowns, wearing tiaras with intricate collars, chokers, and necklaces. Upon entering the gallery, they doffed their wraps, coats, and hats to reveal the finest of visages, with manicured hair, expert makeup, and the palest of skins. They were the most beautiful people I had ever seen; the most beautiful people that had ever existed, and they had come to see my art.

I remember feeling suddenly small, insignificant, and unworthy. I retreated into a corner and watched the affair secreted away from the beautiful people that had come to meet me. I hid because amongst these stunning things, these angelic creatures, I felt my own body, my own features, to be grotesque; my meager attempts at art, at capturing the beauty of the world, wholly inadequate. I had previously thought that capturing the real would had been enough, but now I saw the truth, and it destroyed any illusion of talent that I thought I might possess. My art was nothing, it was inadequate, and it always would be in comparison to these semi-divine spirits that had somehow been embodied in flesh.

My solemnity was broken by a sudden disturbance at the front entrance. Lord Kelso had arrived, and his peers in the Pheme Society parted, like a sea of alabaster, letting him pass. He was, I thought, about twenty; maybe a little older, maybe a little younger, with fine, sharp features and piercing intelligent eyes. His hair was a curious shade of tawny brown and cut in a manner that framed his face and highlighted his cheekbones.

He stood proudly, not defiantly or arrogantly, but upright and proud. When he walked it was as if his feet barely touched the floor, as he didn't so much walk as glide across the room. He wore clothes, of course, and these were as fine as anything else that could be seen in the room. They were still outshone by the person who wore them, and honestly though I think back now that it may have been the finest suit I had ever seen; it did not do the man justice, but I think no suit ever could. Aphrodite herself would have fallen in love with him, and in so doing would have gladly incurred the wrath of the gods themselves.

He strolled through the gallery, pausing in front of each picture, examining it in detail before turning to Scott, who would whisper some words and gesture at the artist who had produced the work. He would then nod and move on. The other patrons appeared disinterested in what he was doing, but I could see them watching out of the corner of their eyes and casting furtive glances in his direction. It was as if they were waiting for something to happen, either for Lord Kelso to find something, or to make a decision.

It was then that I realized there was something terribly peculiar about the Pheme Society, for though they looked young and vibrant, they moved cautiously, they watched intently, and they carried themselves in the most restrained of manners. Some even favored one leg or another or held an arm close to their side or chest. I had seen such behaviors before, amongst those who had come back from the war wounded in some manner; and amongst the very old, who themselves had suffered the slow wounds of time. There was even a woman who, though beautiful and even statuesque, hid half her face from the world behind a thick veil of lace.

As Lord Kelso passed her, his hand touched her shoulder, and she bowed her head and whispered a single lonely word: "Please."

He never looked at her, but his lips parted, and he said in a soft, melodic voice: "I think so, Lady Susurrus, I think so."

There arose then from our patrons the queerest murmuring that passed through them like a wave of adulation. It was at this point that the whole gathering went from merely polite to something more vibrant. It was as if a switch had been thrown and everyone had been given permission to be exuberant. The staid gentry were suddenly lively, more vocal, and freer with their purses. In moments Laird was moving through his gallery hanging small signs on our paintings to mark them as sold. Even the sad half-faced woman seemed to be happy, and I saw the proprietor hang her marker next to one of my charcoal portraits.

"Her name isn't really Lady Susurrus," said a familiar voice.

I turned to find a woman standing next to me, one who looked vaguely familiar, and her voice was one I was accustomed to. It took me a moment to realize that she was Jules Pickering. I hadn't even realized that Pickering was a woman.

"What?" I stammered out in surprise.

"Lady Susurrus, she isn't really a lady, at least not from the north as she suggests. They all play at being titled, and maybe some of them are, but I doubt it. Even Lord Kelso. He claims to be the Irish bastard of the previous lord, an unexpected outcome from his time spent whoring in the Emerald Isles. But it is untrue, I don't care what documents he has as proof."

"How would you know, Pickering?" I still couldn't believe she was a woman.

She beamed a toothsome smile. "Their voices. You can tell by how they speak. My father and grandfather were phoneticists, so they studied speech, accents, and dialects. They could place an Englishman within two miles of his home just by listening to them talk. They taught my mother, and all three of them taught me.

"You wouldn't think that there would be much call for such skills, or that it paid well, but it does. You would be surprised what you can learn about a man by the way he speaks, and what he will pay to keep such secrets. A single word can damage a man's reputation, and a single word can repair it." She twirled around to my other side. "You just need to know the right words."

I shoved her away. I meant to say something cruel and witty, but before I could open my mouth, Scott was there.

"Lord Kelso would like to speak with you, Richard." He looked at Pickering, "Good evening, Jules."

She laughed and departed our company.

I followed Scott out of the Night Gallery and down the street to where Lord Kelso's car sat idling. His driver opened the door and ushered me inside. Lord Kelso was waiting for me, sitting there watching as I stumbled in out of the night.

"Good evening, Mister Pickman." He spoke it as if my name meant something.

As I returned his greeting the car started and motored down the street. "Please call me Richard."

He smiled. "Ah yes, the American penchant for the informal. If I am to call you Richard, you must call me Rian."

"Ryan?"

"No, Ri-an. It is my name. Rian O'Grady. Surely you didn't think my name was Lord?"

I shook my head. "No, of course not."

"It would have been terribly more convenient if my parents had endowed me so. Like the Scotts who name their sons Roy, or the Iberians who optimistically bless their children as Jesus. It just seems so damned arrogant. Don't get me wrong, arrogance is all fine and good, unless it's misplaced; then I find it a damned nuisance." He smirked. "You aren't an arrogant man, are you Richard?"

"I don't believe so, sir."

He nodded. "The other side of the coin. There is misplaced arrogance, and then there are those who have every right to strut about like a peacock and yet don't. You, Richard, deserve to be prouder than you act. You have skill, a talent that has not been seen for more than a generation, and one that is in dire need. I have a proposal for you, one that would benefit you financially and would endear you to my friends and I for your entire life. That is, if you are interested."

I indicated that I was, and once again I was blessed with the hauntingly beautiful smile of Rian O'Grady.

Ten minutes later we were in a district of London I didn't recognize and being ushered into a building I couldn't identify. There were guards everywhere, but as we made our way inside I noticed that every single one of them was blind.

"A few years back there was a rather famous magician who held a horrible secret that he needed no one to see. He trained these men very well. He died, and his secret burned. But the men remained. They may not be able to see, but they are more than adequate for our needs."

I noted the serrated knives strung across their chests and shuddered at the thought of the damage such blades would cause.

Inside the vaulted warehouse I was brought to a vast room, which had obviously once been a warehouse, but had now been converted to an immense gallery. There were hundreds of paintings of various sizes and shapes, and all were hidden behind protective sheets. I could see there were rat traps placed along the walls, and I detected the smell of camphor in the chilled air. I realized that this was not so much a gallery or museum maintained to view art, but rather a mausoleum, the sole purpose of which was to preserve the contents within from the forces of decay.

Lord Kelso made a dramatic gesture with his arm as the lights switched on with a thunderous snap of clicks. "This is the Hallward Collection. Almost every painting he ever did is kept here, the private property of the Pheme Society."

He removed the sheet covering the nearest easel to reveal a large landscape reminiscent of the work of the 18th century master Henry Hogson. I stepped forward and examined it in detail. It was a fine piece, but nothing truly spectacular. I noted the signature and date and realized that this was from very early in his career.

Lord Kelso caught the look on my face and nodded. "Not a particularly exciting piece, but we like to be complete." He dropped the curtain back in place and gestured for me to follow him.

We strolled a few rows further in and stopped in front of another selection. "It was after he began doing portraits that Hallward obtained a true mastery of his field, capturing what he felt and not what he saw."

With a flourish, he removed the covering and flung it to the side. I gasped at what lay beneath, both because of the mastery of style and the grotesque horror of the subject.

The painting was in a rather ornate frame, and the title on the brass plaque read in bold letters, *Gladys, Lady Wooten.* If it was meant to represent a member of the noble court, however, that court must have been in Hell itself.

The thing depicted in the painting was monstrous, a titan worthy of Goya or Bosch, and it may have been at home on any medieval cathedral. It was female, the bosom and manner of dress hinted at that; but the face and features were unreal caricatures. The eyes were small and beady, the ears like those of an elephant, and the gaping mouth bore no teeth, but instead was filled with a dozen wagging tongues. The skin of the thing was warty and random hairs grew out like thick black wires. There were bulbous growths as well, thick pustules that decorated the arms and neck which hinted at a terrible, creeping infection.

As it was both hideous and beautiful at the same time, I stood before it in awe, albeit an awe tinged with sadness. Not just because of its magnificence, but also because of its decay. The canvas had warped in places, particularly on one side of the face, and the frame itself had been crumbled as a result of rot. It was enough to bring tears to my eyes.

My host saw my reaction and placed a comforting hand on my shoulder. "We want you to repair them for us," he whispered in my ear. I opened my mouth to object, but he shook his head. "I've seen your work. Your subject matter may be different, but your style is nearly identical. Scott says you are the best he's seen in decades. Furthermore, he says you also have experience in restoration."

I was flabbergasted, as I had thought my work on the Yvain a secret. "There are dozens of paintings that need restoring. You can begin with this one, as it is the most degraded." He handed me a piece of paper, and on it were some numbers, a rather large value in American dollars. "We will pay you, of course."

"It's very generous, Lord Kelso," I stammered, "but this amount . . ."

He waved my objections away, "That amount is per painting, my dear Richard. And each effort will be reviewed by the whole of the Pheme Society. We are going to make you very rich, Mr. Pickman, and you shall enjoy great distinction, at least among a rather select number of extremely influential people."

I wanted to refuse, I did, but there was so much money and so much pressure. There was no possibility that I could decline, and Lord Kelso made sure that I never really had an opportunity to deny him. In the end, I agreed, and in doing so committed myself to laboring under his thumb for at least eighteen months. At last, I had become a professional artist, only not in the manner I had expected.

***

My work began the very next day. The Elpis Academy was redirected to new quarters and Scott's studio was turned over to me. Three of the blind guards were always assigned to the building, and I was to sleep in the loft above. I could go out if I so desired, but I would be accompanied by a fourth guard who was sighted though never to be allowed inside the studio. It was all so very convoluted,

133

and I felt as if I was in some sort of espionage shocker as documented by the John Buchan. I fully expected German spies to try and infiltrate my unassuming little workshop.

I thought at first that Jack Scott would have been upset by his being ejected from his own studio, but he seemed relatively pleased at the situation and said so that very first day. He was one of the few people who would be allowed to visit when there was a Hallward in residence. I apologized to him for working on the Yvain without his permission, but he assured me that he was pleased with the progress I had made. Indeed, it was based on my work on that very piece that he had recommended me to Lord Kelso.

All he asked is that I finish restoring the Yvain as soon as possible. I suggested that the work was almost done and that I might even finish within the week. He seemed delighted but reminded me to make sure the frame was tight and square before replacing the painting. It felt good to do something nice for the man who had gone so out of his way to help me, and I looked forward to finishing the restoration as soon as possible.

The first painting, the one I had seen in the warehouse entitled *Gladys, Lady Wooten*, arrived that afternoon. It was notably escorted by two more guards, and I found all of this security excessive. Basil Hallward was an excellent artist, but he was hardly known to the general public, and I couldn't imagine anyone stealing one of his paintings.

In the light and with the proper tools I found the damage to be more extensive than I originally thought, but in a way less serious than I had believed. My first job was to remove the painting from its frame to lay it and its stretcher down onto a table. As much as I wanted to embark on working on the actual painting, the first order of business was to excise the damaged pieces of frame and then send them off to be replaced.

If I was going to have one frame repaired, I might as well have a second one fixed as well. I hadn't really looked at the frame for the Yvain before. I had supposed to just replace the thing with another, but now I had a way to restore the old one. It was then that I found the hidden compartment. It was a tube, and inside was an envelope and a shipping label addressed from Allan Campbell in London to Boris Yvain in Paris. There was a note written on the other side that simply said, "Enclosed please find all that remains of your friend. I've done what was written on the note inside his pocket. May God forgive me."

Below these were other words in a different handwriting: "Dedicated to the Restoration of Basil Hallward." Also present, though in a language I didn't recognize, were words that seemed to serve as a kind of epitaph or oath. I put the paper in the pocket of my smock and forgot about it.

I spent more than four weeks working on Lady Wooten and fell into an odd kind of daily routine. I would wake at six and begin my day with coffee and a pastry at a small café around the corner. Then by eight, I would be in the studio tending to the Lady Wooten until one in the afternoon, when I would break for lunch. There was a local butcher shop that made the most wonderful roast beef sandwiches with a smear of grey mustard. I would take mine, along with a bottle of beer, and walk in Hyde Park for an hour.

Afterwards, I would return to the studio and continue my task. It was only after my supper, usually at eight in the evening, that I would stop and put the painting to rest. Supper was at a small restaurant called Simpson's in the Strand, followed by a leisurely walk home, always followed by my guardian. It was only in the late nights that I puttered about with the portrait of Basil Hallward, and then for only an hour or two.

I finished both paintings on the Second of July and let Scott know this on the morning of the Third. He seemed overjoyed and arranged for a viewing by the more senior members of the Pheme Society on the evening of the Fourth. I must admit I had my concerns, but Scott assured me that my work was first rate, and that I had matched the Hallward style most satisfactorily. I did not show him the progress I had made on the other painting, saving that as a special surprise for a later date.

The afternoon of the Fourth came, and the men came to transport the painting back to the warehouse that housed the Hallward Collection. I had hoped that the unveiling would have been at a more prestigious venue, but it was made clear to me that the Pheme Society held their paintings very dear and would not risk them in any way.

I had not forgotten the guards and their wicked blades. It was just before the men arrived that I decided to add the Yvain to the transport crate. I would unveil it as an encore to the Lady Wooten. These people held Hallward in such high esteem, I was sure they would revel in my restoration of his portrait.

It took me hours to make the secret gallery ready for a reception. The work was to be displayed in a small antechamber off the main room. I say small, but this is only in comparison to the vastness that housed the main collection. The actual hall was easily the size of Laird's Night Gallery, if not slightly bigger, and would easily accommodate all the patrons that I expected to attend. There were some perfunctory refreshments and a velvet rope to keep admirers away from the dais that held my restoration; well, one of them, at least. The other I positioned to the back and side so that it too could be seen but would not draw attention from the main attraction.

Guests began arriving at eight, with the circumstance to commence at nine. The procession was much less formal than that of the weeks before, but at the same time there were many more in attendance. I had not thought the Pheme Society to be so large, but it was, and I chuckled to myself that there seemed to be a member for almost every painting in the Hallward Collection… almost, but not quite.

There was something else odd that I noticed. At the previous gathering the guests had been dressed in very stylish, very fashionable outfits, but tonight as they accumulated, I realized that the clothes they wore were decades, perhaps even a century, out of date. It was as if someone had suggested that a masquerade be held, but instead of wearing masks invoking animals or spirits, the theme was the Victorian period. It was so very strange, but I suppose that given the conservative nature of my patrons, a longing for a more glorious time was natural.

As I watched the crowd gather, I saw familiar faces, unfamiliar faces, and one that I seemed to recognize, but couldn't place. It took me a full twenty minutes of furtive glances, deft maneuvering, and eavesdropping to finally realize that it was none other than the Lady Susurrus, but without the partial veil that had hid half her face. I thought at first that her previous appearance had been a kind of grand deception, but as I listened, I realized that it was indeed real, and that she had in the intervening weeks undergone a remarkable transformation, one that the rest of the society seemed to be very pleased with.

Indeed, most of the well-wishers seemed to belong to those members who were themselves wounded in some manner, though there was a curious tone in their voices. It took me some time to recognize the subtext of their comments, but eventually I recognized it for what it was. These people were genuinely happy that Lady Susurrus had recovered, but they were also incredibly jealous.

Just minutes before the fateful hour Lord Kelso arrived looking as stunning as ever. As before the crowd parted for him, and without so much as a word he made his way up to the front of the crowd and assumed a position of authority in front of the covered portrait. He looked about, caught the attention of Lady Susurrus, and beckoned her over.

"This is for your benefit my dear," he said so that all could hear. "You volunteered to take the risks, and I'll admit that they appear to have brought you good fortune. But let us now see what your gamble has wrought, so that others may decide whether to follow in your wake."

He nodded toward me and with a flourish I lifted the sheet and unveiled the restored *Gladys, Lady Wooten*. There came from the crowd a hushed astonishment as they all waited for Lady Susurrus and Lord Kelso to react. There was a suppressed smile on that perfect face as he watched the woman at his side go from hopeful to happy, to crying in joy at what I had revealed.

Cautiously she reached out a hand across the velvet rope as if to touch the source of her ecstasy, but only to withdraw it slowly. "Will it last?" she asked while looking at the man by her side.

He cast a glance in my direction and I nodded. "It shall need regular tending to, but I've repaired all the damage and prevented further decay. When it came to brushwork and subject matter, Basil

Hallward was brilliant. However, his selection of paints and canvas and gesso appears to have been substandard, but it's nothing that cannot be dealt with."

With that statement, I was suddenly the focus of all attention and the gathered crowds were suddenly applauding and calling out my name. It was a moment of pure adulation that I had never felt before. I soaked in their adoration like a long dry sponge, basking in it as if was the brightest sun, or the freshest spring water. I bowed once, maybe twice, as if I was some kind of operatic divo. After a minute or so, I raised my hands and called for the crowd to settle.

"Please, please," I begged them happily. "I am overwhelmed with your response to my work, and for that I am grateful. It was truly a pleasure working on this painting by your illustrious Basil Hallward. I may not be as fond of him as you obviously are, but my appreciation of the man is growing, and I hope to restore many more of his works."

There followed a cordial kind of laughter and a smattering of applause.

"In honor of tonight, in respect to the man who brought me to your attention, and the artist you all admire so much, I have a special surprise."

I scanned the room for Jack Scott but could not locate him. For a moment, I considered aborting the presentation, but I could see that I had captured the attention of the Pheme Society.

It was Lord Kelso that put me over the edge. "Come, come, Richard. You cannot tease us like that and then not follow through. You are a master craftsman, not a common streetwalker. Though I will admit that I have known some craftsmen who were little more than whores, and some whores who were masters of their craft."

139

He rolled his hand in the air to urge me on. Having no choice, I stepped back toward the second covered painting and withdrew the sheet.

"I am pleased to present tonight a second restored piece, a painting by the artist Boris Yvain. And not just any of his paintings, but one of your own obsession: the artist himself, Basil Hallward!"

A hush fell over the crowd as the sheet drifted to the floor. They were stunned into silence, but I could not tell if it was in appreciation, horror, or dismay.

I recognized that the style was not what they were accustomed to and tried to explain. "You will note that Yvain's use of angles and sharp contrast seems to bridge the gap between the symbolists of the last century, and that of cubism, exemplified these days by Picasso and other modern artists. This painting may be a key example of the transition between the various movements, and thus is likely an important if not even valuable work."

As I stopped speaking, I saw Lord Kelso start to chuckle. From that he soon erupted into a hearty giggle, and in seconds the entire room was overcome in laughter and hysterics.

I shrunk back, and this caught the attention of Lady Susurrus who tried to explain through guffaws. "You misunderstand us, Mister Pickman. We are not admirers of my dear uncle, we are his legacy. We do not honor the paintings of Basil Hallward, we are enslaved by them. They are either a blessing or a curse, perhaps both at the same time. We may loathe the gift they give us, but we fear the oblivion of death even more."

I fumbled in my pocket and pulled out the slip of paper that I had found hidden in the frame. "But Yvain seemed devoted to the man

140

and his work. He even wrote a refrain dedicated to the restoration of the painting. I don't understand it, but perhaps one of you will."

It was then that I read those words, those terrible words that I have since learned should never be read aloud. But I nevertheless read them, and in the most eloquent and clearest of voices.

Y'AI 'NG'NGAH
YOG-SOTHOTH
H'EE-L'GEB
F'AI THRODOG
UAAAH

Almost immediately the electric lights began to sputter and wink out, and there came to my ears a tremendous howling, as if the abyss itself had opened up and let loose its legions. There too was a stench; a horrid, fetid thing that hinted at charnel houses and the grave. I stumbled, driven from my feet by the assault on my senses.

I could hear the crowd screaming. They were panicked, and I surveyed the crowd to understand what was happening. Upon doing so I could see Lady Susurrus crumbled into the arms of Lord Kelso, who bore a wicked scowl across his face.

He spoke, but whether I heard what he said or merely read his lips I cannot say. "What have you done, Pickman? *What have you done!*"

It was then I realized I was no longer alone on the dais. There was another figure beside me, one that should not have been. It was an impossible thing: tall and straight, the lines of its arms and legs were unnaturally ordered. There were no curves to the man that stepped out of the frame – out of the canvas itself – and onto the stage. No curves, and no thickness either, the figure was entirely two-dimensional. But it was still terrifying and monstrous, a violation of the very laws of the universe, and there was no denying that it was Basil Hallward restored once more to a semblance of life.

Terrified, I stumbled off the stage and forced my way through the crowd toward the exit. I heard it speak and the words it said weighed heavy on my very soul.

"You disappoint me, my niece. I gave you near-immortality and look how you use it. So much to be done, so much to be accomplished, to be learned and understood and explored. Yet here you are cowering in the arms of Dorian Gray!

"You could have been something special, something unique and astounding in this world, but look at the portrait that reflects the darkness in your spirit. You seem to have squandered your gift and become nothing more than a highly skilled gossip."

A wave of the mob pushed me round to see the confrontation. I was still moving toward the door but now I could see the hideous thing I had unleashed as it towered over Lord Kelso and spoke to him in anger and with retribution in his tone.

"And you, Dorian! Did you think I wouldn't recognize you? I remember what you did to me, how you betrayed me and my friendship. There is a price to pay, sir, and it is time your marker was called."

The mob surged again and forced me out the door just as the monster grabbed one of the lamps and smashed it against the floor. The fire caught almost immediately, and the sheets exploded in flames. The last thing I saw as I was forcibly ejected was the silhouette of Lord Kelso as he raised up a hand, one that bore a long wicked looking dagger. After that, there was only darkness.

***

I awoke in a hospital bed with the police at my side. I had been unconscious for more than a day, and the there were questions to answer. The entire warehouse had gone up in flames. It took ten hours for things to cool down enough for the ashes and walls to be searched.

Witnesses say that dozens of people tried to flee the inferno, but as they ran away the embers must have settled down on them and they burst into flames. They say some few survived by shielding themselves with paintings stolen from the warehouse. The witnesses also say these few did not escape unscathed, however, for as they ran they seemed to smoke as if the fire was smoldering in their clothes.

I answered the detective's questions as best I could but did not speak of the more phantasmagorical things I had witnessed. When it came to the cause of the fire, I suggested that an overly excited guest had kicked over a foot light, thereby setting fire to a woman's dress. In her panic, she ran about the room spreading the flames before anyone could do anything.

The detective seemed to accept what I said, particularly when I asked after the number of injured and dead. "There's the trouble, you see. Witnesses say they saw people burned alive on the street and heard the screams coming from inside the building, but we can't find any bodies." He sighed and closed his notebook. "No bodies, just piles and piles of ash."

I fled London for Boston the very next day. I never heard or saw anything of Scott or Lord Kelso, or anyone else. I resumed my regular life and I tried to paint the portraits and landscapes that I knew would be accepted into the galleries and houses around New England. But no matter how hard I tried I could not bring myself to complete any of these mundane works. I took to wandering, first in the day, but I found this unnerving. I was always looking behind me, trying to identify the queer rustling noise I continually heard amongst the crowds of people who haunt the streets of Boston. I heard it in every crowd, that loathsome rustling of dried canvas rubbing against itself, and the faint crush of flecks of paint falling.

Later, I realized that there were no crowds at night, and I found streets and places where I could be alone. Under such conditions, the rustling ceased. It was in these places that I discovered that there were other things to paint, things that weren't mundane, things made of macabre darkness that should have died out long ago and yet still linger in the shadows of our present modernity.

There are terrors that haunt the untrodden paths of our cities; the remnants of our forests, and the boneyards we have abandoned. I have no doubt of their existence for I have seen them, and I am grateful for that, as such knowledge enabled to learn that whatever fearsome scent they exude seems to keep the queer rustling of burned canvas at a distance. The Pheme Society has every right to a vendetta against me, but if I choose to keep company with things they fear that is their problem, not mine.

"So, there you have it, my friend. You asked for an explanation and I have given you one. Whether you choose to believe it or not, I do not care."

But my friend did believe me. I could see it in his eyes, and I could also see him pondering what to say next. He has always been an introspective man, well-educated in the sciences of biology and chemistry, but not one to scoff at things that were beyond the scope of his own experience. He sat there in silence for a minute, maybe two, and then finally he opened his mouth to speak.

It was my turn to listen enraptured as Doctor Herbert West told me of his own experiences and suggested how the two of us might benefit one another.

END

MANY RETURNS

David MacDowell Blue

Dramatis Personae

Dorian Gray	Carmilla Karnstein	Christine Daae
English gentleman, seemingly in his twenties, very handsome.	Austrian noblewoman, languid, in her twenties (again seemingly).	Swedish music student/singer, nineteen or so, pretty.

Setting

Chateau outside Paris, circa 1890.

Additional Notes

Thanks to my friend Christofer Nigro for insisting I write this.

A few references/explanations. One of the central conceits in this play is that Dorian Gray did not die at the end of the novel bearing his name, but that Oscar Wilde altered events to make the story palatable enough for publication. Hence, the story taking place after the events of said novel. Likewise, the ending of Joseph Sheridan LeFanu's *Carmilla* (which internal evidence suggests cannot have taken place later than 1846) may be rather more ambiguous than is obvious.

The Karnstein Prince, as you may have guessed, is the central character in *The Masque of the Red Death* by Edgar Allan Poe.

Christine Daae is the central character in the novel *The Phantom of the Opera,* and the play takes place a little before the events of that work.

The Chateau Merteuil is a reference to the novel *Les Liasons Dangereuses* by Pierre Choderlos de Laclos.

Jefferson Hope was the murderer in *A Study in Scarlet*, the first Sherlock Holmes adventure.

[A garden maze during a party at a country estate in France. Evening. Perhaps we can hear the sound of night birds, music, revelers not too far away. CARMILLA enters, masked. She removes her mask. Enter two others, making her step into the shadows. First is CHRISTINE, in nice but inexpensive clothes, and with her DORIAN. They carry filled wine glasses.]

Dorian: *[With a perfect gesture]* Voila! The heart of the living labyrinth!

Christine: However did you find your way so swiftly?

Dorian: Experience. A trait as worthless as it is useful. This is hardly my first visit to the Chateau Merteuil.

Christine: *[Absorbs his words, then--]* Living?

Dorian: Yes?

Christine: A living labyrinth you said.

Dorian: The hedges which surround us yet live, even if forced into unnatural shapes. They remind me of my countrymen in that respect. I should clarify. Not merely the English, but all men everywhere.

Christine: Including yourself?

Dorian: Am I not a man, Mademoiselle?

Christine: You are most witty, Monsieur.

Dorian: What a terrible thought. I should loathe being the 'most' anything.

Christine: Ah, but -- have you encountered all men and women, to claim such a thing?

Carmilla: Presumably he has seen enough of a sampling to draw such a conclusion.

[Both of them react to her presence.]

Dorian: Please forgive the intrusion, Mademoiselle...?

Carmilla: Countess.

Dorian: I don't believe we have met.

Carmilla: We have, in fact. *[Switches her attention.]* Earlier this evening I heard you sing, Mademoiselle Daae. I found myself quite moved.

Christine: I am honored, Countess.

Carmilla: You are native to Sweden?

Christine: Yes.

Carmilla: In my imagination that land is a cold and dark realm, where beautiful young people and ugly old ones huddle against the winter. Am I wrong?

Christine: Certainly, parts of Sweden match your description.

Dorian: Both correct and incorrect simultaneously. At once reassuring and surprising. I would offer a toast, but manners preclude such a thing. We have only two glasses.

Carmilla: *[Without looking at him.]* No worries, Monsieur Gray. I ceased drinking wine long ago.

Dorian: Whatever would entice anyone to do that?

Carmilla: It is a secret.

Dorian: I do adore secrets.

Carmilla: Including your own?

Christine: How did you come to know Mr. Gray?

Dorian: Dorian, please.

Carmilla: He and I attended the same murder trial some years ago. The killer had sought revenge on two men and chose a most remarkable method. At gunpoint he made each choose one of two offered pills to swallow. Their choice. And he would himself swallow the pill remaining. Of course, one was harmless, the other a deadly poison. Obviously, his prey each chose death, by coincidence or design.

Dorian: Ah yes, Jefferson Hope. The American. Popular expectation of some frisson of scandal led me astray. It made for dull theatre.

Christine: Would you call this man, Jefferson Hope, a courageous person then?

Carmilla: *[Considers this.]* He believed the universe itself was on his side.

Dorian: Really? You don't suppose he wished to make his crime as exciting as possible, but gambling his own existence in the process?

Christine: But did he believe what you say, or did you merely wish to believe?

Carmilla: An excellent question! What would you say?

Christine: I hardly know.

Carmilla: But between the two possibilities, which would you call the braver?

Dorian: Surely the better question – which of the two is the more intriguing?

Carmilla: *[A beat. She turns her attention towards him.]* You have not aged a single day since then, sir. Not a single day.

Dorian: Nature has been kind.

Carmilla: Nature is never kind.

Dorian: No?

Carmilla: No.

Christine: *[Speaking almost on impulse.]* I should go.

Dorian: But why?

Christine: Forgive me.

Carmilla: Of course.

Christine: *[She hesitates, then speaks.]* You two have solved the maze on your own, with myself a mere follower. My place is not here. I have not earned it. For me, the challenge of finding my way.

Dorian: You speak as if a mere hedge maze were some kind of holy of holies. Surely it is nothing so mundane.

Christine: So much charm. I don't doubt a thousand young singers await you -- better singers than myself. And more beautiful.

Dorian: Those words, my dear Christine, seem almost harsh.

Carmilla: Miss Daae?

Christine: Countess?

Carmilla: I hope one day to hear you sing again—when you have rediscovered the love of your art. May that day come soon.

Christine: Thank you. *[A beat.]* Forgive me, but your eyes -- I do not have the words. Your face so very young, but in them, so much memory. Maybe if I had seen only your eyes -- were you wearing a mask perhaps -- I might mistake you for a very ancient person. But unhappy.

Carmilla: Go. And sing. May angels watch over you.

Christine: Do you believe in angels?

Carmilla: Why not?

[Christine: exits.]

Dorian: One wonders how long she will require to find her way out.

Carmilla: The rest of her life. Not long.

Dorian: Metaphors would seem to be on the menu this evening.

Carmilla: How old are you, Mr. Gray?

Dorian: As delightfully impertinent as I find your query, Countess, I must decline to reply.

Carmilla: Fifty? Sixty?

Dorian: Now you tease me. I am flattered, if somewhat baffled.

Carmilla: Five years. Half a decade, the lifetime of a small child -- you have not aged a single day. Every hair the same shade. Not one hint of a wrinkle, nor the slightest change in complexion. I notice such things.

Dorian: You have the advantage of me, Countess. We have not exchanged even names.

Carmilla: Carmilla Karnstein. I have used a variety of *nom-de-guerres*, but that is my given name. My family is Austrian.

Dorian: Your French is exquisite.

Carmilla: How old are you? Not the mere nineteen or twenty your appearance would suggest. Give me that. One secret. Just one. And I'll repay you in kind.

Dorian: Now I do feel intrigued.

Carmilla: Good.

Dorian: *[A sudden idea.]* One secret in exchange for another?

Carmilla: Yes.

Dorian: Of approximate nature and worth?

Carmilla: Certainly.

Dorian: In whose opinion? Mutual consensus perhaps?

Carmilla: I insist.

Dorian: I eagerly await your offering then and hope you shall force my hand to admit all. Pray begin!

Carmilla: My birth year was 1689. Do you believe me?

Dorian: I do.

Carmilla: My father said I resembled his sister, just as my half-sister Millarca looked rather like a cousin of ours, Marcilla. You perhaps recognize the pattern? A family tradition whose origins no one knows, or if they know refuse to reveal.

Dorian: Anagrams. Although problematical as an art form, not without charm.

Carmilla: Have you read or heard of the Karnsteins?

Dorian: I cannot say I have, at least not without deceit.

Carmilla: You were tempted to say you had, then? *[Dorian: gestures as if to confess.]* There were five of us. Myself and my half-sister. My father's brother's daughter Mircalla, whom everyone called the great beauty. Another Carmilla I had met once before, pretty and nice enough I suppose. And yet another Mircalla, this one from Hungary. I was told she was there, but we never met. Not then nor since. We were the guests of a certain Prince, the de facto head of our family due to the exalted status of his rank. Prince Prospero Karnstein enjoyed a reputation for debauchery. Nothing extreme really, merely extravagant. He threw elaborate parties hinting all sorts of scandal. Had his grandparents not been notorious inquisitors I suspect no one would have noticed. In truth, his genuine sins far exceeded those of which gossip accused him.

Dorian: I will confess now to feeling intrigued.

Carmilla: Don't be. His sins proved sordid and bloody, all about promises of power and immortality with I and my kindred as fodder for something truly ancient; ancient, terrible, and hungry. Quite literally. That was the Prince's greatest scandal, one chroniclers were given orders to remove from any records. I, my sister, the other girls -- we were among the first to die. Not the very first, that was the Prince. In retrospect I can almost enjoy his screams. And as far as I can tell, he remained dead.

Dorian: *[Not quite ready to believe her]* With the attendant implication you, at least, did not. Yet if I may say so, you make for a surprisingly animate corpse. But I listen.

Carmilla: I am no corpse.

Dorian: You claim to have died.

Carmilla: Not dead, no. I am Death itself, Dorian: Gray. Or something very like it.

Dorian: Are you flirting, then?

Carmilla: My kiss has slain more than many wars.

Dorian: *[Feeling his way...]* Are you venomous then? Like some kind of serpent?

Carmilla: Your turn.

Dorian: Dear lady, like the violinist who draws out the final notes, you have delivered me into limbo.

Carmilla: You age no more than do I. Tell me the reason.

Dorian: Have you no patience? How disappointing.

Carmilla: Wait and see for yourself. If you last. Fulfill your word or you hear not a syllable more.

Dorian: *[Waits for a moment, makes a decision]* I bow to your diplomatic skills. My story is simple, too simple in fact for me to truly comprehend it myself. What happened, that I can relate with relative ease. But precise reasons escape me. Quite simply, I made a wish. And my wish came true. A great artist, or at least a very talented one, did a portrait of me. At the time I had reached that point, like a flower at the zenith of its bloom, when soon I would begin to fade. From that hour, as a friend insisted I recognize, my life would be a matter of very gradual but ever-increasing decay. The painting, it had somehow captured my revelation of this fact. Within a year, perhaps mere weeks or even hours, time would begin to eclipse the best that I might ever know, steal away all enjoyment, all pleasure, all joy. Evaporation. Unbearable. So, I made a wish. Or uttered a prayer. Offered a deal, perhaps. Please choose whatever act seems to best capture what I describe. I daresay each would be as truthful as the rest.

Carmilla: What was it you wanted?

Dorian: That all the corruption of age and time and loss of innocence might be visited upon the portrait instead of myself. Thus, my youth and beauty would remain mine forever, while disease and nature had their way with what the canvas now contained. You doubt me?

Carmilla: *[Answering his question]* I simultaneously long to see what your portrait looks like now, and yet to know I would refuse the opportunity if offered.

Dorian: As it happens, I do not allow others to gaze upon it.

Carmilla: Do you yourself ever?

Dorian: Very rarely.

Carmilla: In that, I suspect, you are wise.

Dorian: How refreshing! To speak words sans counterfeit or obfuscation. I feel almost quickened. As if somehow a chain around me had been lifted. What an excessively pleasing sensation, one to which I might almost grow addicted in time. Which would not, in mature consideration, prove at all wise. But the temptation! Such a sweet one! I owe you thanks. And now, your turn, Countess Carmilla.

Carmilla: Oh, no.

Dorian: Please explain.

Carmilla: You have not yet offered equal value.

Dorian: I do not understand.

Carmilla: Consider my words at your leisure. *[She begins to exit.]*

Dorian: *[Suddenly]* Stop!

Carmilla: Why?

Dorian: For the same reason you obeyed. We have as yet so much to share, so many confidences to reveal to one another.

Carmilla: No.

Dorian: I suspect you already know that to be untrue. In fact, I grow certain of it with every moment. Why seek me out this way? Why reveal yourself at all if not for a need for companionship, for the company of a similar mind and soul? To be immortal, unaging, eternal, and unchanging sets us both apart! We are unique -- or at least as near to as to make no true difference. To me you may unveil your most closely held secrets. With me you need never feel fear of disbelief. In me all your solitude may find surcease. Carmilla … whatever forces rendered each of us into this state, they have proven generous enough to push us together. In each other we may have that which I suspect neither of us has ever genuinely known before this hour.

[Carmilla grabs his arm, which causes him considerable pain.]

Carmilla: You presume much.

Dorian: *[Not used to pain, not liking it.]* I offer much!

Carmilla: You offer very nearly nothing at all.

Dorian: If you are Death, as you say, then am I not Life? For all the disease and corruption which should have been my fate as a mortal are drained away! They are no longer a part of my nature! I am more alive than any who has ever walked! We are the opposites which make a whole -- male and female, life and death, ice and fire, day and evening. What truths and pleasures might we find, together?

Carmilla: Do better.

Dorian: Who are your peers? To whom can you speak without the need to pretend?

Carmilla: I am not the only one of my kind. Far from it.

Dorian: But I am the only one of mine! You have before you one unique, a new thing, an opportunity which has never existed ere now. Consider! Am I not as exotic a creature as you may ever encounter? You say there are many who share your nature, yet not one person anywhere shares mine. Am I not singular? Look upon me to view a wonder of this and all the ages of time. I might find another of you, eventually. But wander among epochs uncounted -- you will never find another Dorian Gray. Ponder this, Countess Karnstein.

[Carmilla seems to consider this, then slowly draws Dorian: towards her, forcing him to his knees. Along the way his glass of wine falls to the ground and spills. She bares his throat and sinks her fangs into his throat – then pushes him away in disgust. She spits out his blood.]

Dorian: What is amiss? Tell me!

Carmilla: The truth is always in the blood.

Dorian: What truth?

Carmilla: Truth for truth, Mr. Gray. You've earned that much. I believe your tale of eternal youth, of a magical totem accepting all the signs and consequences of your sins. Until moments ago, I only hoped you spoke the truth. Now I have lost all doubt. But here is another truth, the truth of blood. You called yourself life. No. Quite the opposite. My own life is stolen, taken from others drop by drop or in great gushing feasts. But from you I can take nothing at all. You offer nothing. You died years ago.

Dorian: No. You are wrong.

Carmilla: Dead. Long dead. Empty in fact. I find myself slightly curious about your portrait. Does it feel warm, I wonder? Is that where your life went? If I could smell it, would it seem to be oil and turpentine or to my senses or... something else? Not that it matters.

Dorian: You are lying. But why? There's something you fear, something you don't want to admit!

Carmilla: A pity. I am still thirsty. But then, I always am.

Dorian: I am alive. More than alive! It only seems to you that -- Wait! Come back!

[She exits, ignoring him. He does not follow. Instead, after a moment, he simply reaches over to pick up the empty wine glass and look at it.]

[Curtain]

END

THE D CLUB

Kevin Heim

November 17, 2018

It is no easy thing to see someone you know to be dead walking around a busy intersection. It could be someone that simply resembles a lost loved one, or even a relative of a deceased friend, but that initial recognition, however inaccurate, can be quite shocking. How much harder, then, is it to see someone that you yourself killed? And to know with certainty that it is that same person, and that this same person recognizes you as well?

It was windy out, but the weather had improved somewhat since the beginning of the month. Most locals even considered it unseasonably warm for the middle of November. The outdoor bistro was located far enough away from the Providence River that no additional chill was being felt, and the coffee and biscotti were just right. A playful smile had just started to show on her face as she set her cup down, when *he* strolled over to the table.

"Timmy!" he exclaimed upon recognition. "So good to see you again! It has been far too long! And who is your little friend?"

Doctor Edward Septimus "Tim" Pretorius leered behind his coffee cup but managed to suppress the sneer before standing. "Kyra, this is my longtime acquaintance Prince Charming. Charming, this is Kay."

164

Kay scowled and didn't bother to conceal it. "I'm sure you two have a lot of catching up to do. You'll get the check, 'Timmy?' Don't bother calling, It's unlikely we'll meet again."

With that said, the blonde lady walked up Westminster Street. Or was she brunette? Dorian did a double-take trying to make out her hair color in the mid-day sun, but she had already blended into the crowd.

"Well, that was rude of her," he commented, claiming her chair and her cup. "Oh, this is dreadful. Honestly, why would you even bother with American coffee?"

"She's an American, or at least she used to be, and Americans take their coffee this way," Septimus said as he took another sip of his own drink. "And I need that cup to run some DNA tests, so kindly keep your unclean lips off it. You know you could have waited until I'd finished with her. Your early arrival has quite inconvenienced me. She was a potential candidate for membership."

"So sorry to inconvenience you. I seem to recall you inconvenienced me not long ago, with that business involving those librarians."

"Nonsense! You look perfectly fine. Besides, that was payback for sending those kids from that Berkshire school to my chateau in Mexico."

Dorian feigned shock. "Mexico? That was twenty years ago! I thought we were passed all that. Now, tell me all about Kay. Is she the reason you called me here?"

"Hardly. Kay is someone who turns up now and then, often with a scandal or two trailing her. She's very adaptive; an ultimate survivor type. You'd like her. But she has her roots firmly in the scientific, so nothing you could use against me." Pretorius summoned the waiter.

"Bring my friend a fresh cup of hot water, some milk, and a pouch of Earl Grey. Would you like me to teabag you, or can you do that yourself?"

The quip drew a frown from Prince Charming, a.k.a., Dorian Gray. "If I could do that... I wouldn't be here, would I? Perhaps you should get to the reason you asked me to meet you here. I don't like staying in New England any longer than need be."

Dorian Gray, eternally young; and Dr. Septimus Pretorius, eternally old, stared at each other for much longer than was polite, with neither man blinking. Dorian removed the tea from his cup and added cream, all without turning to look at it. Drawing the cup to his lips, he finally broke.

"Are you ready to admit defeat?"

Pretorius grinned wickedly. "Oh, I don't think that will ever happen. You've made a losing bet this time. What is the score now?"

"You can't bluff your way out of this one. You're not that clever."

"Don't be daft, I am far cleverer than you. But I wouldn't deign to rely on wit and parlour tricks to win; that's your stratagem."

***

Over the years since they've known each other, Pretorius and Gray have had philosophical debates that evolved into friendly wagers, physical contests, and outright attempted murder. Being effectively immortal, both men relished the opportunities to challenge themselves, and lesser men simply aren't worth the time, as they can always be trusted to stay dead when killed.

Their inaugural meeting came about when Pretorius was recruited to join The 500, an exclusive club ostensibly restricted to those who have lived for 500 years or more. Nonsense, of course, as none of the members who have lived more than three centuries even showed up anymore. A much easier way to qualify for membership was returning to life after a medically-confirmed death, as Dorian has done years earlier, and now Pretorius had done too.

Dorian took an immediate disliking to the man, a scientist of ill repute who was quite fond of touting his accomplishments, though they were always achieved through proxies or accomplices, so his name stayed off the record. As a rule, Dorian Gray loathed what passed for progress, and told Pretorius so on several occasions. He even had disdain for how freely Pretorius used contractions and spoke in the common vernacular. Dorian, a native English speaker, had to make a conscious effort to sound modern, and he hated that it came so easily to an elderly Swedish scientist.

Thus, the rivalry began, and soon it became the entire focus of their meetings.

Since The 500 was never an official club, it was no difficult matter to have it renamed The D Club. Pretorius petitioned for the change, pointing out that "D" is the Roman Numeral for 500, and Dorian seconded the move; everyone else in attendance simply didn't care enough to fight it. They all knew the "D" really stood for "Debate," and it was clear that Pretorius and Dorian truly loved the D.

Their battles of wits became the focus of all club gatherings, and many members found themselves betting on Dorian or Septimus to win each new round, based on who had won the previous. Dorian Gray's natural charisma and flippant attitude made him an easy man to support, while Septimus Pretorius had a zealous fervor it was hard not to get caught up in. They debated over the merits of art within a

167

culture, passion over reason as the more efficient motivator, whether nurture or nature was the more important influence on a being, and the potential for magic to beat science or vice-versa. Most recently, this last one had evolved into an exercise in proving which force, magic or science, could be held responsible for the greater number of immortal and near-immortal beings on the Earth.

The current debate began with an analysis of nine immortals that spurned The Club for membership several decades back and moved on to contemporary subjects. As it happened, Captain Jack had just come into the room during the discussion, and the attentions of both men immediately turned to him. Jack, a long-time member of the club who, despite not being particularly fond of either Pretorius or Gray, was nevertheless a huge fan of the D, had never revealed his origins to club members. Hence, Dorian found himself speculating on the Captain's long history in service to the Crown.

He proposed that Jack may be an embodiment of the Spirit of England, a modern day Brutus or John Bull, possibly even of faerie blood. Septimus scoffed at the idea and pointed out that aside from returning to life every time he dies, Jack demonstrated no supernatural abilities at all, and was more likely the result of a scientific anomaly. Jack seemed to enjoy the attention, and he admitted to being the product of a singularity. He further refuted that he was even of British nationality. He confessed that he may have a little fae in him, from time to time, though it was clear he was having them on with this last point.

After that, he started bragging about the conquests he'd had over the centuries, and they had to tune him out when he name-dropped some well-known vampires he'd screwed over, and the other well-known vampires he'd taken them from. Such ribald tales had no place in their discussions.

Then Dorian offered up the example of AW -- the Amazon Warrior (alternately, the Aesir Walkyrie), a warrior maiden known to have been active at various times over the last 100 years, but whose rigid ethics and standards left her morally opposed to the D Club. Gray believed she may be the offspring of an Earth God, such as those found on Kadath or other mystical realms.

Septimus pointed out that not all her appearances were consistent, suggesting a succession of AWs, but had to concede that the current one resembled the original closely enough that she may be the same person, and that her wide range of talents suggested that her existence was beyond the ability of men to reproduce. "Your point," Pretorius declared then.

Dorian arched an eyebrow. "So, it is to be a game, is it? The usual wager?"

"Always." Pretorius smiled at that, reveling in another contest. "To the death!"

And so, they went back and forth, each offering various long-lived individuals for their mutual scrutiny and amusement. Club members were immediately considered off-limits, so as to avoid the uncomfortable positions Jack tried to put them in. So too were aliens, fae, and gods (or as Pretorius classified them: extraterrestrials, extradimensionals, and hyperdimensionals) ineligible, though half-human offspring were still considered for on a case by case basis. Candidates had to be human, to some degree.

The Sharp girl was an easy point for Gray. He brought up her immortality and linked it to a magical portrait of the lady. Pretorius let it go, citing Dorian's intimate knowledge of vanity to be fairly sure he was right about this one. It certainly made sense that her preternatural luck had a mystical origin, much as Dorian's own good fortune did.

Nonplussed, Septimus suggested a scientist they knew by the name Lyndon, who was like Dorian in many ways, but discovered the means to arrest the aging process through an alchemical elixir of life. Though the particulars were not known, his track record suggested this involved harvesting body parts from living 'donors'. Not wishing to familiarize himself with the process any further, Dorian did not dispute the claim.

Dorian begrudgingly mentioned Quentin, a rival of sorts from Maine, who also relied on a painting to maintain his vitality. Pretorius pondered the possibility that all these paintings may have been created with chemically-enhanced pigments, possibly through the use of powdered meteor dust; but Quentin's painting, like Dorian's own, was clearly beyond current scientific explanation, and thus won Dorian another point, as well as some small measure of embarrassment.

So too did he score for submitting the MacLeod immortals. Pretorius had contested the claim immediately; per the rules of the game he had 24 hours after acknowledgement of an entry to challenge it. He was not, however, able to provide any scientific theory that suitably covered all their attributes within the following 30 days. As burden of proof fell to the challenger, the mad scientist had to allow Dorian the points, though he continued to maintain his belief that they may be some form of alien vampire symbiosis.

Pretorius countered with Benton, a protege of his that, though not heard from recently, had made his own immortality through surgical means, unsavory though they were. Unlike several members of the

Frankenstein family he could mention, Benton relied on no magical forces nor assistance from anyone else to maintain his longevity. His isolation may have been his downfall though, as his recent disappearance had been linked to a visit from the Brothers.

The Brothers Band, so called for their tendency to identify themselves using names from rock bands, looked promising for being of Team Dorian, but despite their innumerable deaths, they were only just starting to live past their prime, so it wasn't clear if they were immortal only within the span of a normal human life.

Attempts to send proxies to gather more information on them always led to dead proxies, and the Brothers had proven capable of taking down enemies much more powerful than either Pretorius or Gray, so they had to wait before making a determination. Anyone who had not yet survived beyond fifty years of age was excluded from the Rule of Challenge, in that proof had to be provided by the Defender, and Dorian was not ready to give Septimus an easy victory over such delicious pawns.

Dorian next claimed that a photographer from Queens, New York had recently given birth to himself, but Septimus responded that the shutterbug in question was known to have been scientifically mutated prior to this experience; and that some naturally evolved animals, such as aphids, reproduce asexually to create a being that is genetically identical to itself, thus establishing a scientific precedent for the phenomenon. He then conducted, through an intermediary, cloning experiments on the subject and was able to reproduce the effect, with at least one clone retaining the memories and feelings of its predecessor.

A number of vampires had been suggested, but as Karmilla seemed to have suffered a final death, Dracula proved to be more of an idea than a specific individual, and so many variations existed on what exactly a vampire was, that dealing with them became more trouble than either man found worth the effort. Many strains of vampirism were determined to involve demonic parasites and determining whether or not a scientific symbiosis or the mystical nature of the demon was responsible for the immortal condition was the basis of research for several existing organizations and secret societies. That realization made it clear they would both be wasting their time trying to resolve the problem themselves. It didn't help that several types of aliens, fae, and psychics seemed to self-identify as vampires as well.

Man-made monsters, such as the ones that Pretorius' old friend Henry and his family created, were sometimes deemed scientific (alchemical), and other times magical (necromantic). Others, like the fabled Golem of Prague and the homunculi Pretorius himself had created ages ago, were clearly ineligible due to never having been even partly human.

Surprisingly to both men, certain individuals identified as tulpas, such as Father Christmas, were able to be proven to be scientifically created, despite their use of supernatural abilities. Other so-called "Undead" were considered only if they could return from being destroyed *after* they had already turned, which left ghosts and other incorporeal shades out of the running entirely and made revenants (like the ones found in Haddonfield and Crystal Lake) the most likely beings to be sorted, usually in favor of magic.

***

"Which brings us," Pretorius noted aloud as he reviewed his notepad, "to today's sport. I have leaked information through certain channels of a valuable prize being readied for display at the Lovecraft Arts & Sciences Council, right here at this arcade."

Dorian Gray chuckled. "So, we are to witness a theft, to gage the thief? I assume we will capture the would-be criminal and torture the poor soul, in the name of 'justice?' This does sound interesting, Timmy. Who or what should I be watching for?"

"We've discussed this one before: A werewolf I've dubbed 'Vinnie,' due to his penchant for using aliases with the 'VIN' sound in them. Alvin Howell, Steven Pertwillably, Ivan Scha..." He Pronounced the name *EYE-vun*, the American way, rather than *Ih-VOHN*, to stress the phonetic similarities to the other first names.

"Him? I thought we determined he was a time traveler. Hardly worth torturing someone to death over, though since we are here, we might as well."

"Circumstantially, yes, though there's evidence that suggests his appearances throughout history may not be temporal shenanigans. His whereabouts through World War II have been accounted for, and that is not a period that many would choose to stay in, had they the means to be elsewhere... or else*when.*"

"That leaves the lycanthropy. I know that one is all 'case-by-case' now." Dorian took another sip of tea to hide his disappointment as he recalled losing points for the Talbots, St. Clairs, and Osbornes due to advances in genetic research and the medical diagnosis of LMD, i.e., Lycanthropic Metamorphic Disorder. "Did you not say he was a Daninsky? Unless you've made another break-through, that makes him one for me, if he qualifies at all. Case closed, I'm afraid. Really, I did not expect you to make this game so boring."

"Quit playing the fop. You're too good at it. Or have you forgotten the work he's does at Arkham Sanitarium? That reagent Herbert and the others concocted, scientifically I might add, has been linked to many of our cohorts in the D Club. I still think the Gunny might have been one of those who benefitted from medical treatment by either West or Hartwell."

Dorian's tea, now quite cold, spilled just a little as he set down the cup. "Do not tell me you are considering an invitation for him! He runs with that Taskforce: Ecto crowd these days, detaining restless spirits through whatever you call that kind of science, and he was with the Theurgy Society before that! For all we know he is practicing diablery, devouring trapped souls to prolong his life. Which, I might add, would qualify his immortality as magical."

"No, I would not consider him worthy of membership, any more than I would Captain Rogers. And like Rogers, Vinnie spent a lot of time in the Ordnance, during the 1940s as well as in more recent decades, so he may have been subjected to a super-soldier program or two."

"Was he? I am sure I would have recognized him."

"He was never in the Olympus Initiative, so he didn't do any P.R. missions. My information indicates he was Ordnance Unconventional Tactics: Combat Intelligence Detachment qualified, so he would have most often gone on O.U.T.C.I.De. assignments. There's also the whole 'Anti-Logic' situation, but even I don't pretend to understand what is going on with that one. No, Vinnie is still a mystery, and today I intend to unravel that mystery once and for all."

"Alright, so we are mystery solvers today. Catch me up to speed; how did you leak the information?"

"You'll like this part. I infiltrated one of those online monster hunting networks, where they post their latest kills and file for bounty funds with the Bureau. Vinnie's on one called M*O*N*S*T*A*A*H. I have no idea what the acronym may possibly stand for. This morning I informed him of an artifact he would want to see that will be displayed here in Providence. Vinnie is located on the Massachusetts North Shore, so he ought to arrive here any second."

"You assume much, don't you? What if he is working, or not checking his messages, or just not interested in the bait?"

Pretorius gave Gray a quizzical look, an oversized eyebrow arched high. "You sound worried. Afraid he shall turn out to be another point for me? Or are you afraid of the werewolf? Have you two already met?

"Met? I only know of the brute through your prattlings about him. If I am afraid of anything it would be another wild goose chase on your behalf. Remember that immortal we tracked across Europe for weeks, only to find it was our own Saint-Germain? My point is, you left far too much to chance!"

"Heh, you only say that because you don't know what the bait is yet. Come, the doors to the Lovecraft Arts & Sciences Council will be opening at noon, and I expect our werewolf will be there when they do."

The two immortals then stood, which triggered a waiter to hastily set down the tray he was carrying to bring them their bill.

Pretorius handed the young man a white plastic card with no lettering, computer chip, or magnetic strip on it. "Here, give this to your manager. He'll know what to do with it."

"Sir? I don't think I can take this. We only accept..."

"Get moving! You have only twelve seconds!" The waiter, startled, dropped the card and fumbled slightly while retrieving it from the floor before retreating.

Dorian looked at his companion. "What happens in 12 seconds?"

"The poison embedded in that card will permeate his skin and his heart will stop. I am rather hoping he hands it to the manager before that. No one should be allowed to sell a cup of coffee of such poor quality and live."

Pretorius noticed Dorian glance down at his uncovered hands, and deliberately licked his fingers. "I spent several years building up an immunity to Iocane powder."

***

Inside the building a dozen small shops were beginning to open their doors. Just before they reached Arts and Sciences, Dorian realized he still didn't have an answer as to the lure being used. He was about to mention this when he noticed, rather unceremoniously propped up on an easel, a thick canvas painting, whose subject was the kind of grotesquery one might see crafted by Bernie Wrightson or Richard Pickman. Mutilated flesh with exaggerated features arranged into a roughly hominid design, in a mockery of refined accoutrements.

It was the Picture of Dorian Gray.

Furious, Dorian whirled to face his companion, the concealed pistol he kept in his waistcoat already drawn. "I really do not care how you acquired it. Return it at once or you shall be needing a replacement pair of eyes!"

Doctor Septimus Pretorius, his hair looking wilder than ever, simply smiled. "Well, I couldn't trust that he would show up for a fake. Now, put that away. You're not that good a shot, and I have a gun in my trousers. Before you could fire a second time, I will have spent my entire load." He waved to the man behind the counter inside, a slight man with curly hair, and turned away from Dorian. "I used to think you were cute when you became angry. Now it makes you look trite. Let us both holster our weapons and wait by the--"

Debris pelted both their faces before Septimus could finish his suggestion. The arched ceiling two stories above them caved in directly over their spot, showering them in glass and concrete. They fell to the floor, though without either being seriously hurt. However, before they could fully recover a *very* rough voice murmured to them.

"Stay down. I don't want to destroy this entire arcade, but I will if that's what it takes."

Dorian stared wide-eyed at the hulking shadow with a voice like a rock pulverizer. "Who-- What are you?"

"The doctor can answer that question, but I doubt he can tell you my name. I know who you are, though." The large man, if such a word applied to something so inhuman, hefted both Dorian and Septimus to their feet, only to put his arms around their waists and hold them each horizontally. "Your quarry wasn't fooled by your trick and told his friend Dale. Dale suggested letting me in on the jest, and I just had to be here in person to see it. Now I will take you to *my* lab, in Santa Mira, and we can have more fun."

Pretorius uncharacteristically screamed in terror, "*Nooo!* You cannot do this! I have never wronged you. I've never even met you, though I can tell by your jaundiced skin that you're a Frankenstein."

Their captor squeezed each of them under his arms with rib-cracking strength. "Never call me that! Call me what he called me. Call me *Monster!*"

Lowering his deep voice, the Monster strolled out of the arcade and took them to his van down by the river. "We have indeed met, Pretorius. The body is new, but the brain is the same. And as I told you when last we met, we belong dead!"

END

A GRAY CLOUD OVER CHICAGO

Christofer Nigro

With many thanks to Chuck Loridans for his inspirational creation of the Dracula soul-clone theory for the Children of the Night Timeline **that remains the core of MONSTAAH, the website and group he founded back in 2000!**

Many thanks also to T. Casey Brennan and the ideas he inspired for this novella, and all the inspiration he has provided for many creatives with his work.

Prologue:

The Windy City, October 1976

Dorian Gray smirked in disgust as he traipsed through the decrepit boulevards of Chicago's infamous South Side. His hair was dyed brown, as was often the case, to conceal its normal flaxen hue. He has striven this night to dress as inconspicuously as possible, so his attire did not scream "well-to-do," "high-roller," or, perhaps worst of all, "tourist." A simple sweater, with a dark blue trench coat, denim jeans, and a pair of moderately-priced Nike sneakers comprised his basic attire.

It has taken him some time to get used to the type of attire favored by the people of this time period, which greatly contrasts with the formal wear of the era in which he was born and raised before the portrait granted him an indefinite life extension.

He has often taken on a variety of aliases, so he will not be connected to the "Dorian Gray" of the memoir his late and esteemed friend, the famed and defamed Victorian author Oscar Wilde, composed in the form of a fictional novel. He has always sought to maintain the fiction that the book is a work of fiction. He has thus taken measures to disguise his identity despite Wilde tweaking the ending of the novelized biography -- at Dorian's request -- to falsely claim the subject of the story destroyed the canvassed source of his ill-begotten immortality in a state of guilt-ridden pique -- and thereby destroying himself in the process.

Dorian Gray may have experienced pangs of guilt and remorse between his bouts of manipulation and debauchery since his long-departed, ill-fated friend Basil Hallward created the portrait, but never to the point that he would actually destroy the increasingly grotesque work of art whose mystical properties preserved his youthful beauty and vitality for (at least potentially) all eternity.

For Dorian is his own living picture of his prime, with his portrait taking on all the decay and scars borne by the passage of time, a distinct reversal of the way the laws of the universe work for all but those fortunate (cursed?) few who belong to the secretive Cult of Fama. These are the secret beneficiaries of the goddess Bast and her grand experiment for humanity, and Dorian wasn't to learn of the rest of this group's illustrious number until at least a decade after his own portrait was commissioned.

I.

Dorian Gray's physical senses were bombarded by constant reminders of human mortality and depravity by the crumbling architecture and mind-addled people who inhabited the buildings he passed while strolling down the drafty streets of America's third largest metroplex. He well understood, of course, that these sorely neglected tenements only served as sources of habitation for the impoverished citizens of this area when their place of residence wasn't the local alleyways or parks, the only locales they could sleep free of charge -- save for the local jail where most of them ended up from time to time for charges of loitering, vagrancy, and "disturbing the peace."

Drug addicts walked by Dorian with their emaciated features and rotted teeth, and the most well-dressed and well-fed people he passed were pimps showing off their expensive jewelry and loud-colored wardrobes. Low-level dealers of recreational pharmaceuticals likewise haunted these streets to push their product on the emotionally and physically needy. Regarding the latter, Dorian found great amusement in how much the "crack house" they ran were so like the opium dens he remembered so well from his native England during the gone but always fondly recollected Victorian era.

A big city simply could not be properly considered a big city *sans the purveyors of the poison,* Dorian couldn't help musing to himself as he witnessed the third transaction for "dope" since he began his evening trek. *And so apropos that the opium of the present-day masses refers to their vice of choice as "dope." How ironically scandalous! Did these unsophisticated poltroons actually forget the original meaning of the term "dope," much as they seem to have forgotten the previous understanding of terms such as "queer" and "faggot?"*

As Dorian passed by the corner of Wilson and Sheridan with a rust-eaten street light marking the point, a short but rotund woman he figured to be in her 30s with stringy and frizzy hair approached him. Her face was colored with various types of make-up, and she was garbed in a poorly fitting dress designed to expose her ample cleavage.

"Hey, baby," the woman said as she gripped Dorian's arm. "You look lonely, like you could use some company. Can I take care of you tonight?"

"I somehow fail to see how a lady who so clearly cannot take care of herself could possibly take care of someone else," Dorian snipped.

He attempted to pull away from her, but the small working woman's grip was surprisingly firm, evidently fueled by the strength of her desperation.

"Don't be that way, baby," she pleaded. "Just 'cause I can't take care of myself don't mean I can't take care of a man. I know how to take care of a man. I can show you how good I am at that if you let me."

Dorian pulled his arm free. "Really, now? Are you quite certain that it is my pleasure you are interested in, or even that of your own? Or, is it more akin to a business transaction that you're attempting to conduct here?"

"I mean, we can take care of each other, baby. I provide for your needs, and you provide for mine. It works both ways."

"And you presume to convince me to pay for such services with that clownish make-up of yours and poorly fitting dress that is more designed to expose your sagging bosom than act as protection for the excessive windiness of this city? The most you can offer me here is a bit of amusement, and you have already provided that free of charge. I thank you for the service rendered, and if it is all the same to you, I shall be moving along now."

The woman scowled at Dorian's biting words, then gritted her teeth, followed by the clenching of her fists. She then began pounding them against the young-looking man's chest.

"You don't fucking talk to me like that! Who do you think you are, mother fucker?"

Dorian sighed, then smiled. "I think I am someone who is quickly tiring of your pitiful antics and your repulsive company. Now, kindly step aside or I will begin returning those blows. Do I make myself clear?"

This lady of the night had long grown to become a good judge of her potential clients' likely character simply by the way they carry themselves during an initial conversation. She was left with no doubt that the man with the youthful Adonis-like features before her was fully capable of taking a life and had done so in the past. He was not to be trifled with, and the tone with which he spoke his warning carried the weight of a cargo plane.

After being given pause, the woman stepped aside and struggled to keep tears from streaming down her face. She failed, and her mascara began running down her cheeks like streaking shadows.

"Pathetic," Dorian whispered just loud enough for the belittled and tragic woman to hear as he walked on down the dilapidated neighborhood at a brisk pace.

He had dealt with many prostitutes during his century of immortality, and he always found them easy to manipulate and better suited to satisfying his urges to tear the egos of other people asunder than any of his carnal desires. Moreover, so many of them were already corrupted in his view, which spoiled the fun and challenge he found in pulling the non-corrupt into embracing their inner darkness.

Most importantly, Dorian never needed to pay for that type of company, as many attractive suitors of both genders were often at his beck and call. And most often, they were paying *his* way rather than the reverse. For this reason, he had never had any use for prostitutes, and has tended to treat them as beneath contempt and good for psychological sport more so than anything in the realm of physical pleasure.

Most importantly, however, is that a lengthy dalliance with that woman would have taken precious time away from the actual important matter which had brought Dorian to the Windy City in the first place. Said business had everything to do with the portrait that sinisterly but reliably absorbed all the injuries and depravations that came with the passage of time, at least to those mortals not blessed (or cursed?) by higher forces.

As he and his fellows in the Cult of Fama realized much earlier in the present century, the ordinary wood and canvas of which their portraits were constructed are certainly not free from the relentless forces of decay that inexorably plague most substances in the material world. As a result, these utterly priceless canvases must be periodically maintained. That required the hand of artists with skills at least close to that of his long-departed friend Basil Hallward, the young admirer of Dorian who crafted his ensorcelled portrait and ultimately paid a most dire price for it.

To that end, Dorian's contacts in the art world of his native England informed him of an artist dwelling in America's third largest city that may well serve his needs. It was actually an artiste well-versed in the occult, and his nondescript shop was located just down the corner from the well-known Sheridan Plaza Hotel.

The neotenic immortal couldn't help gazing upwards at the aforementioned inn, standing far taller than any human inhabited structure that graced the streets of his native time period, even if it was still far less impressive than the recently completed Sears Tower. The great architectural accomplishment stood in blatant differentiation to the putrid streets and penurious humans that stood far below it, as if mocking those suffering under a system that produced such glaring dichotomies of wealth distribution.

It was a society that suited Dorian Gray just fine. He was no activist for the good of the many, but an inveterate hedonist determined to live his unending life to the fullest. Testing the lengths of depravity which the lot of humanity restricted to pitiably finite lifespans and fragile biological composition could be driven to was what he eternally lived for. As was the level of debauchery one such as himself with a potentially endless life span and eternal youth could sample through such a vast span of years and cultures.

To the likes of Dorian Gray, consequences were something for lesser beings, the human species that had conceived him before forces from beyond elevated him to something more. He was capable of experiencing love and all the gentler emotions, but he rarely sought these out, for he felt they left him vulnerable in ways that two weeks in one of the fondly remembered opium dens of East London never could.

Sometimes gentler relationships and emotions would enter his life by chance, but he was loath to actually seek them out on purpose. Further, he was oftentimes thankful that the ephemeral lifespan and always fragile mortality of typical human life would tend to make such liaisons in his existence fleeting, sometimes leaving him with a pain and yearning he fervently sought to avoid re-experiencing.

The darkly clothed man, whose very aura made him look eerily out of place yet also strangely at home in this urban cesspool, stepped over various intoxicated bodies collapsed onto the side walk before finding his path suddenly barred by one surprisingly smart-attired young man who attempted to sell him a gold watch. Dorian's only interest was the curio shop at the end of the street, but the would-be gold salesman was as persistent as the lady of the night the youngish-looking scoundrel had encountered scant minutes earlier.

"C'mon, man! Fifteen dollars for one of these is a bargain!"

"Doubtless these time pieces you're vending are 'hotter' than the infernal flames of Hell itself, if I used the slang terminology correctly."

"Huh? What? Wait, if you meant 'hot' as in – stolen – well, the only major steal in this deal is how cheaply I'm offering you such a high-quality number."

"I would think the greatest crime in this attempted transaction lies in your inability to pawn such a counterfeit trinket on one who is not ridden with naivety."

"Counter-what? My man, this is nothing but the finest and purest gold, total sunshine embodied in the physical. Here, take a look at it."

Dorian kept his arms at his side and tucked within the pockets of his trench coat. His right hand was gripped around a concealed Hindu war dagger he picked up while abroad, just in case one of the denizens of these streets decided to be particularly troublesome.

"That was an impressively adroit way of describing the object for someone native to a city such as this, even if the metaphor fell flatter than a tapeworm run over by a cabbie's wheel. And if it is truly metaphors you like, consider the double appropriateness of a bowel dwelling parasite applied to you and your skills as a salesman.

"I have traveled the myriad corners of the world, far beyond this city of man, and even beyond this world itself. So, you can rest assured that I know the difference between actual gold and the fools' gold that fools attempt to pass off as the genuine element."

The stumpy purveyor of not-so-fine gold looked at Dorian for a moment with a baffled expression. "Man, you are one bugged out mother fucker. I'm getting away from yo' ass!"

"Thank the Powers That Be for the smallest of favors," Dorian said aloud with a self-satisfied smirk as his young accoster turned and left him behind.

After kicking aside the legs of a slumbering wino whose limbs were blocking the path to the end of the street, Dorian finally stopped before the odd establishment he was seeking out. A tattered, hand-painted sign that read Gino's Curios was nailed to the storefront to mark the name of the shop. The door was composed of wood with blue paint that had partially chipped off. A soft glow was visible through the pinkish shades that covered the front window, which indicated that a light was on inside the small building.

Dorian smiled at the sight, while a few thoughts crossed his mind as he prepared to enter.

I am gratified to see you're open for business at this late hour, Gino St. Vincent. Because I traversed all the way across the Atlantic to this delightfully debauched city to have you fix my portrait. And I find it quite important to check your progress as often as I can during the week required for you to complete this crucial task.

II.

Dorian Gray pushed open the front door leading into the store section of Gino's Curios, and instantly felt something was amiss. The first indication was the lack of the already familiar jingling sound made by the special metallic wind chimes Gino hung on the inside of the entrance, so he would always be alerted when someone entered the establishment.

The second indication of a problem was Dorian's notice that the wind chimes had been ripped off the door by someone and thrown into a nearby cardboard box filled with ornate decorative rugs. The thin chain used to hang them in place was broken, which made it obvious they had been torn off the door with force, and not removed with any type of care.

As Gino explained to me during our first meeting five days ago, he has much love for those tingling chimes because they are a gift from a treasured person in his past. Never would he have taken them off the door with such callous disregard for damaging them. Nor do I believe he would ever have taken them down at all, and he certainly would not have just tossed them aside so coldheartedly.

The final indication of all not being well in the store was the matter of Gino not being present at his usual perch before the front desk, reading one of his arcane tomes to pass the time between customers.

Dorian found himself extremely concerned, as he had placed his trust in Gino to take good care of his portrait. The man's reputation for discretion and care of such precious items was impeccable to his contacts in England, so Dorian highly doubted that Gino was being neglectful of the proper running of his shop by choice.

Moreover, it was well known that Gino avoided all recreational drug use, including alcohol consumption, which may have disrupted his mental clarity. A person in his line of work simply could not afford such forms of indulgence, as the potential consequences of a misstep in his obligations were too dire to contemplate.

I cannot leave this place without checking on my portrait. That means finding out what may be amiss with Gino. I cannot help but feel dark tidings over his possible situation, and by extrapolation the safety of my portrait -- and hence, my own continued immortal existence.

Dorian looked around the shop, and his bright blue eyes focused upon the portal behind the front desk that led to Gino's work studio and makeshift living quarters. That was where his portrait was located, and nothing would keep the eternally young man from breaking whatever rules Gino had about customers stepping into that area of the small building.

Dorian slid over the front desk, being cautious not to knock any of its myriad skull-shaped implements, crystal spheres, thick books, or shrunken heads to the floor and risk announcing his presence. He quietly stepped into the entrance leading to the enigmatic artisan's private work and living area. After walking several feet through the dimly lit corridor leading into the workplace, Dorian's eyes went wide with horror at the sight he beheld.

A tall man wearing a dark cloak with red lining stood near the far left wall of the studio, his right hand clasped tightly around Gino's throat and holding the morbidly obese man above the ground as if he weighed no more than a pillow case. This dangerous intruder appeared to be in early middle age, with dark hair that was graying at the temples. He had handsome European features, and his skin was unusually pale. His fingernails were surprisingly long with a sharpened appearance.

Gino was alive but gasping for air in the mysterious assailant's steel-like grip. The corpulent man desperately struggled to remove the trespasser's hand from his throat but could not budge those five powerful fingers so much as an inch.

"Where is the amulet, Mr. St. Vincent?" the tall man in black queried with a distinct Balkan accent. It was one that Dorian recognized, and his spine suddenly felt as if it was covered with frost. "I know you have it in your possession, and I shall not leave here without it. Continue trying my patience like this, however, and I will bleed you dry and tear this quaint little shop of yours apart to find it, even if it should take the rest of the evening hours to do so."

No, not him! Dorian suddenly felt a quick pang of panic and looked around the work area for any sign of his portrait. He was still intact, which indicated that his indescribably precious canvas was also. But that wouldn't last if the sinister European in black came across it while thrashing the work room to find whatever bauble the man wanted.

Dorian felt one of the most intense sensations of relief he had ever experienced in his roughly 120 years of life when he noticed the portrait up against the back wall, recognizing it instantly from the distinctive blanket that covered it. Dorian was further immensely relieved that Gino had honored his adamant request to cover the portrait up again after completing a day of work on it. Hence, the European in black didn't see it and recognize it for what it was; if he had, Dorian Gray would have met oblivion before making it to the shop.

"I… I told you," Gino gasped out in response to his brutal attacker's query. "It's… it's in a museum… in Boston. Not… not here."

"You lie!" the man said just before slamming Gino up against the wall, leaving a large round impression in the stucco. The obese owner of the shop gasped in agony as he felt his windpipe beginning to fracture under the pressure exerted by the sinister interloper's inhumanly strong grip.

"I already made inquiries to that museum in Boston, and the inventory records clearly indicate it was shipped *here* at the curator's request! You were hired to examine and verify its authenticity. I already know that Egyptian bauble of mind transference is authentic. And I desire it in my possession. Lie to me again and I will make a feast of your life fluids and search for the item myself!"

The still unnoticed Dorian had no interest in trifling with that European. So, he resolved to stealthily grab his portrait and dash out of the shop with it. But could he do that without gaining the attention of the dark-cloaked European?

That question was to be rendered moot a second later when the tallish man's ultra-keen hearing picked up on the heavy stress-induced breathing of Dorian on the other side of the room. The dark-cloaked man turned to see Dorian standing several feet behind him, and his glaring red eyes flared with anger at the familiar young-looking visage he found himself confronting.

"Gray, is that you? Very interesting meeting you here like this. What would be the odds that we should cross paths again in a part of the world outside our native Europe where neither of us knew the other would be? And to have business in the exact same location, at the exact same time, in a city so large? Truly the Fates mock us with their sense of ironic humor, eh?"

Dorian did his best to stifle his growing anxiety and to appear confident in the encounter before responding. "It is indeed me, Count Dracula. Or, should I perhaps address you as Count Lucien Mordante, a member of a branch lineage connected to the cursed Collins clan whom the *real* Dracula, Vlad Tepes, transformed into one of his many soul-clones?"

The man known in his long *un*-life as both Dracula and Mordante took on a truly savage countenance, his fangs extending menacingly from his mouth.

"Yes, the Cult of Fama is well aware of Dracula-Prime's creation of soul-clones," Dorian continued explicating, "individuals he transformed into psychic vampiric doppelgangers of himself to operate in his stead throughout various parts of the world when he took lengthy slumbers to rebuild his power whenever it was on the wane.

"Some of these soul-clones being quite pitiable failures, whereas others turned out to be quite powerful in their own right, such as Lejos, Denrom, Talbot, Mathias; there was also that weird Chinese wizard Kai, that 'mod' but exquisitely handsome African prince, the long-haired chap who has besieged my good man the Bloody Poet, that silly old scientist who invented the cough syrup that causes mortals to cough … and yourself. It is also well known that you have gone quite rogue since the dark deity Chaos added further psychic memory inserts in your mind to those already implanted by the authentic Vlad Dracula a century past. The former making you think you were an extraterrestrial, like that saucy vampiric she-warrior you often clashed with is reputed to be, correct?"

"Tread very carefully, Gray," Dracula hissed, his fangs still bared. "Have no doubt that despite the lineage of my current host, I am nothing less than the one, *true* Dracula. One day I shall find that portrait bearing your corrupted likeness which grants you the eternal life only we of the vampiric race should enjoy. And when I do, I will tear it to shreds, thereby tearing *you* to shreds in the process."

Dorian forced himself not to cringe upon hearing that, as he could find no caustic amusement in the fact that Dracula was unaware of how close that very portrait was to him at the moment. It was an omission of knowledge on his part, perhaps yet another example of Fate's devious sense of irony, that he needed to maintain at all costs.

"That is quite selfish of you, Count," Dorian replied. "You remind me of those elitist human parasites who believe only their handful should enjoy the amazing wealth that humanity has created in their collective hands since my birth. I love those parasites, do not misunderstand me! But the type of parasite you represent since becoming Undead… well, not so much.

"You may boast of the power and unending longevity of your particular species of immortality, but those of mine need not cower from the sunlight for fear of having our 'eternal' life easily unraveled along with our flesh. Or from a few splashes of holy water; or contact with a little communion wafer.

"And we may still enjoy the finer things in life, such as good cuisine, the sweet taste of wine, and the ecstasy of carnal fulfillment. Whereas you and your kind are forced to subsist on blood alone, behaving like animals in the process of acquiring it, while experiencing no pleasure beside that of the mindless, unending hunt for what lies in the veins of mortals. Vampires of every bloodline can hardly be considered at the top of this world's food chain if they cannot even look the sun in the face or eat and rut as they choose."

Dracula loosened his grip on Gino St. Vincent, whose heavy-set body slumped to the ground with the reverberation of a sandbag. The expert on occult oddities immediately took to his knees and began coughing incessantly while massaging his deeply bruised trachea, relieved that the powerful Dracula soul-clone's attention was no longer focused on him.

"Mr. Gray, now that the Fates have once again graced me with your pestilent presence, I think an experiment is in order. One I have long thought of carrying out following our first meeting. I am already aware, courtesy of a conversation with Lady Karnstein, that your blood is not fit for vampiric consumption.

"However, you can at least sate my curiosity, if not my hunger. Though I am also aware that your portrait allows you to recover from many grievous injuries, I find myself wondering whether it may succeed in putting you back together if your limbs and head were to be torn from your body. What say we now put that to the test? I am certain you must be as curious as to the outcome of such a test as I am!"

Bugger me! Dorian thought to himself as he backed away in a direction opposite to the wall that his covered portrait was situated. He knew he dare not let Dracula know it was present in this workshop. Unfortunately, that wasn't the only problem he now faced here. *Gino must have some objects in this work area of sufficient mystical power to use as a weapon against this fanged cretin. Alas, a sword does not appear to be among them!*

Dorian had long ago learned exactly how incredibly strong Dracula was, and he simply could not afford to let any iteration of the

Vampire Lord get their hands on him. He had no doubt Dracula was fully capable of putting his bodily integrity to the gruesome test he mentioned. And then some.

Dorian's knowledge of magick was largely of the Egyptian variety due to the genesis of his immortality, but it also covered other areas of the mystic arts as well. Nevertheless, he was no sorcerer. *I am by no means comparable to that strange gentleman from Bleecker Street in New York City, but I can make do if need be.*

Luckily for Dorian, Dracula kept his forward pace slow, to accentuate the menace and drag out his quarry's negative anticipation of what was to come in sadistic fashion. If Dorian attempted to run, Dracula could easily morph into the form of a bat or wolf to quickly overtake him before he succeeded in even leaving the shop. The Vampire Lord's quarry fully understood this, and he knew his only chance was in using his astute observation skills to quickly spot something of use, of which there were potentially many in the room.

Just then, Dorian's eyes focused upon a small silvery scepter-like object with the feline head of Bast adorning the end of it. *Yes! Thank you for a mighty* large *favor, Lady Bast! If I can only get to it before the faux Vampire Lord gets to me...*

Before Dorian could even calculate another thought through his ever-scheming head, however, Dracula darted towards him with tremendous speed, seized his throat, and lifted him in the air like a rag doll. The most legendary member of the Cult of Fama had suddenly found himself in a similar predicament to the one Gino was enduring mere moments earlier.

"I see you misjudged my pace as careless indifference to how wily you can be, Mr. Gray," Dracula hissed. "I learned long ago not to underestimate you. Did you think I failed to see you scanning the room for some object to use against me? And yet you *dared* to deride me as you did? As if *I* were the fool, and not you?"

Dracula began angrily shaking Dorian like a leaf, causing the latter to choke and gag as he felt the Prince of Darkness's fingers pressing into his throat like five solid steel monkey wrenches. Despite the attributes afforded to Dorian by the portrait, he didn't possess extra-normal strength, whereas Dracula possessed that in proverbial spades.

Dorian was painfully aware that he needed to think, and think fast, before he was rendered immobile from a broken neck or a crushed trachea. Dracula would then doubtless begin carrying out his intention to tear him to pieces before the power of Bast could undo those terrible neck wounds.

"Your breath… smells like that… of a dog, Faux-Dracula," Dorian choked out. "No wonder… you delight in… taking canine form."

"And you have no breath *at all*, you insolent little sodomite!" Dracula exclaimed as he raised his other hand in preparation to begin the process of dismembering his foe.

"Mr. Gray catch!" Gino suddenly hollered from the other side of the room.

Dorian turned his agony-ridden neck to see Gino tossing the Bast-headed scepter to him. Mustering his formidable will, the eternal miscreant raised his right hand to catch the object… only to have Dracula's free hand snatch it out of the air himself.

"By Hoggoth's shit!" Gino yelled in consternation.

"Shit is indeed the word… you fat imbecile," Dorian said in strained vexation.

"Did you sincerely believe that your reflexes would be a match for mine?" Dracula mockingly queried as he held the scepter in his captive's face.

"One can but hope…"

Little was Dracula aware that this provided him with enough of a distraction that Dorian was able to use his right arm to reach into the pocket of his trench coat and acquire the Hindu dagger on his person. It was a dagger that possessed a razor-sharp tip forged of silver, a metal which is anathema to many vampiric bloodlines, including Dracula's own.

Dorian managed to muster a quick surge of adrenalin-fueled strength to thrust the dagger clear through Dracula's lower forearm in which held the scepter. The startled Vampire Lord was taken off guard by the sudden piercing pain, and as a result he dropped both Dorian and the scepter simultaneously. Dracula resisted being fully debilitated by the wound, however, and he wasted no time in pulling the dagger out of his skewered limb. He then quickly tossed the blade across the room where it could not be easily retrieved.

"I will kill you, Gray!" the Prince of Darkness decreed as his eyes glowed fiery red, and what appeared to be smoke spewed from his nostrils as a twin indicator of his profound level of anger.

"Not… today, Count," Dorian replied while lying on the floor in front of his adversary with the recovered scepter in his right hand.

Dorian pointed the cat-headed portion of the small metallic staff at Dracula and spoke aloud to Bast. "Great Lady grant me the power to strike this grandiose buffoon down!"

Nothing happened, and Dracula lunged towards him.

"Please!" Dorian added to the mystic request, which was then granted as a beam of shimmering elemental energy surged out of the scepter.

This glowing golden energy struck Dracula while he was in mid-lunge and sent him flying backwards and clear through the wall that led into Gino's living quarters. A secondary crash was heard in that other room to signify that the unleashed force of the feline-headed Egyptian deity was so great that the Lord of Vampires continued to be sent involuntarily airborne until he smashed through a further wall leading outside the shop entirely.

"That was far out, Mr. Gray!" Gino yelled as he rushed over to help Dorian to his feet.

"Maybe so," Dorian replied, "but it wasn't so 'far out' that Dracula will not recover in a relatively short period of time. We need to vacate these premises immediately, as I cannot be certain that Lady Bast will heed a second such request of mine, whether I modify it with a 'please' or not. Did you complete the work on my portrait?"

"I regret to say that I have not. But I did repair the frame, and only the picture itself needs to be touched up."

"Then you will complete the reconstructive work once we find a safe haven!"

"I am afraid I cannot do that, Mr. Gray. There is no safe haven from the likes of Dracula in this city now that he is on to me. I am going to have to flee all the way back to my native Italy. I had emergency flight plans chartered to leave at a moment's notice just in case this type of eventuality should arise."

"Then you shall take me with you, and you will finish the task I paid you for once we reach Italy."

"I am sorry, but I cannot do that either, good sir. The flight is available for one only."

"I shall purchase a ticket myself!"

"My apologies, but the cost for such a preemptive measure was not simply monetary in nature, and it is not something you could come up with yourself."

Gino then grabbed the scepter from Dorian's still relatively weakened grip. "Begging your pardon, but I will need this also, now that you demonstrated how it actually serves as a conduit to Bast's power! One cannot be too careful when fleeing from Dracula, you know."

"What about the money I already paid you, St. Vincent? I am not going to just ignore the fact that this extremely important job is incomplete! If you abandon the task, know that Dracula will not be the only immortal being hunting you down."

"Yes, yes, I understand you deserve due compensation. I will give you two things for that. The first is this…"

Gino reached into one of the boxes in his workplace and produced a digest-sized tome with an antique appearance. He hastily handed it to Dorian, who knew just enough of the ancient Sanskrit language to decipher the word "*Crimson…*" on its cover.

"This grimoire, whose name you will surely recognize, is worth far more than any amount of currency you could have paid me, American or otherwise! It is admittedly a far cry from the actual, full-sized tome it is a copy of, but you may be able to make it work for you as you did the scepter. I am thankful Dracula—especially not *that* Dracula (there is more than one, right?)—was unaware I had this in my possession!"

199

Dorian did indeed discern what this small book was a copy of, and he gratified Gino with a satisfied expression. "Very well. But the restoration of my painting is very important, even more so than any such tome…"

"Which leads me to the second item of compensation I mentioned. You already told me how poorly your last attempt at a portrait restoration went for you, and for the rest of that Cult of Famine you belong to, thanks to that Pickman fellow you hired, and I wouldn't want your business with me to end just as badly."

"That would be the Cult of *Fama*, you moronic fool. But do get to the point before I become more riled. Particularly as I am fully aware you made that pejorative grammatical error on purpose!"

"Ha ha! Alright, will do, and this second item of compensation comes in the form of some very valuable information. There is another artist in Chicago who is quite talented and can quickly finish touching up the paint on your picture. He is a young man of Negro descent and lives under impoverished conditions in the dreaded Cabrini-Green Housing Project located on the city's Near North Side. He will thus do the work for a surprisingly low rate by your standards, but do make haste, because his talent is such that the value of his work may rise dramatically any day now."

"I will judge his level of talent for myself, and for that I would require a sample of his work."

"I can provide it."

Gino sauntered over to the section of the workplace where another painting lay, this one with a differently-hued cover concealing it. He removed the covering to reveal a water colored canvas depicting the upper body of a majestic looking male figure dressed in a white and reddish-beige robe, with his right hand pointed upwards; his index

200

finger, middle finger, and thumb pointing up in a holy gesture. The figure displayed dark skin with short, wooly white-ish hair and a matching beard. The background of the painting was sky blue with notable light green shading added to various portions of the canvas.

"Behold Noir Jesus, Mr. Gray!"

Dorian took the painting from Gino's hands and scrutinized it with a glare indicating he was baffled but intrigued.

"The young impoverished artist you mentioned painted this interpretation of Jesus Christ?"

"He did. And fine quality work, I must say. I finagled it from the owner of the local art center, since he told me the painting was rumored to bring fortunate luck to those who displayed it. Didn't work for me, though.

"The man was of French descent, straight out of New Orleans, apparently belonging to that strange-ass 'thieves guild' or some secret organization that's supposed to exist down there in the shadows along with all the voodoo crap and whatnot. And since the version of Jesus in this painting was portrayed as, well, a Negro, he decided it would be cute or something to name the painting 'Noir Jesus' to flaunt the French lingo he's so damn proud to be fluent in."

"I do indeed sense some… strong emanations flowing from this painting. If it bestows good fortune upon those who display it in their place of residence, then it may only work for *some*, and that number would not include individuals like you… or me, Gino. However, this work does serve to convince me of the artist's skill."

"You may keep the painting as a third compensation, Mr. Gray, since I obviously have no use for it if it won't work for me, nor would it likely work for anyone I am likely to sell it to. And far be it from me to sell any of my valued clientele a lemon, eh?"

"I will indeed take this painting as part of your compensation package. But we have belabored the point and tarried here long enough. Give me a name for this artist so we can be off!"

"Just ask for the apartment of Jimmy the Artist. Anyone living there will know of who you speak. Just be careful, as the Cabrini-Green Projects are extremely rough, even for one like yourself who is at home on the dark side of life. But as you said, let's be off before Dracula recovers and makes another play for our throats."

Just prior to exiting his Chicago-based establishment for the final time, Gino ran over to another box and pulled forth a baroque bauble connected to a dull bronze-colored chain.

"I wouldn't leave the Amulet of Transference behind!"

"So, you did indeed lie when you told Dracula it wasn't in your possession."

"Of course, I did! Ha ha! And now that I know how much he wants the amulet, I'll be damned in the Dark Dimension before I let him find it when he returns and thrashes the place in search of it. If anyone is going to use it to transfer a human consciousness into the body of some undead entity, it's going to be me! Or someone I willingly sell it to!

"This amulet is also Egyptian in origin and serves to transfer the minds of people into the heads of one of those cursed mummies that always seem to turn up in hard-to-find sarcophagi. The last time such a mummy was animated like that happened in Boston just a few years ago and ended when the mummy broke some chick's neck and then blew its own brains out, so it's no surprise the curator of the museum wanted to be rid of it!

"Just imagine having to be the guy who had to clean that mess up the next day, and the one who had to explain to the museum owners that their mummy no longer has a head, and somehow became animated and killed some broad who snuck into the museum. And *then* on top of that having to explain to the customers that the Egyptian exhibit no longer has a mummy to make seeing it worth paying for, not to mention…"

"I have no more time for your pointless rambling exposition, Gino St. Vincent! I am now out of here! I would wish you Godspeed, but why should I add another lie to compound those already uttered by you in this place tonight?"

Dorian grabbed his precious portrait along with the canvas of Noir Jesus and ran for the front door. Gino St. Vincent followed close behind.

"Ha ha! I so like you, Mr. Gray! We must do lunch one day should our paths ever cross again!"

"Only if I can lace your food with arsenic before you consume it," Dorian rejoined before running up the street and disappearing into the darkness.

"Ha!" was Gino St. Vincent's only response. "What a personality on that guy! He is surely to die for!" *But maybe not literally, eh?*

The corpulent, oddly-dressed man then paused but a moment to take one final look at his curio shop. "Well, it was a nice business while it lasted but, er, these things happen in my line of work. There will be another shop on another day at another place."

The expert of arcane curiosities then took flight in a different direction, towards a destiny of his own.

III.

Dorian Gray looked at the Cabrini-Green Housing Project with an expression of muted awe. The most notorious low-cost rental complex for the impoverished of Chicago's Near North Side reminded him in some ways of the decrepit streets of the equally infamous White Chapel district in his native London a century earlier, though the majority of people he saw in residence here had dark skin rather than white. Their attire, hairstyles, and manner of speech were also quite distinct from those he remembered to inhabit the less savory, crime-infested areas of the English city where he was born.

However, there will doubtless be individuals of similar behavior, with similar pleasures, vices, and obstacles to be had here as in White Chapel, Dorian quickly and correctly surmised. *Living conditions of this nature will produce such people, the type who are bereft of hope, bereft of trust, and bereft of scruples... much as they are bereft of the material things all people need. But all the amenities they lack will be equaled by a wide abundance of varied talent and ambition.*

Dorian could not help but beam with rapt excitement as he crossed the street of Clybourn Avenue to approach the northern section of the towering, neglect-ridden tenements. Over his shoulders was a duffel bag containing both portraits in his possession, though he had since made a point to stop at the corner of Halsted Street and purchase an item for self-defense. It may be of limited use against many entities of a super-normal nature, but it would work fine against the typical residents of this location if need be. They would be the street gangs and dealers notorious for controlling the neighborhood, but Dorian had long since learned to deal with their type in ways that often required no force.

He had also long since learned to move quietly and unobtrusively through such an area of the city. White people were not overly common here, but their presence was certainly not unheard of, especially if they came in from the swankier areas of the city to purchase pharmaceutical goods. Dorian made a point to spend a healthy amount of the money he had acquired via various means abroad for such drugs to ingratiate himself with the rulers of this tenement cesspit, and to convince them that he was what they called a "high-ender." He was thus treated as a valued customer and worthy of respect for that reason alone. Not to mention his generosity with sharing some of the goods he procured.

"I am hoping to purchase a different sort of service while I am here," he told a member of the powerful gang known as the Soul Lords. "I own a building that requires a mural. I heard I can acquire that from someone called Jimmy the Artist. Point me to his apartment and I will give you a generous finder's fee."

"Whoa, you are totally bitch'n, Mr. Gray!" the colorfully-clad Soul Lord declared. "Give me some skin!"

The gang member held out the palm of both hands, and Dorian went along with the custom by slapping them with his own to signify the gesture of mutual agreement. He then quickly and thankfully remembered that he was obliged to immediately hold out his own palms in similar fashion for a reversal of the move to complete the gesture. *How strange,* Dorian thought. *I can only wonder why a simple handshake no longer suffices to close a transaction in a cordial manner. I would expect such a ritual social gesture developing in a place like Morocco, perhaps, but here in a culture borne out of my native England?*

"My thanks," Dorian said as he handed the young man a fifty-dollar bill. "We are indeed 'cool' with each other."

"You know it, man! And you can find Jimmy on the 5th floor of that building right there," he said while pointing to the correct tenement. "Just be careful, 'cause the elevators are always outta commission, and the lazy ass supers aren't about to get 'em fixed any time before 1985, you know? His family lives in apartment #12. Just go up and knock on the door, he'll find it cool you're offerin' him a job. He won't work for us, he's too goodie-goodie for that with his mom all down with the church an' all, 'specially after the leader of Satan's Knights done shot his scrawny ass two years ago."

"Oh, really? He was shot? Is he still mobile and able to work?"

"Yeah, man. The bullet just scratched his shoulder or some shit like that. He can still walk, and he can still paint."

"Good, and I do thank you again for your good service."

"Hey, no worries. You keep bringin' the cash, we'll keep providin' the stash."

Ah, what passes for witty repartee in this place, Dorian thought to himself with a smirk as he headed for the designated building. *It is quite fortuitous, though, that for everything that has changed from the world I was reared in, so much has also remained the same.*

Now That Dorian had made "good" with the current reigning street gang in the neighborhood, and had achieved the equivalent of VIP status, he could move about unmolested and conduct his *real* business on the grounds.

***

Young Jimmy Jr. was surprised to hear a knocking on his door at 10 PM in the evening, but he never hesitated to answer it anyway. The lanky youth sat up on the pull-out couch bed that he shared with his younger brother Mike in his family's two-bedroom apartment.

"Isn't it your turn to get the door, Mike?" he asked his sibling.

"Don't be pulling that jive on me," Mike replied. "You know I answered it yesterday and the day before. Stop being so lazy for once."

"Hey, if you worked as hard as I do creating all of those artistic masterpieces as the Da Vinci of the ghetto, you would be tired by ten in the p-m too."

"Get the door, Jimmy, before whoever it is wakes up Mom or Selma. I swear, sometimes I wish everyone would just barge right in like Mom's best friend always does."

"Yeah, yeah, hold your haughty little horses…"

Jimmy stood up in his patented red long john pajamas and retrieved his equally patented denim bucket hat that was his constant trademark. *I wouldn't look like myself in anybody's company without this little number,* he thought silently as he placed it on his head.

Jimmy casually walked to the door and opened it, to find the trench coat-wearing Dorian Gray on the other side.

"Are you the 'Jimmy the Artist' I have heard so many complimentary statements about?" Dorian asked, recognizing Jimmy based on how he fit the general description provided by Gino St. Vincent.

Jimmy let out an exasperated sigh. "Sorry for my look of disappointment, but I was hoping it was some foxy Avon lady coming by late at night, for a date with Kid… Dy-no-*mite!*"

Dorian could only respond with a befuddled stare. "I repeat my previous question. Are you Jimmy the talented artist whom I was told resides here?"

"I guess that depends, mister. You aren't a collection agent for the supermarket that I'm running up a month-long tab for Kool-Aid on, are you?"

"I am no such thing. My name is Dorian and I am looking for an artist of your reputed caliber to hire for an important job."

"By job, do you mean… something that pays? As in, real money that can keep us with a fresh supply of Kool-Aid for the remainder of the winter months? Not to mention pay the rent and get Mike into law school?"

"That is exactly the type of pay I am offering here."

"Then by all means, step into our humble abode, take off your funky trench coat, and stay for a while as you tell me about this lucrative job you're offering."

By this point, Mike was also sitting up in bed. "Jimmy, should you let that cat in? We have no idea if he's legit or totally bogue. Hell, he could be here to rob us for all we know."

"I think, Mike, that robbers tend to rob places that have things worth taking. And does this dude seriously look like the robber type? He looks to me more like the type that *hires* people to rob places, not someone who does the job himself. Er, no offense there, mister; I think that came out a bit wrong."

"None taken, for I can understand your reticence."

"Wow, do you ever talk seditty! Um, not that I meant that in a bad way. Are you a professor of language or something like that?"

"Yes, something like that. Now, onto my job offer."

Dorian put his duffel bag down and unzipped it. He first retrieved the Noir Jesus painting and uncovered it.

"Does this look familiar, Jimmy?"

"Whoa-ho! Mike, look! It's Noir Jesus! I didn't think I would ever see this painting again! Where did you get that?"

"I… purchased it from the gallery. That is how I learned of your work and realized you would be an exemplary choice for my needs."

"For a fan of my work who wants to pay for more of it, how can I say no? What are your requirements from the kid?"

"I require you to touch up another painting, one that was rendered by another artist long ago but is now fading. I need it restored to its former level of artistic quality. Can you provide that service?"

"I believe that is well within my repertoire of skills. How about you sit down on the couch—er, bed—and show me the painting while I fix you some Kool-Aid. Mike won't mind the company, he's used to having someone beside him there. Just not usually someone who is white and dressed in a trench coat instead of long johns."

"Let me speak for myself, Jimmy!" Mike stated firmly. "But… well, Dorian seems like a righteous cat to offer you legitimate work, so I have no problem with him taking a seat on our bed. Or with drinking our Kool-Aid."

"I must confess to being rather intrigued by this Kool-Aid beverage you continue to mention with such reverence," Dorian said as he sat down. "Surely it cannot be as sweet and sensuous as wine. Now, that is truly the nectar of the gods!"

"Well, Dorian, my man," Jimmy replied, "I can rightly assure you that Kool-Aid is pretty damn sweet, considering all the sugar it has! And it may not be the nectar of choice for the gods, but it's totally and truly the nectar of the ghetto! As for sensuous, well, I get that from kissing my girl Henrietta, so I don't really need to get it from my Kool-Aid."

"And not to be rude, Dorian," Mike interjected, "but there is only one God. That painting Jimmy made a few years ago represents him. And he's black!"

"I meant no disrespect by referring to 'God' in the plural," Dorian noted, hoping to remain in the good graces of Jimmy's family, at least until the all-important work he had commissioned was completed. "But I can greatly appreciate your brother's interpretation of Jesus. And though you do not acknowledge any of the legendary pantheons of deities, I am familiar with those worshiped by the ancient Egyptians, and *they* were black as well."

"Really?" Mike asked.

"Truly, my friend," Dorian replied. "Might you be familiar with Bast? She is a goddess from the Egyptian pantheon that is rather… dear to my heart."

"No, but I am sure going to find out more about her and the rest of the Egyptian gods," Mike noted excitedly.

"And look, this is a white guy saying that!" Jimmy said as he stood in their glorified kitchenette mixing the Kool-Aid powder with water in a large plastic pitcher. "So, he can't be all bad if he shows so much respect for the brothers and sisters of Egypt."

"Do you respect Jesus also?" Mike queried to their unexpected house guest.

"Why, certainly," Dorian replied with just a slightly forced smile. "And your brother's interpretation is most impressive and inspiring."

Jimmy then walked in the front room carrying a tray with the pitcher of Kool-Aid and three plastic cups. "Well, here is the Kool-Aid, or, as we like to call it: ghetto juice. You've seriously never had it before? Where do you come from, Planet X?"

"Actually, I hail from England. I had thought my accent would have given that away."

"Oh, well, that explains it. I guess Kool-Aid hasn't found its way to the home of Winston Churchill yet."

Dorian took a sip from the cup he was given. "Interesting taste. It cannot provide the punch of wine due to its lack of fermentation, but it provides a fair simulation of a fruit taste."

"If you wanted more 'punch' in your Kool-Aid, I can always make you the fruit punch flavored instead of the cherry. That is, if we have any left, considering how Mike always drinks all of it up like he was a diabetic fish."

Mike became chagrined at his brother's accusation. "Yeah, like you don't always drink down all the cherry *and* the grape flavors, Jimmy!"

"Me? You're the one with the hollow leg! And you're not the one who has to share a sleeping space with a brother who pisses the bed because he drinks so much Kool-Aid during the day!"

"Jimmy, you weren't supposed to say that in front of anyone! I should sock you in the eye for that!"

"Now, gentlemen, there is no need for any acrimony between brothers here," Dorian intervened. "I have been privy to the personal foibles of many in my time, and I can assure you that compared to so

211

many others I have known, the shame of bed urination pales in comparison."

"'In your time?'" Jimmy asked with confusion. "You don't look any older than me, Dorian."

"What I meant by that was," Dorian quickly lied, "I have seen much in my short time on this world despite only being alive for such a paltry number of years."

"Oh," Jimmy said. "Well, how about you show me the painting you need my artistic genius applied to."

"Yes, the painting." Dorian hesitated before reaching into the duffel bag to produce it. "I must warn you, it… is not exactly a pleasing sight. Its artist intended for it to represent… well, a metaphorical rendering of human evil, and how much of it one can accumulate over a long lifetime."

"I can dig that!" Jimmy declared. "So, take it out of the bag and lay it on us!"

"To be frank, it may be best if your little brother didn't see it," Dorian advised.

"Oh, c'mon!" Mike complained. "I am not a sissy! I went to see *The Exorcist*, that movie based on a true story about a girl who spazzed out after getting possessed by a demon, and I sat through it all the way with no problem, even when other people in the audience were screaming and fainting all around me…"

"Quiet about that, Mike," Jimmy said, indicating that he should lower his voice. "You know I wasn't supposed to take you to see that picture."

"… Yet it was Jimmy who fainted halfway through the movie! The first time was when that girl projectile puked, and then again when she stabbed herself with the cross down here…"

Jimmy began getting visibly queasy. "All right, Mike, no reminders of that. I only fainted because it was so damn warm in that theater!"

"*Sure*, you did, Jimmy! I'm telling you, Dorian, my brother may criticize me for pissing in the bed after drinking so much Kool-Aid all day, but *he* pissed himself in the middle of the theater! And I'm telling you, it smelled *nasty*! Ha ha!"

"Listen, you little pipsqueak, I would slap you in the face, but you're so short I'd probably end up just swatting air!"

"You just try it, Jimmy, and…"

"Gentlemen!" Dorian interceded firmly. "We have work to do, correct?"

"Sorry about that," Jimmy apologized.

"Yeah, Dorian, I'm sorry too," Mike followed up.

"All is forgiven," Dorian said. "Jimmy, I suggest that you brace yourself before I unveil the canvas, as I do not want you to soil that luxurious full-body sleeping garment of yours."

"Ha ha!" Mike chortled upon catching on to Dorian's scathing irony.

"And Mike, while I have full confidence in your ability to handle the sight of this portrait, I must confess to not being comfortable with anyone seeing it other than those who absolutely must for professional purposes. Begging your forgiveness, but this portrait is… highly personal in a way I would rather not describe, and I am here on business, which is between your brother and I."

Mike sighed. "Yeah, okay, I guess I understand. I don't want Jimmy missing out on a job because I can't be mature about something."

213

"I thank you, Mike. That is… 'righteous' of you, I believe to be the proper phraseology. Now, Jimmy, please do prepare yourself as I specified."

"I am nothing if not prepared when it comes to business," Jimmy assured him. "Lay it on me, dude! Let's see the masterwork I will be applying my masterful skills to restore to its former majesty."

IV.

"Ooohhh, man!" Mike said a few seconds after Jimmy hit the floor. "I told you!"

Dorian grumbled, unable to conceal his frustration. "Mike, fetch me a glass of cold water from what passes for your kitchen so we can revive him. And please get him a change of clothing! This is extremely important work I am hiring him to conduct, and Jimmy is the only one at hand who can do it!"

Mike did as requested and Dorian wasted no time in splashing the chilled water on Jimmy's face. He started awake, shaking the droplets of water from his face and hair.

"Mike! I had this horrible nightmare that I looked at a frame and saw a painting of Selma without her make-up on staring back at me! Please let me pass out again!"

Dorian glowered and pulled the feather-light young man back to a standing position with a single heave.

"Jimmy, you must get on your feet and remain there for the duration of this job!" he insisted. "I hired you for this task, and I expect you to make good on this professional obligation. I never said it would be an easy job, which is why I am paying you $200.00 for it. Did you ever earn that much for a single job before in your entire misbegotten life? Are you not a top notch professional? If your answer to both is in the affirmative, then kindly get the job done! After which, you are free to pass out and remain in that state for the rest of your life for all I care!"

"All right, all right," Jimmy said. "Just help my 'missed gotten self' stay on my feet and move me towards my work area."

"Where is your studio located?" Dorian enquired.

"Right there," Mike said as he pointed to the far end of the front room near their apartment's side windows. "Right where you see his canvas with the paint brushes on it."

"Why am I not surprised?" Dorian asked himself aloud. "Let us go there now and get this job completed."

***

Over the course of the next two hours, Jimmy went to work on restoring the portrait, and his burgeoning talent shined like a newly minted coin in the eyes of Dorian Gray throughout. Gino St. Vincent had already repaired the frame, but this young artist from the ghetto provided all the touch up to the canvas required to keep the portrait viable for at least the next few decades to come. Provided Dorian kept it safe and out of the sight of meddlers, of course. And preferably, out of his own sight as well, considering what it represented and the darkness its every change chronicled in nightmarish detail.

"And that is that," Jimmy said as he completed the final essential stroke of the brush. "But I just gotta know, Dorian: why would you want to keep something like, um… *this*… in tip top shape? It looks like something that would have given Lon Chaney nightmares!"

"Once again, that is a personal matter," Dorian replied.

"Suit yourself, man. You're the customer. And you can bet your uppity vocab I appreciate the business!"

"You are truly a rising star in the heavens, Jimmy. I am duly impressed with your attention to detail. Is that painting over there a representation of your family?"

"Yeah, the second one I whipped up. The first one had my dad in it, but after we lost him not too long ago, well, my mom wanted that painting in her room. So, I came up with another one without Dad to fill the gap in the front room, leaving the one with him to keep my mom company. We miss him like no one's business."

"I see. Well, my full condolences for the loss. How did that happen, if you can forgive my forwardness in asking?"

"Yeah, it's okay. Car accident, while he was returning from out of state to see about a job. It was a bummer of the maximum degree with how it affected the family, but my mom has always been strong, and if my father taught us anything, it's how important it is to stick together during hard times. And that we could get through anything as long as we did stick together."

"I... see. Interesting and evocative platitudes, I must say, my newest friend. Which behooves me to ask: What do you do to unwind and have your share of fun?"

"I paint, I watch the variety shows on the boob toob -- when it's working, that is, especially since all the good stuff seems to be on cable these days, and we'll be damned if this household can spare the cash for that—and I hang with my main men from the crib."

"Do you ever frequent the taverns that the streets of this fair city have to offer?"

"I don't think my mom would be too happy with that. I'm too skinny to hold down the booze anyways."

"Nonsense. I have seen thinner than you throw back many a lager in times past. I think, Jimmy, you need to get out on the town, and I am the one to help you enjoy yourself properly. You are, I dare say, too decent for your own good."

"And I'd like to stay that way. I think the world doesn't have enough decent people as it is."

Dorian smirked. "That is one perspective. Another would say there may be too many good people, or at least those playing at being good, suppressing their inner nature and depriving themselves of a full life that is destined to be all too brief. Do you want to be one of those individuals, Jimmy?"

"I think I'm still a bit too young to decide exactly what I wanna be yet, other than the best and most dyno-mite artiste the world has seen since De Vinci and Van Gogh ran the show."

"That is precisely my point. Other than being an artist, you know not what you want out of life. And I assure you I have known many an artist in the past and having such a vocation has never precluded having a full and rich life. As a matter of fact, my extensive experience in such matters has taught me that enjoying life to the fullest and experiencing all there is to experience in this world is crucial to an artist developing their skills to their fullest."

"If you say so."

"I more than say so, Jimmy; I *know* this to be so. Now, let us build your life experience, and therefore enhance your skills as a famous artist in the making, by taking to the streets of this city tonight. A city like Chicago has much to offer in that regard. Come, it shall be my treat."

"Well, it is sort of late…"

"There is no better time to take to the taverns and byways of such a city than the hours after midnight and prior to the onset of dawn. More pleasures await in such an environment than those readily available during the daylight hours. So, let us waste no more of this terrific night on meandering discussions and take to the streets together."

"Mom may be worried if she wakes up and I'm, well, you know, not here."

"You told me yourself that your mom, as well as your sister, sleeps like a proverbial rock, a comparison that has been proven to be apt throughout my visit this night. And your younger brother Mike has long since slipped into peaceful slumber on that sofa-cum-bed you share with him. Let us depart this confining apartment and see what I can get you into this evening. The streets of Chicago eagerly await our presence."

It was obvious to Dorian that Jimmy found something "off" about him. The young artist's upbringing in a location like Cabrini-Green and a rearing from good parents—one of whom was now sadly departed—gave him an instinct for such things. The deceased James Henry Sr., the man who raised his younger namesake, couldn't possibly have been more different than the strange youngish-looking man who so unexpectedly turned up at the doorstep this night.

But Dorian was nothing if not persistent, and a veritable expert at breaking down the barriers between one's better side and its baser counterpart. And he was fully aware that the recent loss of a beloved parent had left Jimmy in a vulnerable emotional state, which may provide just the "opening" that Dorian could slither through to exert his will.

"Um, look, Dorian, I really *really* appreciate the business and all, even if I did have to spend two hours looking at whoever or whatever I was looking at on the canvas, but…"

"And I, in turn, appreciate the hard work you did on such abrupt notice, and what your senses had to endure in order to fulfill such a business obligation. That is why you deserve to enjoy some good times, and why I wish to show my gratitude for your work by treating you to that. You have recently suffered a terrible loss, and I would be remiss if I failed as your newest friend to provide you with the succor that would take your mind off it."

"You want to give me… a lollipop?"

"What? No, I said succor, not 'sucker.' Listen to me, Jimmy, and listen well. Your recent tragic loss has shown you how fleeting and capricious life can be. How suddenly and without notice it can be taken from you. I believe your father, were he here now, would want you to live your life to the fullest before the Reaper inevitably arrives, even more unannounced than I did earlier this evening, and decidedly less welcome, to take his due and thereby deprive you of any further opportunities to enjoy the precious gift that is life. I would think your sire's demise would have made this evident."

"Yeah, well, I do think Dad would have wanted me to live a full life and all that, but I'm not sure he would have in mind what you have in mind, you know."

"Bollocks, my friend."

"'Butt licks'?"

"No, *bollocks*, which would be English slang for *bullshit*, Jimmy. I am guessing you are fully acquainted with the latter metaphorical term?"

"Oh yeah I am. Especially around this neighborhood."

"I presumed as much. And I further presume your father could not fully enjoy his life in the manner in which you now can, as he was attached and tied down to his role as a provider to a wife and children."

"Wait a minute now, my dad never complained about…"

"And I am certain he would not have complained about you enjoying your life in a way his obligations did not permit him to. And one day you will have those same obligations. Possibly. But let us tarry here no longer with this pointless dialogue. Just endeavor to *live* and let me show you how that is done."

Dorian approached the door leading out of the apartment and extended his right arm in a beckoning motion to Jimmy.

"Come now, Jimmy, before you talk yourself out of it. Seize the moment, for it may never come again!"

Jimmy was almost overcome by wariness, so he hesitated. But *almost* was the operative descriptor in this situation. Dorian's words were cringe-inducing, but at the same time, strangely *compelling*. He *knew* what he was talking about, even if a prominent part of Jimmy's psyche disliked what the seeming young man was talking about.

"Okay, but, like I said, my mom has enough on her mind right now, so I really prefer she not wake up and find me, well, you know… not here."

Dorian looked at Jimmy with another of his disturbing yet endearing smirks. "Now, Jimmy, do you lack all confidence that I will have you back safely and soundly in this tenement hovel of yours well before your mother awakens?"

Jimmy took a few moments to ponder that question.

"Well, I guess it wouldn't hurt to go out just for one night. Just for an hour. Or two. I mean, hey, it's not really *that* late."

"That is the spirit, my new friend. Let us be off, for the evening city awaits us."

And off they went into the dark boulevards of Chicago, neither fully anticipating what was in store for them there.

V.

Dorian's and Jimmy's evening excursion into the more unsavory regions of the Windy City took them to the South Side, which the former quickly arranged via a taxi service. Jimmy was both impressed and chilled by the safe passage afforded to both Dorian and himself in and out of the Cabrini-Green turf by the Soul Lords.

"Those guys totally like you," Jimmy noted to his ersatz friend during the cab ride. "And just so you know, I don't exactly mean that as a compliment."

"Ha!" Dorian responded. "I have ways of making friends in the highest of places, my dear lad."

"I just wish you had ways of making friends with speech instructors who could give you a crash course on 'Standard Layman.'"

"Ha ha! You are a funny young man, Jimmy. I anticipate a jolly good time with you this evening."

"Do they still say 'jolly' in England? Over here, we only use that word these days when referring to Santa Claus."

"Ah, good old Father Christmas. An annoying git, that one."

"You talk about the dude as if he were, you know, *real* or something. Didn't your parents ever bother to tell you the truth about that by the time you were ten?"

"Oh, Jimmy, my friend, if only you knew the *actual* truth."

"Huh?"

"Let us just say that the universe is a more fascinating and complex place than you imagine. But enough about that. Our first stop is at the warehouse I rented since my arrival in this city."

"Is that where you stashed your beer, or something?"

"No, no, we will get our 'beer' in the company of others, at the proper establishments. The warehouse is for the safekeeping of these two valuable portraits, one of which is entirely your work; the other being the work of my departed friend Basil, which you so professionally embellished this night."

"I'm not sure I like hearing about one of your 'good' friends being, um, 'departed.' I hope that didn't happen to your man Basil during a night on the town with you. Like, you know, the one I'm on with you right now."

"Ha ha! Oh no, not at all. Poor Basil's demise ensued under different, more complicated circumstances than one such as this. Also not worth discussing, as we have other interests to take up our attention."

"You call everything 'complicated.'"

"As things tend to be in this universe."

Moments later, the portraits of Noir Jesus and Dorian's own all-important canvas, The Portrait *of* Dorian Gray -- not that Jimmy could possibly have recognized it as such -- were placed in a superlatively secure warehouse. There they would later be retrieved by Dorian, just before he made his departure from the Windy City. That, at least, was the plan. As it would turn out, however, only *one* of those two canvases would be successfully retrieved. That, however, is getting well ahead of things in this tale.

***

Dorian and Jimmy strolled down the dimly lit street of Englewood, heading towards a bar with the ironic name of

Englewood's Best. Its exterior showed signs of being run down, but its shimmering red neon sign served as a blazing welcome mat to all who wanted to drink, play pool, and consort with the city's less than reputable elements. That population segment included Dorian Gray among their number on this night, though earning money and getting sauced were not part of his evening itinerary.

"Do you think it's really a good idea to go for a drink here, Dorian, my man?" Jimmy asked as well-warranted tremors of fear crept across his lanky form like serpentine undulations.

"As a matter of fact, I think it is," Dorian replied as he stared at the glowing sign.

"Do you know the rep of this place?"

"I am eager to find out exactly what that 'rep' happens to be, and by way of direct experience rather than the hearsay tales of others. This, my friend, is where we shall begin teaching you the finer indulgences in life."

"Couldn't we have just stopped at McDonald's for some of those indulgences?"

"Absolutely not. The vices that establishment offers pale in comparison to those we may find here. Follow me."

Dorian headed towards the door but was forced to sidestep when it was pushed open from the inside as a tall, burly bouncer in a dark shirt hurled an inebriated man out into the street.

"And don't let me catch your fuckin' ass in here again!" the bouncer screamed.

"The charm of this place has touched me already," Dorian said with a grin.

"You better hope none of the rowdies in there end up touching you instead!" Jimmy lamented.

"No need to get me unduly excited before I even enter the place, Jimmy. Let us go inside and seek all the enjoyment this little backwoods tavern can offer. You need a helping of that considerably more than I do."

The young artist and the not-so-young-yet-young-looking scoundrel entered the establishment behind the bouncer, to behold rows of chairs and the smell of stale, spilled beer permeating the atmosphere. These seats were filled with a plethora of individuals who seemed to exude impropriety as if it were a gaseous emission.

Dorian wasn't the only one in his party of two to pick up on those palpable sensations.

"If the sleazy vibes in this place were any thicker, you couldn't cut them even with a samurai sword," Jimmy lamented.

"Ha ha. Indeed," Dorian replied. "And such a blade would be a katana, my dear boy. But getting back to matters of relevancy, do you not see all this establishment has to offer us?"

"Actually... no. But you lead the way."

"Then I lead you here..."

Dorian motioned for Jimmy to follow him to the bar. There they were greeted by a server who was a highly attractive African-American woman in her 20s, with a bushy afro that was tinted three different colors and filled with golden glitter that gave the colors a nearly iridescent luster. Her attire consisted of a pink tube top and tight denim jeans, all doing a good job of accentuating her body's curves and exposing generous amounts of her smooth dark skin for all to admire. It wasn't difficult to see how she was basking in all the attention this brought to her direction.

"Hello, sweet mama," Jimmy said with a star-struck countenance at the sight of this woman.

"Hey!" she replied. "What will be your pleasure tonight?"

"Um...?"

"I believe the lady is inquiring as to what you want to drink, Jimmy," Dorian clarified. "But do not hesitate to interpret that question of hers precisely as you were doing."

Jimmy shook his head to bring his mind out of what his mother might call "the gutter."

"Um, I'll have the breast drink you can offer here."

Both the woman and Dorian burst out laughing in tandem.

"What? I meant, the *best* drink you have to offer here!"

"Of course, that is what you *actually* meant," Dorian said with all due sarcasm. "It pleases me to see you so transparently enjoying yourself before you have partaken even a single drop of the spirits, Jimmy."

"Little man there probably thinks you're talking about sharing some tongue with a ghost," the young woman quipped. "But, to answer his question about the best drink in the house, that would be a Ketel One. How 'bout I get you a shot of that? It's 100 proof, so even a single shot of that shit will get your pleasant mood started."

"My friend will absolutely be having that," Dorian interceded as he slapped several bills down on the table. "In fact, it may be prudent to purchase five of those shots for him. The ways in which he needs to loosen up are legion."

"I like the way you talk, white boy," the woman said. "You sort of remind me of my father."

"Huh?" Jimmy said as he shook his head in befuddlement.

Dorian began laughing again.

"Oh, I meant because my father is a college instructor," she elucidated while filling up the shot glasses with vodka. "I didn't mean it the way you're thinking, man."

"Are you absolutely *certain* of that, little miss?" Dorian enquired with a laugh.

Dorian and the stunning bartender then shared another boisterous laugh.

"Um, oh… um," was Jimmy's initial response. "Maybe… maybe I should take a seat, since my friend here is generous enough to pick up the tab for both of us."

"Why do you want to go and sit over there instead of up here?" the woman asked while placing the filled shot glasses on the bar table in front of them. "Am I too hot for you to handle, little man?" She bent over the counter as she asked, making a point to expose an plentiful degree of her cleavage as she did so. "Don't ya like me at all?"

"I like them perfectly fine," Jimmy replied while staring at her exposed anatomy. "I mean, I meant, I like *you* totally fine! Because, you're, well, you know… fine!"

The woman and Dorian shared a third raucous laugh together.

"A man I once met named Freud would have envisioned you as a walking verification of certain theories he developed!" Dorian snorted at his young companion.

"Maybe it's my hair that turns you off then?" the woman queried to Jimmy, still teasing him.

"Um, no!" he blurted. "I'm a professional artiste, so I have no problem getting into all of those colors."

The woman tilted her head in a puzzled fashion. "Say what?"

"I meant, I've seen hair like that at the circus before, so I'm completely down with it."

"*What?*"

"I meant, I always dig colored hair on the ladies! You must have done yourself up for the Bud Billiken Parade and liked your hair that way so much you just kept it like that, er, right?"

"Wrong, toothpick! I never go to that boring parade, and it was months ago anyway. The colors would have been faded by now if I just left it like that for months, and you would now be seeing a lot of ugly ass dark roots. I just like my hair to be colored. Do you got a problem with that or something?"

"No! I mean, I noticed your cleavage before I ever even saw your hair, so they stick out… I mean, your *hair colors* don't stick out compared to your boobs. I mean… I meant, I think I need to go and sit down so I can find the time to yank my foot out of my mouth."

Dorian and the woman released another joint deluge of uproarious laughter.

"Jimmy, you totally slay me," Dorian said. "It is beyond obvious how much you needed this little soiree tonight. By all means find us a table, while I complete payment to…"

Dorian pointed to the woman, to indicate he was fishing for her name, to which she said, "Monica."

"Ah, yes, *Monica*. Exquisite name for a truly exquisite woman."

"Why, thank you," she replied. "Someone sure is on the make tonight!"

"Astute observation, but that would hardly be limited to this night only."

Jimmy shook his head and walked towards the nearest empty table he could find. He sat down and briefly removed his denim hat to wipe his brow. The anxiety he felt in the bar was causing him to perspire, and he found himself thankful that he took the time to spray deodorant on his arm pits while changing out of his pajamas to accompany Dorian on this nighttime excursion.

It was then that the seat across from Jimmy on the table was taken. But it wasn't by Dorian, who remained at the bar trading flirtatious comments with Monica.

The young man who joined him in Dorian's stead was terrifyingly familiar. This newcomer wore a denim jacket with a decal sewn into the shoulder area that bore the gawking visage of the red-colored and horned common cultural conception of the Devil. It was a symbol that Jimmy immediately recognized as the official emblem of the notorious street gang called Satan's Knights.

It was a street gang for which Jimmy was an unwilling conscript two years earlier, and the young man before him was none other than its feared leader, who had proudly earned the street moniker Mad Dog.

This was, in fact, the same gang leader who shot Jimmy two years earlier, nearly killing both him and the father that he later lost through unrelated means mere months ago. He could never forget the bushy but well-maintained afro, the thin moustache, and savage glare, as he nearly died the last time he had laid eyes upon it.

"See, I told you it was him, Mad Dog," said a tall young African-American man also wearing the emblem of the Satan's Knights; a man whose lankiness nearly rivaled that of Jimmy. "You can't forget the face of a fuckin' jive ass turkey like that."

"I got eyes too, Neck Bone," the gang leader said in a voice reeking with authority. "Jimmy and I haven't had the honor of seeing each other in two years now, ever since Satan's Knights had to yield

Cabrini-Green to the Soul Lords. So, we got some catching up to do. Right, Jimmy?"

Jimmy tried focusing every erg of his will into not fainting again. "Y-yeah, Mad Dog. And, uh, hi, Neck Bone. Good – good to see you again, right? How is Sweet Pea doing? He was one of your main men, Mad Dog."

Neck Bone walked up to Jimmy and thrust his index finger a mere half-inch from the space between his eyes. "Ty done got himself stabbed to death. On the same night you was supposed to come with us to rumble with the Warlords."

"I'm sorry to hear about your man getting taken out like that," Jimmy sputtered nervously but with genuine sincerity. "He was, um, cool. But, you know, I couldn't join that fight on account of the fact that Mad Dog sort of, well, shot me."

"Because your old man got in *our* way when we was *on* the way to the rumble!" Neck Bone said with another angry thrust of his finger. "You just lucky Mad Dog's bullet didn't hit yo' ass in the skull instead of the shoulder. Right, Mad Dog?"

"Be chill, Neck Bone," was the leader's cool reply. "Go get me another drink and let Jimmy and I do our... catching up."

Neck Bone complied with what was obviously a direct order with no further hesitation. However, his ire was merely replaced by that of Mad Dog, whose own attention was considerably more fearsome to confront.

"You bailed on us that night, Jimmy," was the gang leader's first statement. "A man who runs the war council for Satan's Knights doesn't forget shit like that."

"Hey, I know," Jimmy stammered, "and I compliment your good memory. I mean, not that I'm glad you remembered me, I meant...

ugh. Look, Mad Dog, my dad was killed in an accident some months ago."

"Then it looks like you got in the way of my bullet for nothing."

"You're wrong there, man. I'm really glad my getting in your way like that helped my family get two more years to spend with my dad. As I heard it, when he saw you get off the hook for blowing me away, he let you off easy. Even felt bad for you when he saw your mom tell you that she hated you and wished you were never born."

Jimmy jumped with a start when Mad Dog slammed his hands down on the table, causing a glass left behind by previous patrons fall to the floor and shatter. That caught Dorian's attention at the bar.

"I didn't need your old man's pity," the leader of Satan's Knights said, "and I didn't need *anything* from my mother either, least of all her love and support."

"I think you're joshing me there, Mad Dog."

The bush-headed young man grabbed Jimmy by his shirt and pulled him across the table top until he was looking Mad Dog face-to-face.

"Watch yourself, pencil dick. I told my fucking mother right then and there that I didn't need nobody. She didn't want my help taking care of my younger sibs, then fuck her! I didn't leave her on purpose like my dad did!"

Mad Dog was interrupted when a shot glass was slammed on the table. He and Jimmy looked up to see Dorian standing beside them.

"And to think you told me that you had no friends to speak of in a place like this, Jimmy," Dorian said with a flippant tone. "By all means introduce me to this interesting acquaintance of yours."

"Fuck off, you prissy faggot!" Mad Dog insisted. "This is between me and the boney one here."

"And *this* 'bony' one too," interjected Neck Bone, who was also attracted by the commotion. "Want me to make this jive ass mother fucker get out of your face, Mad Dog? I'm here to see to it that you ain't got to deal with the little things."

"Yeah, why don't you take this faggot into the bathroom and teach him not to fuck with me," Mad Dog agreed.

"You got it, man…"

"Now, gentlemen, there is no need for any of this," Dorian said in a calm, festive tone. "If your leader wishes for alone time with Jimmy, I would be more than happy to retreat to the bar to have a drink there, and to buy one for your lackey, here."

"Wait, what does this dude think I lack?" Neck Bone asked.

"He meant you're under my authority," Mad Dog replied, "and there's no disagreeing with that. Go back to the bar with this peckerwood and keep an eye on him, make sure he stays out of my shit, so I can talk to Jimmy without having to kill his white boyfriend first. I don't wanna get blood on my jacket if I can help it, 'cause I just got it washed yesterday."

"You got it, man!" Neck Bone assured his leader. "You can totally count on me. C'mon, dude."

Dorian acceded to the request… at least to all appearances. He made a quick, wry grin at Jimmy before walking away, using that along with his confident demeanor to indicate he had things well in hand. Jimmy was simply hoping Dorian would get him out of this however he intended to do it before Mad Dog took things to the next level. Until then, he would have to do his best to de-escalate the street warrior's rage with fancy words of his own.

He found himself really wishing his father would walk into the bar, as he could always count on his dad to bail him out of things like this. But he knew that was no longer possible, so he had to rely on Dorian instead. Or, failing that, on himself.

Mad Dog wasted no time in continuing the conversation. "Now, where were we before your faggish white friend interrupted us, Jimmy?"

"I, uh, think you were calling your mother names that would make a sailor blush, and ranting about how you didn't need her or anyone else."

"Yeah, thank you for keeping my place in the conversation for me." Mad Dog loosened his grip, allowing the thin 19-year-old to slide off the table top and back onto his bar stool. "You're better than a book marker. Just as thin and light as one, too. Now, maybe you can take a few minutes to explain to me why I shouldn't just pull out my .22 and finish the job right here and now."

"You, uh, might get blood all over that outta sight jacket of yours?"

"That's one. But you better try again, because I'm only giving you another minute before I get bored with the amusement of hassling you and move onto spilling the blood. Can you dig that?"

"Yeah, yeah, I can totally dig it. My grave, that is. Look, Mad Dog, I think it was a jive deal that you ended up with a dad like yours. But, man, look at the potential you got. I can totally see you leading a Chicago faction of the Black Panthers and doing something for the brothers and sisters instead of taking things from them. You know, like their lives and assorted bodily fluids?"

"You're failing to make a convincing case, Jimmy. All my life, things were taken from me. Why shouldn't I be one of the ones who does the taking, instead of one of the jive ass turkeys like you who're on the opposite end of that deal?"

233

"I know you think I'm some kind of sissy, and I'm sure as hell not a fighter like you. Or like my dad was. But my mom and younger siblings lost our dad too. He didn't leave like yours did, but he was still taken from us. Like you almost took him from us two years before that. Like you almost took *me* from *them*.

"But maybe there's a way to give to others without being a sissy who gets things taken from them. Do you think the Fruit of Islam are a bunch of sissies? How 'bout the Black Panthers? What about Malcolm X? And didn't Martin give it all up for us despite not being a fighter, and despite not ever taking shit from anyone?"

Mad Dog actually seemed to ruminate on Jimmy's words a moment before replying. "You may be a born preacher, skull bones, but not me. I'm a warrior. That's my calling."

"But, man, there's a lot more to being a warrior than just taking people out. It's fighting for something more than just yourself. Okay, maybe that is preaching, but sometimes we need to throw the words at people."

"I fight for Satan's Knights, and they *are* a bigger thing than me!"

"Well, um, I can't agree with that, Mad Dog. I think the Knights are just an extension of you, if I'm making sense there. Please tell me I'm making sense…?"

Mad Dog sighed and shook his head. "Someone, please kill me now."

"I should be so lucky," Jimmy whispered to himself.

"What?"

"Erm, I meant I should be so lucky to be as handsome as you."

Mad Dog cocked his head. "Are you some sort of faggot or something?"

Then it was Jimmy's turn to shake his head. *Dorian, you better think of something to get me out of this, 'cause I am fast running out of things to say here!*

VI.

Back at the bar, Dorian engaged his unasked-for host Neck Bone in conversation as he looked around the room, hoping to find just the right person for the scheme he was concocting.

"So, Bone Head, my newfound friend, by all means tell me about the joys and tribulations of life in a street gang," he said with convincing cordiality.

"The name is 'Neck Bone,' man," was the gang member's irritable reply. "And Satan's Knights is a really far out gig, you see? Nothin' some faggot like you would ever know about."

"Why, of course not. The thought of me being involved in some darkly exclusive organization is just beyond the pale."

Dorian did his best to refrain from smiling with anticipation for when his plan came to fruition. Particularly after he noticed a certain large, fancily dressed man step into the bar. It was a man that Dorian had never met personally, but one whose reputation on Chicago's South Side was so well known and feared that Dorian could not help overhearing more than one person point the man out when he visited the bar on his first night in Chicago five days previous.

It took the purchase of just a few drinks to get those people to tell Dorian the full story of that intriguing individual, such as the fact that his name was Leroy.

The immortal Englishman tapped the wooden counter of the bar to get the bartender's attention. "Monica, would you be a dear and bring a round to Leroy over there on me. And also, be so kind as to attach this thank you note I just scribbled onto this folded napkin when you do."

Monica's eyes nearly rolled inside her head. "Him? *Seriously?* Dorian, if you go both ways, then I wouldn't advise you to send overtures to this particular guy…"

"Oh, yes, most seriously. I do owe him for picking up a previous tab of mine, so it's all well and good."

"Did he *seriously* pick up a tab for you?"

"Monica, just do it, please. Here is the cash for the round, and here is a generous tip for you, to go along with the other sort of tip I plan to give you later. After all, I do not want to be rude to Neck Bone here by delaying the continuation of our charming conversation for too long."

"Well, alright. And thanks for the tip. This one now, and the other one later." Monica grinned impishly at Dorian as she filled a pitcher of beer and proceeded to take it and the note over to the man called Leroy.

Dorian returned the grin and then renewed his attention on Neck Bone. "Now, what were you saying, Mr. Boner?"

"That's *Neck* Bone, man. And I was saying that I'm starting not to like yo' ass at all."

"Truly? Was there actually one point since we met when you actually were fond of me? I am sorry I missed any statement from you which may have indicated that. Also, in regard to the specific part of me that you said you're beginning to dislike, I must say I am not used to hearing anyone make a negative critique about my buttocks upon becoming acquainted with them."

"Huh?" Neck Bone stood up, nearly knocking over the stool he was sitting on. "You're one mental mother fucker, ya know that?" He then brandished a switchblade. "I think I'm gonna cut yo' face."

Suddenly, Neck Bone was interrupted by the angry approach of Leroy. The tall and thin gang member tended to fear nothing when Mad Dog was around, but his emotions couldn't help making an exception in this particular case. Especially since he, like everyone who frequented the South Side of Chicago, was all too familiar with Leroy and his much-feared reputation.

"So, you think I look like a faggot in my suit?" Leroy spat close to Neck Bone's face.

"Huh?" Neck Bone's incredulity was genuine. "I didn't say shit 'bout you, man."

"Neck Bone, you may as well be a man and own up to that indiscretion," Dorian said. "I felt I had no choice but to send this gentleman a message and inform him of the ill-advised drubs you directed at his attire, even though I can fully understand that you wanted to look powerful and fearless to your leader in the gang you belong to. Nevertheless, as one who respects Leroy and his reputation, I would never have risked any ill will from him by keeping your opinion of his attire from him. That would just be dishonest!"

"So, you did say that shit about my clothing, huh?" Leroy's nostrils flared with rage, almost giving him the features and disposition of a junkyard dog. "This clothing that cost more than your entire wardrobe? And that silly ass sticker on your cheap ass jacket don't make you look half as tough as you think you it does! Not to me, mother fucker! If you were even half as tough as you think you are, you would've had the balls to come say that shit about me to my face!"

Neck Bone was all but trembling with fear and was highly tempted to call out to Mad Dog. But he couldn't look like a coward in front of the leader of Satan's Knights, and he needed to show he was worthy of his station as Mad Dog's right-hand man. Hence, he forced himself to turn his switchblade in the direction of his fearsome accoster.

"You… you back off, mother fucker! Back the fuck off or I'll… I'll cut you open!"

Without saying another word, Leroy grabbed Neck Bone's blade-wielding wrist and twisted it, making an audible cracking sound in the process. Before he had a chance to scream from the broken ulna, Leroy slammed his fist into the gang member's face, shattering his nose and sending his gangly body flying on top of the bar counter. He then quickly reached and pulled a razor blade from one of his socks.

"You mean cut me open like this?" Leroy sliced the flesh of Neck Bone's forehead, ripping a gash in the skin clear across the crown of his skull.

After that, Neck Bone abandoned all pretense of being able to gracefully take what was being wrought upon him, and he screamed in agony. This immediately got the attention of every single patron and employee of the bar, including Mad Dog and Jimmy. The former turned to see what happened to his second-in-command, and this caused him to leave the company of the young artist and dart towards the bar to deliver retribution.

For Dorian's part, he was simply looking in the other direction and casually sipping a glass of Canadian Club whiskey.

Leroy saw Mad Dog rushing towards him, recognized the devil emblem on his jacket, and turned to meet the approaching challenge. Both he and the gang leader were fast on the draw, and the two immediately found themselves standing a mere four feet apart with a firearm pointed at each other's faces. It was a classic stand-off.

As both were distracted, Dorian motioned for Monica to come over to him, as Neck Bone continued to writhe and scream on the bar's counter top.

"May I please borrow your cigarette, dear?"

Monica complied with the request. "Um, okay, I can see why you might really need a drag right now."

"Oh, I do not smoke at all. At least, not cigarettes."

"Then why…?"

Her question was answered when Dorian turned and grabbed the pain-wracked Neck Bone by the throat, holding the glowing cherry of the lit cigarette above his face.

"Neck Bone, my friend, I see you enjoy throwing the word 'faggot' about. Are you aware of what a 'faggot' originally referred to? No? Well, it was a *burning* ember."

He then pressed the lit end of the cigarette directly down on the gang member's open head wound. The glowing cherry made a sizzling sound as it burned into the exposed hypodermis.

Neck Bone screamed in even worse agony than before.

Dorian's countenance was suddenly taken over by a look of mock self-recrimination. "Oh, bugger! How clumsy I am! Here, you may have my whiskey in compensation."

With that, Dorian picked up a shot glass filled with Canadian Club and poured its 100 proof contents into the screaming Neck Bone's gaping mouth, causing the stinging liquid to fill inside his esophagus.

"Oh, whatever is the matter with me today and my dreadful clumsiness?"

He next snatched a newly lit cigarette directly from Monica's fingers and dropped the glowing end into Neck Bone's mouth. The smoldering cherry ignited upon contact with the gang member's alcohol-filled mouth and throat, before his saliva had time to sufficiently dilute it.

As a result, Neck Bone released one last incredibly intense scream as he spewed flame for a few seconds. That scream was quickly choked off, however, when the flesh of his lips, gums, inner mouth, and throat became a swollen mass of scar tissue. He passed out within a mere few seconds.

Monica put her hands over her own mouth and gasped in shock at the sight. Dorian politely handed her back the cigarette after taking one final look at the twitching, torture-ridden form of Neck Bone as consciousness rapidly and mercifully left him.

"Thank you for the use of this, luv. And Neck Bone, you should cheer up, mate. I doubt you will be running off your big, sycophantic mouth ever again, and that can only make for an improvement in your deportment. You may even find yourself invited to the occasional party that isn't paid for by your gang of ruffians. I would refrain from putting any spicy food in your gullet any time soon, however."

He then turned to witness the armed stand-off between Leroy and Mad Dog.

At that moment, Jimmy finally worked up the nerve to run over to his companion of the night's events.

"Man, is the dude facing off against Mad Dog who I think he is?"

"If you are surmising as I believe you are, then the answer is most certainly yes."

"Hooo man! This guy is supposed to be the baddest man in the whole damn town! And Mad Dog seems bent on dethroning him! We need to make like we're trying to break Frank Shorter's record at the Olympics and head for the door before the bullets start flying! I think I've 'lived' enough for one night! And I'd like to keep on living if you don't mind!"

"For once, I cannot find fault with your plan, Jimmy. Let us make haste…"

However, as Dorian turned towards the front exit of the tavern, he found another tall, dark-attired individual standing before him and barring their way. It was not only another figure of terror-inducing familiarity, but one whom Dorian had already run afoul of several hours earlier.

"Did you think you could elude me for long, Mr. Gray?" was Dracula's sole question as he glared at the object of his wrath.

Dorian frowned. *Wonderful. This is most certainly not what I what I need right now.*

Jimmy turned to his unwanted compatriot. "Uh, Dorian, can I feel safe to assume this newest acquaintance of yours is the same type of bad news as those other two over there?"

"Incorrect," Dorian answered. "He is countless magnitudes worse 'news' than that pair combined."

"I was afraid you were going to tell me that. This evening out with you just gets better every minute."

"You have no quarrel with this young man, Dracula," Dorian said to the powerful soul-clone of Vlad Tepes. "Let him go, and then we may settle things."

"Dracula?" Jimmy bellowed incredulously. "First you tell me Santa Claus is for real, and now Dracula too? Just my luck it had to be the guy in the black cape instead of the one in the red coat who dropped in to prove your point."

"The boy may *not* go, Mr. Gray," the Vampire Lord said angrily. "While it is true I have no quarrel with him, you were foolish enough to just reveal he is of concern to you. That means my quarrel now extends to him by association."

Jimmy covered his face. "Thanks a bunch, Dorian."

Dorian knew he had to think fast. He found himself feeling prickles of guilt over Jimmy becoming part of Dracula's wrath due to convincing the young artist to go out on the town with him in the first place. He knew he shouldn't be concerned about anything other than safely extricating himself from this situation, but for some reason, he was unable to entirely divest himself of consideration for the adolescent at his side.

If only I could get my hands on the crimson-covered tome in my pocket. But I will need to read the incantation on the dog-eared pages aloud, while simultaneously concentrating on the proper image. I must buy us some time.

It was then that Dorian spotted the burly bouncer in the corner, doing his best to direct patrons out of the establishment before the situation between Mad Dog and Leroy, two fierce men with even fiercer reputations in Chicago, finally exploded. Dorian almost grinned as his devious mind immediately hatched a plan.

VII.

Leroy and Mad Dog began growing mutually tired of the armed stand-off between the two of them.

Hence, Leroy offered a solution to the seeming impasse. "Dude, we can stand here forever, or just one of us can pull the trigger and hope the other guy's finger don't contract and wipe out the one who shoots first. Or, we can toss the pieces and settle this man-to-man. Unless, of course, you know who I am and are too chickenshit to do that."

Mad Dog became irritated, as Leroy had hoped. "Man, I *do* know who you are, and I ain't scared of you. Your rep ain't so hot anymore since that guy whipped your ass when you put the make on his wife."

Leroy grumbled with rage. "That injury to my rep only lasted 'till it got around who that guy actually *was*. Then I had no reason to feel any more shame over losing that one. If you really think I ain't shit, then let's toss the guns into the back room on the count of three and see if you can take me out knuckle-to-knuckle. So, what's it gonna be? You gonna walk the walk, or just keep talking the talk, like the little pussy ass faggot I think you are?"

Mad Dog gritted his teeth as he trembled from the rage-induced adrenalin pouring through his veins. "You don't get to run the war council of Satan's Knights by being a pussy, mother fucker. At the count of three, you dig?"

"You better believe I dig, asshole. Now let's see if you're not too much of a pussy to keep your word. One… two… *three*."

The very moment which the final number was uttered by Leroy, the two dangerous men kept their mutual word and simultaneously tossed their firearms into the open door of a back room. There the lethal objects bounced off a wall and clattered down a long flight of stairs leading to a dark storage cellar. No one would be retrieving those weapons any time this evening. The two of them then immediately stepped into a fighting stance, their weapons now a combination of savagery and street skills rather than bullets.

**

"Sir!" Dorian screamed as loud as he could to the bouncer standing about fifteen feet behind him. "Oh, sir, my friend and I cannot leave the establishment because this gentleman in the cape is barring our way and threatening us!"

The already flustered bouncer was by that point close to the edge of his temper due to the night's events, much as Dorian surmised. The powerfully built man left his post and ran towards Dracula, and the former's chunky hand came down on the vampire's shoulder a few seconds later.

"I've had enough of this shit tonight! Get out the way and let these guys leave!" he bellowed. "Then your ass is outta here too!"

Dracula's response was to turn, bare his fangs, and hiss in a raging fury at this mortal rabble who dared lay a hand on him, let alone having had the audacity to give him orders. The bouncer of this South Side bar wasn't easily scared but suffice to say he came close to losing his bowels at the sight of the Count's protruding fangs and glaring red eyes. Not to mention the incredible aura of menace his countenance exuded.

"You dare touch me!" were Dracula's only words as he backhanded the heavily built security man with his closed fist.

The soul-cloned Prince of Darkness struck with a speed that the usually alert and athletic bouncer had no hope of evading. The blow landed with such force that the 260-pound man was knocked completely off his feet, ultimately flying backwards over a dozen yards distant as if blasted out of a circus cannon. His body slammed into the wall with superlative force, creating numerous zig-zagging lines of lightning-shaped cracks on the linoleum in the process. The security man released one brief gagging sound upon impact, and then fell to the floor unmoving.

"Whoa-holy-shit!" Jimmy exclaimed. "That was… dy-no-*mite!* Um, I meant… Dorian! Do something, man! I'm not about to go the distance with this cat! I think even Mohammed Ali or George Foreman would be in trouble here!"

When Jimmy turned his head, he noticed that Dorian had made good use of the distraction by getting the paperback-sized book out of his hands. The tome had also been successfully flipped open to the particular location he had doggie-eared earlier that day.

As he began pronouncing the incantations on the page facing him, struggling to get those words scribed in an ancient language pronounced with full phonetic fealty, Dracula couldn't help but catch notice of the cover. And his scarlet-hued eyes, matching those of the tome's cover, opened wide with an expression that almost seemed akin to… fear.

"No… How did you gain possession of *that*?"

Unfortunately, Dracula proved as fast as ever, and he lashed out with the reckless abandon that comes with desperation. This swat of the hand -- what people on the streets would one day christen a "bitch slap" -- sent Dorian sprawling through the air with a momentum similar to that wreaked upon the bouncer moments earlier.

The airborne immortal crashed into the edge of the bar, and he felt his spinal column crack upon doing so, and then crack even more as he bounced and landed on the hardwood floor. He had no idea how long it would take his mystically enhanced body to fix that type of damage, and he could only hope it would do so before Dracula had descended upon his hapless form to rip it to pieces.

"Jimmy..." Dorian managed to croak out despite the debilitating agony he was in. "Jimmy... run! Get out...!"

Though Dorian had dropped the book as Dracula intended, it nevertheless got caught in the momentum of the blow and slid underneath a table in the eastern corner of the bar. Only Jimmy saw exactly where it landed. He had never seen that book before, nor did Dorian mention it or its purpose to him, but he had just seen enough to realize the tome could evidently be used by his dubious friend to defeat Dracula. It was already clear to him that Dorian was much more than he seemed to be, which could be absolutely anything if he had personages like Dracula -- and evidently *Santa Claus* -- among his acquaintances!

Does this guy have tea with the Tooth Fairy too? Or puff reefer with Puff the Magic Dragon? I gotta book from here right now, 'cause Mom and the family don't need to lose me after we just lost Dad. I was a total maroon to go with Dorian when, like, every single alarm system ever installed in my brain was going off. What were you thinking, *Jimmy? Would Dad be proud of you if he knew you went out with a guy like that? A guy who actually knows* Dracula, *for shit's sake?*

Jimmy turned to get out of there as fast as he could before Dracula -- the *real* Dracula, mind you -- or Mad Dog, if he came out on top of his scuffle with Leroy, came after him.

Just as he reached the door, the fledgling professional artist stopped. Something gave him pause, a nagging feeling in the back of his head that actually overcame the extreme flight instinct that was demanding he leave with all due haste.

Okay, okay, I know I shouldn't have brought my skinny ass here. But I did come here, and that's not gonna change. And even though Dad wouldn't be proud of me for hanging out with Dorian, would he be proud of me for... well, just abandoning him to the fangs of doom like that? And after he sort of put himself on the line for me?

C'mon now, Jimmy No way do you want to mess around with a cat like Drac. Or stick around while Mad Dog is still here. I'm not that Van Helsing dude, or someone like Leroy, or the leader of the Warlords, or someone equipped to handle guys like them. I'm just... me. And I'm not a brave hero! And I really wanna see Mom and the rest of the family again, and I don't want them to have to deal with losing me on top of losing Dad.

With that decided, Jimmy finally reached for the doorknob to the front exit.

His hand froze upon touching it, though. He hadn't made up his mind after all. His conscience had given him a complete pause. And it was also thoughts of his dad that made him actually stay, rather than leave.

Okay, maybe I'm not brave at all, but... Dad sure was. He wasn't afraid of anything or anyone if they needed to be faced. He stood up to Mad Dog in my defense. And I don't doubt in the least he would have stood up to even Dracula if it meant helping a friend and doing the right thing. And I would want him to be proud of me. And...

"Aw, shit..." Jimmy whispered to himself as he turned around and ran towards the table at the eastern end of the bar where he saw the book slide under.

He needed to retrieve it and do what he could to help Dorian. No matter what the possible cost.

***

Much to Leroy's surprise, Mad Dog managed to get the first punch in, and it sent the bigger man reeling. However, much to the gang leader's chagrin, it didn't send him to the floor. Leroy turned, spit out a wad of blood, and turned back towards Mad Dog. A reddish sheen was visible over his teeth as he delivered a menacing smile.

"Is that the best you got, kid?" he taunted. "Maybe we should rename your gang Satan's Pussies, huh?"

As he hoped, Mad Dog yelled with rage and recklessly lunged at Leroy. He thus ran headlong into two of the much-feared man's blows, the first of which cracked one of his teeth, and the second of which sent him flying off his feet to land on the floor several feet away.

"Hah! Thought you were so fucking tough! Now I'm gonna stomp the shit out of you!"

Leroy then moved to make good on that statement, and he sent his left foot down on the unmoving body of the afro-topped young gang leader. As it turned out, though, Mad Dog was more resilient then he expected, and recovered faster than most other men Leroy had faced.

The head honcho of Satan's Knights caught his larger opponent's right leg as it descended upon him in the grip of both hands. Mad Dog then twisted it to the side to take him off-balance and leaped forward to bite into his upper thigh.

Leroy had luckily moved aside just enough to avoid having those teeth sink into his testicles instead of two inches down on his leg. That didn't mean he wasn't spared a painful wound, however.

Leroy gritted his teeth and managed to stifle the full force of the howl of pain his lungs wanted to release. He had now discovered why this gang leader had earned the epithet of 'Mad Dog': He never hesitated to use his teeth during a fight.

Leroy, however, had likewise earned his formidable reputation with good reason. His tolerance for pain was amazingly high. He reached down, lifted Mad Dog in the air as if he weighed no more than a few pounds, and slammed his body down against the hardwood floor.

Despite his namesake, the gang leader couldn't help but release Leroy's leg from his teeth upon the body-jarring impact. Leroy then lifted Mad Dog almost completely over his head, with no discernibly greater effort than before, and hurled him clear over the bar. The gang leader's limp form only halted its flight after smashing into the many bottles of liquor on the shelves behind it. He then fell to the floor seven feet below, landing out of visible range behind the counter.

"Hah!" Leroy howled as he rubbed his bleeding thigh just beneath his torn custom pants. "That'll teach little cockheads like you to get cock-headed with me!"

No sooner did he say that then he was struck on the bridge of his nose by a bottle of Chango thrown at him from behind the bar counter. Leroy's nasal cartilage was slightly deviated, and a trickle of blood streamed out of his left nostril. He teetered but ultimately remained on his feet, however, and turned to see a bloodied and battered Mad Dog pull himself up from behind the counter and jump on top of it in a manner reminiscent of... a dog gone mad, for want of a better description.

"Still too stupid to just stay down, huh?" Leroy said as he held out his arms in a taunting manner. "Well, don't just stand there acting like the animal you are, then! C'mon! Let's finish this, mother fucker!"

Mad Dog was only too happy to oblige, and he howled with near-animalistic ferocity as he leapt from the bar counter at his boastful opponent. The leader of Satan's Knights was apparently unconcerned about the many small shards of broken class embedded in various portions of his face and hands, not to mention two missing teeth, as he did so. Leroy met the attack with equally imposing force, and the vicious battle between these two formidable men continued.

***

"Hey, um, you back away from my man, Dorian!" Jimmy shouted as he held the crimson-covered book in front of Dracula. "Or, I'll... read stuff out of this book! And I know ya'll don't want that for some reason, right?"

Dracula turned around at the sound of Jimmy's voice mere seconds before he would have torn the felled Dorian to pieces.

"Do you presume to threaten me, you emaciated little fool?" Dracula said with his fangs bared and his eyes practically glowing a fiery red.

"Um, yeah, I guess I sorta am," Jimmy replied while focusing every iota of willpower he had to maintain the confrontation.

"Look at me and obey me!" the Vampire Lord insisted as waves of mesmeric force radiated through his eyes to those of the youth artist. "You are now in my thrall. Hand me the book."

"Ummm… uhhh…" was all Jimmy could utter as he felt his will being wrested from him, and all he could now think of was complying with Dracula's demand. "Dorian… do something…!"

Despite Jimmy's fading will, he succeeded in distracting Dracula long enough for Dorian's mystically augmented metabolism to correct the spinal damage. He forced himself to his feet, a soft cracking sound being vaguely audible as he did so to mark the last of the dislocated vertebrae being pushed back into its proper place. Dorian gritted his teeth hard to avoid screaming in pain and alerting Dracula to his recovery.

Dorian moved as quickly as he could over to wear Monica was standing and watching the proceeding events in a state of confusion over how she should intervene.

"I need your cigarette again, luv!" he said as he pulled it out of her fingers once more. "And this shot glass full of whiskey. Also, get out of here after you see me do what I am about to do!"

Jimmy's hand shook like a tree branch buttressed by gale force winds as he struggled to resist handing Dracula the all-important book. The Lord of Vampires seemed to fear just moving in and pulling it from his grasp until he was certain that the young man's will was fully subservient to his own. It was a battle that Jimmy would obviously lose within a few seconds.

Or so it would have had Dracula not been suddenly distracted by having his right shoulder doused with whiskey.

"Have a high-quality Morley on me, my dear Count!" Dorian shouted as he touched the burning cherry of the cigarette to the heavy proof liquor splattered over Dracula's cloak.

The cape immediately burst into flames, and Dracula bellowed in pain and anger as he felt his pale undead flesh burning beneath the fabric of his cloak. His hypnotic hold over Jimmy was immediately broken.

"Aarrghh! Curse you, Dorian!" the Count hollered as he urgently sought to tear the burning cape from his shoulders. "I shall make you wish you *were* capable of dying!"

Dorian ran behind Jimmy and caught him underneath his arms as he almost toppled over upon being abruptly freed from Dracula's mesmeric spell. He also caught the book as the artist dropped it.

"Huh? Wha' happened?" Jimmy asked as he shook his head to bring himself back to his full senses.

"Dracula and his accursed hypnotic eyes happened," Dorian said as he pulled his friend towards the door. "Now, let us extricate ourselves from this place while he burns!"

Dracula succeeded in tearing the cloak from his back and threw it over the bar counter, where its flames could scorch him no longer. The clothing beneath it was still afire in several places, so the Vampire Lord deliberately fell to the floor and rolled over several times until the fire was successfully smothered. He then jumped up to his feet and ignored the severely seared skin on his shoulder, neck, and back as his blazing eyes turned towards the fleeing Dorian and Jimmy.

"Gray!" he shouted with unfettered rage, as wisps of smoke were emitted from his nostrils to match those still billowing out from his burned clothing.

Before he could rush after the two with his inhuman speed, he was suddenly knocked off his feet at the same time he heard a loud booming sound. He looked up from the floor to see Monica holding a shotgun she had just retrieved from the back of the bar counter, its double barrels still smoldering.

"Stay down, mother fucker!" she screamed while latching back the gun's action to load the second set of shells.

"You filthy wench!" Dracula yelled as he sat up. "I will suck you dry for that!"

Dracula's then flew back to the floor as the next blast struck him in the torso just as he pushed himself to his feet.

Monica now realized the shotgun wouldn't stop him for keeps, so she took advantage of the dramatic but temporary effects wrought by the second blast to retreat into the door leading to the tavern's basement, where she was aware of a back entrance to escape from.

Sorry, Dorian, but I did all I could to distract that cocksucker to buy you a little time. But no way am I gonna stop a fucker who gets up again after two shotgun blasts. I'm sorry, baby, but you're on your own after this.

***

Minutes earlier, and several yards on the other side of the bar, Mad Dog and Leroy continued to grapple. The former seemed to be losing ground steadily, but he recouped that setback by suddenly headbutting his opponent in the face. It worsened the injury to the septum that Leroy had already received, and this caused him to release Mad Dog and back away.

253

The gang leader was quick to viciously press this advantage by delivering two quick punches to Leroy's face in rapid succession, which sent the man with the rep staggering even further. But he still didn't go down despite the blood now tricking out of both nostrils, as well as dripping down his chin from a smashed lip. Undaunted and still determined to stay on the offensive, Mad Dog rushed his '6'4" opponent and took another swing.

By this time, however, Leroy was recovered enough to block the gang leader's next intended clout. He returned a blow to Mad Dog's stomach, causing him to keel forward; and immediately followed that up with an uppercut to his chin that sent the supreme Satan's Knight flying on top of and over the bar counter again.

"Be smart and *stay* down this time, fool!" Leroy demanded despite keeping his fists clenched and maintaining a fighting stance just in case.

As it turned out, Mad Dog still wasn't finished. He shrugged off the effects of that epic blow in less than thirty seconds and was deceptively crawling about on all fours behind the counter with the intention of taking his foe in a surprise move.

"Keep thinking you won, mother fucker… we'll see who goes down in the final round…" he whispered to himself while picking up a broken bottle in his hand, intending to use the sharpened edges in his next assault. *Fuck the hand-to-hand agreement. I'm taking this cocksucker down however I have to. Fun and games are over now. But I know he carries razors and brass knuckles, so I gotta do this careful.*

That act in progress was interrupted, however, when a door leading to a storage locker behind the bar counter opened and a mysterious figure walked in. He appeared to be African-American and dressed in a dark green robe with symbols evocative of various African cultures. He put his hand on Mad Dog's shoulder while the urban warlord was still down on his knees, a move that startled the gang leader and caused him to swing the business ends of the broken bottle at the strange man.

"What the fuck is…?"

But oddly, the sharpened edges had no discernible physical effect.

The enigmatic interloper then spoke in a voice that was simultaneously piercing and comforting. "Cleon, I believe it is time you listen to what young Jimmy said to you earlier this evening, when he advised you to consider taking your life in another direction. Your true calling may indeed lie on a path quite different from the self-destructive road you are now speeding across."

"Huh?" Mad Dog responded. "How the fuck do you know my real name? Are you one of Jimmy's boys? You don't look like the type anyone would see outside of a fucking mosque, and far as I know, he don't swing to Farrakhan's tune. And why didn't the glass just cut you?"

Despite being startled and baffled by this strange man's unexpected appearance in a situation most sane people would go out of their way to steer clear of, Mad Dog could nevertheless feel an overwhelming sense of peace radiating from the stranger. These emanations seemed to affect him on a deep level of consciousness, resulting in a strong calming effect despite leaving his will completely under his own volition.

"I am indeed one of what you may call young Jimmy's 'main men,'" the stranger explicated, "though he would envision me in a different form, but with a similar archetypal purpose. He has yet to meet me 'face-to-face' in this manner, however, despite his being the inadvertent catalyst for the chain of events that have allowed me to manifest here so directly. But how I came to be here is not of paramount importance at this time. Rather, the moral crossroads you now find yourself standing in front of merits our attention."

Mad Dog was even more incredulous, but only for a moment. "Huh? What? You mean to tell me, you're... *him*? But, you just can't be him, man!"

"But I am indeed 'him,' Cleon. I have simply taken a form more suitable to your personal sensibilities. I cannot and would not force you to choose any particular road ahead of you, but I do urge you to follow Jimmy's earlier advice to step off your current path with these Satan's Knights and to strongly consider becoming one of the Black Panthers. Their mission could use a staunch warrior like you, and the human race could only benefit from another of your ilk directing your talents in a more positive direction."

"And what do I get out of this, huh, wise man?"

"You most likely get a much longer life, something now lost to your friend Tyrone, and something your friend 'Neck Bone' came close to losing tonight as well; a chance at reconciliation with your mother and siblings, and to have the opportunity to truly care for them in an honorable way; and to never become the type of man your father was. On your current path, however, you are straying from all of these options, and actually becoming a worse man than your father ever was. Is this truly the legacy you want to leave to the world?"

"Don't preach to me about 'doing the right thing,' man! Where were you when my mom and me and my sibs really needed you, huh? Tell me that!"

"I was always here, Cleon. You just refused to embrace me. I am now simply doing so in a more *direct* fashion, courtesy of the energies your friend Jimmy has inadvertently unleashed. Please consider this change of direction. I know it shan't be easy, but the strength of will you have focused into becoming one of the most dangerous gang leaders in this particular city indicates you have all the courage and fortitude one can hope for to accomplish such a change of direction."

"Yeah? And what if I don't have any kind of faith in you?"

"Having faith in me is not nearly as important as having it in yourself. And moreover, I have full faith in *you*."

Mad Dog listened to the words carefully. He dropped the broken bottle and let it smash down to the floor.

"Leroy is gonna be on top of me any second now, I can't…"

"You can, actually. I have suspended time as you normally experience it until you make your decision. Take hours from your own perspective if you must."

Mad Dog took the equivalent of 20 more minutes, thinking and mulling over many possibilities and considerations. Finally, a decision was made.

"Alright, man. I think… I'm going to leave the gang and approach the Panthers, see what they got going for them. No promises, but I'm gonna try. What about my main man Neck Bone, though? I can't just leave him."

"You can actually do that as well. He is unconscious and is now out of this fight. You may contact him at another date once you have fully pulled yourself out of this direction, and I suspect that after tonight's tumultuous events, he shall be amenable to major changes in his life as well. He has always looked up to you; it is your time now to become the kind of man he *should* be looking up to when next you meet."

"Alright. I can dig that."

The former Mad Dog reached his hand to take the one offered by the strange man, who then helped him to his feet. Next, the man led him safely through the portal leading into the storeroom and out onto the streets, where he would depart from both the bar and the life he led up to this point and time soon began once again moving in synch with the world he knew.

Leroy would be convinced he simply never got up again after being knocked over the bar counter. The former Mad Dog no longer cared what he thought, however.

"Hah! I knew it!" Leroy shouted at the silence now confronting him from the bar. "Who's the man, right?"

He then turned to see Monica motioning to him from a hidden spot behind the door leading to the cellar and out the back entrance.

"Leroy, c'mon!" she said, barely loud enough for him to hear. "We need to get the hell out of here before that vampire dude comes after us."

"I'll get out my brass knuckles and kick his ass! Just like I did those gang members!"

Monica knew she had to find the right words, since even Leroy would be hard-pressed to come out on top of a tussle with an enraged Dracula.

"Help get me out of here, and you can spend time partying with me tonight instead of fighting with some other dickhead. And I mean, *all night* with me."

She winked flirtatiously to make her point both crystal clear and more appealing. Monica actually looked forward to a tryst with such a man, and she also knew he had at least one vehicle outside that could make for a quick getaway.

"Okay, you talked me into it, babe!" Leroy said as he headed into the cellar towards the back exit with her. "Which one of my cars do you want to cruise back to my place with: My custom Continental or my El Dorado? I'm not picky!"

VIII.

Dorian exited the front of the bar with Jimmy's arm around his shoulder. Before letting the semi-renowned artist of the ghetto stand on his own, he wanted to make certain that his young companion was fully recovered from the dizzying after-effects of Dracula's mesmerism.

"Jimmy, are you able to fully stand?" Dorian asked.

"I think so," Jimmy replied with a voice suggesting he was now completely lucid. "What the hell did that cat do to me? I feel like I just drank about ten pitchers of fermented Kool-Aid."

"He mesmerized you. Never stare him directly in the eyes, or he can entrap your will."

"Geez, is there anything this guy *can't* do?"

"Dracula has his share of limitations, but that is not for you to be concerned with right now. We need to flee this area post haste. We must try to hail a cab."

"Around here? Cabbies know better than to take any fares around here. We'd be more likely to hail a horse and carriage in this neighborhood!"

"Ah, the memories…"

"Huh?"

"Not relevant, I was just reminiscing. Alright, then we must get as far as we can on our own. Do you perchance know how to – what is the proper terminology? – 'hot wire' a vehicle?"

"You mean… steal somebody's wheels?"

"If you feel such a strong word fits the deed, then yes. Do you have such skills?"

"Dorian, I've done more things I'm not exactly proud of in just a short two hours on the town with you than I did in, like, all nineteen years of my life combined! I'm done with all of that!"

"You fool! There is no time for moral posturing in a dire situation such as this! We each risked all for the other! Would you like all that to have been for naught? I am doing what I can to get you home intact tonight, before your mother awakens after dawn, as promised!"

"Maybe I can make it home on my own, then? Your help has been full of more compromises than there are holes on my old socks. And you'd be amazed at how many pairs of socks I go through in just a month!"

Dorian grabbed Jimmy by his shirt and pulled him closer. "Jimmy, you had best abort that stubborn moral preening of yours and listen to me, or you will force me to knock better sense into you!"

Jimmy glanced behind himself as the corner of his eye caught a curious flash of movement.

"Um, Dorian, when you came in from London, did you bring some of that city's famous fog with you?"

"What are you talking about?"

Dorian looked over the young man's shoulder to see a billowing, almost luminescent cloud of mist seeping through cracks in the tavern's front window and detouring in their direction with apparent purpose behind it.

"Oh, bugger," the immortal uttered with trepidation.

"You need not waste the effort it would take you to strike down that young accomplice of yours, Mr. Gray," came a chillingly familiar Balkan accent from the center of the roiling foggy mass.

"Allow me to administer such blows to the lot of you instead. It will be my pleasure to expend that energy myself."

After finishing that declaration, the fog began whirling about until it quickly coalesced into the completely tangible personage of Dracula. His shoulder and neck still bore the scar tissue of third degree burns, but they had already healed to an extent that would not have been possible for any mere mortal.

"Did he... just come out of that fog?" Jimmy asked.

"Actually, young man," Dracula replied as he viciously bared his fangs, "the fog *was* me. It is but one of the many alternate forms I have at my disposal. You will experience the same once I sire you into the ranks of the Undead."

"That don't sound good!" Jimmy lamented while shaking in his boots. "I think I would rather stay non-dead than become un-dead, or whatever you call whatever it is you are!"

"Your preferences are subservient to my own, you silly little mortal peasant," Dracula said as he continued moving forward.

Dorian pulled the red-covered tome out of his trench coat pocket with surprising swiftness, determined to open it to the marked pages and again use its power against this dangerous soul-clone of the Lord of Vampires. He managed to do so with such speed, in fact, that many mortals would likely have been taken by surprise.

Unfortunately for him, though, the soul-clone categorized by some researchers as Dracula-Mordante was no mere mortal. Like many members of the various Collins clan branch lineages who have been cursed to experience similar macabre fates, Count Lucien Mordante had become something both far more and far less than human when Vlad Tepes transformed him into one of his soul-clone doppelgangers.

Before he knew it, Dorian's arm was grasped by the rogue Dracula soul-clone at the exact same moment he brandished the tome. Such was the power of the Count's pulverizing grip that Dorian felt his wrist being crushed before he could get the book opened to the appropriate pages.

"Did you think to catch me unawares with that abridged version of the Book of Chaos, Mr. Gray?"

"Need I... answer that rhetorical... inquiry?" Dorian asked as he struggled to resist giving into the pain of his carpal bones being splintered under Dracula's clenched fingers.

Jimmy backed away instinctively, torn internally over what course of action he should take: Flee, or stay and attempt to help Dorian again? Should he once more risk his life for the debauched young man with arcane acquaintances and knowledge, who attempted to pull the young artist into his world with such potentially catastrophic results? Should he run while Dracula and Dorian are busy trying to destroy each other, and reach what passes for the safe haven of his project apartment before his mother wakes to find that her beloved son has joined her husband in the arms of death?

It took him nearly five seconds to break through the conflicting thoughts and come to a satisfactory conclusion.

"Sorry, Mom," he whispered aloud. "But your oldest can't just leave a friend hanging like this. Not even a, erm, friend like Dorian."

It was then that the sensation of a warm hand came upon his shoulder, followed by the utterances of another familiar voice, only this one being extremely welcome to hear. And one Jimmy had never expected to grace his ears again.

"Don't worry, son," came the voice of his deceased father, James Sr. "I'm here, and you ain't got to deal with either of those bums on your own."

Jimmy turned to see that his senses hadn't deceived him. It was his father! No longer alive, but somehow *there*, looking as robust and healthy as ever, but with what appeared to be a radiant aura thinly outlining his form.

"D-dad?" Jimmy began sobbing with tears of joy streaming from his eyes, as a powerful feeling of warmth and security suddenly enveloped him.

"Yeah, Junior, it's me," James Sr. replied with his characteristic grin.

"But... how...?"

"I can't say I can even answer that, son, but all I do know is that you can thank that gentleman behind me for getting me from the other side to here."

Jimmy looked over the shoulder of his father's image to see the same robed figure that appeared before Mad Dog back in the bar a short time ago. Only this time, within a moment of Jimmy looking upon him, the mysterious stranger's form seemed to shimmer and take on the appearance of one he could much more readily recognize: the white-and-reddish robe-adorned figure of Jesus Christ.

However, it was not the Caucasian image of Jesus commonly depicted on Christian statuary and paintings, but rather Jesus as presented on the canvas created by Jimmy's artistic brush: Noir Jesus, reflecting his Middle Eastern roots as noted in *The Bible*.

"Greetings, James the younger," the figure of Jesus said with a comforting smile.

Jimmy's jaw fell wide open. "You… you're… you're… *him!* I mean, first I learn Santa Claus is supposed to be real, then Dracula, and now… I mean, well, I never doubted *you* were real! I just never expected to see you on this side of the… I mean… you're Jesus!"

The spiritual embodiment of the Christian faith smiled and raised his hand to calm Jimmy "I am indeed the one of which you speak. And my friends have always called me Yeshua. You may do so as well, if you wish."

"If—if only I could get your autograph for Mom! You know, to sign her Bible, or something! And—and, Dad is here too! How is this even possible?"

The apparition of James Sr. turned towards the glowing figure that allowed him to manifest in such an etherically vigorous form on this side of the veil.

"Junior has a damned good question there, Mr. Jesus, sir. Pardon my French."

Jesus smiled again in response. "Ha ha! That is quite alright, my friend. Harsh actions have always been far more off-putting to me than harsh language under flippant circumstances. And do call me Yeshua. I always preferred the name given to me by my mortal parents than the one assigned to me by the Greeks."

"Wait!" Jimmy shouted. "How come I can't see Dorian and that Drac cat anymore?"

"I can't answer that one either, Junior," James Sr. responded.

"Worry not, for I *can* answer it," Jesus assured them. "I have pulled both of you out of the time frame you normally experience. After this introduction runs its course, I will bring us back in synch with those other two, so we can deal with the situation at hand in a linear fashion."

"Wow," Jimmy said. "This power would sure have been useful to have during the days I had to wake up in the morning for school!"

Jesus laughed. "You truly have the gift of mirth, young Jimmy! Now, let us rejoin the progression of time you are familiar with, so we can, as you might say, 'take care of business.'"

Not even a second more seemed to pass before Jimmy turned to once again see Dorian struggling with Dracula. And the situation seemed to be occurring at precisely the same moment he had previously "left" it, as if time had simply been switched off and then on again. Much to his relief, the manifested apparitions of both Jesus and his deceased father remained at his side.

"Thank God, I mean, um, *you*, Mr. Christ, Yeshua, sir... that you and my dad showing up when I needed you wasn't just me hallucinating! I was worried maybe Dorian spiked my Kool-Aid with LSD or something! I sure wouldn't put anything like that past him!"

"We are most certainly both here, James the younger," Jesus assured him. "No hallucinogens need claim credit for this manifestation."

Dorian was now down to his knees as Dracula exerted more bone-crushing pressure to his wrist, attempting to get him to drop the mystical tome in his hand. The young-looking immortal continued to resist, but he realized he would soon have no working bones left in his forearm with which to grip the book.

"Yield to me, Gray!" the Vampire Lord demanded. "Drop that tome and *yield* like the troublesome rabble you are!"

Dorian was trembling intensely under the pain, but he still summoned the extra will required to make a verbal response to his adversary. "Fuck you... to Hell, vampire!"

"What that prissy white dude just said!" James Sr. exclaimed in agreement as his ethereal form ran up to Dracula. "You threatened my son! Now you get to deal with me! I'd tell you to step outside if we weren't already outside!"

Dracula looked up in bewilderment at the new player on the scene. He quickly recognized a discarnate human spirit wrapped in semi-dense ethereal matter to grant him a temporary semblance of 'solidity' on the material plane, and the spectre's introductory words made it clear who he was in relation to the people that crossed him that night.

Dracula hurled Dorian aside with a casual toss, causing him to fly several feet to the left until he struck the cylindrical metal form of a street light. The impact was accompanied by the sound of his entire rib cage splintering, and he fell onto the curb of the street unmoving. The Vampire Lord then turned to face the new challenge in front of him.

"The departed but materialized sire of the young man Jimmy, I presume," Dracula said. "You certainly do not resemble any possible relation of Mr. Gray."

"Damn straight I'm Junior's father!" James Sr. clarified with strong conviction. "And damn straight I'm no relation to that jive ass Mr. Gray. You made a big mistake threatening my son. Now I'm going to threaten *you!*"

"Do you truly believe that any insipid spectre short of Detective Corrigan himself, no matter how suffused with etheric force, could present any sort of obstacle to me?"

"I'll answer that one by putting my 'insipid' foot up your aristocratic ass!"

Jimmy began jumping up and down while excitedly simulating punching moves. "Knock him off this block, Dad!"

James Sr. possessed enough quasi-solidity that he was capable of grasping Dracula, and the two promptly locked arms. Since the former was now embodied only in astral form, it was not a contest matching physical strength in any fashion, but rather the power of his will to overcome against that possessed by the Vampire Lord.

Dracula psychically projected his indomitable will against that of James Sr.'s, who found the etheric substance granting his astral form of sufficient 'density' to interact with the material plane beginning to disintegrate under the Prince of Darkness's mighty psychic onslaught.

"You will bow to me, you mongrel fool!" Dracula insisted as his eyes shined a fervid scarlet while he emanated more psychic force.

"You're sure no slouch, Dracula," James Sr. said as he continued to resist. "I'll give you that. But this is my son you're threatening. And I don't care if you're the king of vampires, or the king of the gypsies! No one threatens my son without answering to me! It don't matter if he's a punk off the streets of Chicago or from wherever in the European boonies you come from!"

Dracula found his own undead form trembling under the determined astral pushback of James Sr.'s steadfast refusal to yield to any force, no matter how powerful, that would imperil one of his own.

Before the battle could be decided, Dracula's distraction by the opposition provided via the shade of James Sr. allowed Dorian Gray ample time to both fully heal from his crushed rib cage and to recover the crimson-covered tome. He stood behind Dracula and read aloud the words from two particular pages in the middle of the grimoire, which he now had the time to take proper effort to pronounce correctly.

"Yeildum… Mosophenes… Erid Chaos… Ephrem Nyarlothotep…"

Dracula's form was suddenly surrounded by what appeared to be whirling vortices of flame that caused him to scream in agony.

"What…?" He turned to see Dorian standing behind him and holding the tome. "Curse you, Gray! You will suffer beyond your darkest nightmares for this…!"

"It would seem you are about to do enough suffering for both of us, my dear Count," Dorian uttered as he smiled and closed the tome in an accomplished fashion.

The fiery whirling dervishes finally seemed to consume the very air around Dracula, and the echo of his threats were the last sounds any being present on the deserted boulevard would hear from the Vampire Lord as he appeared to be swallowed by the very air itself. The seeming rift in the folds of reality itself then abruptly imploded upon itself with an obscene 'whooshing' sound as the fiery tendrils accompanying the phenomenon dispersed and faded.

"Whoa!" Jimmy hollered. "That… was… *dy-no-mite!"*

"It was that, and so much more as well," Dorian said as he took a deep breath and smirked in satisfaction.

"What did you do to him?" Jimmy queried.

"This particular soul-clone of Dracula fancied himself a worshiper of Chaos," Dorian responded. "That being an Old One in the form of a universal concept of cosmic unpredictability and anarchy of physics. This book is a copy of a larger tome inscribed with the spells of the very Chaos-worshiping cult this particular Dracula soul-clone took leadership of. The spell I just used served to open a portal to the very nether-realm where Chaos exists in a raw personified form. I offered up Dracula himself as a 'sacrifice' to this being of dark cosmic personification. Since Dracula worshiped this sentient force, I thought it was a simple matter of cordial amicability that he should drop in and keep this deity company in person for a while."

"I have no idea what you just said," Jimmy replied, "but it totally *sounded* like something that cat deserved!"

"It was totally that, my friend," Dorian concurred.

"So, this is Dorian," the still manifested apparition of James Sr. said. "It would be my pleasure to properly introduce myself to him."

He walked up to Dorian and held out his ethereally manifested hand. Just before the youngish-looking immortal could take it, though, James Sr. pulled his hand away, curled it into a fist, and punched Dorian in the face. The astrally simulated kinetic force acted much like an actual punch, hitting with enough force to bloody its recipient's nose and send him sprawling to the pavement.

"That's what you get for pulling my son into this mess of yours!" James Sr. decreed while pointing down at Dorian. "He's a good kid, someone his mom and I are proud to have raised. I can't take a direct hand in that no more, but I'll be damned if I'm going to leave this world for the second time without setting *you* straight for your part in this! You had your business with Junior, he gave you what you paid for, now you leave him alone! If you don't, you can bet your uppity fuppity vocabulary I'll find a way to come back and give you a foot to go along with my fist! And take a guess where that foot is gonna go?"

Dorian slowly returned to his feet as the trickles of blood that flowed from each nostril ceased their scarlet dribbles.

"Sorry, Dorian," Jimmy said as he stood beside the manifestation of his caring father's spirit. "Like I said, I appreciate your business, and I do gotta thank you for bailing me out of the trouble you got me into in the first place, but… my dad is right. I don't want to be what you are, and I hope one day, you won't want to be what you are anymore either. Can you dig that?"

Dorian simply looked at the young artist and said nothing in return.

Jimmy then turned to his father's still lingering apparition. "Dad…"

"Son," James Sr. replied with tears of pride in his eyes. "Just look at you now."

"Dad, this super-bizarro trouble I got into tonight was totally worth it if I meant I got to see you one last time. We… miss you, Dad."

James Sr. beamed with further pride. "I dunno if I can agree it was good in any kinda way that you got into this sort of trouble, but I'm glad it led to me getting to talk to you face-to-face like this again. I miss you, your mom, Mike, and Selma more than a man of my limited education can put into proper words."

"You never needed anything like a formal education to be one of the smartest and stand-up dudes I ever knew, Dad."

James Sr. smiled again. "I love you, son. I think… I have to get going now." Those were his last words as he felt the energies keeping him on this side of the veil fading away, signaling his inevitable return to the wonders of the astral plane.

"I love you too, Dad!" Jimmy said just in time for his father's shade to hear them before his senses—and his simulated form—shifted from the material plane back to their astral counterpart.

271

Jimmy forced himself not to cry, and only lost that struggle for a minute. He turned to find the figure of Noir Jesus still glowing and manifested before him.

"Thank you for all that, Yeshua."

Jesus smiled. "No need to thank me. It is what I do."

"Well, I had to anyway," Jimmy replied. "How did you do all this whacked out stuff?"

"It all derives from that painting of me you created a few years ago as you measure the passage of time," Jesus explained. "There are many psychically charged locales in a city this size, and you managed to tap into one of those reservoirs in such a way that the painting you created became a conduit to my energies.

"When your 'friend' Dorian Gray acquired the painting and put it in close contact with his own portrait, which was a conduit to great ancient forces as well, it allowed me to tap those various forces to augment the conduit bearing your interpretation of my image.

"In short, it enabled me to not only manifest here in an embodied form for an extended period, but it gave me sufficient energy to bring your father's spirit here, and briefly invigorate it with sufficient energy to enable him to act on your behalf as he did.

"But you have had enough to deal with this evening as it is, young Jimmy. Your taxi is now approaching to take you home before dawn breaks."

"Wait," Jimmy said. "I didn't call a taxi. There ain't even a pay phone in this neighborhood that actually works! And I sure don't have the dough to take me from here all the way back to the North Side even if I could call a cab…"

"Worry not," Jesus interjected. "I 'called' the taxi for you myself. As for payment, worry not about that either, as I will give you sufficient cash to pay for your trip right here, with a generous tip included."

Jesus handed Jimmy the precisely calculated amount of money he would need to cover the trip, with a good extra amount to serve as a gratuity for the driver.

"Wow! You just blinked that out of, um, nothing?"

"Not as such. I am not the divine equivalent of the United States Federal Reserve. I collected this amount out of Mr. Gray's collection of American currency. I believe he would agree this is the least he could do for you after getting you embroiled in this morning's events."

Jimmy took the cash and gave a wide beam as his taxi pulled up to the curb. "You pick-pocketed Dorian? Ha ha, that is... okay, I said it enough already tonight!"

Jesus raised his fist and shouted, *"Dy-no-mite!"*

"You know it, man! I'm gonna make sure I save up enough to get me and the family tickets to see *Jesus Christ Superstar* the next time it comes to the stage on State Street!"

"Ha! Very good. Be well, Jimmy. There will be more challenges in your future, as they are required for you to grow and progress as a person. That is the way of the universe, a set of laws above the control of all beings such as myself. But I shall always be here to help guide you along your path, no matter how dark it may appear to become at times."

"I'll hold you to that," Jimmy said as the taxi took off for the Cabrini-Green Project on the city's Near North Side.

As the excitement and elation wore off, Jimmy sobbed with tears of both joy and sorrow at seeing his father again, only to have to say good bye once more as well.

After quietly entering his apartment, he quickly dressed in his pajamas, laid beside his brother on his usual side of the pull-out bed, and drifted to sleep within seconds. Upon waking a few hours later, he strived to rationalize his memories of the previous night's events as nothing more than a dream. He had only the money Dorian paid him and his brother's shared memories of Dorian's visit as incontrovertible proof that the visit alone had actually occurred.

***

Several minutes earlier, as the taxi departed the street, Jesus decided to use the remaining supply of energy that fueled his manifestation to have a short discussion with Dorian.

"A word, Mr. Gray."

"A sense a dreary sermon coming on," Dorian said as he folded his arms and rolled his eyes. "I steer clear of churches for good reason, I'll have you know."

"That is quite alright," Jesus replied. "We could carry on this discussion anywhere in the universe, and even beyond."

"Truly wonderful to know. Allow me to speak my piece first. I am not the one who takes the blame for creating a universe of this nature. One filled with rampant brutality, and the ravages of age, disease, darkness, and decay. One which makes our too-brief lives often too tumultuous to properly enjoy, filled with numerous types of pain both emotional and physical.

"Yet you would expect us to just ignore all of this, be 'good' according to cryptically written scriptures in a holy book that are subjectively interpreted according to all-too human clergy seeking to maintain power over the lives of others, the same type of power they claim to afford to your supposed 'father' alone. When all along, it is *they* who are the 'God' of which they speak, using a fear of his wrath and a desire to gain his favor to bully compliance from the herd.

"A clergy who use the alleged 'Word of God' to serve their own interests and to lead as exalted a life as most mortals could ever hope to achieve on his miserable plane. This being an exploitative situation that is apparently just well and dandy from the point of view of God, since he never appears to step forth and contradict said claim in any fashion. Nor do you, his 'son,' or avatar, or representative, or whatever your connection to Him is supposed to be. Your followers and clergy alike cannot seem to make up their mind on that.

"But now, you are going to judge me for taking the measures that I did to become one of those few mortals who managed to shield himself from such a brief but protracted conscious existence of pain and turmoil, and to enable me to enjoy the pleasures that the material plane does have to offer. Pleasures which so few can enjoy for any length of time before age or one of innumerable possible health calamities overtakes us and forces us to watch others enjoy these pleasures from the sidelines. And only presuming we will even have the financial means to fully enjoy these pleasures in the first place, as such amenities do not come cheap.

"Evidently, all of this is fine in your eyes as long as we continue to worship you and give you the emotional energies you require to be a 'God,' correct?

"And dare I surmise you would overlook any breach of ethics I may have committed if I had done the deeds while dressed in the clothing of one of your clergy, and spending a good share of my time on this world sitting atop a marble pedestal and preaching fidelity to a set of strict morals which those in power are never expected to follow?

"Should I strive to be above all reproach, and agree to suffer with all the joy and pride that is somehow supposed to bring?

"Is that what you are going to lecture me about now? Or is hypocrisy something you consider to be reserved for mere mortals as well?"

"In actuality, Mr. Gray," Jesus calmly replied, "I neither expect nor desire worship or subservience from you. Nor anyone else, for that matter. Those who profess to follow me are often no better than you, and sometimes even much worse. I cannot propose to be your personal savior. The only personal savior you can ever truly have is *yourself*.

"My story is a guide of self-sacrifice. A willingness to suffer not because there is anything inherently wonderful, or beautiful, or glamorous, about such pain and suffering. But rather, to endure my share of this plane's turmoil so that others would have to suffer *less* of it. To lead not by decree or demand, but by example. To encourage others to do the same so that the entire species of humanity improves and rises above the need to suffer in order to grow and evolve.

"I have no judgment to place upon you, Mr. Gray, but only words, as per my stated intention. You have been granted a gift that very few other mortals ever manage to achieve at this point in your species' evolutionary history and development. Consider using it wisely, lest you one day end up being harshly judged by no less than *yourself*. The only true personal savior you could ever have is likewise the most difficult judge you could ever face. And face that judge you eventually will, because no being in existence can expect to exist forever, no matter what type of forces they may have lucked into."

Jesus then turned to walk away, only to stop in order to convey one last quick message.

"By the way, Dorian, I also took it upon myself to relieve you of the portrait that James the younger created to represent my image. I believe it can be of better use in the possession of individuals other than yourself, since it would be of no use to you whatsoever. That is why you will no longer find it stored alongside your own charming portrait at the storage place you rented. I thank you, however, for putting it in a place where it was able to accomplish much good tonight, even if you did so under no deliberate intention. After all, everyone must start somewhere."

With that final point given, the figure of Jesus was seen to step into a grimy alleyway at the end of the street and seemingly vanish from existence. Or, at least from this plane of reality.

Dorian stood on the deserted streets, now long since cleared of every person, with a look of resigned consternation on his visage. The emotions behind that mien were not truly possible to discern, and his thoughts at this moment were to go unrecorded.

Upon hearing the blaring sound of approaching police sirens, he sauntered into the middle of the street to recover the scarlet-covered grimoire lying underneath the street light which Dracula had thrown him against.

"The inhabitants of this city gave no exaggeration when they told me the constables of this jurisdiction take their sweet time to arrive following a reported conflagration," he said to himself while he walked over and picked up the book.

Dorian Gray smiled as he looked closely at the words exotically scrawled on its crimson-hued front cover. "Now, I wonder what sorts of fun I can have with this little book, hmmm?"

END

DORIAN AT THE GROVE; OR FINDING DORIAN WITHIN

T. Casey Brennan

Part One: Dorian Melts

This is the story of Dorian at the Bohemian Grove; but it isn't.

I just made it up, but I had a good reason. In 1959, I started in the seventh grade at Swamp School in Kenockee Township (in rural Michigan) so it must have been around then that I found *The Picture of Dorian Gray* in Daddy's books. Mama said I had to make Daddy like me more, and I had just spent four years in a Catholic school trying to be more like the real Brennans who had adopted him in 1906, and it hadn't worked. This wouldn't either, but I didn't know that then.

So, I found the chest of books. They had been his college textbooks in Ann Arbor at the University of Michigan, in the 1920s, and the others that he and his classmates had read in that bygone enlightened era: Kant's *Critique of Pure Reason* (I understood *some*; after all, I'm in Mensa); Will Durant's *Story of Philosophy* (I didn't read much past the chapters on Socrates, Plato, and Aristotle); Gustave Flaubert's *Madame Bovary*; and Oscar Wilde's *The Picture of Dorian Gray*.

But Daddy wasn't going to like me all the time no matter how well I could read his old books. Mama and Daddy were married in 1938 and I was born in 1948. So maybe Daddy wasn't Daddy, but I didn't know that then, and I also didn't know that his "hypnosis lessons" would someday lead to something really, really bad.

But it was 1959, and I was still learning how to pick up girls, and *The Picture of Dorian Gray* was helping. In a future, grown-up world, adults would insist that every portrayal of Dorian Gray would reflect Oscar Wilde's own gay lifestyle. But any adolescent brave enough to read it knew it was a book about a guy that could *really* pick up girls. So I learned, and more bad things happened, and then I saw Dorian melt. This was how all of *that* happened.

In the summer of 1959, Daddy got involved with an Osteopathic physician in Michigan who was also a professional hypnotist and a self-described official of the CIA's Project MKULTRA. He wanted children to experiment on; and later, he wanted to kill President Kennedy, and Daddy said he could help with both those things. And so could I. The CIA could have found no better place to conduct their Project MKULTRA experiment than Kenockee Township, Michigan. It was a back woods rural area; many residents were barely semi-literate, preferring the back-breaking labor of bare-subsistence farming to the education that might have given them equality with the middle class.

The first girl must have been some country cousin to Eddie Rickenbacker. Her name was Kathy and I wrote a poem about her in 1953. Her brother Jerry showed me who Batman was that same year. In 1959, or '60, or '61, sometime after I started back attending the one-room school, my parents took her to Project MKULTRA to be drugged, raped, and groomed for killing. She didn't work out, but I did. Was she truly related to the famous general? What would it matter? Though we were of the blood, that would not assuage them, would not spare us, would not save us; we were the sacrificial lambs, the price our parents paid for services, they would force their bodies and their drugs and their murders upon us.

There was no escape, not through guile or courage or regality -- we were their living weapons and there was no escape. Soon John Kennedy would die, but in 1961, I watched Dorian Gray melt.

Part Two: The Funny Boy and Donny and *Famous Monsters*

Sometime before I met Donny at Swamp School (who gave me my first copy of *Famous Monsters of Filmland*, the one with Gorgo on the cover), I met the funny boy (who looked just like him) at a campground in St. Ignace. The funny boy acted like a standard country kid of that era except sometimes, he said, he predicted things. One day he said his father had named his rifle or shotgun, or whatever it was he used for hunting the food he put on the table. He said it was named "Old Caintuck" but since they weren't from Kentucky, it wasn't clear why. Then he said, mystically, "Old Caintuck will outlast your parents love for you."

So, after Donny gave me *Famous Monsters* #11, and I watched the Dorian Gray movie they had something to do with, it occurred to me that the final image of Dorian Gray therein looked more like melting wax than a man dying. Later on, I would talk about Donny giving me *Famous Monsters* #11 at a comic book convention in Mt. Clemens, Michigan in 2015, where I shared a panel with fellow Warren alumnus Basil Gogos, who had done the Gorgo cover. I never saw Donny or the funny boy again. So, Kathy got raped, and Daddy turned bad and Dorian melted, and here's what happened to me.

On November 22, 1963, Daddy comes into my room. He says we are going to see the same hypnotist who raped Kathy (except, we don't remember that by then). He drives us really fast to the airport in Yale, Michigan (which all the JFK researchers found out didn't exist when I first wrote about it in 1996), and the hypnotist is waiting. When they drape me over the rifle, I fire only one shot, but nonetheless it is the shot that ends the world. They have told me that I must start the shooting or die, and I was unable to trick them in that also. I fired deliberately to miss, but it hadn't mattered. Unable to push the rifle from the window as I had dreamed, I had only signaled the actual shooters from their various spots.

My dad was an expert marksman and he thought he would be the one to shoot, not me. But it had all been a trick to see if I would comply, even though I loved the President, and comply I did. So, I was there and I was at the 2014 Fantasticon and I almost made this party too. Years ago, James Roth introduced me to Larry Silver - just on the social media site Facebook - leading to a series of posts on Larry's Facebook page by me... over and over, "James R. wants you to get my *Social Worker* song on the radio in New York" -- referencing a thoroughly objectionable song produced by my band, FRANKENHEAD!

Larry put up with it for *years*, then blocked me from his Facebook page! I was even invited to the new building to get free champagne! One of the first families with mixed Indian blood came and got blocked by security. Larry came down and apologized and gave him the champagne. But even that led to more blood, and I didn't get to go to the Bohemian Grove after James invited me either.

Part Three: A Death in the House of Roth; and Dorian Visits the Grove

To those few who were aware of it, it was, of course, the highest of honors that modern society could possibly bestow upon me. The Bohemian Club had begun among journalists, then somehow reached the elite and powerful of the world as the years and decades passed. Oscar Wilde had placed their annual festival, the Bohemian Grove, first on his list of things to see when he came to America in 1882. To be invited to it at all is amazing, but to be invited by one of the most powerful banking families in the world -- what could possibly go wrong?

But, I had caused a death in the house of Roth. I did more than write the comics he liked. I got his father killed. When I wrote of my JFK involvement in 1996, alluding to a CIA AIDS MKULTRA Operation Paperclip connection, young Amschel Roth *bought* the Paperclip File. His intention was to cure AIDS, crash the stock market, and destroy the world economy. In the ensuing panic, credit would be as important as agriculture in a world struggling for recovery. The house of Roth would take over the world in *fact* rather than fantasy.

Walking in an open field, in a foggy dawn or dusk, is like this... you can see the fog so dense up ahead. But once you're there, it's gone. You can only see it in the distance. The power of the House of Roth is like that. The closer you get, the more you realize that it was just an illusion. So on the 8th of July, 1996, Amschel Roth was suicided by the CIA.

Rather than pretend some sort of inside information on Amschel's obvious murder, I would prefer to begin this way. Abbie Hoffman said you could riot against them, Cesar Chavez said you could organize labor, Jane Fonda said you could go to Communist Vietnam and party, long before the Nike executives thought of it. But David Carradine -- and his TV show -- claimed that you could defeat them with mind-over-matter, even deflect spears that way. So it was inevitable that they would murder Carradine also.

What was alarming was the *way* in which Carradine was murdered. First Carradine was suicide by hanging. Then, as the stage was set, the Carradine verdict became auto-erotic asphyxiation, even though his hands were tied. The intent is to preclude further investigation. If one investigates the apparent suicide, the "real" story comes out and is far more appealing than the truth (murder) because it is so sordid.

The question is, does this also apply to Amschel's suicide. If not, why such a minimal report on his death, even by his own company? Did the Roths fear that the slanderous -- and false -- accusations that would surround an investigation of his death would be more damaging to their fog-bound House than what they already faced? So, James Roth did *not* ask Larry Silver to get my *Social Worker* song on the radio; that was just a joke. But he did invite me to the Grove, and this is what happened next.

Those who entertain conspiracy theories may suggest that I was invited as an ersatz Oswald, and that it was implied that I would bring my main financier at the time, as a substitute for his widow, a woman of royal background whom I often call "The Princess," with a similar name and nationality to the widow of the falsely accused assassin. All to front off the CIA, who would also be there, for murdering his father. But that was not to be because I collapsed and needed surgery a few weeks before, the Princess was attacked, and her arm broken. I had even learned that I could have taken her as far as the Clubhouse up front, though regrettably (and perhaps illegally) only men can join in the festivities in the forest. So even that worked out with lots of people hurt.

But what if it hadn't? What if T. Casey had gone anyway, even with Amschel unavenged, and the Princess injured, and JFK unsolved? What if he had found Dorian within, just as he'd wanted in 1959 when he first learned to pick up girls? What if T. Casey had lost all that idealism and emotion he had felt in the Warren comics he had written in the '70s; or, not lost, but misplaced somehow? What if the blood no longer mattered? What if he only needed a place to rest? What if he found Dorian Gray within the Grove Eternal? Could he go then, even washed in the tears and blood of the fallen?

Epilogue

The Grove has always been there. Before time and space, before the universe was created, the Grove was there. It was a place the powerful could go to rest. For that one moment we could forget what little people could never bear to know: actions can have consequences. We are powerful... all of our actions have consequences. I've *always* been there. So has Dorian Gray; Dorian from the book, and Dorian within.

Me.

END

A SHADED TIMELINE

Robert E. Wronski, Jr. and Christofer Nigro

I love timelines. And I love crossovers. Some of the most fun timelines I've had the pleasure to read or compose involve immortals. There are such wonderful opportunities for many authors to fill in the gaps over a lengthy timeline, and plenty of opportunities for these immortals to have encountered many other notable characters of fiction.

I have a bit of notoriety for crossover chronologies. I created The Television Crossover Universe website, and I've written The Horror Crossover Encyclopedia, which covered a bit of Dorian Gray. When Christofer Nigro asked me to write a timeline to accompany this anthology, I was very pleased to accept.

I've had the pleasure of diving further into the continued legacy of Oscar Wilde's creation, and got the opportunity to have a sneak peek at the other stories held within this volume, to make this timeline as complete as possible.

This has also been an interesting exercise for me in playing within someone else's sandbox. Though the "Wild Hunt Universe" (WHU) is very similar to my "Horror Universe" (HU) and "Television Crossover Universe" (TVCU), there are slight differences. It was a fun challenge in making sure I was adhering to the rules created for Wild Hunt Press, rather than my own standards.

And of course, keep in mind that we consider the ending of Oscar Wilde's novel to be invalid, for Dorian Gray's legacy to continue over the ages. Clearly many other authors have agreed, as they continue to write more stories featuring the immortal. The conceit that Oscar Wilde was a friend of Dorian Gray that wrote his biography while presenting it to the public as a work of fiction but changing the ending to make it seem as if he destroyed himself, was utilized by Big Finish for its popular audio book series The Confessions of Dorian Gray, which is considered canon in the WHU.

Please, please, please do not read this timeline until you've read the various tales in this anthology. Major spoilers will be found here, as I've placed the stories found in Darker Shades within this timeline, so we can see where it all fits.

--R.W.

Also, please note that like all timelines, this one is necessarily a work in progress that will eventually go "out of date" with the info provided. Hence, supplements to it will likely be provided in future editions of this work, or possibly in a standalone fashion. Nevertheless, this timeline takes the published & produced saga of Dorian Gray right through the year 2017, which has just recently slipped into the expanse of past history as of the release date of this edition in 2018.

Next, I'd like to take several words to thank the staff of Wild Hunt Press and crew of contributors to the anthology for their invaluable edits and suggestions to help make this timeline the best it could possibly be. For that reason, special thanks for important entry contributions should go to Micah S. Harris (for his info on *The Beast Within*) and Kevin Heim (whose eye for detail caught numerous incorrect details and helped the main authors clean up the mess they could sometimes leave behind).

Finally, I want to thank James Bojaciuk, author, podcast extraordinaire, and CEO of the great indie publishing outfit 18thWall Productions, for his amazing contributions to the very complicated differentiation and connections between the comic book and cinematic versions of the League of Extraordinary Gentlemen. Thanks, dude!

Without further pause, let us get to the timeline's main content!

--C.N.

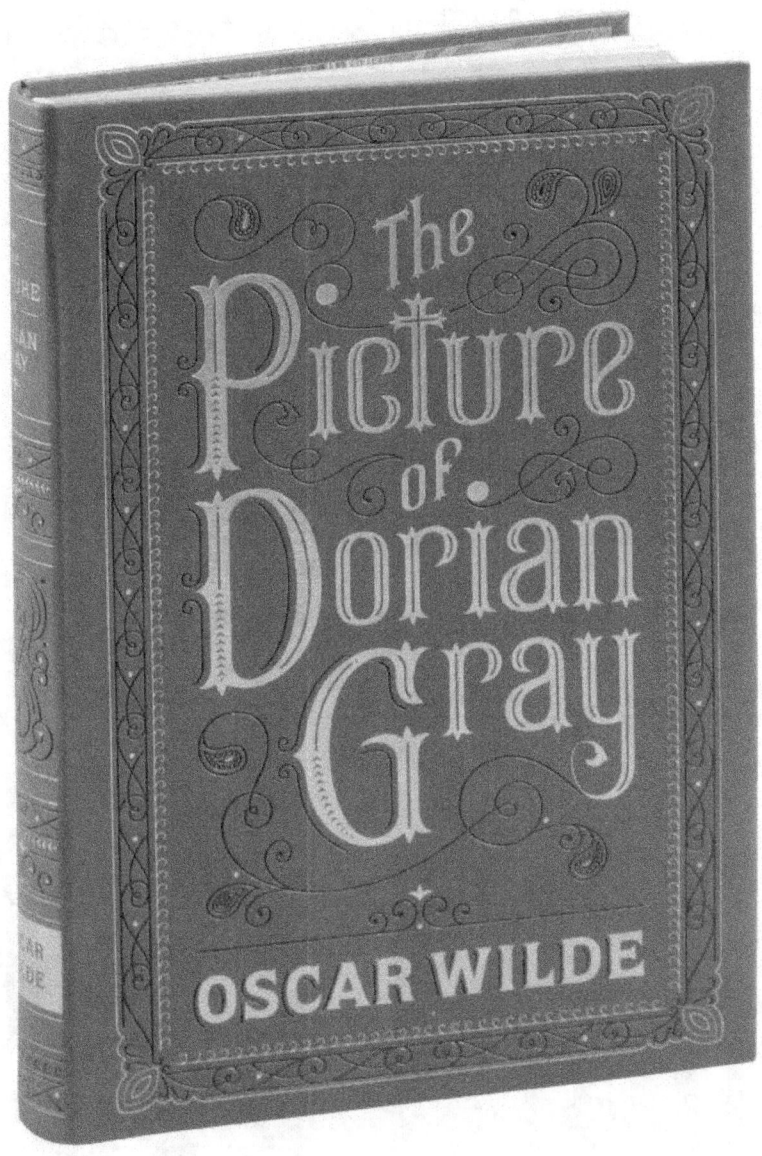

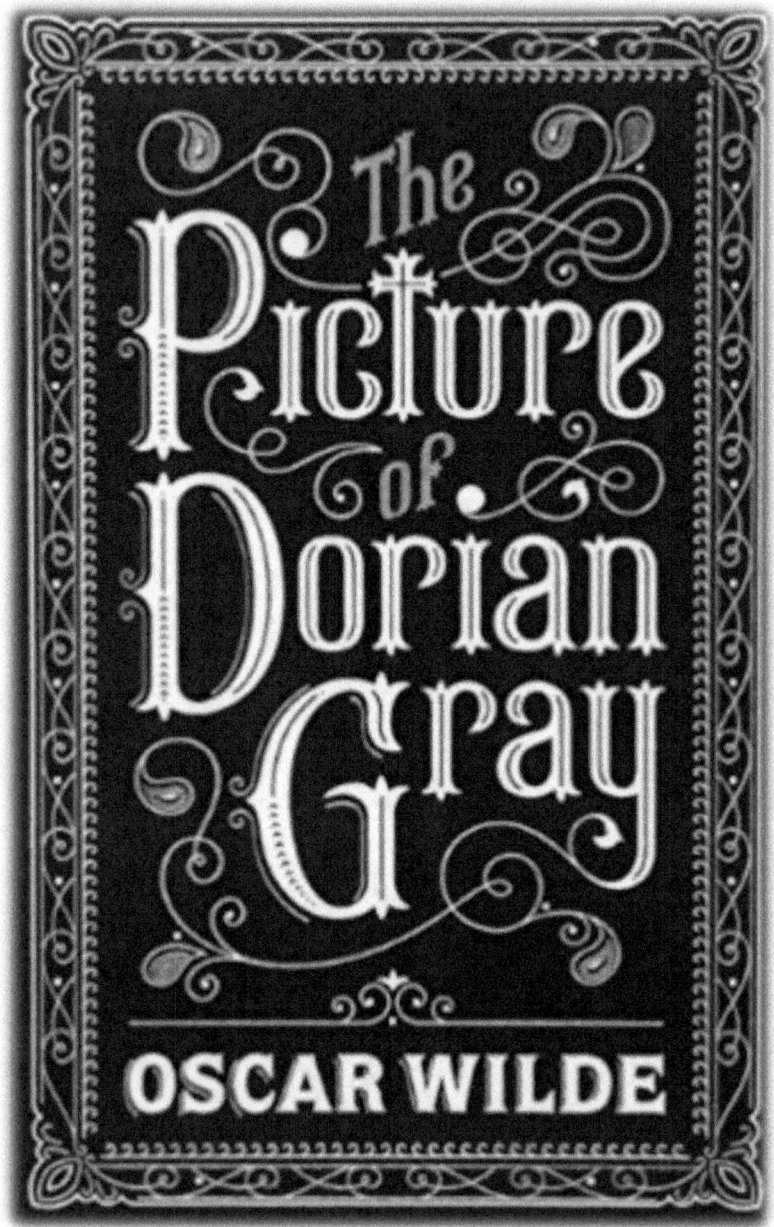

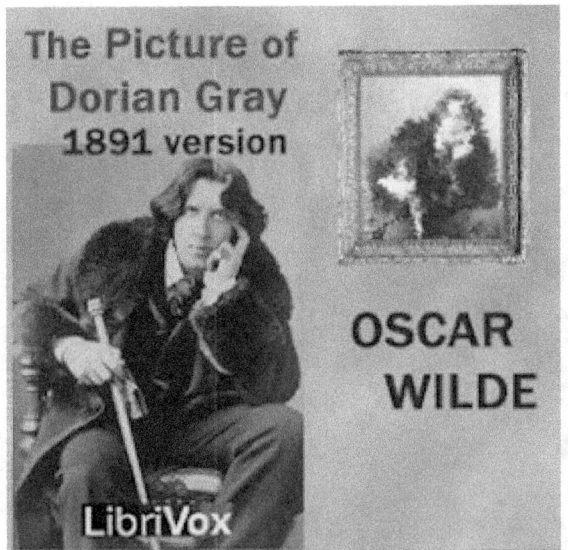

MAIN TIMELINE

Mid-1700s--*THE BEAST WITHIN: A TALE OF BEAUTY'S PRINCE* (novella by Serena Valentino) --Authorized juvenile novella by Serena Valentino that is a prequel/retelling of Disney's version of *Beauty and the Beast*. An engagement portrait of the already cursed but not yet transformed Prince begins to reveal the beast inside him that his handsome appearance hides from the world. The engagement is soon off. The painting is the work of a mysterious "Maestro," whose anachronistic musings on art link him with the Aesthetic movement and Oscar Wilde; and are clearly intended to cast the Beast's portrait as a precursor to Dorian's.

This may be a reference to an alternate reality, the one where a non-toon version of Disney's interpretation of the classic story took place or may have been an alternate event that was similar to the one from the "classic" version of the tale. The preponderance of different source versions detailing the unfortunate Prince who became a Beast may suggest a succession of such events whose differences were tweaked to make them appear as a variant of a single "core" tale for various published, filmed, or theatrically choreographed retellings; or there may indeed be a solitary event in WHU canon whose details have been tweaked according to the whims of anyone who may have been retelling it at any given time.

November 8^{th,} 1852--Dorian Gray is born on his parents' family estate in Kew, London.

Late 1850s - early 1860s--Dorian's constant loneliness causes him to contact a disembodied entity of some sort that calls himself Brendan Doyle. The true nature of Doyle is unknown, but he seemed to feed off the emotional energies of Dorian's loneliness, and he may be a conscious thought form (i.e., a tulpa) brought into full existence over the course of several years. Dorian considered him an imaginary friend he created to relieve his loneliness, and this may indeed have been how Doyle's existence began. Nevertheless, as years passed, the negative emotions that Doyle fed on caused him to eventually develop a sadistic and even homicidal personality. See *THE CONFESSIONS OF DORIAN GRAY:* "RUNNING AWAY WITH YOU" below.

1863--Dorian Gray's sister Isadora is born.

1864--Dorian's father dies, and the mental anguish of the loss sends his mother into a mental breakdown. She is institutionalized, and Dorian and his sister are raised on the estate by their aunt and uncle.

1867--*THE CONFESSIONS OF DORIAN GRAY*: "RUNNING AWAY WITH YOU" (audio drama, Big Finish) --This story is set in 1879, based on the premise that Dorian's portrait was painted in 1882. But based on the timeline we are using here, this would take place in 1867. This story details the circumstances of Dorian's aunt and uncle hiring housekeeper Constance Harker to take care of him and his sister. She was overly strict with Dorian, making the young man's life quite miserable, and even causing him to run away once. At one point, when his guardians were away, Harker seduced him, taking his virginity and providing him with an experience that forever resulted in his affirming belief that youth was the only thing worth having, and age was an evil to be avoided at all costs.

Because of these powerful and conflicting emotions shared between Harker and Dorian following that experience, the latter's tulpa friend Brendan Doyle used its resulting energies to manifest in his usual form of a small boy, but now having the energy to temporarily take on a somewhat corporeal state. Upon manifesting, Doyle pushed the woman down the stairs to her death. This incident traumatized Dorian, causing him to break all psychic ties with Doyle, and to forcibly suppress the incident.

Approximately 1870--Birth of Quentin Collins (*DARK SHADOWS* TV series).

Quentin Collins

The Portrait of Quentin Collins

1870 - 1889--*LIPPINCOTT'S MONTHLY MAGAZINE* -- "THE PICTURE OF DORIAN GRAY" (novel by Oscar Wilde) -
-Dorian Gray, a man who only cares about looks and self-satisfaction, wishes (whimsically) that he could sell his soul to maintain his youth. He gets his wish, and a painting of him instead ages while he remains immortal, free to live a life of sin.

Dorian will return for crossover goodness (or badness, if you will.)

And ok, hear me out. *The King in Yellow* won't be published until five years after *The Picture of Dorian Gray*! But Dorian is seen reading (and keep in mind this story starts in 1890 but continues for some years) a book that seems to be *The King in Yellow*. A later crossover in this book called "In Memoriam" will cross the two and will support that Gray is indeed reading a tome that hadn't been written yet. Pretty nifty, huh?

Note that the story by Micah S. Harris in *Darker Shades* reveals that the film adaptation of this novel is also in the WHU, telling the same story with a different perspective. The events of the book and film should be considered the same events and equally valid. Further note the only part of this story that isn't canon for the WHU and this timeline is the ending, as we must presume that Dorian survived for the remainder of this timeline (and this anthology) to work. Again, keep in mind that the WHU includes the Big Finish audio drama series *The Confessions of Dorian Gray*. Big Finish also adapted the original novel. The audio drama adaptation is set in 1872. *Confessions* makes it clear that Oscar Wilde of the WHU wrote *The*

Picture of Dorian Gray as a fictional account based on the true events that happened to his friend Gray in 1882.

However, Wild Hunt Press also relies on the timeline established by Win Scott Eckert and continued by Sean Lee Levin for their *Crossover Universe* volumes, and this timeline author (R.W.) also holds to that timeline in most cases. Thus, I have kept the events as taking place from 1870 to 1899 as established by Eckert. Based on evidence in other stories Dorian did experience the events of the novel, at least up to the blackmailing of Alan Campbell to dispose of the body of Basil Hallward.

Also, valid for this timeline are *The Uncensored Dorian Gray*, which includes the parts Wilde had written that had been edited out of the original published version; and *The Darker Passions: The Picture of Dorian Gray*, a novel by Amarantha Knight (later republished under her real name, Nancy Kilpatrick), which added erotic scenes to the original story. It was part of Kilpatrick's Darker Passions series that provided erotic augmentations to other horror classics, including Stoker's *Dracula*). Neither of these expanded versions contradict the original published story. Most adaptations that are set in the same timeframe can be considered the same story from different perspectives, rather than alternate timelines.

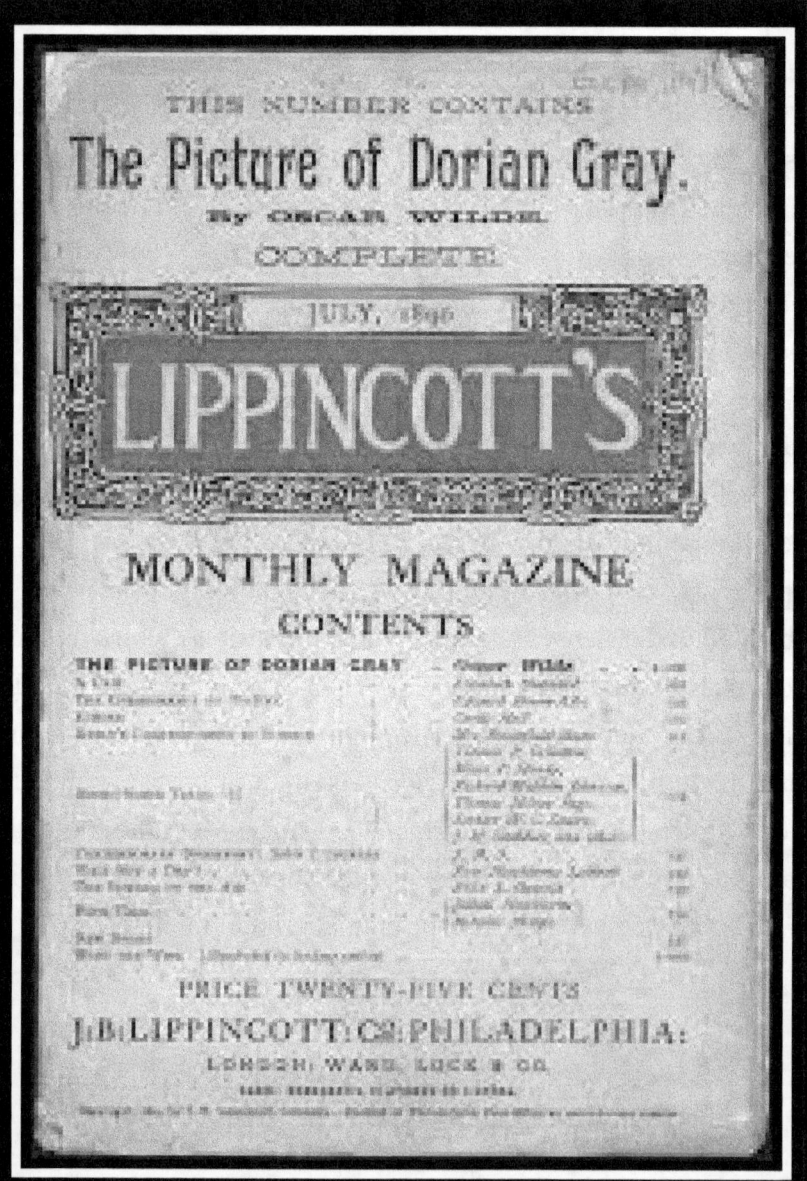

Summer 1878--*TALES OF THE SHADOWMEN VOLUME II: GENTLEMEN OF THE NIGHT* --"ANGELS OF MUSIC" (short story by Kim Newman) --Years before Charles Townsend came up with the concept (or perhaps in this world, Charles never did), Erik, the infamous Phantom of the Opera, gathers together three "angels," a trio of beautiful mystery solving young ladies to work for him as private investigators. His angels are Christine Daae, Trilby O'Farrell, and Irene Adler. Buy the books. They rock. (*The Shadowmen* books are available on Black Coat Press' website.)

Erik is from *The Phantom of the Opera* by Gaston Leroux. Christine is from *Phantom* also. Trilby is from a book of the same name by George Du Maurier. Irene is the lovely nemesis and lover of Sherlock Holmes who appeared in several of his stories by Sir Arthur Conan Doyle. It would be fitting that in the WHU, *Charlie's Angels* would be so altered as to take place in Victorian era Europe led by an infamous horror icon.

There are many crossovers in this story, but there are two I'd like to briefly note. One of the figures seen in this story is Count Ruboff from Universal's 1925 film version of *The Phantom of the Opera*, but not the original novel. We should assume that both the book and film are the same story, perhaps told from two different perspectives, thus with slight alterations. Also, another character that appears is Basil Hallward, who is from *The Picture of Dorian Gray*.

1880s--*BERNICE SUMMERFIELD: SHADES OF GRAY* (audio drama, Big Finish) --Flashbacks

June 1887--*DORIAN GRAY: DARKER SHADES*-- "PORTRAIT OF A LADY" (novella by Micah S. Harris) --This story is set in an alternate timeline to Micah's tome *The Eldritch New Adventures of Becky Sharp*. Rebecca is from William Makepeace Thackeray's classic novel *Vanity Fair*. In this story Becky, who has taken over the role as ruler of Kor after having helped dispatch Ayesha, She Who Must Be Obeyed (from H. Rider Haggard's novel *She*), is in England for the Queen's Golden Jubilee, and a secret mission for the Diogenes Club. Her immortality becomes revealed, making her the subject of inquiry and desire from three men, one of which is Dorian Gray. This story conflates Oscar Wilde's novel with the film adaptation and establishes that Basil Hallward was intentional in his work, using Egyptian magic as a worshipper of the Egyptian goddess Bast and a member of the Cult of Fama. Finally, the villain's henchman who attempts to help put Becky in wax is

Ygor, or Igor, particularly the version of the character from the 1932 film *Mystery of the Wax Museum*. And more crossover information from the author himself:

Most of the aliases that Becky finds in Lyndon Thackeray's drawer are names of Thackeray characters from his other books.

Barry Lyndon, of course, is from William Makepeace Thackeray's novel *The Luck of Barry Lyndon* – thus we now have "the Thackeryverse" since Barry and Becky have met. To my knowledge, this is the first time anyone has done this. Or particularly cared to.

Now the metafictional fun and games get interesting: *Barré Lyndon* was the pen name of a writer named Alfred Edgar, who was obviously riffing off Thackeray's character/novel for his *nom de plume*. He did the screenplay for the classic *War of the Worlds* film adaptation by the great George Pal from the '50s. He was also a playwright whose work included *The Man in Half Moon Street*. It's a play about a scientist who has learned the secret of immortality by extracting an organ from the human body, but it only keeps him young for so long; then he must do it again periodically, and that always means murder.

A couple of critics, including Kim Newman, have seen Barré Lyndon's story as a riff on *The Picture of Dorian Gray*, but using science instead of supernatural means to keep the titular protagonist young. Notably, the movie version of *The Man in Half Moon Street* was released the same year of MGM's 1945 cinematic adaptation of *The Picture of Dorian Gray*, evidently an example of a rival studio doing a similarly themed picture to cash in.

The Man in Half Moon Street was later remade by Hammer Films as *The Man Who Could Cheat Death*, relocating the story to nineteenth-century France. Which is why in my story it is implied that Dr. Lyndon Thackery is headed there at the end. Part of my game here, of course, is to give the character a name that is a homage to the writer Barré Lyndon, the fictional character Barry Lyndon whence he got *his* pen name, and the creator of Barry Lyndon, William Makepeace Thackeray, who also created Becky Sharp.

In his script for the sequel to the classic Dan Curtis '70s' telefilm *The Night Stalker*, genre great Richard Matheson used the basic concept of *The Man in Half Moon Street* for *The Night Strangler* -- but made the unaging man with his bodily extraction experiments a Civil War doctor named Dr. Richard Malcolm. I suggest the same name was an alias for my version of Barry Lyndon in "Portrait of a Lady" when we are told that Barry Lyndon actually faked his death at the end of the Thackeray classic and fled to America.

When he returns to England after the Civil War in my "Portrait of a Lady," "Richard Malcolm" now has the metatextual moniker of Dr. "Lyndon Thackery."

Following the character's progress, then, after the events of "Portrait of a Lady," Lyndon Thackery / Richard Malcolm / Barry Lyndon survives Becky's stab in the eye and flees to France where he heals, adapts a thick accent (not French), and becomes "Georges Bonnet" for Hammer's *The Man Who Could Cheat Death* where he continues sculpting. He apparently dies in this movie before the Meonia can find him and release the Templar's Black Madonna on him, as is Becky's suggestion.

However, somehow the old boy got away with it at least one more time because during the 1970s in *The Night Strangler*, Carl Kolchak meets him as Dr. Malcolm Richards, where he is living in an underground city in Seattle. So, after "dying" in France, Georges Bonnet / Lyndon Thackery / Richard Malcolm / Barry Lyndon / Redman Lyndon / mysterious white man from lost African civilization – *this guy* returned to the States, switched his old Civil War era name around to Malcolm Richards, and *finally* dies the final death, having lived long enough to see a man on the moon and a U.S. President impeached. Good times. Yes, he would have also witnessed *Good Times* become a prime-time television hit. Maybe at this point, he felt he'd at last seen it all, and decided he was shuffling off the mortal coil for good this go 'round.

Of course, you can see how irresistible it was to me in writing a story in a Dorian Gray anthology to have Dorian find a rival in another fictional character apparently inspired by him. My transformative incarnation, Dr. Lyndon Thackery also makes this ersatz immortal Barry Lyndon, the creation of William Makepeace Thackeray who, as mentioned above, also created Becky Sharp herself. No wonder Dr. Lyndon felt so possessive of her!

And of course, "Portrait of a Lady" takes place in an alternate universe to that of my novel *The Eldritch New Adventures of Becky Sharp* and the events of all other previously published Becky stories, but, according to Chris [Nigro], is canon in the WHU.

Circa 1888--*THE CONFESSIONS OF DORIAN GRAY*: "ONE MUST NOT LOOK AT MIRRORS" (audio drama, Big Finish) - -London. Oscar Wilde meets Dorian Gray.

1889 - 2013--*THE WILDE PASSIONS OF DORIAN GRAY* (novel by Mitzi Szereto) --This novel also confirms that Dorian's death was fictionalized in Wilde's biography-disguised-as-novel, and that Dorian has continued to live into the modern day.

Winter 1890--*REHEARSALS FOR OBLIVION, ACT I -- TALES OF THE KING IN YELLOW*: "IN MEMORIAM" (short story by Roger Johnson and Roger M. Price) --Some friends who believe Dorian to be dead perform "The King in Yellow" in his honor. OK, I mentioned it before, but it bears repeating. In *the Picture of Dorian Gray*, Dorian seems to be reading *The King in Yellow*, even though *Picture* was written five years prior to *King*. Pretty spooky.

Circa 1890--*MANY RETURNS* (playlet by David MacDowell Blue) --Dorian meets Carmilla Karnstein and finds himself drawn to her, until a certain revelation disturbs him.

The Carmilla who appears here is a cousin of the version from J. Sheridan Le Fanu's classic 1872 eponymous vampire novella, and the same version who first appeared in David's 2014 stage play by that name. Many of the various female vampires of the Karnstein clan have used the name "Carmilla" or other variations of "Mircalla," and have been seen in many sources, including Hammer's Karnstein Trilogy of lesbian vampire films from 1970-71. This film trio starts with *The Vampire Lovers* and continues with *Lust for a Vampire* and *Twins of Evil* (the latter being the earliest in terms of chronology).

Another female vampire of the Karnstein clan appeared in the Hammer Film *Captain Kronos – Vampire Hunter*. The Karnsteins were of a different vampiric strain than the one that spawned Dracula, which accounts for their different weaknesses (the Karnstein strain are resistant to direct sunlight, though they are irritated and weakened by it). Another Hammer movie to feature vampires from the same strain as the Karnstein clan was *Vampire Circus*.

This one act play is filled with crossovers. Carmilla is, of course, from the eponymous 1872 novella by Joseph Sheridan Le Fanu. Dorian is accompanied when he encounters Carmilla by Christine Daae prior to the events of *The Phantom of the Opera*. Carmilla mentions her family, including the Karnstein Prince from Edgar Allan Poe's short story "Masque of the Red Death." The story's setting is the Chateau Merteuil from *Les Liaisons Dangereuses* ("Dangerous Relationships" in English), the novel that inspired the films *Dangerous Liaisons* and *Cruel Intentions*. (The latter is a modernized version, while the former is a more faithful adaptation.) Carmilla and Dorian's first encounter was at the trial of Jefferson Hope, following the events of the Sherlock Holmes adventure, *A Study in Scarlet*.

1892--*PHOENIX RISING: A MINISTRY OF PECULIAR OCCURRENCES NOVEL* (novel by Pip Ballantine & Tee Morris) -- An agent hears rumors that the warehouse holds a certain painting.

Television Crossover Universe crew member James Bojaciuk identified the Ministry of Peculiar Occurrences as the precursor to Warehouse 13. Later, the authors have come across James' theories and approved of most of them, including other crossovers in this novel with "The Fall of the House of Usher," *20,000 Leagues Under the Sea*, Dr. Silence, Sherlock Holmes, *My Name is Bruce*, Gemma Doyle, *Pirates of the Caribbean*, and Dorian Gray.

The only area where the authors disagreed with James Bojaciuk is the debunking of Dr. Silence as Mycroft Holmes.

1895--*THE KING IN YELLOW* (a collection of interconnected stories by Robert W. Chambers) --This is several stories, all involving the supernatural and a play that is fictional in the real world, called "The King in Yellow." See the entry for *The Picture of Dorian Gray* for a very interesting note about this book.

1897--*DARK SHADOWS:* "804" (TV show episode) --A portrait of Quentin Collins is painted against his will, by artist Charles Delaware Tate. The portrait and thus Collins himself are cursed by the magic of Count Andreas Petofi, who has made the artist's canvases so that they cause the person painted to become immortal, while the portrait ages and the evil acts are captured within the portrait.

In *The Picture of Dorian Gray*, Dorian is painted by Basil Hallward. In Micah S. Harris' tome *Slouching Toward Camulodunum*, it's revealed that Tate was a student of Hallward. However, it's Petofi who creates the magic behind the portrait of

Collins. Micah has pointed out in "Portrait of a Lady," found in this anthology, that Egyptian magic was behind Hallward's talents for capturing the soul as he did in his paintings; and Peter Rawlik's short story "The Hallward Restorations" (also in this anthology) demonstrates that Hallward has done many such paintings. It must be that Petofi is using the same Egyptian magic in conjunction with the stylings created by Hallward.

May - August 1898--*THE LEAGUE OF EXTRAORDINARY GENTLEMEN* (six-issue comic book limited series by Alan Moore and Kevin O'Neill, America's Best Comics) --Five unique individuals -- Allan Quatermain, Dr. Henry Jekyll/Edward Hyde, the second Captain Nemo (Prince Dakkar), the first Invisible Man (Prof. John Hawley Griffin), and Mina Murray are gathered together by British Intelligence agent Campion Bond (grandfather of James Bond; or at least the first of them) and find themselves caught in a war between Professor James Moriarty and Fu Manchu (here referred to as "The Devil Doctor" to cover copyright issues).

Boy oh boy. Where to start? This tale brings in *The War of the Worlds*, Dorian Gray, Dr. Caligari, Varney the Vampire, and Poe's Mummy from his short story "Some Words with a Mummy." There are, of course, many, many more. I suggest if you are curious, first read the book. I doubt you'll find them all, but it's more fun to read it first. Then, refer to Jess Nevins' *Heroes and Monsters: The Unofficial Companion to the League of Extraordinary Gentlemen*.

The version of Captain Nemo who appears in both the comic book and movie version of *The League of Extraordinary Gentlemen* is Prince Dakkar, the Hindu anti-hero who first appeared in Jules Verne's novel *The Mysterious Island*, and seems to be distinct from the original, Caucasian version seen previously in Verne's novel *20,000 Leagues Under the Sea*. Since "Nemo" means "nobody" in Latin, this provides a strong hint that "Captain Nemo" was an alias used by different individuals who utilized a version of the *Nautilus* super-submarine; and maybe by other sea-going anti-heroes and villains as well.

The original Invisible Man is the demented scientist from H.G. Wells' eponymous novel. Only his last name, Griffin, was given in Wells' novel, and the name "Hawley," presumed to be his first name, was introduced here. It is accepted by WHU canon that this is his middle name, since "John" has been given as his first name in other sources. Reconciling the conflicting first names in this fashion was done by Dennis E. Power for Part 1 of his outstanding online series of articles "Invisibles: Revealing the Unseen History of the Griffin Family" with a good degree of input by Matthew Baugh, Win Scott Eckert, and Chuck Loridans, and incorporated into Eckert's and Sean Levin's Crossover Universe (CU). It is similarly considered canon in the WHU, which takes much of its continuity from the CU and is indebted to the work of the four authors listed above.

(As of this book's publication, Dennis's article could still be accessed at: http://www.pjfarmer.com/secret/invisible/im1.htm)

John Hawley Griffin's son, John "Jack" Griffin, was to become the Invisible Man of the classic 1932 Universal film of that name (a few details of those events were tweaked by the filmmakers to make it appear to be an adaptation of the novel rather than a separate tale).

Allan Quatermain is the Great White Hunter adventurer who was the featured character of several novels by H. Rider Haggard beginning with *King Solomon's Mines.*

Dr. Henry Jekyll and his monstrous alter-ego Mr. Edward Hyde first appeared in Robert Louis Stevenson's classic novel *The Strange Case of Dr. Jekyll and Mr. Hyde.* In the novel, Jekyll's Hyde form was diminutive and lacked superhuman strength but was still quite vicious and dangerous; in this series, however, his Hyde form has evolved/mutated into a more than seven-foot-tall brutish being of great superhuman strength, and the capacity & propensity to eat human beings and even aliens like the Martian Sarmaks. Subsequent appearances of Hyde in other sources maintained this enhanced form, including the opening sequence of the film *Van Helsing.*

Mina Murray is the main female victim/protagonist of Bram Stoker's iconic horror novel *Dracula* and was divorced from her husband Jonathan Harker by this point in time, thus having dropped the use of his surname. The Vampire Lord wasn't mentioned by name in this limited series, but simply referred to as "a foreigner" who had "ravished" Murray. Murray's character had come a long way between the events of that novel and her being elected leader of the League, and part of her evolution was seen in the two novels *Mina: The Dracula Story Continues* and *Blood to Blood: The Dracula Story Continues* by Elaine Bergstrom (who also used the pen name Marie Kiraly).

Campion Bond was an original creation of writer Alan Moore for this series. Though he didn't serve as M in the movie, he did show up at the end of the novelization, presumably to "whip" the new imposter team into shape for the British government, just as he had done for the previous team of bona fides (see the respective entries for the *League of Extraordinary Gentlemen* movie and novelization down below for the long story behind that).

August - September 1898--*LEAGUE OF EXTRAORDINARY GENTLEMEN VOLUME II* (six-issue comic book mini-series by Alan Moore and Kevin O'Neill, America's Best Comics) --When the Martians invade Britain, on the front lines of Earth defense are the League of Extraordinary Gentlemen. I refer you to Jess Nevins's *a Blazing World: The Unofficial Companion to the League of Extraordinary Gentlemen Volume II*. Dorian Gray is referenced in this story, among the numerous crossovers.

The octopoid Martians seen in this novel are the Sarmaks, a.k.a., the 'Molluscs,' from H.G. Wells' classic sci-fi novel *The War of the Worlds*. The Mars of this limited series was depicted in an early sequence of the first issue that featured crossovers of numerous different Martian races culled from a variety of classic literary sources. This included John Carter from Edgar Rice Burroughs' series of novels beginning with *A Princess of Mars;* and Lt. Gullivar (sometimes spelled "Gulliver") Jones from Edwin Lester Arnold's novel *Lieut. Gullivar Jones: His Vacation*. Though the humanoid, Arab-like Hither people of the latter novel were depicted as lazy and unproductive, their contradictory depiction as warriors led by Carter and Gullivar against the Sarmaks may simply be explained by the contention that the two military men from Earth managed to rally the usually apathetic people against the invaders by convincing the Hithers of what an extreme threat the octopoid invasion force presented to the red planet.

It has been established by various creative mythographers that the Sarmaks not only had a dimensional iteration within the Edgar Rice Burroughs Universe (ERBU) outside of Barsoom's solar system, but also in the CU proper, and hence within alternate versions of the CU like the WHU. As editor Gordon Long very helpfully pointed out to this author (Christofer Nigro – thanks, dude!), this interdimensional status of these faux Martians was first established in the 1976 novel *The Second War of the Worlds* by George H. Smith.

In this alternate reality period piece, the Sarmaks made a second invasion attempt on a different Earth, which was no less than Annwn, Earth's counterpart in the ERBU (where Barsoom, the counterpart of the WHU's and CU's Mars, exists). It's an Earth which, during the late Victorian/Edwardian era, was slightly less advanced technologically than the Earth we know (and which the WHU and CU proper are a reflection of), but where magick is still in prominent use. And the people of Annwn also ended up getting assistance in thwarting the Martian invasion from a dimension-hopping Sherlock Holmes and Dr. John Watson (referred to in the book as "Mr. H" and "Dr. W").

Annwn first appeared in Smith's 1969 novelette *Kar Kaballa*, where a foreign invasion of that Earth's British Empire by a nation of Mongolian cannibals was fended off partly with more extradimensional assistance from the Earth of the WHU or CU proper (probably analogues occurred on both Earths due to their similarities) in the form of an American arms merchant hocking Gatling guns (never invented on Annwn!). Many thanks to Amazon commentators Ralph E Vaughan and Barry C. Jacobsen for this info!

Annwn made its final appearance under George W. Smith's pen in his 1978 novel *The Island Snatchers,* which makes the saga of the Earth of the ERBU a trilogy. Many thanks to colleague and fellow creative mythographer Jay Lindsey for this important tidbit of info.

The Sarmaks also seem to have made interdimensional incursions into the Marvel Universe (MU), thus creating the divergent post-apocalyptic world of the early 21st century seen in *Amazing Adventures* Vol. 2 #18-39, courtesy of writers Roy Thomas & Gerry Conway and artists Neal Adams (initially) & (later) Don McGregor and a host of various other artists. In that alternate version of MU, the Sarmak invasion was opposed by the crusading human warrior Killraven (real name: Jonathan Raven) and his team of Freemen.

Other Martian species from different sources who appeared in the first issue of *The League of Extraordinary Gentlemen* Vol. 2 #1 includes the Sorns (a.k.a., Séroni) from C.S. Lewis' Space Trilogy, beginning with *Out of the Silent Planet*; and references to *Kane of Old Mars*, which is part of Michael Moorcock's long-running Eternal Champion series. The many humanoid Martian races seen in Burroughs' books refer to their world (i.e., Mars of the ERBU) as Barsoom, and their counterparts in Lewis' trilogy refer to it as Malacandra. The Sarmak invasion was clearly shown to be interdimensional, with the hostile multi-tentacled 'Molluscs' using it as a base from which to launch another invasion, this one to the Earth of the WHU (and CU proper). This idea originated with the curators of the CU, which the WHU closely follows in major respects.

It would therefore appear that the dimensional version of Mars seen in this book is Barsoom, which has been established by creative mythographers Win Scott Eckert and others to exist in an alternate reality called the Edgar Rice Burroughs Universe (ERBU). It has also been suggested that Gullivar Jones' version of Mars was likewise Barsoom, as was Malacandra and the Mars of Moorcock.

However, it's possible, as per a theory of this anthology's editor and co-author of this Timeline (Christofer Nigro), that each of these versions of Mars were from distinct alternate realities vis a vis the numerous alternate and strangely inhabitable versions of the Red Planet seen in novels such as Robert Heinlein's *The Number of the Beast*, Larry Niven's *Rainbow Mars*, Harry Turtledove's *A World of Difference*; and Philip José Farmer's *World of Tiers* series, where an artificial version of Barsoom was created. If this is true within the context of the multiverse connected to the WHU, which is a parallel version of the CU, then the Mars seen in *The League of Extraordinary Gentlemen* Vol. 2 may indicate a multi-dimensional invasion of the Sarmak against multiple quantum variants of Mars, with John Carter and Gulliver Jones marshalling denizens from these various versions to Barsoom, where the invasion was most concentrated, just as the Sarmaks began their interdimensional invasion to possibly multiple dimensional versions of Earth.

However, this is a concept that has nothing to do with the subject of this anthology, so it will be mentioned no further here, but will likely be taken up in a future volume from Wild Hunt Press that directly deals with Mars.

**Autumn - December 17, 1899--*DARK SHADOWS*: "THE
SKIN WALKERS" (audio drama, Big Finish) --**New York.
Features the Lowell Foundation, which monitors the activities of

Dorian Gray in Big Finish's audio book series *The Confessions of Dorian Gray*. Quentin Collins has left Collinsport for a better life.

1899--*THE LEAGUE OF EXTRAORDINARY GENTLEMEN* (a.k.a., "*LXG*," film) --An aged adventurer is called upon to lead a League of Extraordinary Gentlemen when a mysterious masked personage who calls himself the Fantom (also sometimes spelled "Phantom" for obvious reasons) threatens to incite war in Europe. This film takes the very basic premise of the comic book and goes in a wildly different direction from there.

Because of that, many fans of the comic hate this movie. However, I feel if taken on its own merits and not compared to the comic, it's a great fun action crossover film. The League of this motion picture consists of Allan Quatermain (from a series of novels by H. Rider Haggard, starting with *King Solomon's Mines)*; Captain Nemo (the Hindu version from *The Mysterious Island*; not the prior Caucasian version who appeared in *20,000 Leagues Under the Sea,* both by Jules Verne); Mina Harker (*Dracula* by Bram Stoker); Rodney Skinner (a thief who has taken the invisibility formula from the original Invisible Man, a.k.a., John Hawley Griffin, the antagonistic protagonist of the eponymous novel by H.G. Wells); Dr. Henry Jekyll and Edward Hyde (*The Strange Case of Dr. Jekyll and Mr. Hyde* by Robert Louis Stevenson); Dorian Gray (*The Picture of Dorian Gray* by Oscar Wilde); and Tom Sawyer (from a series of novels by Mark Twain, starting with *The Adventures of Tom Sawyer*; the version of Sawyer seen in this film was more akin to the young adult incarnation of the character seen in Twain's novel *Tom Sawyer,*

Detective).

The team reports to M (a precursor to the one James Bond reported to). After his long trip from Africa to London, Quatermain makes a remark about "Around the World in 80 Days" (this being a reference to the momentous event accomplished by the protagonists of Jules Verne's eponymous novel). The villain is the Fantom (keep reading for the full skinny on him). And spoiler, there is a character from Sherlock Holmes as well.

Normally, I'd place a film that is so contradictory to the canonical source material in an alternate reality. However, we really like Dorian Gray, and the events of this movie can be fully compatible with this timeline following some diligent tweaking and para-scholarship research. Thus, the brain trust of Wild Hunt Press, the contributing authors of this anthology, MONSTAAH, the TVCU Crew, and some others, have banded together to figure out how this could fit. If we watch the film's events as occurring exactly as we see it on screen, but change who the actual characters were, it can work. This explanation is canon for the version of events that take place in the WHU. Whether this likewise counts for the CU proper remains to be seen at this writing, as its prime curators are Win Scott Eckert and Sean Levin; and the same must be said for the Monster Hunter Universe (MHU; you may not have heard of it yet, but you will).

First, let's deal with the "Allan Quatermain" of this film, and how we settled on a logical stand-in for him: he was Colonel Sebastian Moran, the accomplice of Prof. James Moriarty introduced in Sir Arthur Conan Doyle's short story "The Final Problem." We came to that conclusion thanks to the able assistance and ruminations of James Bojaciuk, author and CEO of 18thWall Productions. In short, Moran would be the only Great White Hunter archetype who would be alive at that time and have the requisite skills and characteristics to fit the bill. He would be advanced in age, as the character was portrayed in the film, and would have reason to hide in Africa while hiring another man to impersonate him in case his location was discovered. This also correlates with his appearances in the Big Finish audio dramas, and the machinations of The Society, which James (Mr. Bojaciuk, not Professor Moriarty!) contends was likely the brain behind the Fantom's siege in *LXG*. Further, Moran was later shown to be one of the chief players in The Society, and he was certainly a major presence in whatever organization eventually emerged from the real Prof. Moriarty's scheme – see David McDaniel's Man from U.N.C.L.E. novel *The Dagger Affair*, for instance.

The Big Finish audio drama *The Ordeals of Sherlock Holmes* (these Holmes adventures are likewise considered canon in the WHU) made it clear there was a specific but exceedingly rare Afghani flower that can significantly extend the human life spend and regenerate most wounds, which could explain both Moran's continued vitality despite his age by 1899-1902 and the clear implication at the end of the film that he was soon to rise from the coffin he was placed in after his death. He would simply have been in a catatonic state while the healing process took place, and his time being shipped back to Africa in the coffin would have provided him with that opportunity. This makes sense, since Moran turned up alive circa 1902 in Doyle's short story "The Adventure of the Illustrious Client."

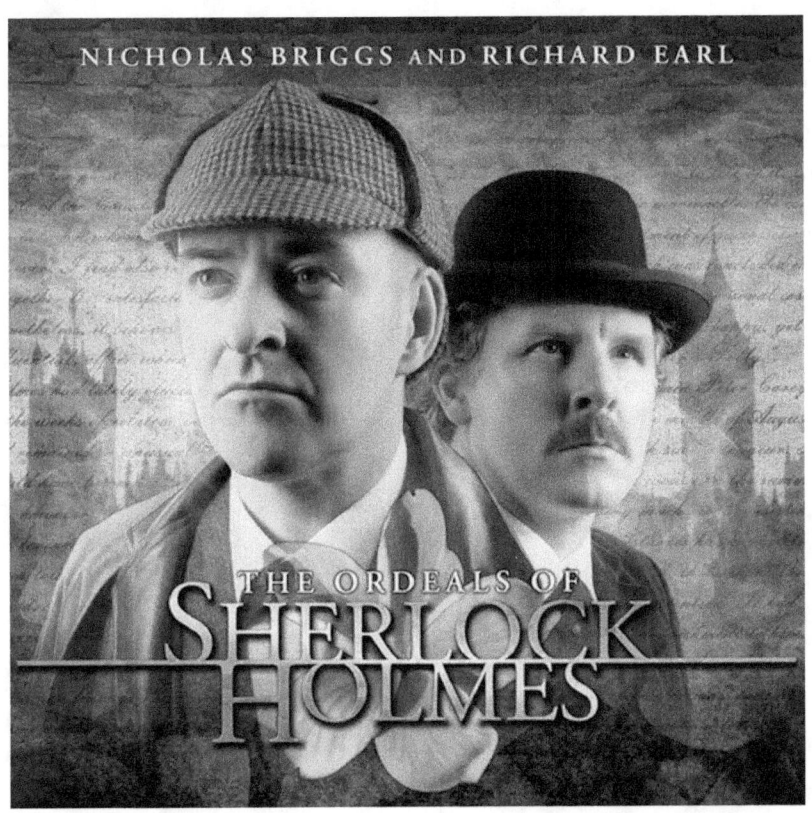

Next, we confront The Society introduced in the Sherlock Holmes audio dramas from Big Finish being the force behind The Fantom. Their goal to initiate a World War by spreading various forms of chaos, as shown in Big Finish's audio dramas *The Judgment of Sherlock Holmes* and *The Sacrifice of Sherlock Holmes* correlates strongly with the actions of The Fantom. Their reasons for trying to secure samples of Hyde's formula and "Mina's" vampiric blood may have been part of the plan they later initiated in 1921, when they used an agent spread by blood-mingling to transform people into inhuman madmen, as well as the creation of the "Hounds."

In fact, this is similar to the effects of the Hyde-25 drug seen being spread around London in the 1890s, as shown in the "Night of the Jackass" stripe serialized in Warren Publishing's *Eerie* comic magazine (more on that below).

Next up is the "Captain Nemo" of the film. Contributor Kevin Heim provided the deciding determination for this stand-in: He is The Persian, albeit the original version who first appeared as the trusted servant and frequent partner-in-mayhem of The Phantom of the Opera in Gaston Leroux's eponymous novel.

It makes sense for The Persian to be given the guise of the Prince Dakkar version of "Captain Nemo" by M and the agency of the Crown they served for this mission. It has been theorized by the editor of this anthology (and co-author of this Timeline) that the true Phantom of the Opera, a greatly feared member of Europe's underworld, collaborated with M behind the scenes due to the former being incensed that his identity was appropriated by the unknown individual – likely under the auspices of The Society, as noted by James Bojaciuk – to carry out their mad scheme in London. The Society may have mistakenly believed that the Phantom of the Opera was either a frightening urban legend, or that his main base of operations in Paris was sufficiently far away from the U.K. that he would overlook his identity being used for someone else's nefarious schemes. Big mistake.

Erik the Phantom had more than enough contacts to help him locate the *Nautilus* super-submarine during a time when Prince Dakkar had left it docked somewhere hidden, perhaps when he was back in his native India on an urgent personal matter of some sort. Erik also possessed more than enough engineering skills to learn how the *Nautilus* operated, and to teach these functions to The Persian and the crew of support staff hired by them.

331

"Mina Harker" of *LXG* is Vampirella, the heroic vampiric she-warrior, who has appeared in multiple comic book series published by Warren, Harris, and Dynamite from 1969 to the present. More specifically, this is Vampirella in her periodic human guise of chemist Ella Normandy. Even though she began her monster-fighting career between 1969 and 1971 (at least in her familiar incarnation), during the '70s Vampi has used one of the Mirrors of Merlin in the possession of her ally, the vampire hunter Conrad Van Helsing, to time travel back to the late 19th century on a mission as chronicled in contributor T. Casey Brennan's "Shadow of Dracula" story arc from Warren's *Vampirella* Vol. 1 #19-20. Since Vampi has found reason to time travel to that era before, she may have taken on the guise of Mina Harker rather than Ella Normandy at the British government's behest during the events of this film (for the reason why, see below).

Also, since Vampi's origin is still murky to the point where we cannot say for certain exactly when she first appeared in the Earth dimension, the faux Mina from *LXG* may have been a Vampirella who was indigenous to that era, especially if creative mythographer John A. Small's theory that Vampi was originally the tough, whip-wielding Western hero Lady Rawhide before turning into a unique type of vampire after being bitten by one of Dracula's thralls, a female vamp named Carmelita Rodriguez, happens to ring true in the WHU. That theory is covered in Small's article "Kiss of the Vampire," which can be read online.

At this writing, it can be found at:
http://www.pjfarmer.com/chronicles/smallvamp.htm.
It can also be read in its published form in *Myths for the Modern*

Age: Philip José Farmer's Wold Newton Universe, edited by Win Scott Eckert (Small has credited Win, Dennis E. Power, Chuck Loridans, and Matthew Baugh for providing him insights and info towards building that theory).

Note: The great anthology of articles was published prior to the Wold Newton Universe (WNU) appellation being reserved specifically for the works of the late, great author Philip José Farmer, with the broader expansion of the concept begun by Eckert having been christened the Crossover Universe (CU) and covered in an extensive timeline published in four volumes, the first two by Win himself and the last two to date by Sean Levin. The Wild Hunt Universe (WHU) is inspired by the CU and is a close alternate analogue to it.

The fact that "Mina Harker" of this film was depicted as a chemist is further evidence in favor of a possibly extratemporal Vampi operating in the guise, since on her first trip back in time in her Ella Normandy identity, she posed as a laboratory assistant to chemist Boris Van Helsing, the elder brother of famed vampire hunter Abraham Van Helsing. Since Vampi had to learn to use lab equipment to formulate her blood serum substitute, she likely became a good amateur chemist. Skill in chemistry was never attributed to Mina Murray/Harker in any other source, including either Bram Stoker's *Dracula* or the comic book version of *The League of Extraordinary Gentlemen*.

The "Mina Harker" of this movie displayed a power that Vampi never demonstrated in the comics, which was to control the will of bats and mentally command swarms of them to attack her enemies. There could be various ways of accounting for this discrepancy, including a temporary chemically-induced augmentation of her natural vampiric powers provided by the British government through M to make her a more efficient agent for the duration of her service to them. She also appeared to fly without transforming into a bat, something she was unable to do in the comic books (in the 1990s she learned to fly in humanoid form by manifesting two gigantic bat-like wings), but this could have been creative license on the part of the filmmakers.

"Dr. Jekyll" of *LXG* is Claude Bishop from the Warren Comics series "Night of the Jackass," which was serialized in their horror anthology comic magazine *Eerie* (the entire series was collected in *Eerie* Vol. 1 #115). In that series, Bishop was a cynical and bitter man from Wales who helped others battle the destitute residents of 1890s London that used an illegally distributed chemical variant of the original Dr. Henry Jekyll's formula, called Hyde-25, to transform into mutant psychopaths who exacted brutal vengeance on the hapless residents of the Late Victorian society they believed had abandoned them to poverty and homelessness. In the last part of the series, the increasingly unbalanced Bishop used the Hyde-25 chemical on himself, causing him to mutate (a process called "going jackass" in the series). He became the first individual to take the formula that didn't die within 24 hours of the mutagen taking effect thanks to the inventor of the chemical, Dr. Bertha Astruc, injecting him with an experimental antidote that seemed to revert him back to his normal human form.

However, it was revealed in *Hyde-25* #0 by Harris Comics that the original chemical had permanently altered Bishop's chromosomes, resulting in his descendants being born with permanent "jackass" traits. One of them, Samuel Bishop, used his "Jackass" attributes to become a government-controlled monster hunter during the 1990s, having once teamed with Vampirella.

The theory that Bishop was the Jekyll/Hyde stand-in was formulated by creative mythographers Kevin Heim and Henry Covert that the Jekyll/Hyde, who later found a variant of the Hyde-25 serum developed by either Astruc or a member of the true Jekyll clan that could trigger the transformation again. This time, however, the metamorphosis was more extreme, so that his general physique and level of superhuman strength approached that of the actual Edward Hyde after his form had later mutated in similar fashion. These superhuman traits, along with the characteristic psychotic behavior of someone under the influence of this mutagen, were exhibited by later individuals who synthesized a variant of the Hyde formula, such as Dr. Calvin Zabo during the 1960s.

The Invisible Man of this film was the only doppelganger who was overtly portrayed as such, rather than attempting to conflate him with Prof. John Hawley Griffin, the first member of that infamous clan to use the invisibility formula to become the titular menace of H.G. Wells' eponymous novel (he was directly referenced in the novelization of this movie). Hence, this job was already done for us. He was revealed to be Rodney Skinner, a dangerous but relatively scrupulous and loyal spy working for the Crown who had absconded with some of the first Prof. Griffin's formula. The villainous version of the Invisible Man seen in this film, an agent working for the Fantom who likewise stole the invisibility formula, was revealed in the novelization to be the Fantom's main henchman Sanderson Reed, who was seen in the first act of both the movie and novelization (but only identified as the evil Invisible Man in the latter).

The "Tom Sawyer" of the film is the grandson of Mark Twain's Tom Sawyer. The date of this film is too late in time for the original Sawyer to still be a young adult at this point, but there is good reason to suspect that a grandchild might have grown up to become a U.S. Secret Service agent.

Creative mythographer Gordon Long, a Wild Hunt Press staff member who aided with the research and para-scholarship for this anthology, made the following observations regarding the connection between the Tom Sawyer of Twain's novels (i.e., "Book Tom") and the version seen in the *LXG* movie (i.e., "Film Tom"). These observations made note of an interesting tidbit of supplementary info provided in the novelization of *LXG*, which told the same story as the film version but with a few more details revealed:

Tom Sawyer: [Actor] Shane West was about 24 when he filmed *LXG*. So, he was born circa 1875. The original Sawyer tale is set about 1845, when Tom is about 12. Now, Book Tom's dad isn't in the picture. This leads me to suspect that Book Tom might not have been in his son's life; and the son, who likewise named his own son Tom (this would be Film Tom), wasn't around either. As such, you can see why "Allan Quatermain" would be like a father figure to him. I am not proposing that these three fathers are shiftless wanderers like

Huck's dad, Pap; rather, they seem to be wandering adventurers who are good guys-- Book Tom is a good guy with wanderlust, as is Film Tom, who is a government agent.

In one of Twain's sequels, *The Adventures of Huckleberry Finn*, he runs an elaborate operation to free Jim the slave; he has a Jules Verne-like adventure in *Tom Sawyer Abroad*; and solved a murder in *Tom Sawyer, Detective*. Film Tom, in the novelization of *LXG*, mentions he was once a detective. Oh, and in a version of *The Mysterious Stranger*, Tom and Huck have adventures with Satan. All in all, the Sawyer men have a clear legacy of being wandering adventurers in the classic Wold Newton [pulp] style.

Now let's get to the story behind the Fantom. As noted above, he claimed to be Prof. James Moriarity, the "Napoleon of Crime" and arch-nemesis of Sherlock Holmes, who first appeared in Sir Arthur Conan Doyle's "The Final Problem." This faux Moriarity attempted to cash in on the notoriety and feared reputation of the Phantom of the Opera by posing as him, a detail confirmed in the novelization of this film. Despite taking Erik the Phantom as a model, the Fantom nevertheless utilized a modus operandi that was more inspired by the dreaded Fantômas, another notorious member of the criminal underworld who called Paris of that era home. This classic French pulp villain appeared in a series of 44 novels written by Marcel Allain (1885–1969) and Pierre Souvestre (1874–1914). Subsequent exploits of Fantômas have been published by Black Coat Press since the turn of the current century, including short stories featuring the character in various volumes of the annual *Tales of the Shadowmen* anthologies since they began being published in 2003.

Both the original Fantômas and the Fantom served as inspiration for the career of a second super-criminal who called himself Fantômas and was active in Paris during the 1960s. This version of the villain displayed his influence from the Fantom by wearing a blue mask and black gloves, the use of various technological devices, and acting much more "over the top." The 1960s version of the Fantom – who simply called himself Fantômas -- had his exploits chronicled via a trilogy of movies in French cinema directed by André Hunebelle, the first being released in 1963.

The Fantom was eventually to reveal himself as "James Moriarty," though that clearly could not have been the real deal. So, who was the "Moriarity" of this film regarding WHU canon? This was likewise explained by James Bojaciuk in a manner that works for both the film's plot and for canon in the WHU, which also connects him to The Society from Big Finish's Sherlock Holmes audio dramas: mind-altering techniques were clearly within the means of The Society, so it was likely the faux Moriarty was simply a skilled member of that organization who was brainwashed into adopting and actually believing this false identity, all to cash in on the Phantom of the Opera's reputation and to eventually bedevil Sherlock Holmes.

Finally, we get to the truly relevant member of this team of doppelgangers: Who was the stand-in for Dorian Gray in this film, and what connection to the real Dorian may he have had?

Much research points to a temporal (or time) clone of another individual who was known to have acquired immortality based on a portrait being painted of him, though in his case this was also done to suppress his curse of lycanthropy. That individual would be Quentin Collins, the anti-hero werewolf of the *Dark Shadows* mythos. This conclusion came with the aid of anthology contributor Kevin Heim's para-scholarly musings, with additional input from contributor David MacDowell Blue.

The major question to be answered here is how this can be reconciled with two things seen in the film. First, the death of the "Dorian Gray" at the end of this movie via the destruction of his immortality-sustaining portrait during his sword battle with Vampirella, a.k.a., the faux Mina Harker of this movie. Second, the swordsmanship skills wielded by Dorian during the above described battle, which surpassed the capabilities of the Quentin Collins we know.

As conjectured by the editor and co-author of this work (Christofer Nigro), most likely the portrait-dependent immortal posing as Dorian Gray in this film was a divergent "time clone" of Quentin Collins, i.e., a doppelganger who was created because of the "mainstream" Quentin's forays through the alternate timelines referred to in the *Dark Shadows* chronicles as Parallel Time.

As contributor David MacDowell Blue, an expert on all things vampiric, explains when asked about the possibility of this: "There were several Quentin Collins in the family, but only one (evidently) with a magical portrait. His great uncle (and namesake) built a 'stairway through time' which could have had all sorts of bizarre side effects."

One of the side effects of these travels through time resulted in a divergent temporal counterpart, or "time clone," of the portrait-owning Quentin Collins to end up on the timeline of the "mainstream" WHU at some point in the 18th century. The exact circumstances of how that happened remain unclear at this writing.

Importantly, though, his portrait functioned differently in one prominent way from what was apparent with the real Dorian Gray. Whereas the latter depended on keeping his portrait physically intact to maintain its immortality-conferring benefits, this temporal counterpart of Quentin Collins was unable to look directly at the unwrapped canvas of his portrait otherwise he would be instantly destroyed, with the painting shedding all its accumulated "scars" and reverting to its original youthful appearance. In the divergent timeline from whence this version of Quentin Collins hailed, the portrait either received an additional curse via the handiwork of its creator Charles Delaware Tate and the vile warlock Count Petofi or had a new one conferred upon it later from sources unknown, possibly occurring *after* he and the portrait entered the "mainstream" timeline.

Nevertheless, this time clone of Quentin was forced to take on various aliases to avoid running into the various members of the Collins family native to that timeline and era, particularly the portrait owning man of that name to which his existence directly diverged from. Now let us consider how Vampirella was also known to have traveled back in time, during which she was forced to take on different identities to prevent scribes of that period from making paradoxical recordings of her existence prior to her emergence in her familiar guise circa late 1960s. Hence, she would have had ample opportunities to encounter this doppelganger of Quentin Collins in one of his previous guises. This would have led to their combination of sexual liaisons and falling outs.

That provides the explanation as to why Vampi, in her guise of "Mina Harker," and the time clone of Quentin Collins in his guise of "Dorian Gray," recognized each other upon the former's excursion back to 1899 from (presumably) some point in the future for the mission that brought them together in *LXG*.

But how did the Quentin Collins time clone acquire the swordsmanship skills that his counterpart who was indigenous to the "mainstream" timeline lacked?

That could be explained simply. At some point, the Quentin Collins time clone contacted and joined the Cult of Fama. He would obviously have been using some other guise at the time (it would be a long time before he took the identity of Dorian Gray). During his association with the Cult towards the last three decades of the 19th century, he met the real Dorian Gray and the two struck a deal. Dorian taught the Quentin time clone the art of swordsmanship – which he learned quite well, and quickly at that (Quentin Collins was a natural fighter) – in exchange for the latter agreeing to do him a favor whenever the need may arise in the future.

341

When The Society attempted to recruit Dorian Gray into their ranks for the events leading towards New Year's 1900 in London, the real Dorian wanted no part of that, as his own debauched interests did not include widescale destruction or taking over the world. He also did not want to run afoul of The Society, however. Hence, he called in his favor: The Quentin Collins time clone took on his identity while the real Dorian quietly exited the country for fun times elsewhere in the world (some of which was recorded in the Big Finish audio series). It was something the far more power-hungry Collins man had no problem with at any rate, as he believed he could use the favor he owed to his advantage by standing in for Gray in this instance.

The plan which The Society had for him, of course, was for "Dorian" to infiltrate the imposter League that the Crown hastily pulled together to challenge the Fantom. It was then that he met the time-traveling Vampi in her Mina Harker guise, and the two were able to recognize each other right through their respective disguises due to their history together.

Why didn't Vampi recognize "a" Quentin Collins when she met the version indigenous to this timeline many decades later during the *Dark Shadows/Vampirella* mini-series published by Dynamite? It is possible Vampi had discovered at some point that she hadn't slain the "real" Quentin Collins on her native timeline, and thus knew he wasn't the "same" individual, technically speaking; or, the events of this mini-series occurred prior to her going back to the late 1890s.

There are two more important and interrelated questions to be considered here prior to moving on to the next entry.

Why might the Crown want to establish a doppelganger League to handle The Society-backed threat of the Fantom? Why not the originals? That is simple enough to answer. The team consisting of the Real McCoys had split up following the tumultuous events of the second *League of Extraordinary Gentlemen* comic book series.

Why recruit individuals to serve as effective doppelgangers of the first team, instead of just forming an entirely new team that didn't pretend to be otherwise? The Crown clearly wanted the team to be able to pass itself as the original personas, albeit with Dorian Gray and Tom Sawyer added to the mix, to prevent The Society from knowing that the main team was no longer protecting London. Their major victories against the real Prof. James Moriarity and the Martian invasion established quite a rep for them, and the British government wisely wanted that psychological advantage to be retained against the likes of The Society. This did indeed end up giving the new crew an extra edge to aid them in succeeding, despite the unexpected betrayal by the "Dorian Gray" stand-in.

This film has been referenced as fictional in other timeline chronicles. It has also been paid homage to numerous times in other films and on television. Further, it has also been spoofed in *Lust for Dracula*, *The Venture Bros.*, *The Simpsons*, and *2 Broke Girls*.

1899--*THE LEAGUE OF EXTRAORDINARY GENTLEMEN* (a.k.a., *LXG*, novelization of the film by Kevin J. Anderson, working from James Dale Robinson's screenplay) –This novelization of the movie version tells essentially the same story, but with details added, some of which shed some supplementary light on certain events that weren't made fully clear in the film, including some pertaining to the faux Dorian Gray (i.e., the Quentin Collins time clone). Other details were added from the comic book version, along with references to or recollections of past recorded incidents related to the real individuals whom this "imposter" League were impersonating. This included Tom Sawyer lamenting that the childhood friend of his killed by the Fantom was Huckleberry Finn. That was either apocryphal, or a reference to the possibility that this Tom's childhood friend was the original Huckleberry Finn's grandson, but we may never know for certain and the matter is too irrelevant to this anthology's focus to conjecture upon further.

These details were likely added by the Kevin Anderson of the WHU to further conceal the fact that these were not the bona fides they purported to be, while others were false info added to attempt to build bridges between the novelization of *LXG* and the very different story told in the comic book. A prominent example of false info added to make such connections was an attempt to say that Prince Dakkar (i.e., The Persian posing as him for this adventure) was the same "Captain Nemo" as the Caucasian holder of that alias who controlled the *Nautilus* in Verne's *20,000 Leagues Under the Sea* (he was not; there are some creative mythographers who long ago conjectured that the first individual to take that alias was the original Prof. James Moriarity; a third is conjectured to have been Arthur

Gordon Pym, the maritime adventurer from Edgar Allan Poe's novel *The Narrative of Arthur Gordon Pym of Nantucket*).

Also, additional crossover references to fantastic individuals and elements in the European Victorian era were made, such as refs to amontillado (the titular liquor of Edgar Allan Poe's short horror story "The Cask of Amontillado") and the astronomer Ogilvy's discovery of "flashes" appearing on the surface of Mars that signaled the Sarmak/Mollusc invasion fleet seen in H.G. Wells' *The War of the Worlds* (which actually occurred a year before 1899, and was an incident that involved the League of Extraordinary Gentlemen whom this new team was impersonating; hence, its reference here was anachronistic and obviously just a detail added by the author).

Regarding Dorian Gray, in this book it was said that Gray had had a falling out with his friend Oscar Wilde, implicitly due to the way the author portrayed the former in his biography disguised as a fictional novel. This is known to be false, since it has been made clear in other sources, including the Big Finish audio drama "This World Our Hell," that Dorian had no problem with Wilde's honest depiction of him, and that he had tweaked the ending at his friend's request.

Most likely, the disguised Quentin Collins time clone made that comment either to humor the teammates he was about to betray, or to secretly discourage them from mentioning anything to Wilde about becoming acquainted with his friend "Dorian" should they run into the author, who could have compromised the ruse (actually, there was no chance of that happening, since Wilde was then exiled to

France and in poor health; he would die of meningitis the following year in Paris, with the real Dorian Gray at his side; it's possible, however, that the Quentin Collins time clone was unaware that Wilde was permanently expiated from London, as well as the status of his health).

It was also revealed in this novelization that the faux Dorian Gray had copies of the brutal and perverse oeuvre of the Marquis de Sade, along with illustrated guides to sadomasochism, in his personal library. This provides further indication that the Quentin Collins time clone was a nasty customer who made a good stand-in for Dorian Gray, and was thoroughly corrupt even by the real Gray's standards (not that anyone who owns copies of such books are automatically evil and corrupt, but the observed behavior of this character made it clear that the matter was true in his case).

**Circa 1900--*THE CONFESSIONS OF DORIAN GRAY*:
"THIS WORLD OUR HELL" (audio drama, Big Finish) --**
Dorian visits Oscar Wilde on his deathbed in Paris.

**1900--*THE CONFESSIONS OF DORIAN GRAY*:
"BANSHEE" (audio drama, Big Finish) --**County Meath. Dorian
visits a haunted house in Ireland.

Circa 1911--*THE WORLDS OF BIG FINISH*: "THE ADVENTURES OF THE BLOOMSBURY BOMBERS" (audio drama, Big Finish) --Dorian makes a cameo at the end of this Sherlock Holmes mystery.

December 25th, 1912--*THE CONFESSIONS OF DORIAN GRAY*: "GHOSTS OF CHRISTMAS PAST" (audio drama, Big Finish) --When Dorian's portrait is stolen, the thief blackmails Dorian to kill the Great Detective, Sherlock Holmes.

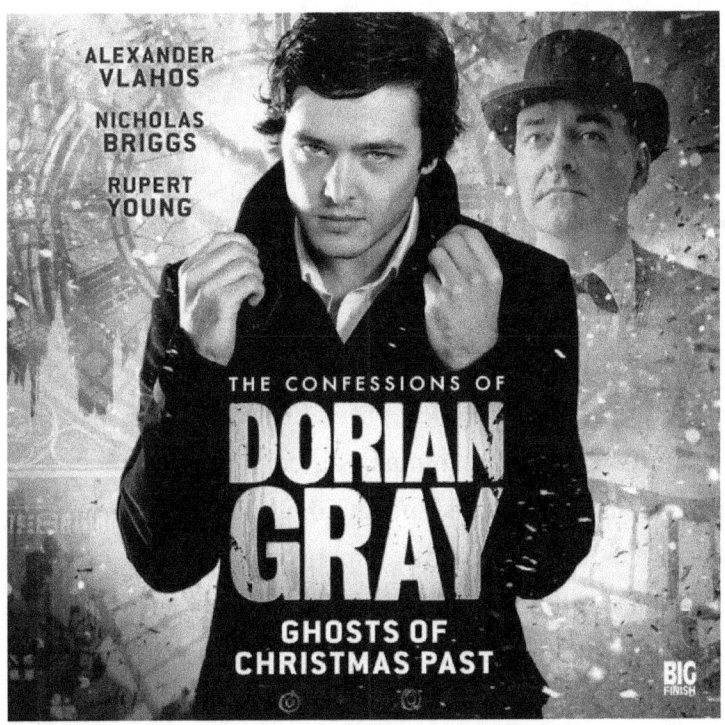

1913--*THE CONFESSIONS OF DORIAN GRAY:* "THE IMMORTAL GAME" (audio drama, Big Finish) --Brighton. Gray encounters Jekyll and Hyde.

1913--*LOST GIRLS* (graphic novel by Alan Moore and Melinda Gebbie, first six chapters originally serialized in Steve Bissette's *Taboo* magazine; later published in complete form in various formats by Tundra and Top Shelf Productions) –Three women previously depicted as girls in classic children's fantasy novels -- Alice Liddell (now Lady Fairchild; of Lewis Carroll's *Alice's Adventures in Wonderland* and *Through the Looking Glass*), Dorothy Gale (of L. Frank Baum's *The Wonderful Wizard of Oz* &

DORIAN GRAY: DARKER SHADES

subsequent books in the series), and Wendy Darling (of Neverland, from J.M. Barrie's *Peter and Wendy*) meet, share stories of their youthful sexual exploits, and engage in new ones with each other and various individuals they meet in Austria at the Hotel Himmelgarten as World War I begins. One such "flashback" exploit involves an encounter with Dorian Gray and Basil Hallward.

Since the erotic exploits these three older versions of Alice, Dorothy, and Wendy tell about their pasts differ markedly from the fantastic adventures chronicled in many other sources. As these events portray dramatic but mundane analogues of their recorded youthful exploits, with the fantastic elements present only in metaphorical fashion, it's quite possible these are alternate universe versions of the characters, and not the iterations from the WHU, or even the CU proper. If such is the case, then the Dorian Gray and Basil Hallward who make a brief but notable appearance in the story are likewise alternate reality versions. However, this appearance of Dorian Gray is nevertheless included here for the sake of completism, allowing readers to interpret it as they wish.

1915--*THE CONFESSIONS OF DORIAN GRAY*: "ANGEL OF WAR" (audio drama, Big Finish) --France. Dorian in World War I.

Winter - Summer 1919--*DORIAN GRAY: DARKER SHADES* -- "THE HALLWARD RESTORATIONS" (short story by Peter Rawlik) --A Boston artist, Richard Pickman, finds himself hired by a mysterious society to restore the paintings of Basil Hallward. SPOILERS: Go back and read the story first in this very anthology!

The man who hires the artist is Dorian Gray, calling himself Lord Kelso. Hallward's soul had been trapped within a portrait, and then released using some very Lovecraftian phrasing. The story is being told by the artist to his friend, Dr. Herbert West, and they conclude to conspire together in the future. Richard Pickman is, of course, from H.P. Lovecraft's short story, "Pickman's Model." Herbert West is from Lovecraft's novella, "Herbert West—Reanimator." This story further ties into Peter's continuing series of Lovecraft inspired novels, which includes (to date) *Reanimators* and *The Weird Company*.

October 1920--*THE CONFESSIONS OF DORIAN GRAY*: "THE PRIME OF DEACON BRODIE" (audio drama, Big Finish) --Edinburgh. Dorian reunites with a WWI comrade.

Summer 1921--*TALES OF THE SHADOWMEN VOLUME 2*: *GENTLEMEN OF THE NIGHT* -- "A JEST, TO PASS THE TIME" (short story by Jess Nevins) --A mysterious person sends the world's greatest thieves out to get the fabled Moonstone. This story by Jess Nevins is packed full of subtle and overt crossovers. You could simply buy the book and read it yourself, but unless you are familiar with film and literature of the era, chances are you won't catch them all yourself. Basil Hallward from *The Picture of Dorian Gray* is among the many crossover references.

1927--*THE WORLDS OF BIG FINISH*: "THE FEAST OF MAGOG" (audio drama, Big Finish) –Dorian Gray and Sherlock Holmes meet again, and work with the WHU version of real life occultist Evan Morgan. This is a continuation of the story started in "The Adventure of the Bloomsbury Bomber" and is part of a bigger *Worlds of Big Finish* crossover event that also features Iris Wildthyme, Abby & Zara, Vienna Salvatori, and Bernice Summerfield.

1929--*THE CONFESSIONS OF DORIAN GRAY*: **"HIS DYING BREATH" (audio drama, Big Finish)** --London. Dorian is accused of a string of murders.

Summer 1933--*A BOOK OF WIZARDS* -- "SORCERER CONJURER WIZARD WITCH" (short story by Kim Newman) --Charles Beauregard of the Diogenes Club becomes involved in a wizard war. As usual, Kim Newman packs another story chock full of crossover goodness. Let's discuss who we have here.

By now, I don't think I need to explain Lovecraft's Cthulhu Mythos or Dracula. Carnacki is the famed Ghost Finder.

Chandu is the main character of a 1930s radio series and two film serials. Both the serials and the radio show are considered different perspectives of the same series, so the Chandu of this tale is the character from both radio and film.

The Magician is a 1908 novel by W. Somerset Maugham. It is a story loosely based on true life occultist Aleister Crowley.

Rosemary's Baby is a classic movie (based on a novel) about a woman impregnated by the Devil.

"A Visit to Anselm Oakes" is another story featuring a character based on Crowley, this time written by Christopher Isherwood.

The Black Cat is another classic horror film.

Casting the Runes is a collection of ghost stories by Montague Rhodes James.

The Picture of Dorian Gray is Oscar Wilde's classic tale of the man who was immortal, while his picture aged.

Varney the Vampire; or, the Feast of Blood by is one of the earliest vampire tales (first serialized from 1845-47), written by James Malcolm Rhymer and Thomas Peckett Prest (the latter today often described as "the Stephen King of his era"), with the vampire Sir Francis Varney being one of the oldest vampire characters in literature, predating Bram Stoker's *Dracula* by 52 years.

Pandora and the Flying Dutchman is a tale of a woman named Pandora (who isn't the one with the box), who becomes involved in events involving the legendary ghost.

The Department of Queer Complaints from Carter Dickson is a secret group that solves cases that are unusual and unexplained.

"Green Tea" is a story by J. Sheridan Le Fanu, the author of *Carmilla*, another classic vampire book. And speaking of which, *Carmilla* is, of course, one of the first vampire books to have survived to today, having preceded Stoker's *Dracula* by decades.

The Vampyre is the book, authored by Dr. John Polidori (previously mis-credited to Lord Byron), which features the vampire Lord Ruthven, who not only likely wrote *The Ruthvenian* (the vampire bible), but may also have been Angelus, a.k.a., Angel (real name: Liam) from the classic TV series *Buffy the Vampire Slayer* and its spin-off *Angel*.

Dr. Silence is Algernon Blackwood's occult detective.

The Dream Detective is Sax Rohmer's occult detective, Morris Klaw.

The Secrets of Dr. Taverner are the collected short story adventures of "the occult Sherlock Holmes," written by real life occultist and ceremonial magician Dion Fortune, who also happened to be a prolific author of both fiction and non-fiction. Dr. Taverner was based on Fortune's real-life mentor in the magical arts, the Irish exorcist and Freemason Theodore Moriarity (no relation to the infamous mathematician and crime lord by that name!). Hence, Taverner can be considered the WHU counterpart of Theodore Moriarity.

And *Some Ghost Stories* is a reference to a collection of stories from Alfred McLelland Burrage.

Suffice to say, all those series are in the WHU.

1939--*THE CONFESSIONS OF DORIAN GRAY*: "MURDER ON 81ST STREET" (audio drama, Big Finish) --New York. Dorian encounters the Golem of Prague. This is a creature of folklore, revealed to exist within the WHU.

1940--*THE CONFESSIONS OF DORIAN GRAY*: "THE HOUSES IN BETWEEN" (audio drama, Big Finish) --London. As bombs fall, Dorian's past is catching up to him.

December 24th, 1947--*THE CONFESSIONS OF DORIAN GRAY*: "FROSTBITE" (audio drama, Big Finish) --New York City. Dorian encounters Mina Harker (evidently the real one), revealing a long-standing enmity between the two.

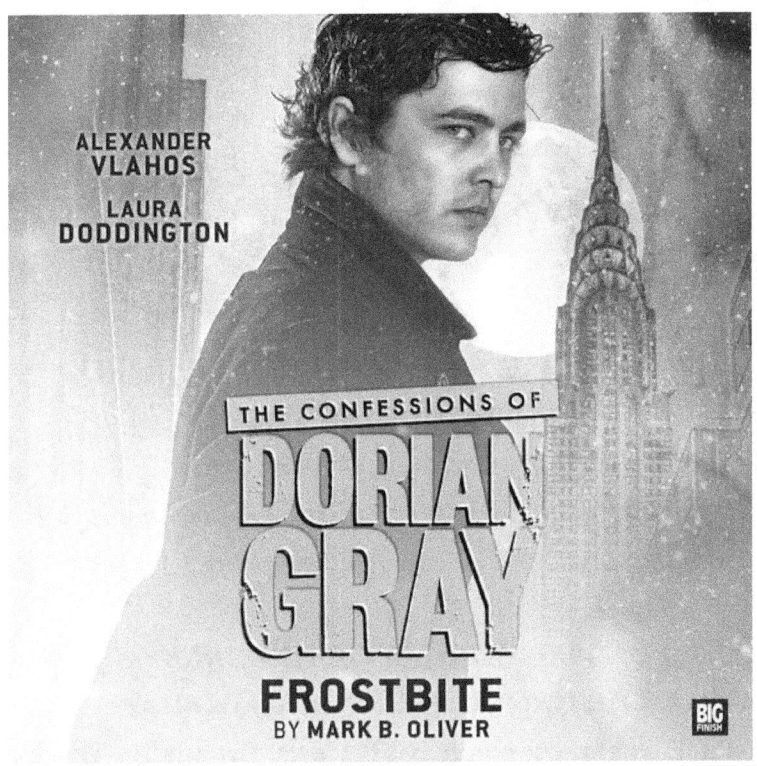

1948--*THE CONFESSIONS OF DORIAN GRAY*: "THE VALLEY OF NIGHTMARES" (audio drama, Big Finish) --Los Angeles. Dorian in Hollywood.

1948--*DORIAN GRAY: DARKER SHADES* -- "DORIAN AT THE GROVE; OR FINDING DORIAN WITHIN" (short story/memoir by T. Casey Brennan) --Birth of author and anthology contributor T. Casey Brennan.

1949--*THE CONFESSIONS OF DORIAN GRAY*: "THE LIVING IMAGE" (audio drama, Big Finish) --England. Dorian wishes his life was more mundane like the couple he meets on a train.

1956--*THE CONFESSIONS OF DORIAN GRAY:* "THE TWITTERING OF SPARROWS" (audio drama, Big Finish) -- Dorian is in Singapore.

1959--*DORIAN GRAY: DARKER SHADES* -- "DORIAN AT THE GROVE; OR FINDING DORIAN WITHIN" (short story/memoir by T. Casey Brennan) --Future author T. Casey Brennan discovers Oscar Wilde's *The Picture of Dorian Gray*. His father becomes involved in the CIA's notorious MKULTRA Project.

November 22nd, 1963—*DORIAN GRAY: DARKER SHADES* -- "DORIAN AT THE GROVE; OR FINDING DORIAN WITHIN" (short story/memoir by T. Casey Brennan) --Death of JFK, and T. Casey's possible involvement in it due to the coercive machinations of the MKULTRA Project.

1964--*THE CONFESSIONS OF DORIAN GRAY*: "THE LORD OF MISRULE" (audio drama, Big Finish) --England. Dorian is a rock star, as so many immortals seem to become in the late 20th century.

1965--*DARK SHADOWS*: "THE DARKEST SHADOW" (audio drama, Big Finish) --Dorian meets Quentin Collins, and they have a conversation.

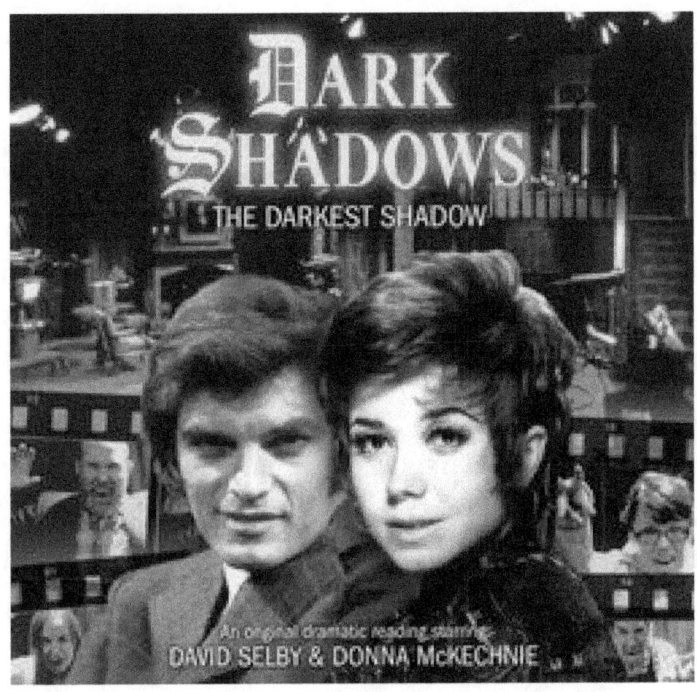

1968--*THE CONFESSIONS OF DORIAN GRAY*: "THE ENIGMA OF DORIAN GRAY" (audio drama, Big Finish) -- Salford. Returning to one of his old universities, Dorian has his first encounter with artificial intelligence.

1970--*DARK SHADOWS* (TV series) --By this period, the portrait of Quentin Collins had been painted over with a landscape. Dr. Julia Hoffman receives the picture from Angelique, who is married to the current owner of the painting, Sky Rumson. Julia uncovers the hidden portrait beneath and uses it to prove her theory that amnesiac Grant Douglas is an immortal Quentin Collins.

Spring 1973--*THE EVIL IN PEMBERLEY HOUSE* (novel by Philip José Farmer and Win Scott Eckert) --Patricia Wildman is the daughter of the late Doctor Clark Wildman, better known to the world as the globe-trotting adventurer, scientist, surgeon, crime-buster, and Renaissance man, Doc Savage. After the death of her husband, Patricia learns that she is heir to the estate in England known as Pemberley House, the very same house made famous from the novel by Jane Austen, *Pride and Prejudice.*

She travels there to claim her inheritance, where she finds herself being attacked by thugs and dealing with a legendary ghost, as well as strange distant relatives who all seem to have shady motives. This book is part of a series of stories featuring Patricia Wildman, the daughter of Doc Savage. In the book, Patricia refers to her father's adventure on an Antarctic expedition, a reference to the sci-fi novella *Who Goes There?* by John W. Campbell Jr., later made into various movie versions titled *The Thing* (the full title of the 1950s film version was *The Thing from Another World*), as well as a Dark Horse comic book mini-series based on the 1982 John Carpenter film version; a prequel to Carpenter's version, also titled *The Thing,* was released in 2011.

Patricia also speaks of one of his colleague's Antarctic expeditions, as told in Lovecraft's novella *At the Mountains of Madness.* Also, in the Pemberley Library is a copy of the book *De Vermis Mysteriis* from the Lovecraft mythos. Another book is *How I Did It* by Victor Frankenstein (descendant Frederick Frankenstein in the WHU), originally from the film *Young Frankenstein.* And another is *The Ruthvenian,* named for Lord Ruthven, from Dr. John

Polidori's *The Vampyre*. Pemberley House also has a painting by
Basil Hallward, from *The Picture of Dorian Gray*.

1974--*THE CONFESSIONS OF DORIAN GRAY:* "FREYA" (audio drama, Big Finish) --Scandinavia. Dorian and a woman he is attempting to rescue are hunted by something.

1974--*THE CONFESSIONS OF DORIAN GRAY*: "THE ABYSMAL SEA" (audio drama, Big Finish) --Greece. Dorian and his paramour Alyssa take a vacation to save their failing relationship, and encounter something in the sea.

October 1976—*DORIAN GRAY: DARKER SHADES* -- "A GRAY CLOUD OVER CHICAGO" (novella by Christofer Nigro) --Dorian is in Chicago trying to get his portrait restored once more. This leads to an unlikely friendship with J.J. Evans (of the TV series *Good Times*) and encounters with old foes of both: Dracula-Mordante (a powerful soul-clone of Vlad Dracula, i.e., Dracula-Prime); and Mad Dog, leader of the dangerous Chicago-based street gang Satan's Knights. This story is crossover heavy. I may miss a few, but hopefully not since the author is also the editor for (and co-author of) this timeline. **Note:** Spoilers totally abound in this entry, so you should read Nigro's novella first!

Jimmy and Mike are WHU versions of siblings J.J. and Michael Evans from the sitcom *Good Times*. Satan's Knights, their lethal leader Mad Dog, and his gangbanger lackeys Neck Bone and Sweet Pea (the latter revealed to have died at a point prior to this story) are from the classic two-part episode of *Good Times* called "The Gang." Jimmy's sister Selma and mother are referenced, but not seen (Selma is a WHU counterpart of Thelma Evans from *Good Times*). James Sr., the Evans' deceased patriarch, appears as a ghost summoned to the Earth plane to defend his son from Dracula in the last act of this novella. The Noir Jesus painting is a WHU version of the canvas from the "Black Jesus" episode of *Good Times* (where it's referred to eponymously). These characters have been re-named to make it clear they are pastiches of the familiar sitcom family, and not the "originals" as seen in the TV series.

This story makes the soul-clone theory of Chuck Loridans canon in the WHU. The soul-clone theory appears on the *MONSTAAH* website created by Chuck Loridans (in an article describing the soul-clone theory and the Children of the Night Timeline, both authored by Chuck), and now maintained by Christofer Nigro (who has incorporated it into articles of his own, as well as the Trinity of Terror Timeline, which he built from the foundation of Chuck's timeline). The soul-clone theory has been used as a crossover convention by Win Scott Eckert and Sean Lee Levin for their Wold Newton Universe and Crossover Universe websites; and their books in the four-volume series, *Crossovers: A Secret Chronology of the World.* It has also been used by this timeline co-author, Robert E. Wronski, Jr., for his *Television Crossover Universe* website and books, and for *The Horror Crossover Encyclopedia* published by 18thWall Productions. This story, also for the first time, makes certain soul-clones from the *MONSTAAH* website canon in the WHU.

For the record, the soul-clones Dracula-Lejos, Dracula-Latos, Dracula-Grodimn, Dracula-Grimpod ("the silly old scientist who invented the cough syrup that causes mortals to cough"), Dracula-Denrom, and Dracula-Kai (the first four from the Universal movie & TV horror stable; the last two from Hammer's cinematic stable) were first identified and coined by Chuck Loridans for his "Children of the Night" Timeline on the original MONSTAAH website. They have since been included in WHU canon by this timeline's co-author Christofer Nigro for his "Trinity of Terror" Timeline, which is an extrapolation of the framework introduced by Chuck. Dracula-

Mathias was identified and coined by Mike Ongsingco for his "Castlevania Timeline" that first appeared on the original MONSTAAH site (and since incorporated into the "Trinity of Terror" Timeline). The soul-clones Dracula-Mordante, Dracula-Mamuwalde, and Dracula-Rominoff were identified and coined by co-author C.N. of this timeline.

Without further ado, let us meet the soul-clones mentioned in this story:

Dracula-Lejos: Lejos is the Dracula seen in the Universal films portrayed by Bela Lugosi. This timeline co-author Robert E. Wronski, Jr. had previously felt, as expressed in *The Horror Crossover Universe*, that the Universal Dracula portrayed by John Carradine in the two *House of...* films (Universal's *House of Frankenstein* and *House of Dracula*) was the same Dracula portrayed by Bela Lugosi, but MONSTAAH identifies them as being distinct soul-clones.

Dracula-Lejos

Dracula-Latos: The Dracula portrayed by John Carradine, both in the Universal films and movies outside of Universal's oeuvre (such as *Billy the Kid Versus Dracula*), is the soul-clone Chuck Loridans has christened Dracula-Latos.

Dracula-Latos

Dracula-Mordante: Mordante is the Dracula soul-clone appearing in this story, and hence is not Dracula-Prime, i.e., the original Dracula, Count (formerly Prince) Vlad Tepes Dracula himself. This soul-clone was introduced in Warren Publishing's comic magazines during the early 1970s, both as a brief love interest and recurring major nemesis of Vampirella in her own magazine's strip; and in two solo series of is own, the first in *Eerie* and the second in *Vampirella* (the latter strip was, interestingly, the only series in that comic headlined by a male).

In *The Horror Crossover Universe*, I (Robert E. Wronski Jr.) had established the Dracula from that series to be the true Dracula, but this story invalidates my previous theory. This novella notes that Mordante is also said to be part of the Collins family. This is a reference to *Dark Shadows*, but also a nod to anthology contributor T. Casey Brennan, who had intended Warren's version of Dracula from *Vampirella* to be inspired by Barnabas Collins in appearance and mannerisms once he took over the writing on the character (Dracula-Mordante was created by Archie Goodwin, though T. Casey tweaked Archie's origin account for the Vampire Lord and introduced new elements into his saga, such as the Conjuress and his conflicted persona).

According to author Christofer Nigro's Dracula-Mordante Timeline on the *MONSTAAH* website (soon to get a new home!), Mordante is also the Dracula seen in the films *Dracula 3D* (2012), *Bram Stoker's Dracula* (1992), and comics from Atlas/Seaboard (*Fright* #1), Eternity Comics (*The Ghosts of Dracula* mini-series),

Harris Comics, and Dynamite Entertainment. Dracula-Mordante was proposed for MONSTAAH by Christofer Nigro and was introduced on The Trinity of Terror Timeline. The Trinity of Terror Timeline incorporates Chuck Loridans' original Children of the Night Timeline and includes additional material added by Nigro that is only applicable to the WHU. Both timelines can be found on the *MONSTAAH* website, with Chuck's original timeline also having its own home on WordPress (as of this writing, it can be located at: https://childrenofthenightclassic.wordpress.com/2016/04/06/main-page/).

Dracula-Mordante facing off against the Blood Queen.

Dracula-Denrom: This is the Dracula portrayed by Sir Christopher Lee in the Hammer film series, beginning with *Horror of Dracula* [a.k.a., *Dracula* 1958] and continuing through all but the final Hammer Dracula film (Lee's last film for Hammer being *The Satanic Rites of Dracula*).

Dracula-Denrom

Dracula-Grodimn: The soul-clone referred to as "Talbot" in this story. He was the version of Dracula as portrayed by Lon Chaney Jr. in Universal's *Son of Dracula* film (and the first to be seen using the "Alucard" alias). Chaney, of course, also played Larry Talbot in *The Wolf Man* and all subsequent Universal films portraying the character. Dracula-Grodimn was thought up by MONSTAAH creator Chuck Loridans for his original Children of the Night Timeline. He was referred to as "Talbot" in the story because part of Chuck's theory -- since incorporated into the CU proper as well as the WHU -- is that Dracula-Grodimn was Sir John Talbot Jr., the older brother of Larry Talbot, who was reported as recently killed in *The Wolf Man* but was actually transformed into a soul-clone by Dracula-Prime.

Dracula-Grodimn (Sir John Talbot II)

Dracula-Mamuwalde: This is the African Prince Mamuwalde, who was transformed into a soul-clone by Dracula-Prime when he made the mistake of meeting with the Vampire Lord (not realizing what he really was) circa 1780 in an ill-fated venture to acquire the Count's aid in ending the slave trade. The Prince was insensitively nicknamed "Blacula" by the Count before being placed in a coffin, where he slumbered in suspended animation and was later accidentally awakened in Los Angeles circa 1972. Mamuwalde's willpower was sufficient that he retained most of his own memories and personality traits despite Dracula-Prime's attempt to implant imprints of his own during the soul-clone creation process and was thus a "failed" soul-clone and thus his own vampire from the get-go. Dracula-Mamuwalde's saga was told in the 1972 film *Blacula* and its 1973 sequel *Scream, Blacula, Scream*, where he was depicted onscreen by William H. Marshall.

Dracula-Mamuwalde (a.k.a., "Blacula")

Dracula-Kai: Kai (sometimes spelled "Kah" in English) is a Chinese wizard and Taoist monk who was transformed into a soul-clone by Dracula-Prime circa 1804. For a century, this soul-clone served as the High Priest of the Temple of the Seven Vampires, controlling a Chinese strain of the Undead to prey upon peasant farmers in rural regions of China. At the end of that reign, the Kai soul-clone and his vampiric legions were defeated by Prof. Lawrence Van Helsing, his son Leyland, and Hsi Ching & his seven siblings, a family of formidable martial artists. This was depicted in the 1974 Hammer/Shaw Brothers co-production *The Legend of the 7 Golden Vampires* (released in America five years later by Dynamite Films as *The 7 Brothers Meet Dracula*, its title referred to as *The 7 Brothers and their One Sister Meet Dracula* in the U.S. trailer to acknowledge the female sibling of the Ching family, Mei Kwei; it was released in Far East theaters as *Dracula and the 7 Golden Vampires*). Dracula-Kai was portrayed in the film by Chan Shen.

Dracula-Kai

Dracula-Prime transforming Kai into a soul-clone.

Dracula-Rominoff: This is the soul-clone that battled Prime Slayer and monster hunter *par excellence* Buffy Summers in the classic episode of *Buffy the Vampire Slayer* entitled "Buffy vs. Dracula," and is also known as the version of Dracula most often featured in DC Comics. Dracula-Rominoff has continuously battled his dhampiric warrior daughter Eva (known as both "Daughter of the Dragon" and "Daughter of Dracula") through the centuries as shown in various comic books published by Dynamite, including the *Eva, Daughter of the Dragon* one-shot (but who first appeared in the *Army of Darkness: Ash vs. the Classic Monsters* story arc, a.k.a., *Ash vs. Dracula*, originally published in *Army of Darkness* Vol. 1 #8-11; Eva has been a recurring ally of monster hunter Ash Williams ever since – and that Ash is none other than the famed protagonist of *The Evil Dead* and *Army of Darkness* movie, comic book, and video game franchises). Dracula-Rominoff is also the soul-clone who appeared in Top Cow's *Monster War* mini-series; and the version of the Lord of Vampires who, decades prior to beginning his antipathy with Buffy Summers, became an enemy of her vampiric ally and former arch-foe and paramour Spike, as mentioned in "Buffy vs. Dracula" and finally depicted in IDW's *Spike vs. Dracula* comic book mini-series.

This particular soul-clone is distinguished by his long mane of hair with no gray in it, and lack of moustache. This differentiates him from Dracula-Mordante, who is never depicted with long hair, but is instead closely cropped to his head and short; and quite often seen to be graying at the temples. Like Dracula-Mordante, Rominoff is quite a powerful soul-clone, and seems to have all Dracula-Prime's powers, including his full array of shape-shifting abilities (something not all the soul-clones possess). Dracula-Rominoff was been depicted onscreen by Rudolf Martin, both on "Buffy vs. Dracula" and the 2000 film *Dark Prince: The True Story of Dracula.*

Dracula-Rominoff

Dracula-Mathias: The 11th century warrior-alchemist Mathias Crongvist, who became the mighty Dracula soul-clone, is the central figure of the long-running *Castlevania* video game series produced by Konami, as well as its various comic book and anime spin-offs. Dracula-Mathias was accepted for MONSTAAH by Chuck Loridans based on Michael Ongsingco's Castlevania Timeline, and Chuck posted the original version of Ongsingco's timeline on the original website (it remains online at this writing on the reconstructed *MONSTAAH* website by Christofer Nigro and will follow the site to its new upcoming home on WordPress).

Dracula-Mathias (Mathias Crongvist)

Dracula-Grimpod: This rather wacky, failed but charming soul-clone was an eccentric elderly scientist/inventor whose actual quirky but harmless personality proved too much for Dracula-Prime's forced personality implants to actually turn evil (but he nevertheless believes himself to be Dracula due to those implants!). Grimpod invented a chemical enabling him to resist burning up in sunlight and a blood substitute serum similar to the one utilized by Vampirella. He was later integrated into a family of similar quirky but harmless monsters who were christened... the Munsters. And Grimpod became known as none other than Grandpa Munster.

Dracula-Grimpod (a.k.a., Grandpa Munster) holding one of his many chemical inventions.

The mystical book seen in this story comes from Warren's "Vampirella" series in the eponymous comic magazine. It is referred to there as *The Crimson Chronicles*, the *Necronomicon*-like tome used by Dracula-Mordante as the head of the main worldwide Cult of Chaos. The "mad god" Chaos and his human minions have been a major adversary for Vampi since her earliest days, and a version of Chaos has also appeared in the *Castlevania* video game series.

The "Bloody Poet" was William the Bloody, a.k.a., the anti-heroic vampire Spike from the TV series *Buffy the Vampire Slayer*, it's spin-off *Angel,* and a plethora of comic book follow-up series.

One of the characters appearing in the bar fight scene is Bad, Bad, Leroy Brown, the "baddest man in the whole damn town." He is from Jim Croce's classic eponymous song.

A character uses the term "Pardon my French." While this may seem anachronistic, considering the term didn't become popular until it was introduced in the 1980s film *Ferris Bueller's Day Off,* consider that Ferris lived in Shermer, a suburb of Chicago, where the events of this story take place. It could be that the phrase started in the projects of Chicago, and as with much of pop culture, made its way from the ghettos to the suburbs and then eventually nationwide.

This tale also ties into two other stories within this anthology. There are references to the Cult of Fama from Peter Rawlik's short story "The Hallward Restorations"; and the power drawn from the Egyptian goddess Bast to mystically enchant the Cult's immortality-conferring portraits is a concept introduced in Micah Harris' novella

Portrait of a Lady.

And Morley Cigarettes appear here. Morley appears as a cigarette brand in numerous television shows and films, most notably *The X-Files* and *Buffy the Vampire Slayer*.

There is also a reference to Gambit of the X-Men via the Thieves Guild from the Big Easy in New Orleans (though the X-Men exist in a much different form in the WHU than in the "mainstream" MU).

And though not necessarily crossovers, it should be noted that this story confirms the existence of Santa Claus in the WHU; and likewise confirms the existence of Jesus Christ, or at least (in my opinion – R.W.) a tulpa representation of Jesus.

1985--*PICTURE OF EVIL* (novel by Graham Masterson) -- Dorian doesn't appear but the portrait does.

1986--*THE CONFESSIONS OF DORIAN GRAY:* "THE HEART THAT LIVES ALONE" (audio drama, Big Finish) -- Whitby. Dorian meets his vampiric lover Tobias Matthews for the first time.

1987--*QUEST FOR DREAMS LOST* # 1 (Literacy Volunteers of Chicago) -- When two movers find that the contents of the moving truck are missing, contents that include valuable artifacts, they call on real heroes to help. Leonardo of the Teenage Mutant Ninja Turtles is sent to Central Park to retrieve Excalibur. This version of the Turtles is the original version created by Eastman and Laird.

According to the film *Turtles Forever*, they exist on the divergent timeline called Turtles Prime.

Of course, many of these mini-stories in this one-shot seem to exist in alternate realities, but considering that one person owned all these artifacts, surely, he is a man who can summon heroes from throughout time and space. Excalibur is from Arthurian legend, and thus doesn't count for crossovers since Arthurian legend in one form or another seems to exist in the history of practically every timeline.

The Trollords travel to one of the Hell Dimensions to face Charon at the river Styx to retrieve his staff. The Trollords were from an independent comic about three trolls that cheated death and thereafter find themselves pursued by the Grim Reaper while at the same time working to convince humans of the value of their lives. Due to the nature of this story, it's impossible to determine which timeline the Trollords come from, but they certainly exist within the larger Wild Hunt Multiverse (WHM). Charon, the mythical skeletal ferryman, comes from Greek mythology, which follows the same rules as Arthurian legend.

Matt Sinkage (from the independent comic *Silent Invasion*) recovers the Picture of Dorian Gray. *Silent Invasion* is an alien conspiracy story set in the 1950s that fits nicely into the main WHU timeline, which is good since obviously the Picture of Dorian Gray is solidly in the main WHU.

Adventurers from "The Realm" retrieve the ruby slippers from the Wicked Witch of Oz. *The Realm* is about a group of friends who are transported to the dimension of Azoth. The heroes may originate from the Earth of the main WHU, but at least a divergent timeline thereof; and Azoth is certainly a pocket dimension within the WHM. It's clear that the MGM film version of *The Wizard of Oz*, i.e., Oz-MGM (in contrast to Oz-Prime, which is Baum's official version, as well as many other dimensional variants), is quantum-tethered to the WHU; though Oz-Prime, Oz-WNU (the Oz from Philip José Farmer's novel *A Barnstormer in Oz*), and many other variant versions of Oz that have appeared in the myriad sources are likely quantum-tethered to it also. Of note, some of the Oz realms have ruby-colored slippers that were used for dimensional transport by Dorothy Gale, such as Oz-MGM; Oz-Prime and others, however, feature silver-colored foot gear that perform this function. Dorothy clearly had a counterpart in the WHU, and the Oz she visited must have been a pocket reality within the WHM. One problem with this story being about the film version is that the Wicked Witch should be dead, but more than one Oz sequel has portrayed a resurrected Witch.

The Wordsmith is sent for the ring of the pulp hero called The Shadow, and the story also involves the Phantom Detective, another masked pulp hero. The Wordsmith is an independent comic about a writer during the Great Depression. The Shadow has been well established as a character in the WHU. This story brings in the Phantom Detective. It's clear from the story that the Wordsmith, The Shadow, and the Phantom Detective coexist in the same timeline, which would be the main WHU.

Reacto Man retrieves the Time Machine (from the eponymous novel of H.G. Wells). Reacto Man was a superhero from an independent comic. Since the Time Machine from H.G. Wells is well established in the WHU, Reacto Man is likely also from the main WHU timeline.

Eb'nn is a raven bounty hunter from a Wild West reality of anthropomorphic talking animals. This pocket reality must exist within the WHM. He is sent to retrieve the Maltese Falcon, an object from a novel by Dashiell Hammett that was originally serialized circa 1929 in the detective pulp magazine *Black Mask*, and which introduced Dashiell's sleuth character Sam Spade (it also has a well-known film version). The Maltese Falcon and Spade also exist in the WHU.

J.B. Space of the Aniverse goes after the Pied Piper's pipe. The Aniverse is a futuristic reality of anthropomorphic talking animals which must be a part of the WHM. The Pied Piper has been established via *Tales of the Shadowmen* to be a character in the WHU that can travel through time. The Pied Piper is part of a real legend that was recorded in a classic poem by Robert Browning called *The Pied Piper of Hamelin*.

This comic features all heroes from independent comics and was created as a fundraiser for the Literacy Volunteers of Chicago.

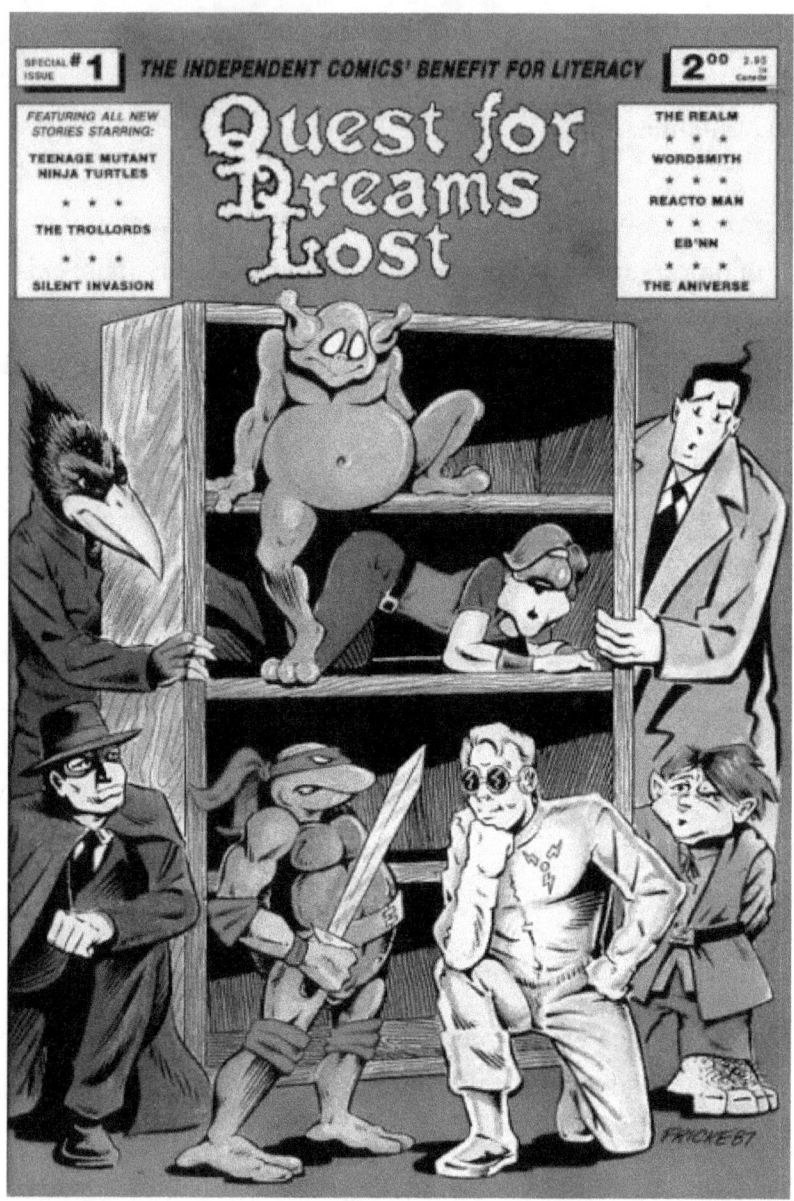

October 1989—*HELLBLAZER* VOL. 1 # 23–24 -- "LARGER THAN LIFE" (comic book, Vertigo/DC) --Jerry is a collector of unusual artifacts. Many of these are famed items of history and legend. He's even gone so far as to start collecting items from other realms. But when he starts collecting items from the Realm of Fiction, the entities of that reality come after him, and he needs the aid of John Constantine.

Hellblazer and the other Vertigo series were only loosely connected to the mainstream DC Universe (DCU). For the most part, they maintained a separate reality, and instead of operating on "comic book time," things moved in a normal time frame. Jerry has a copy of Jorkins' notes, the *Unaussprechlichen Kulten,* and the *Necronomicon* in his collection (all from Lovecraft's Cthulhu Mythos). He also has a coffin implied to be that of Dracula, and Dorian Gray's portrait.

Additionally, he has the Maltese Falcon (everyone seems to have had it at one time or another!) and remnants of the ship that chased Moby Dick (the deadly white sperm whale from Herman Melville's novel *Moby-Dick*). From other realms, he has the Mad Hatter's Hat (from Alice Liddell's Wonderland) and the corpse of the Tic-Toc Croc (of Neverland, the home dimension of Peter Pan as written by J.M. Barrie).

Jerry's shop is in the same town as the Admiral Benbow Inn, meaning they are in Black Hill Cove from Robert Louis Stevenson's classic pirate novel *Treasure Island*.

The collector also has other items from fairy tales and folklore. The Realm of Fiction is a pocket realty within the WHM where imaginary characters exist, and it may be related to the Ideaverse and H.P. Lovecraft's Dreamlands.

1995--*DARK SHADOWS* (TV series) --Barnabas Collins and Dr. Julia Hoffman have travelled to 1995 from the year 1970 where they find Quentin Collins still young and immortal, and quite mad. Of course, the portrait is also still intact.

1996--*DORIAN GRAY: DARKER SHADES*-- "DORIAN AT THE GROVE; OR FINDING DORIAN WITHIN" (short story/memoir by T. Casey Brennan) --T. Casey Brennan writes about his involvement in the CIA's notorious MKULTRA program and the JFK assassination.

October 31st, 1996--*THE CONFESSIONS OF DORIAN GRAY*: "TRICK OR TREAT" (audio drama, Big Finish) --London. Dorian didn't decorate, and thus is visited by the Trick or Treater.

Summer 1997--*WITCHBLADE: SHADES OF GRAY* #1-4 (comic book, Dynamite Entertainment and Top Cow Productions) --Detective Sara Pezzini is pursuing a murderer, but it's unclear just who the murderer may be. Dorian Gray is one of the suspected killers in this story and claims to know of a past wielder of the Witchblade.

The villain of this story isn't Gray, but rather the Comte de Saint-Germaine, a real historical figure who has been fictionalized in literature to become an immortal supernatural villain. Gray makes

399

statements that imply that he was Jack the Ripper, Spring-Heeled Jack, and Mister Hyde. There's enough evidence from other stories in the WHU to prove otherwise, but the statement still indicates that those figures were real in the WHU.

Of course, Jack the Ripper was a real serial killer, who has had an extensive mythology all his own created around him. He is known to have had many copycats and individuals filling that role in the WHU in addition to whoever the "real" (i.e., original) Jack the Ripper may have been.

Spring-Heeled Jack was a much more mythical figure than Jack the Ripper, more along the lines of the one of the many mysterious anomalous humanoids reported in paranormal lore and literature who has, like Jack the Ripper, since been incorporated into horror fiction in various incarnations. Unlike the other infamous Jack, the spring-heeled one cannot be categorized as a serial killer, as he had only one alleged murder attributed to him, that of a young prostitute named Maria Davis whom he allegedly hurled off a bridge at Jacob's Island in 1845. However, this claim has never been substantiated, nor was Davis' actual existence; the report can be traced back to Peter Haining's notorious 1977 non-fiction book *The Legend and Bizarre Crimes of Spring Heeled Jack*, which has been critiqued for reportedly fabricating some claims (including the one involving "Maria Davis") that have since become embedded in Spring-Heeled Jack lore (i.e., "fakelore").

Most of the actual recorded reports simply have Spring-Heeled Jack assaulting and terrorizing women, doing everything from groping them, to pulling their hair, to scratching them and/or tearing their clothing with his metallic claws, or even projecting what has been described as a bluish-colored bolt of "flame" in their faces which stunned and temporarily blinded them (according to the reports); at other times, he simply appeared before them and frightened them. He also occasionally assaulted men (including soldiers in one case, and many anomalous humanoids are alleged to invade military bases).

Starting in the 19th century, the character of Spring-Heeled Jack was converted into an anti-hero of sorts in various works of fiction, including a variety of penny dreadful serials thru the pens of many authors between the 1860s and 1880s, all titled *Spring-Heeled Jack; The Terror of London* (with a variety of spellings of his name & punctuation variants); and Frederick Hazleton's 1863 play *Spring-heel'd Jack; or, The Felon's Wrongs*.

Spring-Heeled Jack

Mister Hyde is from Robert Louis Stevenson's novel *The Strange Case of Doctor Jekyll and Mister Hyde* and already has a significant presence in the WHU.

Also, this story would seem to bring in a version of Sara Pezzini and the supernatural Witchblade weapon which she, and several predecessors, have wielded into the WHU.

1998--*THE CONFESSIONS OF DORIAN GRAY*: "HUMAN REMAINS" (audio drama, Big Finish) --London. Dorian finds a monster haunting a hospital.

1998--*SMOKE AND MIRRORS* -- "THE WEDDING PRESENT" (short story by Neil Gaiman) --A modern retelling. Dorian doesn't appear. Other retellings ended up in the alternate universe (AU) section, as alternate universes where the events are real but take place in later years and sometimes with genders swapped, but in this story, there are references to how the events are like the Oscar Wilde novel.

In the other retellings, the original Dorian Gray story doesn't exist as real or fiction, so I'm presuming that this story does take place in the WHU, and that the characters involved assume the novel that Wilde wrote based on the real Dorian is a fiction (much as the public does).

December 1999--*THE CONFESSIONS OF DORIAN GRAY*: "THE MAYFAIR MONSTER - PART 1" (audio drama, Big Finish) --London. People think the end of the world is coming, and they may be right.

January 2000--*THE CONFESSIONS OF DORIAN GRAY*: "THE MAYFAIR MONSTER - PART 2" (audio drama, Big Finish) –London. Conclusion of the 2-part audio drama.

February 2005--*HEX AND THE CITY* (novel by Simon R. Green) --John Taylor is hired to investigate the origins of the Nightside. Taylor and his secretary dine at a restaurant that serves exotic animals, including some acquired from Wonderland. Wonderland, of course, is one of the magical realms connected to the WHU. The Nightside is a nexus of time and space, chronicled in-depth in Greene's popular series of novels and short story collections.

There is a club that caters to all the various creatures that have been created by the Frankenstein family over the years. An auction is selling Dorian Gray's mirror. A later *Nightside* tale reveals it has the power to kill immortals.

Taylor reveals that his mentor was Thomas Carnacki. Taylor says his phone was once possessed by Kandarian demons, which originate from *The Evil Dead/Army of Darkness* film, comic book, and television series franchise.

Below the city, a boat guide is Erik, a.k.a., the Phantom of the Opera.

As usual, there is Cthulhu cult graffiti on the walls of the Nightside.

The Nightside uses tana leaves as a drug. Tanna leaves were important in the Universal film series featuring Kharis The Mummy. It may be prudent to point out that there were two different Universal Mummy characters during its Golden Age of Horror, the first being Imhotep, who appeared only in Universal's first film *The Mummy* (1932); and Kharis, who evidently had no connection to Imhotep and first appeared in the Universal film franchise starting with *The Mummy's Hand*. This is the version that the tana leaves were associated with. Okay, if one wants to get technical, Universal had *three* Mummy characters, if one were to include Kharis' alleged cousin Klaris, who appeared in *Abbott and Costello Meet the Mummy* (1955; the duo's last film together).

Imhotep I (in his guise as Ardath Bey)

Kharis

Klaris

Klaris teaches the hapless Freddie Franklin who's the boss prison-style.

The super-technical could even, in fact, argue that Universal has *six* major Mummy characters, if one were to count the three introduced long after the Golden Age had ended, during the past few decades, which will be noted here for those who may be interested in these broader aspects of the WHU:

The pulpish, action-adventure reboot of Imhotep, *The Mummy* (1999), which became popular enough to spawn a franchise trilogy (though the rebooted Imhotep only appeared again in the second film, *The Mummy Returns*), an animated series, a video game, and a spin-off film, *The Scorpion King*. The above is all considered canon in the WHU. The reboot Imhotep is considered to be a different cursed Egyptian sorcerer of the same lineage as the first, who lived at a different time but suffered a similar fate to the other due to that curse having a hereditary aspect.

Imhotep II

The fifth Universal Mummy had his origin in the ancient Far East, not ancient Egypt: The First Emperor of Qin, a.k.a., the Dragon Emperor, of the WHU (like Imhotep, he had a "real universe" counterpart) who was cursed by an ancient witch only to be revived in the 20th century to grapple with archeologist and adventurer Alex O'Connell, the son of archeologist/adventurers Rick and Evie O'Connell, who decades earlier had grappled with the Imhotep of the previous two films in the franchise. This underscores a theory by some creative mythographers that certain familial lines have a quantum-influenced "destiny" to be a certain type of adventurer, e.g., monster hunters (note the Van Helsings and Belmonts for two other prominent genealogical examples). The First Emperor of Qin appeared in the third and final film of Universal's reboot Mummy franchise, 2008's *The Mummy: Tomb of the Dragon Emperor*.

First Emperor of Qin (a.k.a., The Dragon Emperor)

The sixth Universal Mummy was the cursed ancient Egyptian sorceress princess Ahmanet (of the WHU). This femme fatale was freed in the 2010s to plague the Earth anew in Universal's ill-fated horror action-adventure flick *The Mummy* (2017), which was an aborted attempt to create a new rebooted Universal Monster shared universe franchise called "The Dark Universe."

Princess Ahmanet

Three allegedly authentic Maltese Falcons are sold. This coveted object is from Dashiell Hammett's classic detective novel of the same name, which has been filmed twice to date, and even received a cinematic comedic sequel with 1975's *The Black Bird*.

Maltese Falcon (or one of them, anyway)

It appears that Willy Wonka and Rick Blaine have opened establishments in the Nightside. Willy Wonka is the uber-eccentric genius and uber-wealthy industrial purveyor of candy and other sweet treats from Roald Dahl's classic children's book *Charlie and the Chocolate Factory*. It was later prominently filmed as *Willy Wonka and the Chocolate Factory* (and again three decades later under its original title), which essentially told the same story as in the book so is cross-canonical, with any differences being attributed to artistic license on the part of the filmmakers. The book's sequel, *Charlie and the Great Glass Elevator*, was never filmed, apparently because it was considered too weird. As for Rick Blaine, he is the savvy American expatriate who ran a popular ritzy Morocco nightclub during World War II in the classic film *Casablanca*.

There is a Prospero and Michael Scott Memorial Library. Prospero is from Shakespeare's play *The Tempest*. Michael Scott is from the American version of small screen series *The Office*. Scott is not dead, by the way.

Shadows Fall is mentioned as the possible new home of a god.

Nightside's homeless live in Rat's Alley, a reference to T.S. Eliot's poem "The Waste Land." As author and anthology contributor Micah Harris has noted regarding Elliot, "given the patchwork nature of the poem, he may be lifting it from somebody else's writing."

Also living in Rat's Alley are robots with positronic brains, a concept first proposed in the works of Isaac Asimov. Such synthetic A.I. systems were brought to full success by the 24th century of the

Classic Star Trek Future Time Track courtesy of genius roboticist Prof. Noonian Soong in the form of his twin male androids, the villainous Lore and the benevolent Data/ The latter of these went on to achieve the rank of Lieutenant Commander in Starfleet of the United Federation of Planets, and to become the Chief of Operations/science officer (third-in-command) of the Galaxy class starship *Enterprise* (Starfleet's flag ship); and its immediate Sovereign class successor, both under the command of the celebrated Captain Jean-Luc Picard. Data's saga was told in the television series *Star Trek: The Next Generation* and four motion pictures (the last of which, *Star Trek: Nemesis*, depicted Data's courageous sacrifice of his own life to save his crewmates), as well as a slew of novels and comic book series, as well as video games, which are part of WHU canon or not on a case-by-case basis. Lore's saga was told in the *Star Trek: TNG* episodes "Brothers," "Descent" Parts I and II, and "Datalore." Note that the Classic Star Trek Future is but one of many possible alternate future time tracks of the WHU.

Taylor says that he learned about fighting poisons with broccoli from the travelling doctor. He's referring to the fifth Doctor of *Doctor Who* fame, a Time Lord from a distinct universe – often called the Whoniverse – whose time-traveling exploits have invariably taken him to numerous different universes and timelines, including that of the WHU and CU proper. Later, a flashback to the 1960s features the second Doctor and his companions.

Taylor is warned about the Eaters of the Dead, a reference to a Michael Crichton novel about a Hindu abducted by Vikings.

Taylor is called a Moonchild, a reference to an Aleister Crowley novel about a wizard war.

Another drug of the Nightside is taduki, a favorite of Allan Quatermain.

In the 1960s flashback, the immortal gender-swapping nobleman/woman Orlando, of Virginia Woolf's classic 1928 novel *Orlando: A Biography*, is seen. Orlando was revealed to be a member of one of England's League of Extraordinary Gentlemen teams predating that of the most familiar 1898 version first written about by Alan Moore in the two eponymous comic book mini-series. He/she met up with Mina Harker and Allan Quatermain in Moore's and Kevin O'Neill's graphic novel follow-up *The League of Extraordinary Gentlemen: Black Dossier*, which featured an alternate universe Orlando alive during the 1950s on the same timeline where the political events of George Orwell's novel *1984* took place; and where he/she was revealed as a former lover of both Harker and Quatermain in his/her different gender identities.

December 2006 - Present at Time of Writing--*THE SECRET KNOTS* (web comic by Juan Santapau) --It's some sort of supernatural mystery. It's online. Go read it yourself if you want to know. One of the storylines involves Dorian Gray, thus bringing the Secret Knots into the WHU.

2007--*THE CONFESSIONS OF DORIAN GRAY:* "THE FALLEN KING OF BRITAIN" (audio drama, Big Finish) -- London. Dorian's workmates are dying in their sleep, and Dorian must find out why.

**December 2009 (likely just after The Unnatural Inquirer) --
JUST ANOTHER JUDGEMENT DAY (novel by Simon R. Green)**
--The Walking Man is the embodiment of the wrath of God and he
has come to the Nightside. Nightside's new authorities hire John
Taylor to stop him. The Walking Man is shown to be so powerful
that he can easily destroy a Lovecraftian horror while walking down
the street without even slowing down. (I guess God trumps Cthulhu
after all.) It's possible, from the standpoint of this anthology's editor
and co-author (that would be Christofer Nigro), that The Walking
Man, as an aspect of the wrath of God -- meaning the Supreme Being
of the Universe, not the Christian Jehovah; *The Bible* sort of
conflates the two, though the latter seems prevalent in the Old
Testament outside of Genesis, whereas the former seems more of the
focus in the New Testament -- may be an alternate guise of the being
depicted in DC Comics as The Spectre, albeit in his "raw" form,
untethered to a human soul (or the soul of some mortal sentient
being); and thus without his power and vengeful, one-sided mindset
tempered by connection to the spirit of a human (mortal) host.

As is typically the case in one of Greene's Nightside novels,
crossovers that tie numerous characters, groups, and franchises into a
single shared universe, or in some cases between numerous realities
in the greater multiverse converging on a single interdimensional
locale, abound. These include a Dorian Gray reference that is
significant to this timeline, but the rest will also be listed here for
readers who may be fans of a shared universe concept; in this case,
the WHU and the various other realities it may intersect with at

times. And let's face it, this anthology was produced with such fans in mind, considering the crossover-heavy nature of the Dorian Gray tales that comprise the meat of this volume.

Shoggoth's Old and Very Peculiar appears again. Zhang the Mystic, a member of the Adventurer's Club, is said to have battled Elder Gods. The Shoggoths are monstrous spawn of the cosmic entities from Lovecraft's "Cthulhu Mythos," which have sometimes been referred to as the Elder Gods, the Old Ones, and various other monikers suggesting antediluvian histories and origins. They even had their own series of stories in the horror anthology comic magazines published by Skywald in the 1970s (those mags being *Psycho*, *Nightmare*, and *Scream*). Of course, other ancient and powerful entities of a dark and decidedly manipulative-to-humankind nature have likewise been called the Elder Gods, so each mention of that name must be taken on a case-by-case basis and scrutinized according to the source material.

Shoggoth (or one variation thereof)
Pic courtesy of Martin Kacl

John Taylor and Suzie Shooter fight an evil Victor Frankenstein from a mirror universe. This is not the same Victor Frankenstein from the main WHU timeline. Taylor mentions that Frankenstein is a common name in the Nightside and that he has encountered many of Victor's descendants and their creations. This supports the theories of authors Mark Brown and Chuck Loridans that many of the Frankensteins and man-made monsters seen in fiction are Victor's family and their numerous monsters, rather than always being the same Victor Frankenstein and one single Monster. This theory comprises a significant portion of Loridans' Children of the Night Timeline and has been adapted into Christofer Nigro's Trinity of Terror Timeline, both of which are on the MONSTAAH website.

The mirror Victor finds a way to control the citizens of the Nightside by learning that the actions of people in one reality dictates the actions of their doppelgangers. Taylor compares this to Dorian Gray's picture, where Dorian's actions are reflected within the portrait.

The sewers of the Nightside have giant ants, like those from the classic 1950s sci-fi film *Them!* and the not-so-classic 1970s horror film *Empire of the Ants* ("very loosely based" – as, in name only – on the short story by H.G. Wells, which actually featured a deadly but ultra-intelligent colony of ants, not those of gigantic size; it's the contention of WHU canon that both tales "occurred" but describe entirely separate events in their respective time periods).

426

The Adventurer's Club has a stuffed Gill Man, the monstrous aquatic menace from Universal's film franchise. starting with *The Creature from the Black Lagoon.*

Jacqueline Hyde is at the Adventurer's Club. In the previous *Nightside* novel, she was mentioned in *The Unnatural Inquirer* as being in love with her male Hyde alter-ego. There is an old Victorian drinking song called "Dr. Jekyll's Locum." One of Suzie's neighbors is Sara Kingdom, a character who first appeared on *Doctor Who* during the first Doctor's run.

Janissary Jane, a character from Greene's *Secret Histories* series of novels, appears at the Adventurer's Club. The Walking Man mentions the Drood family from *Secret Histories.*

Past members of the Adventurer's Club mentioned in this book include an interesting variety of individuals from various sources, such as Doctor Syn, Salvation Kane, and Owen Deathstalker; their respective histories will be noted below.

Doctor Syn (Doctor Reverend Christopher Syn) is a late 18th century vicar who moonlighted as a smuggler hero and protector of the residents of Dymchurch, a village and civil parish located in the Shepway district of Kent, England, in a makeshift scarecrow disguise. Syn's activities often centered upon the eerie Romney Marsh area, which was a center for smuggling tobacco products and liquor from France to avoid excessive taxes on the common people by the local corrupt government. His exploits were recorded in a series of novels written by Russell Thorndike in the early 20th century, beginning in 1915 with *Doctor Syn: A Tale of Romney Marsh* (which was actually the last story in the series chronologically; Doctor Syn's chronologically earliest adventures begin in the second novel of the series, 1935's *Doctor Syn on the High Seas*).

Doctor Syn has also been identified as a member of the first League of Extraordinary Gentlemen to be formed by the British Crown, a version led by Lemuel Gulliver (of Tom Swift's novel *Gulliver's Travels*). He served that first league both in that guise and in his alter-ego of Captain Clegg (see below), as made clear via photos in both the comic book and movie versions of the late 1890s teams.

Doctor Syn has likewise appeared in several new stories – in both the latter guise, or as The Scarecrow – in short stories appearing in Black Coat Press' annual *Tales of the Shadowmen* anthologies, published since 2003.

Doctor Syn has also taken on two other prominent and famous guises, these being:

The Scarecrow of Romney Marsh, i.e., "The Scarecrow," an alias that Syn took on after becoming the leader of rebel smugglers against the corrupt government officials (when he wasn't hunting down and terrorizing his former best friend and former wife for hooking up with each other and eloping, that is), by designing a scarier scarecrow suit decorated with luminescent paint for chilling effect, and recruiting a group of spookily-garbed and code-named confederates on horseback called the Night Riders (also referred to as "Demon Riders," as some of the more suspicious townspeople believed Syn to be a manifestation of the Devil himself to punish evil-doers).

Syn's Scarecrow alias first appeared in Disney's made-for-TV productions about the character, initially airing as a three-part series *The Scarecrow of Romney Marsh* within their weekly show *Walt Disney's Wonderful World of Color* (this was 1963, so whenever a television series was released in color it was considered such a big deal that the network totally had to mention this in the show's title). It was later edited together as a full-length feature in various formats with a variety of title modifications for release in Britain, home video (by the 1980s), etc. The series was twice adapted into comic book form, first by Gold Key for a three-issue run and then serialized within *Disney Adventures* (publisher obvious).

Captain Clegg (with which he also used the faux identity Parson Blyss), was a guise Syn took as seen in an eponymous Hammer Film depiction of the story (released in the U.S. as *Night Creatures*), where "Blyss" was incorrectly recorded as being killed. This is the identity that Syn utilized during his piracy days out in the Caribbean, which was where he first met his trusty ally, Mr. Mipps.

Wild Hunt Press editor and creative mythographer Gordon Long expressed this interesting theory regarding Doctor Syn: "Due to the Same Actor Principle, I believe that Doctor Syn is an ancestor to John Drake/Number Six, due to Patrick McGoohan playing all three roles."

Scarecrow of Romney Marsh (a.k.a., Dr. Syn)

www.alamy.com - DXKRBK

The Scarecrow of Romney Marsh and his crew

(Why so many pics of Dr. Syn's alter-ego? Because he's a cool character, that's why!)

Salvation Kane was likely meant to be Robert E. Howard's Puritan monster hunter/adventurer Solomon Kane; and Owen Deathstalker is from Greene's futuristic sci-fi *Deathstalker* series.

At a gun shop is the Darkvoid Device, also from the *Deathstalker* series. (Remember that the Nightside exists outside normal time and space.)

The Adventurer's Club also has an arm of Grendel, the man-eating monstrosity slain by Beowulf, the medieval Danish hero of Nordic legend, from the eponymous epic poem (since adapted into film, prose, comic book, and likely many other mediums).

2009--*THE CONFESSIONS OF DORIAN GRAY*: "INNER DARKNESS" (audio drama, Big Finish) --Iceland. Dorian finds himself stranded in the middle of nowhere.

July 2010--*WAREHOUSE 13* (TV series) Season 2 Episode 4 -- "AGE BEFORE BEAUTY" --Warehouse 13 is an unassuming warehouse in the middle of nowhere containing the most dangerous artifacts in the world. It is guarded by a special branch of the secret service who also search for and capture other artifacts still out there. This series fits into the WHU well.

In this episode, the agents investigate when supermodels begin aging rapidly. The picture of Dorian Gray is in the warehouse, and it has aged and gotten uglier, implying that Dorian has continued to exist as an immortal and in committing evil acts. Since Dorian has subsequently had the portrait in his possession, it can be surmised that it was only temporarily in the possession of the Warehouse 13 crew.

2011--*DOWN THESE STRANGE STREETS* -- "HUNGRY HEART" (short story by Simon R. Green) --A *Nightside* story. Taylor is hired by a witch to recover her heart. Crossovers include: Dracula, Bring *Me the Head of Alfredo Garcia*, Dorian Gray (that mysterious unexplained mirror), and Varney the Vampire.

2012--*THE CONFESSIONS OF DORIAN GRAY*: "THE PICTURE OF LORETTA DELPHINE" (audio drama, Big Finish) --Dorian encounters another immortal product of Hallward's work.

2012--*THE CONFESSIONS OF DORIAN GRAY*: "RUNNING AWAY WITH YOU" (audio drama, Big Finish) --Kew. Dorian's childhood home has been turned into flats.

Around the Mayan Prophecy of December 21, 2012--*PROPHECY* # 1-7 (comic book series, Dynamite Entertainment) --The story of how the 2012 apocalypse, predicted centuries ago by the Mayan calendar, was averted. This is the first major companywide crossover event from Dynamite. This story involves the soul-clone Dracula-Mordante, the immortal dhampiric (half-vampire; half-human) warrior Eva ("Dracula's Daughter"), and Vampirella, with the Vampire Lord noting that Eva only "claims" to be his daughter. This may possibly square with the editor's theory that her sire was the powerful soul-clone Dracula-Rominoff (more on him can be found in the list of soul-clones further above in this timeline). The fact that there appeared to be no enmity between the Dracula and Eva who teamed up to save the world during the incident recorded in the *Prophecy* mini-series, and Dracula-Mordante didn't seem to recognize her despite acknowledging her parentage claims, give further credence to this theory.

The characters involved in this crossover are Vampirella; "Warrenverse" Dracula (Dynamite Entertainment); Eva, Daughter of Dracula; Re-Animator (i.e., Dr. Herbert West, though not likely the original); Dorian Gray and his famous portrait; Purgatori; Pantha; the Deadites (i.e., demonically possessed human corpses from *The Evil Dead/Army of Darkness* film & comic book franchises); Hunchback of Notre Dame; Evil Ernie; Red Sonja; Conan the Barbarian; Allan Quatermain; Athena (Dynamite Entertainment); Sherlock Holmes; Indiana Jones; the Three Musketeers; The Phantom; Green Hornet;

Flash Gordon; the Lone Ranger; Zorro; Project Superpowers.

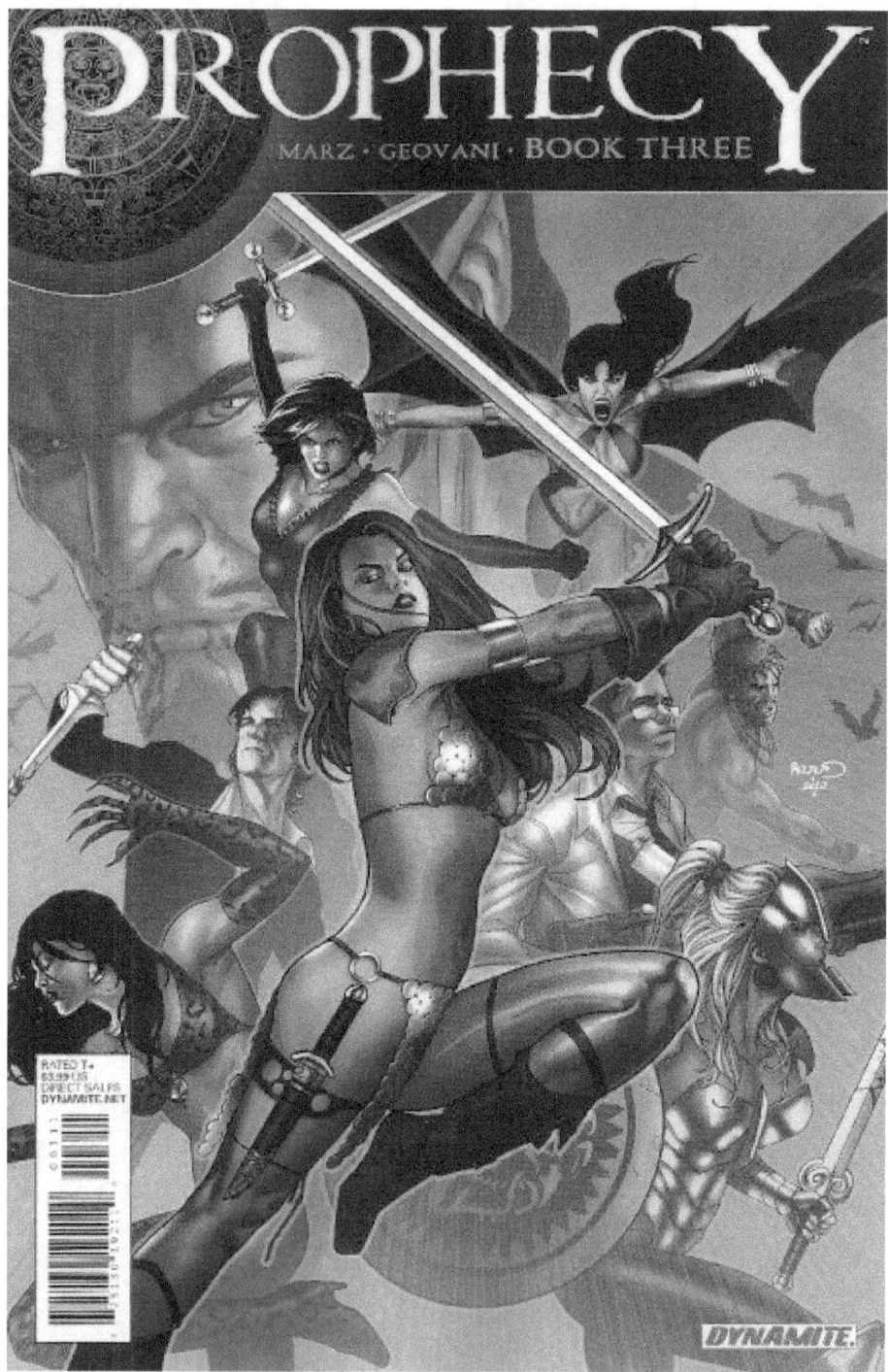

2012 –*THE PORTRAIT OF DOREENE GRAY: A CHIHUAHUA MYSTERY* (novel by Esri Allbritten) – The second of Allbritten's series of novels featuring the quirky team of town-traveling paranormal investigators who chronicle their findings for *Tripping* magazine (the first novel was 2011's *Chihuahua of the Baskervilles*, also obviously based on a famous mystery novel with paranormal overtones [or so it seemed on the surface]; and also featuring a Chihuahua). In this exploit the crew comprised of intrepid editor Angus MacGregor, dedicated skeptic Michael Abernathy, and photographer Suki Oota travel to the town of Port Townsend, Washington to investigate the mystery of the titular Doreene Pinter Gray, who never seems to age, though her portrait painted many decades earlier by her identical twin sister Maureene gets literally weighed down by the ages in her stead… only to revert to its original youthful appearance upon the real Doreene's murder. And yes, Doreene's pet chihuahua Gigi also appears, since author Allbritten loves chihuahuas.

Though this story only bears a peripheral connection to the Dorian Gray saga, it arguably warrants a spot in this timeline for the completists among Gray's fans and researchers. How peripheral is that connection, exactly? Read the book and judge for yourself! And does the *Tripping* staff of Boulder, Colorado fit into the WHU? Time will tell, and because this author (Christofer Nigro) leans towards the inclusive, I decided to include the entry in the main timeline for the time being.

December 2012 (a few days after *A Hard Day's Knight*, and between *Secret Histories* novels for *Heaven's Eyes Only* and *Live and Let Drood*) --*THE BRIDE WORE BLACK LEATHER* (novel by Simon R. Green) –John Taylor is about to marry Suzie and retire as a private investigator to work as an official for the Nightside. However, events get interrupted when the Sun King arrives, threatening to end the eternal darkness of the Nightside. John turns down a case from Katherine Karnstein, who wishes to find her lost innocence. Katherine is likely from the same family as Carmilla, the titular lesbian vampire from Sheridan Le Fanu's classic novella. (Some names are rare enough that their very mention denotes a crossover).

There is a Jekyll and Hyde reunion dinner, which is not only for the Jekyll family, but for anyone who has used the formula. In the Nightside, that's a lot of people. Any of those Jekyll family members or Hyde monsters who have appeared in past stories may have been present at the function.

John mentions that Bettie Divine was involved in the Lovett Pie Show fiasco, a reference to Sweeney Todd, the "Demon Barber of Fleet Street," who was a Victorian serial killer that dispatched his unwitting victims on his barber chair. Todd first appeared in the penny dreadful *The String of Pearls.* Mrs. Lovett was Sweeney's partner-in-crime, who would help him dispose of the bodies by processing them into meat pies she would sell to unwary customers at her shop. The story, which has become something of an urban legend, has been filmed several times, and this reference brings Sweeney into the WHU.

An immortal has discovered that he can kill other immortals with a shard of glass from the mirror of Dorian Gray. Yet another reference to Gray's mysterious mirror, which must have been imbued with mystical properties every bit as fascinating as his infamous portrait. Further investigation into its origin and nature is quite warranted.

A former member of the Carnacki Institute is consulted. The Carnacki Institute is from Green's *Ghost Finders* series. John mentions that Thomas Carnacki was his mentor.

John sees a vampire ventriloquist's dummy, which may be from the *Middleman* episode "The Vampiric Puppet Lamentation."

Taylor mentions being grateful that his last civilian case doesn't involve the Maltese Falcon, and adds, "which is a very real object, in case you were wondering." Several stories mention the Maltese Falcon in a way that could be taken as a pop culture reference or as a real object. Since this story is meant to be the finale of the *Nightside* series, it was nice of John (and Green) to let us know for sure the intention before ending the series.

At the Immortals' Ball, stuffed Morlock is served. Morlocks are bestial former humans from a far distant alternate future, first appearing in H.G. Wells' novel *The Time Machine*, and they appear frequently in the *Nightside* series.

Orlando, the gender-changing protagonist of Virginia Woolf's novel *Orlando: A Biography*, is present at the ball.

Like most *Nightside* stories, this one has many references to Green's *Secret Histories* series. However, in this case, there is a major plot point that ties the two series together. Part of the reason that the Sun King is drawn to the Nightside is because of the events which destroyed the immortal Drood family in Green's novel *For Heaven's Eyes Only*. When a ghost bar vanishes, so do those who were inside, including the Amber Prince.

When John and Suzie finally get married, characters from *Shadows Fall* are guests.

One of the characters has the special glasses from John Carpenter's classic sci-fi film *They Live*, which allows him to see aliens through a human disguise. Based on the short story "Eight O'clock in the Morning" by Ray Nelson, the movie told of those special lenses allowing certain people, starting with the drifter Joe Nada, to discover that the elite human ruling class are extraterrestrials in disguise, and use the mass media to manipulate the public into accepting their status quo. Since this difference would be sufficiently dramatic from the real world which the WHU reflects to an outward surface degree (e.g., fossil record, social development, politics, economics, pop culture, basic recorded public history), it can be surmised that this secret invasion occurred on an alternate Earth that had interdimensional connections to the Nightside. Of course, counterparts of this alien race, and those special lenses, may exist in the "mainstream" WHU sans the successful clandestine invasion.

The Bride of Frankenstein appears at the Immortals' Ball, and thanks John for his recent battle with the Victor Frankenstein of the mirror reality. This may be the Universal version, last seen before this in David Jacobs' Universal Monster novels *The Devil's Brood* and *The Devil's Night* (themselves follow-ups to Jeff Rovin's novel

The Return of The Wolf Man). Or, it may be one of the various other "Brides" created through the centuries by other members of the accursed Frankenstein clan who have appeared in different sources; this includes the female creature from the 1974 movie *Andy Warhol's Frankenstein* (released in England, and better known on video today, as *Flesh for Frankenstein*); the titular female protagonist from the 1985 horror film *The Bride* starring Sting; and the four-armed warrior version introduced in the comic book *Seven Soldiers: Frankenstein* #3 (DC Comics), created by Frederick Victor Frankenstein I (her two additional arms were grafted onto her much later by a madman called the Red Swami, who wanted her to resemble the Hindu assassin goddess Kali for his death cult), and intended to be the mate of Johnnie Frankenstein, the name for the Frankenstein Monster copycat whose exploits have most often been depicted by DC Comics from the 2000s to the present.

Some extended info will now be given on the intriguing Monster copycat Johnnie Frankenstein, for those readers who may be interested in some of the broader aspects of the WHU beyond that of Dorian Gray (feel free, of course, to simply skip to the next entry if you have no interest).

This Monster copycat who would eventually come to be called Johnnie Victor Frankenstein was reputedly created by Frederick von Frankenstein I (grandfather of the titular scientist from the film *Young Frankenstein*), a reprehensible member of the dreaded clan who duplicated the experiment of his close cousin Victor Frankenstein I several years earlier, this time with a combination of galvanic energies and water taken from the enchanted Fountain of

Life.

This member of the Frankenstein family did not duplicate his cousin's experiment simply to find a means of reversing death, but to create a powerful undead servant to commit any number of dark deeds at the behest of his demented and brilliantly dangerous "father." The Monster fled from his evil creator soon after being brought to life and refusing to do his bidding, only to spend many years avoiding his sire's relentless attempts to re-capture him. At some point he gained an enchanted blade called the Sword of Michael, which is empowered to effect supernatural beings and magical barriers as a result of being inscribed with sigils belonging to the eponymous archangel in his warrior aspect. This Monster's origin has been told in *Seven Soldiers: Frankenstein #1* and *Frankenstein, Agent of S.H.A.D.E. #0*, details from each of which combine to comprise his WHU origin.

The Monster who has since come to be known as Johnnie Victor Frankenstein (or just "Frankenstein" in DC Comics, and to much of the public) then became a crusading but secret champion against monster-oriented dangers and other strange paranormal phenomena, at times working under the auspices of the covert U.S. government agency called Project M, which was an adjunct to the Bureau of Paranormal Research and Defense, whom the demonic hero Hellboy has worked for. As of the 2000s, he has worked for two sub-units of Project M: The first, as leader of the modern version of the Creature Commandos; and the second, as a member of the team of clandestine special operatives code-named simply the Seven Soldiers, the latter of whom were brought together to counter the alien invasion of the

Sheeda. His adventures were chronicled in such series as *Seven Soldiers of Victory* #0-30, *Frankenstein and the Creatures of the Unknown* #1-3 (which took place on an alternate timeline), *Frankenstein, Agent of S.H.A.D.E.* #0-16, and the later issues of *Justice League Dark* Vol. 1. Of course, these adventures in printed form contained many exaggerations as far as canon in the WHU is concerned (though may have occurred in a more "literal" sense in the DCU proper).

[**Editor's Note:** The WHU is primarily a pulp hero & monster universe, with pulp heroes/villains, monsters, horror heroes/villains, pro-wrestler heroes, vigilantes, and super-spies being the dominant players, with a strong smattering of sci-fi and fantasy elements, e.g., aliens, space heroes/villains, time travelers, faeries, etc., thrown into the mix. Its rules of reality are very similar to Eckert's and Levin's CU, save that it allows for much more characters from numerous genres and mediums, including those from sitcoms, medical dramas, crime dramas, family dramas, soap operas, dramedies, video games, commercials, etc., et al. Super-heroes in the WHU (like in the CU proper) are relatively few in number, less conspicuous than in, say, the Marvel or DC Universes; are usually considerably less powerful versions of their counterparts in the latter two realities, with origins and activities more akin to glorified pulp heroes.]

Johnnie Frankenstein is not to be confused with other man-made monsters chronicled by DC Comics, specifically the following three.

The first was Pvt. Elliot "Lucky" Taylor, a soldier active during World War II whose body was blown to bits on the battlefield, only for Project M to revive him as a mute flesh golem similar to that of the various Frankenstein Monsters by utilizing the techniques of Frederick von Frankenstein I (whose journals had been located) and genome grafts from the original Frankenstein Monster (i.e., Adam Frankenstein of Mary Shelley's novel *Frankenstein; Or, the Modern Prometheus*), which had been recovered from a location in New York City during the 1920s where he was struck and severely injured by a locomotive while battling the vampire Angel (see *Angel vs. Frankenstein II*, published by IDW Publications). Taylor served as a member of the original Creature Commandos during World War II, a position he carried out with heroic distinction until sacrificing his undead existence to save the life of team member Dr. Medusa, whom he was secretly in love with.

The second was the result of Johnnie Frankenstein and his four-armed former mate/wife The Bride (not to be confused with the similar albeit two-armed and much more famous creation of Dr. Henry Frankenstein and Dr. Septimus Pretorius in the Universal film *The Bride of Frankenstein*) attempting to use a combination of Frederick von Frankenstein I's techniques and Project M's scientific resources to create a "son," who simply became known as the Spawn of Frankenstein. The use of genome grafts from Johnnie Frankenstein resulted in the "son" having some of his memories, and the "newborn" thus believed he was created and being pursued by Frederick von Frankenstein I; and that his "parents" were creations of the vile scientist designed to capture him. Hence, the errant "son" escaped after trying to kill them, and instinctively made his way to the Arctic (where Johnnie once journeyed for an extended period, in psychic imitation of the first Monster, during the decades he was fleeing his creator).

The Spawn of Frankenstein was later seen there in 1942 during an encounter with Kalla of the Dzyan race as shown in *Young All-Stars* #18-19, where he told her was the original creation of "Victor" Frankenstein (something he likely still actually believed). Kalla quickly fled his company, though, and the distraught Monster later ended up frozen in suspended animation. He was recovered and revived by scientist Dr. Victor Adams in 1972. This Monster then engaged in some adventures of his own, once battling against and then alongside the mysterious entity known as the Phantom Stranger to oppose two powerful Deadite demons (the Deadite demons, which possess and reanimate corpses as material vessels for wreaking havoc on the material plane, are from *The Evil Dead* and *Army of Darkness* franchises of films, comic books, video games, and TV series). His exploits were chronicled in the DC comic *The Phantom Stranger* Vol. 2 #23-30. The Spawn of Frankenstein later fell under the thrall of the powerful soul-clone Dracula-Rominoff, where he battled Superman and the Batman of that era (Bruce Wayne Jr.). He was evidently eventually destroyed during one of these conflagrations. The Spawn of Frankenstein, like his "parents," was quite brilliant and capable of speech.

The third was the apparently youthful flesh golem of limited intelligence and stilted speech patterns who was referred to simply as Young Frankenstein (not to be confused with the much more light-hearted Monster copycat created by Frederick von Frankenstein's grandson, as seen in the film *Young Frankenstein*). He was first seen in the 2000s battling alongside that decade's iteration of Teen

Justice, a group of American youths with mutant powers and special skills who unite against the forces of evil from time to time (the earliest version of the club emerged during World War II to challenge the Axis powers, and had their exploits chronicled in highly exaggerated from under a variety of names from the 1940s up to the present by both DC and Marvel comics, including the "Young Allies," "Kid Commandos," "Teen Titans," "Young Justice," "Young Avengers," "New Warriors," "Champions," etc., and were similar to non-mutant groups of adventurous teens such as the Newsboy Legion, the Boy Commandos, and the Teen Brigade). Young Frankenstein was evidently dismembered during one such conflict. His origin is unknown, but he is believed to be one of the various graft "clones" created from the necrotic but power-charged skin cells of the Frankenstein Monsters, likely Johnnie Frankenstein.

Pvt. Elliot "Lucky" Taylor

Johnnie Frankenstein

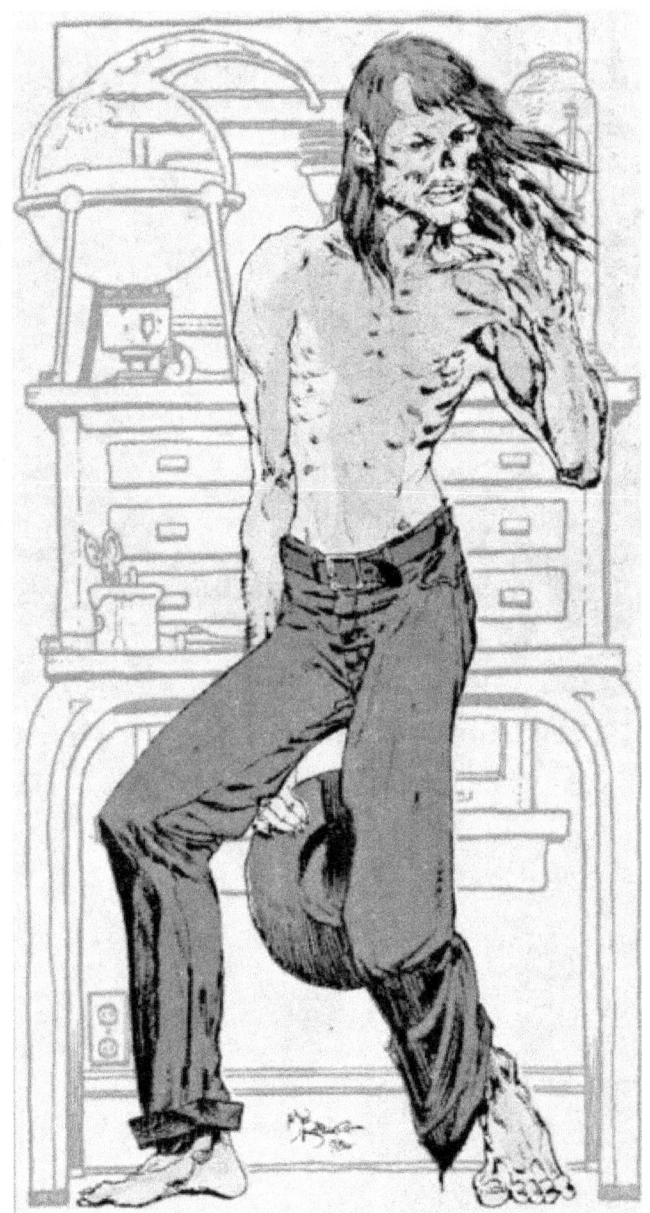

The Spawn of Frankenstein

Henry Frankenstein of Visaria's Monster

Henry Frankenstein & Septimus Pretorius's "Bride of Frankenstein"

Frederick Victor Frankenstein I's "Bride of Frankenstein" (following her additional modifications by the Red Swami)

June 30, 2014--*DARK SHADOWS*: "THE DARKEST SHADOW" (audio drama, Big Finish) --Amanda gets a part playing herself in a movie about the events of the past at Collinsport. This audio drama is from the folks that brought us *The Confessions of Dorian Gray*. They have created a story that combines two of their audio series. This episode also makes it clear that film versions of the events from Collinsport exist within the WHU, though without most of the public suspecting they are more than mere fiction.

2014--*THE PICTURE OF DOREEN GRAY* (stage play by Maggie Fox and Sue Ryding, LipService Theatre) --This play tells the spoofy tale of yet another woman named Doreen Gray – not to be confused with the similarly named (but differently spelled) titular character of *The Portrait of Doreene Gray: A Chihuahua Mystery* novel by Esri Allbritten (see individual entry for 2012) – this time a contemporary British citizen who is a long-time radio deejay and TV presenter who becomes irritated at the loss of her once steady work after she hits middle age and her youthful beauty begins to fade. This changes when she comes across an old self-portrait she drew of her then younger self decades ago in a college art class, and the picture seemingly comes to life and agrees to "swap" ages with her.

Doreen then goes through a series of laughable misadventures when her restored youthful appearance doesn't quite synch with her aged inner self that ultimately cause her to demand a "re-swap" with her portrait persona, and to appreciate what middle-aged women have to offer the world. This is a problem that never seemed to befall Dorian or other immortals of both genders, I should point out, e.g., Becky Sharp, which may be due to the retention of a "young at heart" personality in their individual cases (something that Doreen Gray lost on the inside as she aged).

If this play can indeed be fit into the WHU canon (and I'm giving it the benefit of the doubt for the nonce), then it may suggest that both Doreene and Doreen Gray were close relatives of Dorian Gray whose quantum lifelines somehow ended up "caught" in a synchronistic manner by the Egyptian magicks Basil Hallward employed when creating Dorian's canvas. This would have caused Basil's enchantment to "infect" paintings made by other individuals (or at least appear to do so, as in the case of Doreene's twin sister Maureene), including even self-portraits like the one Doreen crafted in her youth. Of course, the effects in these other cases could be somewhat different, such as the apparent independent consciousness displayed by Doreen's younger portrait, which may have been "animated" by an aspect of her own persona that was mystically "imprinted" on it decades earlier due to the backlash effect of Basil's enchantment, but which only became "activated" by the specific type of strong emotions her aging self was feeling when she came across that self-portrait decades later.

It may also be possible that Basil Hallward's painting created a much stronger synchronistic backlash than surmised above, somehow imprinting a quantum level Event Duplication on many other individuals whose only connection to the original Dorian Gray was the coincidence of having the same first and last name, or a female variant of the latter in the case of females (names have a lot of power in the realm of magick). This may have ensured circumstances would arise that someone would create a painting of them at a key point in their youth, and that in turn acted as a catalyst for a mirror sequence of events to occur. Why no one in the recorded sources ever seemed to acknowledge this strange synchronicity with the events recorded in Wilde's novel (believed to be fiction by the general public, but actually describing real events in the WHU) is unknown; however, this may be due to one of the effects of such a powerful synchronistic mystical backlash, particularly one enhanced by the magick of a mighty deity like Bast.

If there is any merit to this author's theory of Synchronistic Event Duplication, then how these various individuals would experience this quantum catalyzed chain of events will vary according to their personal quantum signature. In other words, some would experience the events in an edgy, "horrific" manner (as did Dorian Gray); whereas others with a quantum tendency towards "the funny" – a situation experienced by many individuals whose lives were chronicled in sitcoms and cinematic rom coms, for example -- would experience them in what average people would consider a comedic fashion, as did Doreen Gray. Others, such as Doreene Pinter Gray, might experience them as a combination of the two.

The events of this play may prove to only be able to take place in an alternate reality upon further research, but until this author conducts said research, it will remain in the Main Timeline section.

Doreen Gray

DORIAN GRAY: DARKER SHADES

2014--*THE CONFESSIONS OF DORIAN GRAY*: "BLANK CANVAS" (audio drama, Big Finish) --Two years after Dorian's alleged death (again), burglars break into his home and find someone they didn't expect. Spoiler: It's old Dorian.

2014--*THE CONFESSIONS OF DORIAN GRAY*: "THE NEEDLE" (audio drama, Big Finish) --Dorian uncovers a centuries old conspiracy.

2014--*THE CONFESSIONS OF DORIAN GRAY*: "WE ARE EVERYWHERE" (audio drama, Big Finish) --A serial killer uncovers Dorian's secret.

2014--*THE CONFESSIONS OF DORIAN GRAY*: "ECHOES" (audio drama, Big Finish) --Dorian is alone on the Tube (that's subway for us Yanks) when he's confronted by phantoms.

2014--*THE CONFESSIONS OF DORIAN GRAY*: "PANDORA" (audio drama, Big Finish) --Dorian is concerned by a psychic who may be too good.

2014--*THE CONFESSIONS OF DORIAN GRAY*: "HEART AND SOUL" (audio drama, Big Finish) --Dorian finds a circus involved in human sacrifice.

2014--*THE CONFESSIONS OF DORIAN GRAY*: "DISPLACEMENT ACTIVITY" (audio drama, Big Finish) --Dorian agrees to help Victoria Lowell to learn the truth about his return from the dead. The fact that Dorian is established to have died and been resurrected means that some of the other tales regarding deaths of Dorian Gray are not necessarily invalid. It may be that he has died and been resurrected on more than one occasion.

2014--*THE CONFESSIONS OF DORIAN GRAY*: "THE DARKEST HOUR" (audio drama, Big Finish) --Finale of Season 3 featuring Old Dorian's resurrection.

December 2015--*THE LIBRARIANS* -- "AND THE IMAGE OF IMAGE" (TV series episode) --The Librarians seek out Dorian Gray when young clubbers are affected by mysterious events.

The Librarians

2015--*THE SPIRITS OF CHRISTMAS – THE CONFESSIONS OF DORIAN GRAY:* "DESPERATELY SEEKING SANTA" **(audio drama, Big Finish)** --Dorian encounters Santa Claus!

December 24, 2015--*THE SPIRITS OF CHRISTMAS – THE CONFESSIONS OF DORIAN GRAY:* "ALL THROUGH THE HOUSE" (audio drama, Big Finish) --Dorian finds himself in a haunted hotel.

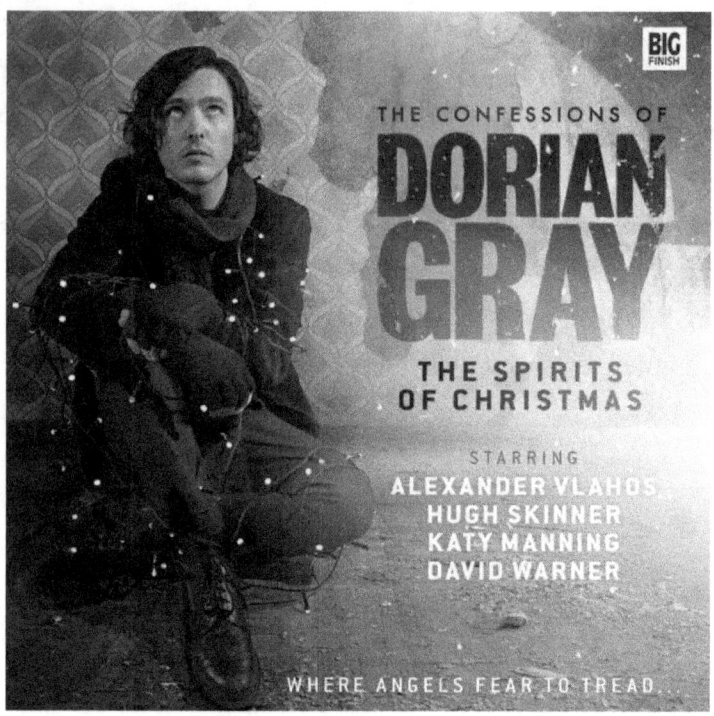

2015--*THE CONFESSIONS OF DORIAN GRAY*: "EVER AFTER" (audio drama, Big Finish) --In the final episode of *The Confessions of Dorian Gray*, Dorian dies (for good?). This happened when he apparently destroyed his portrait to free the spirit of Constance Harker, his former housekeeper and first sexual partner, from further psychological torment by the tulpa Brendan Doyle, which had likewise latched onto the matrix of the home.

2016--*DR. DOA* (novel by Simon R. Green) --A *Secret Histories* novel. Eddie Drood has been poisoned. Crossovers? Of course. And of course, there are the usual references to Green's other series: *Nightside*, *Shadows Fall*, and *Ghost-Finders*. Eddie and Molly also visit the headquarters of Black Heir, from Green's *Ishmael Jones* series, newly joining Green's "Greenverse" franchise.

Lovecraft references: Cthulhu graffiti, Shoggoth's Old Peculiar, and the Overnet (a mystical version of the Internet) has copies of *The Necronomicon*, the *Book of Eibon*, and *Mysteries of the Wurm*.

Eddie meets with Persecution Smith, who is clearly Solomon Kane. Harry Fabulous from the Nightside appears. He is the man to see if you want Martian Red Weed (H.G. Wells' *The War of the Worlds*); or want your picture painted like Dorian Gray, meaning that Fabulous has some connection to Hallward's process using Egyptian magics. That latter reference makes this novel of relevance to this timeline.

Molly claims to know how to find the real Maltese Falcon. The novel of the same name where this much coveted item first appeared has already been mentioned more than once in this timeline.

There is also reference to the Droods battle at Castle Frankenstein in a previous novel, including the dragon's head obtained at that event. Eddie also mentions that teleporting feels like travelling through a Hell Dimension. This may be both a Buffy the Vampire Slayer and X-Men reference. *Buffy the Vampire Slayer* coined the term "Hell Dimension," while Nightcrawler of the X-Men does travel through Hell when he teleports.

Note that in the WHU, Kurt Wagner is a demon raised on Earth by a family of German gypsies and is not a human mutant. Further, the "X-Men" as such do not exist, and are actually a motley team of odd, usually metahuman individuals called the Legion of the Strange who have banded together for mutual protection and family-like camaraderie since the early 1960s. Reports of their stories have been collected and published in highly exaggerated form by both Marvel and DC Comics from 1963 all the way up to the present; they were called the X-Men by the former, and the Doom Patrol by the latter. This is a concept worked up by creative mythographers Kevin Heim, Dennis E. Power, Pete Coogan, and Henry Covert, and has been incorporated into the WHU by the editor of this anthology.

A group of scientists have failed to find the means for immortality. Frankenstein's notes were a dead end, though they are hopeful to get advice from the Spawn of Frankenstein. This may be a reference -- from a WHU context, mind you; not necessarily Green's intention -- to the specific title given to the copycat Frankenstein Monster depicted in DC Comics during the 1970s, who had a back-up feature in *The Phantom Stranger* Vol 2 (starting with issue #23).

November 19, 2017—*DORIAN GRAY: DARKER SHADES*-- "THE D CLUB" (short story by Kevin Heim) --Nope, Dorian did not die for good, though his "friend" Septimus sure thought so. Dorian meets with Dr. Edward Septimus Pretorius. Pretorius is both the character from Universal's classic film *The Bride of Frankenstein*, but also a character in the film *From Beyond*, which is the movie version of H.P. Lovecraft's short story by that name. The two incidents are different enough that they could have occurred on the same timeline, with the short story taking place early in the 20th century and the movie by that name occurring in the 1980s. Pretorius only appears in the latter, and his actual first name of Edward is revealed there (Septimus is the middle name he was most well-known by).

They are both members of the D Club, an elite covert establishment for immortals. The two of them have an ongoing bet, as they try to track fellow immortals with Dorian gaining a point for each one who acquired their longevity via supernatural means, and Pretorius a point for each who acquired this enviable attribute scientifically.

The purpose for their meeting this day is to study another potential immortal, "Crazy" Ivan Ronald Schablotski (known in other circles by aliases such as Steven Pertwillaby and Agent Verdigris), and to that end they attempt to lure him to the Lovecraft Arts & Sciences store located at the Providence Arcade in Providence, Rhode Island (which has a real-life counterpart!).

Their plan is foiled by the appearance of the Frankenstein Monster previously seen in another of Kevin Heim's published short stories, "Redux of the Living Dead," here revealed to have the brain of the Monster from Universal's first few Frankenstein films (*Frankenstein* 1931; *The Bride of Frankenstein*; *Son of Frankenstein*). In *the Ghost of Frankenstein*, the Monster's brain had been removed and replaced by that of the evil hunchback Ygor. This story reveals that the Monster's brain survived in the skull of another man-made monster. The Monster is currently living in Santa Mira, California, a setting that originated in the 1956 sci-fi film *Invasion of the Body Snatchers* (based on Jack Finney's 1954 novel *The Body Snatchers*) but has since appeared frequently in various works of published, filmed, and televised fiction.

As Dorian arrives, Septimus is having lunch with Kyra Zelas (whom he has nicknamed Kay) from Stanley G. Weinbaum's short story "The Adaptive Ultimate."

Septimus is revealed to have been behind the scenes to the events of the 2015 episode of *The Librarians* featuring Dorian ("And the Image of Image" – Season 2); while Dorian is said to have been behind Pretorius' encounter with Gen13 and Generation X in that one-shot intercompany crossover between Image and Marvel ("Generation Gap"), though obviously the WHU version of those events occurred differently, with different players involved than those in the published sources.

As the club and bet are discussed within the story, several crossover references are made, which include: *Doctor Who*; Wonder Woman/Valkyrie (where in the WHU, DC's Wonder Woman and Marvel's Valkyrie are the same character, but also that every different version of Wonder Woman has been a separate character existing within the same universe under a different name); *Vanity Fair* and Micah S. Harris' version of Becky Sharp (including a reference to Harris' novella within this anthology, "Portrait of a Lady").

The Luck of Barry Lyndon (novel by William Makepeace Thackeray) and *The Man of Half Moon Street* (movie) -- Barry

Lyndon is the same character in both the novel and the movie.

References to *Dark Shadows* (Quentin Collins from the TV series and excursions in other mediums, including comic books and audio dramas); *Highlander* (film and TV franchises); the Frankenstein mythos; *Supernatural* (TV series); *Carmilla* (novella); the Dracula mythos; Spider-Man (a pastiche here referred to as the Shutter Bug); Father Christmas; the Wolf Man (Larry Stewart Talbot) of the classic Universal film franchise; the New Mutants (a "kid" spin-off of the Legion of the Strange in the WHU); *La Marca Del Hombre Lobo* (a.k.a., *The Mark of the Wolf Man,* a.k.a., *Frankenstein's Bloody Terror),* and every werewolf movie featuring Waldemar Daninsky or one of his ancestors of the same name, cursed with lycanthropy to become El Hombre Lobo, a.k.a., the Spanish Wolf Man); Peter Rawlik's novel *Reanimators*; *Halloween* film franchise; and *Friday the 13ᵗʰ* film franchise.

There are also references to the works of Philip José Farmer and mention of the theories that there are numerous vampire strains, explaining why so much vampire fiction can coexist in the same reality with different rules for vampires; and references identifying the existence of many monster hunting organizations, with some being named, including M*O*N*S*T*A*A*H (with asterisks properly included), created by Chuck Loridans and mentioned in various sources, with future publications planned. Others included:

The Ordnance, OUTCIDe (Ordnance Unconventional Tactics: Combat Intelligence Detachment -- the military division of the Ordnance consisting of the Navy SEALs, Army Rangers, and Green

Berets who work for it), the Theurgy Society, and N.E.G.A.T.E. (North East Ghosthunters Alliance: Taskforce Ecto) were all created by author Kevin Heim for his various timelines, and slated for future publications;

Monster Hunter International is from Larry Correia's series of novels;

The BPRD (Bureau of Paranormal Research and Defense, a.k.a., The Bureau) from Mike Mignola's *Hellboy* comic book series and various spin-offs, including its own series. It may be another abbreviation for the Monster Control Bureau from Larry Correia's *Monster Hunter International* novels;

Bureau 13 is from GameTek's video game series.

"Crazy" Ivan Ronald Schablotski has appeared in the published and online writings of Kevin Heim, and he has counterparts in various realities (where different aliases may be used), such as the MHU (Monster Hunter Universe), the TVCU (Television Crossover Universe), the WHU (where he is most often identified as Steven "Steve" Pertwillaby), and likely the CU proper. Most of his MHU appearances (at least) will have analogue events in the WHU. Ivan's first published appearance was in the short story "The Christmas That Almost Wasn't Christmas" in the *Psychopomp 2012 Christmas Special* from Psychopomp Press. Ivan's extensive history and exploits in the TVCU can be found on Kevin Heim's painstakingly and ongoing-ly updated timeline on the Television Crossover Universe blog, one of the most popular features ever on that popular site:

http://www.televisioncrossoveruniverse.com/2014/04/some-people-call-me-crazy-april-fools.html.

His excursions throughout the time stream and various dimensions mean he is likely to pop up just about anywhere, any time – even into the Dragonstorm Universe (this author's kaiju/sentai Earth) under his "Agent Verdigris" alias, where he made two memorable cameos in my kaiju novel *Megadrak: Beast of the Apocalypse* from Severed Press and ended up becoming a legend in a world he never made.

**"Crazy" Ivan Ronald Schablotski invading…
somewhere.**

The Lovecraft Arts & Sciences – where Dorian and Pretorius *tried* to meet Ivan!

Dr. Septimus Edward Pretorius first appeared in Universal's classic 1935 cinematic monster epic *The Bride of Frankenstein*. He has since appeared in subsequent sources (though not necessarily connected to the character from his inaugural appearance), which includes the following for those readers who may be interested in the recorded saga of Pretorius in the WHU (if not, then please feel free to skip over the next five paragraphs!).

In the story arc of Skywald's "Frankenstein II" series that was serialized in the horror comic magazine *Psycho* #4-6, Dr. Pretorius, in a tale which this author has theorized on the MONSTAAH website to take place circa 1888 (two years after the events of *The Bride of Frankenstein*), had captured the severed but galvanically re-animated head of Aloysius Frankenstein – who had alternately used the forenames "Victor" or "Henry" throughout the series; Aloysius was another member of the Frankenstein family [a cousin of both Victor Frankenstein I and Henry Frankenstein I] involved in the clan's ghoulish experiments of creating flesh golems from pieces of different human corpses stitched together chimerically – as part of an attempt to force the bodiless but still living scientist to reveal his secrets to him (the now thoroughly maddened Pretorius seemed determined to learn the re-animation secrets of the Frankenstein clan, having evidently scrapped his own techniques which he used to create The Bride alongside Henry Frankenstein I).

This ultimately led Pretorius to a team-up with Erik the Phantom of the Opera and an ill-fated encounter with Aloysius Frankenstein's own man-made monster, the copycat Monster I refer to as "V.H. Frankenstein" (as he took both the forenames "Victor" and "Henry" at different points, just as his creator did) – and the main featured star of Skywald's "Frankenstein II" series.

Professor Septimus Pretorius

The immortal Pretorius has also appeared – using his middle name Edward – in the 1986 film *From Beyond*, where he has moved on from experiments in creating artificial organic humanoid life to joining the Miskatonic University staff and using a Tillinghast Resonator (first introduced in the H.P. Lovecraft tale of the same name as this movie, but referring to a similar but different incident) to breach interdimensional space into "The Beyond" – and unleashing more madness as a result, both on himself and everyone unfortunate enough to make his professional acquaintance (including a beleaguered young student descendant of the original Crawford Tillinghast, inventor of the first such resonator).

Professor Septimus Pretorius and a set of his homunculi.

[**Side note:** The Tillinghast Resonator, it should be noted, has implications in various universes – including the WHU and the MHU -- for being behind the infamous Philadelphia Experiment of World War II (based on a real life legend and the subject of various speculative books and films). This incident had the U.S. Navy engage in a very ill-fated attempt to use such a resonator to confer both visual and radar invisibility upon an entire manned battleship, Instead, the device teleported the hapless crew through time and space and caused other ill effects upon their return such as disrupting their physical corporality and inducing severe bouts of insanity. Another such device, actually named as such, appears in Charles Stross's novel *The Jennifer Factor*.]

Pretorius may also have aided another member of the Frankenstein clan (Ludwig Frankenstein I, called "Victor" in his film appearance, another close relative of Victor I and Henry I) in creating a mate, Prima, for the latter's male flesh golem at some point during the mid-19th century, as seen in the 1973 TV mini-series *Frankenstein: The True Story*. In this source as televised, Pretorius was referred to as "Dr. Polidori," which may have been either a guise he took on, or the screenwriter paying homage to Dr. John Polidori, the personal physician of Percy Bysshe Shelley, who was present with the classic Romantic poet and his young wife Mary Shelley during the fateful rainy day indoors circa 1816 when it was suggested they pass the time by writing horror stories – and Mary Shelley penned what would soon be published as *Frankenstein; Or, The Modern Prometheus* (Dr. Polidori's contribution was the far less well known but no less important horror novel *The Vampyre*, which introduced Lord Ruthven; Percy Bysshe Shelley, and the also present poet Lord Byron, evidently never finished the tales they started). Another appearance of Pretorius, this time in Germany circa the late 1980s, was chronicled in German author Akif Pirinçci's 1989 novel *Felidae* (and its 1994 animated film adaptation), where his name was spelled/pronounced "Preterius"; and where he was seen performing vile scientific experiments on a cat named Claudandus.

Pretorius in *Felidae*.

Alternate reality versions of Pretorius have also been recorded, such as the one from the Anno-Dracula Universe that appears in Kim Newman's novel *Dracula Cha Cha Cha*, where he is revealed to be consorting with that reality's version of Herbert West I (a.k.a., the original Re-Animator). The iteration of Septimus Pretorius seen in the Universal Monster novel *The Bride of Frankenstein: Pandora's Box* published as part of Dark Horse's series of prose novels featuring the Universal Monsters was also quite possibly an alternate reality version (as at least some of those novels clearly were). A gender-swapped version of the Professor called Jane Pretorius who was the boss/mentor of contemporary scientist Dr. Victoria Frankenstein in the ITV British telefilm *Frankenstein* (2007). A particularly mad version of Dr. Pretorius – this time attended by purple and ebony garbed minions -- was the arch-nemesis of the dimensional iteration of Stanley Ipkiss, a.k.a., the bizarre super-hero called The Mask, who headlined the TV series *The Mask: Animated Series*.

Other references include: Lovecraft's Mythos, Captain America, Buffy the Vampire Slayer, *The Princess Bride*, Dale Parker (a monster hunter character created by John Lindsey, another author who was to contribute to this anthology, but scheduling didn't allow it), the Avengers, and the Teen Titans; the latter two are combined as a single organization, as this is not the Marvel or DC versions, but consists of the U.S. government's various mostly covert and periodic teaming of special operatives.

The name of such teams will vary according to which pulp hero/monster universe any given tale takes place within, though a good number of alternate realities will have analogues of the same events, but with subtle differences at times. In the MHU, where author Kevin Heim's stories generally take place, this team is called the Olympus Initiative; other versions of Marvel and DC teams that combine into pulp-friendly iterations in this reality include the Secret Society of Mystic Defenders and the All-American Squad. In the WHU, they have been known by designations such as the "All-Star" teams or "Justice League" initiatives; in addition, there are more clandestine teams such as the Order of Secret Defenders. They have sporadically been brought together throughout the decades since the first was gathered by the government in the early days of World War II.

These teams were clearly inspired by Britain's League of Extraordinary Gentlemen and their French and German counterparts, the Mysterious Men [Les Hommes Mystérieux] and the Twilight Heroes [Die Zwielichthelden], respectively (these latter two teams were introduced in Alan Moore's and Kevin O'Neill's graphic novel *The League of Extraordinary Gentlemen: Black Dossier*, America's Best Comics).

DORIAN GRAY: DARKER SHADES

December 15th, 2017--A very attractive man absolutely did not pay co-author and prime timeline architect Robert E. Wronski, Jr. a visit and "convince" him to rewrite this timeline to make Dorian Gray appear to be a character of fiction.

2100s--*BERNICE SUMMERFIELD*: "SHADES OF GRAY" (audio drama, Big Finish) --Flashbacks.

27th Century--*LEGION*: "SHADES OF GRAY" (audio drama, Big Finish) --Bernice Summerfield, the original future space archaeologist companion of The Doctor (of *Doctor Who* TV series fame) from the alternate universe that has been called the Whoniverse, hops around time to various alternate timelines, and encounters Dorian Gray! Wild Hunt Press holds that since this included alternate timelines and time travel, Bernice and Dorian may originate from different universes, thus keeping the Whoniverse separate from the WHU. The story's framing sequence is set in the 2600s. The appearances of Dorian are at various points in his past. There are also references to Big Finish's *Dark Shadows* audio drama series.

ALTERNATE REALITIES

***CREEPY* Vol. 1 #44— "DORIAN GRAY: 2001" (comic book story by Al Hewetson and Bill Barry, Warren Publishing)—** Devon, England. This odd alternate universe tale, penned by the late, great comic book auteur (and later co-founder of Warren's rival black and white, horror anthology comic magazine publisher, Skywald) Al Hewetson, brings us a variation of Dorian Gray that is more or less a variant of the character in name only. In an alternate timeline of the year 2001 – about thirty years in the future from the publication date of this story – a "future" version of Britain is plagued by a type of vampire that has resulted in paranoid, police-state measures being invoked to handle the problem (meaning, more innocents will be taken down than actual guilty parties). Here we have a bloodline of vamp with the familiar fangs, depraved bloodlust, and immortality, but sans any apparent superhuman strength or anything akin to shape-shifting powers; mesmerism is possibly implied in the scene where this version of Dorian menaces a young paramour named Trisha.

Yes, in this version we have a Dorian Gray who has achieved his eternal youth courtesy of the "curse" of vampirism, and whose wealth is obtained by being a ruthless munitions manufacturer of nuclear weapons and germ warfare (I know, "WTF!", right?). His sinful behavior is derived from a combination of his status as a predatory vampire and as an Evil Capitalist. Basil Hallward of this reality is an apparent law enforcement agent of the "Federation" (what may pass for the British government of this timeline), who ruthlessly hunts down and exterminates vampires – both real and suspected – in small 'hover-copters.' Their method of choice is stringing the poor wankers they hunt down on rope and blasting them through the heart with spear-like projectiles fired from apparently electrically powered, high-tech pistols (I couldn't make this up! Only Al Hewetson could!). This is all done right there on the spot Judge Dredd-style, with nothing resembling due process taking place (thus suggesting this may occur earlier on the Judge Dredd timeline, prior to the nuclear catastrophe that resulted in the formation of Mega-City One by the time of the 22nd century).

Basil appears older than Dorian in this story, and apparently has nothing to do with his friend's immortal "affliction," thus making him a Basil Hallward whose name and homoerotic-laced friendship with Dorian is the only thing he has in common with his counterpart from Oscar Wilde's novel and the "mainstream" WHU.

Needless to say, it all ends poorly for the vampiric Dorian after his loyal friend and erotic admirer Basil, the fanatical vampire-hunting agent of the U.K. Federation, discovers the sordid truth about his favorite munitions industrialist. I won't spoil the ending completely, except to say that this reality's vampire bloodline is not immune to the horrific effects of biological warfare agents.

Al Hewetson was clearly a major fan of Wilde's classic tale of a Faustian bargain made to attain eternal youth, as he also scripted a more straightforward comic book adaptation of the story for Skywald's *Scream* #6, published just a few years later.

***ANNO DRACULA* (series of novels, short stories, and comic books by Kim Newman)** --In 1888 (listed by Newman as 1885), during the events of Bram Stoker's novel *Dracula*, events diverge, and Dracula(-Prime) defeats Abraham Van Helsing's team and then marries Queen Victoria, causing a major alteration in the socio-political world for the next 125 years and beyond.

This is a divergent timeline, but not a parallel universe. In my theory (this is Robert E. Wronski, Jr. speaking here), a parallel universe is created at the dawn of time at the same time as the main universe and other parallel universes. They may evolve similarly, but they are separate. Meanwhile, each universe has a main timeline, and at each moment, there are an infinite number of divergent timelines created from the main timeline. When thinking of divergent timelines, try picturing a fork in the road. Both paths lead in different directions, but they both start at the same point, and once were the same road. The Anno Dracula Timeline has shown to be an alternate timeline of the main WHU (and similar universes, such as the CU and Monster Hunter Universe [MHU], etc.).

For the record, the complete *Anno Dracula* series (as of the end of 2017), all prose novels unless otherwise specified, consists of *Anno Dracula*; *Anno Dracula 1895: Seven Days in Mayhem* (comic book mini-series by Titan, which is in canon); *The Bloody Red Baron: Anno Dracula 1918*; *Judgement of Tears: Anno Dracula 1959* (a.k.a., *Dracula Cha Cha Cha*); *Coppola's Dracula* (novella from the anthology *The Mammoth Book of Dracula*); *Castle in the Desert: Anno Dracula 1977*; *Andy Warhol's Dracula: Anno Dracula 1978 - 1979* (novella first published in *The Mammoth Book of Vampires*); *Who Dares Wins: Anno Dracula 1980*; *The Other Side of Midnight* (novella from the anthology *The Vampire Sextette*); *You are the Wind Beneath My Wings: Anno Dracula 1984*; and *Johnny Alucard*.

Basil Hallward from *The Picture of Dorian Gray* appears in the first novel, and again in *Judgement of Tears: Anno Dracula 1959* (a.k.a., *Dracula Cha Cha Cha*).

***THE RETURN OF DORIAN GRAY* #1-2 (comic book mini-series, Daedalus)** –This tale, which most likely occurs in an alternate reality to the WHU, takes place at the dawn of the Edwardian era circa 1902. It deals with a Dorian Gray who has somehow grown old to match his chronological age and discovers that the spilling of the blood of men eviler than himself on the painting gradually restores his physical youth. Hence, he sets out on a mission to find such individuals for their blood, which brings him into conflict with this reality's version of the original Invisible Man (most likely John Hawley Griffin) – who finds himself with the equivalent predicament: the effects of his invisibility process are gradually eroding, leaving him in a ghastly state as his bones and internal organs become discernable.

Daedalus is a company the Netherlands and this mini-series, despite its story taking place in London, England, is not yet available in English at this writing, and is difficult to find.

***DORIAN GRAY* (film)** –This 2009 production tells an alternate version of *The Picture of Dorian Gray*. The events are similar on this timeline but with notable differences. A major example of such deviations from the WHU series of events as depicted in the novel and other sources is the relationship Dorian starts with Lord Henry Wotton's young adult daughter Emily after he returns to London and visits his old friend and other acquaintances over twenty years after first acquiring his immortality.

MARTIN MYSTÉRE #63 – "OPERATION: DORIAN GRAY"
-- and #293 (comic book series, Sergio Bonelli Editore) – Martin
meets Dorian Gray in both stories; and in the second, he meets Oscar
Wilde as well.

This character, created by Alfredo Castelli, began as the same-named grandson of Allan Quatermain, growing up to follow the old man's footsteps as an adventurer and investigator of occult mysteries. From 1978-1981 his exploits appeared in the Italian weekly magazine *Supergulp*.

After that mag ran its course, the character was revived under a variety of subsequent names depending on what language the comic was printed in, including Doc Robinson, Martin Mystère, Martin Y, and finally in the U.S. under his Dark Horse incarnation as Martin Mystery. Other iterations of the character have since appeared in different mediums, including video games (see entry below) and a French animated series, with this dimensional version of Martin being a high school teenager accompanied by younger versions of his Neanderthal sidekick Java and lover Diana, the latter of which became his step-sister in this reality! The adolescent dimensional version of Martin crossed over with another French animated series, *Totally Spies*, in the latter show's episode "Totally Spies Much?"

I place the Martin Mystery crossovers with Dorian Gray in the alternate reality section of this timeline since there are so many versions of Martin under different names, and he tackles various alternative history versions of "real life" mysteries and folklore legends such as the "true" story behind the 1908 Tunguska, Siberia explosion; Santa Claus; the Loch Ness Monster; and the Golem of Prague. Hence, not only do these various versions of the character likely conflict with each other, but the "truth" behind the above mysteries and folklore likely contradict explanations provided in certain sources established to be in the WHU (though some mysteries, such as the nature of Santa Claus, can have multiple "explanations" depending on the interpretation). Also, except for the Dark Horse mini-series that was published in English, these other tales of Martin have yet to be translated into English at this writing, thus making it so this co-author (Christofer Nigro) was unable to read the stories to determine the potential WHU canonicity of any of these stories.

Since Martin has dealt with established WHU items such as the *Necronomicon,* and his earliest version (at least) establishes him as the grandson of WHU icon Allan Quatermain, he likely has a dimensional counterpart in the WHU, but which version it may be (if this version has already been seen) has yet to be determined. Hence, I will presume the versions of Dorian Gray and Oscar Wilde encountered by him in the above issue to be alternate reality versions, at least for now.

***MARTIN MYSTÉRE: "OPERATION: DORIAN GRAY" ("CRIME STORIES: FROM THE FILES OF MARTIN MYSTÉRE"* for its North American version); (video game, GMX Media for its European version; The Adventure Company for its North American version)**– This is a video game version of the story from *Martin Mystère Monthly* #63 and can be presumed to tell the same story in a different medium, and possibly from a somewhat different perspective.

I am indebted to the U.K.'s *International Hero* website for the info on Martin Mystery.

MARVEL ILLUSTRATED: THE PICTURE OF DORIAN GRAY #1-6 (**mini-series, Marvel Comics**) –Legendary comics author Roy Thomas and artist/inker Sebastian Fiumara brings us a faithful adaptation to Oscar Wilde's novel, leaving out nothing save for that which may be considered extraneous filler. Why does this author (Christofer Nigro) include it here in the Alternate Realities section, then? Only because it may imply there is (or was) a version of Dorian Gray in the "mainstream" Marvel Universe (MU, i.e., Earth-616 as officially designated by Marvel). If so, then this version of Dorian Gray has an origin story more or less identical to his counterparts in the WHU, the CU proper, the Ideaverse (see entry for

DEADPOOL KILLUSTRATED #1-4), and likely various other alternate timelines. However, no subsequent appearances in "mainstream" MU sources to date may suggest that in the MU, he truly met his end as described at the conclusion of both Wilde's novel and this adaptation. Alternatively, his demise in that grisly fashion may likewise have been mis-reported by the Oscar Wilde of the MU, and Gray of Earth-616 simply hasn't been subsequently depicted since. If the latter is the case, then his backstory in the MU is likely quite different in at least some ways than described in the main body of his WHU Timeline, and Gray's counterpart there has gone out of his way to keep a low profile.

CALEDONIA **(TV series)** --A comedy series about Dorian and other classic monsters and horror characters as modern day Scottish police detectives. Dorian is a selkie in this timeline, which is a being from Scottish folklore that shape-shifts between the forms of a human and a seal.

DEADPOOL: KILLUSTRATED **# 1 - 4 (mini-series, Marvel Comics)** --In an alternate reality, Deadpool realizes he is fictional, and decides to destroy everyone in every reality until he reaches his "creators" in the real world. This story involves Dorian Gray among many others. However, they all exist in alternate universes across various time periods. Likely none of these exist in the main WHU timeline but are all probably connected to the larger Wild Hunt Multiverse – or, more specifically, they exist in the Ideaverse (described in the Marvel Database website as Earth-TRN388), where "fictional" characters exist precisely as described in their written literature. Hence, this was not the Dorian Gray of the WHU, or even of the CU proper; nor of the "mainstream" MU (i.e., Earth-616), if such exists, which he may, and if so, was introduced in *Marvel Illustrated: The Picture of Dorian Gray* six-issue mini-series by Marvel.

DORIAN: AN IMITATION **(novel by Will Self)** –The events of *The Picture of Dorian Gray* takes place in June 1981. This is one of many timelines where a familiar series of events take place in a different period, with the nature of the events necessarily receiving a historical tweak as a result.

EL RETRATO DE DORIAN GRAY **(Mexican telenovela)** --In a world where the Spanish conquered the world, another version of the Dorian Gray story occurs within the context of this alternate timeline's historical differences.

THE FACE OF DORIAN GRAY **(music video by Robert Marlow)** –We get a glimpse at a timeline where a 1920s era version of *The Picture of Dorian Gray* took place.

GOTHICA **(TV series)** --This was a series in the same tone as *Once Upon a Time* that never aired, but a pilot was created. It tells modern reimagining's of Dracula, Edward Hyde, Frankenstein, and Dorian Gray.

PARTY MONSTERS **(film)** --This movie, in post-production at time of writing, is too goofy to place in the main timeline. Dorian, Dracula, Edward Hyde, Erik the Phantom, and Frankie the Monster are housemates living in modern day Los Angeles.

PENNY DREADFUL **(TV series)** --We tried. The brain trust of MONSTAAH, THE TVCU Crew, and Wild Hunt Press worked on trying to fit *Penny Dreadful* in the main timeline, because we loved it so much. It just didn't work, sadly.

***PORTRET DORIANA GREYA* (telefilm)** --Another TV movie from Russian TV. In this version, Russia has apparently taken over the world, and Dorian is gender swapped again.

***SHERLOCK HOLMES IN ORBIT* -- "THE MOUSE AND THE MASTER" (short story by Brian M. Thompson)** --A man attends a seance with several notable figures. Because of the characters involved, and references in the book to their individual chronologies that don't match up, this must take place in a divergent timeline. Malcolm "the Mouse" Chandler investigates seances attended by John Watson, Count Dracula, Alice Liddell (from Wonderland), Henry Jekyll, Dorian Gray, and Phileas Fogg.

***THE SINS OF DORIAN GRAY* (telefilm)** --TV movie that updates the Dorian Gray story to the 1980s and gender swapped.

***DORIAN GRAY* #0-4 (comic book mini-series, Bluewater Comics)** –Admittedly, neither author has read this currently hard-to-find 2012 comic book series yet, but its synopsis from the publisher as quoted from the Atomic Avenue website (source: http://atomicavenue.com/title/39790/Dorian-Gray) strongly suggests an alternate universe from the "mainstream" WHU: "The Grays are a cursed family. Dorian Gray IV, the last of his line, struggles with the realization that his personal demons are exactly that - a supernatural force that plagues not only the Grays but many of society's wealthiest families. Convinced his redemption is only secured through ridding the city of demons called the Morbi, Dorian launches an ongoing crusade for his soul."

The WHU canon is certainly not averse to the Gray lineage being cursed due to the actions of Dorian Gray (the first?), as the universe is filled with cursed families (e.g., the Karnsteins; the Collins; the Frankensteins; the Talbots; the Daninskys; the Vorhees). However, a succession of members of the family bearing the forename Dorian carrying on and dealing with the curse as described in this series has yet to be fully discerned in proper para-scholarly fashion, so it remains in the Alternate Realities section for now. The Morbi variant of demonic entity may well prove to have counterparts in the WHU even if this series must remain confined to an alternate timeline, though.

SLOUCHING TOWARD CAMULODUNUM AND OTHER STORIES -- "SLOUCHING TOWARD CAMULODUNUM" (novella by Micah S. Harris) --Becky Sharp teams with Sâr Dubnotal (the anonymously published hero of French pulp fiction from the early 20th century) to enact revenge upon Helen Vaughn (from Arthur Machen's novella *The Great God Pan*) and her demonic father, and to rescue Sharp's little girl.

Author Micah S. Harris has reported to me (Robert Wronski, Jr.) that this story, a continuation of *The Eldritch New Adventures of Becky Sharp*, is part of a divergent timeline to the WHU. With the new novella found in *Darker Shades* (*Portrait of a Lady*) he has sort of done a "soft reboot" of his further adventures of the character from William Makepeace Thackeray's 1848 novel *Vanity Fair*, to work his version of the character into a more compatible shared universe. The divergence starts with Chapter Two of *Eldritch New Adventures*. However, this story still has some great crossovers and revelations.

One might explain this divergent timeline as being some sort of "Television Crossover Universe" due to its inclusion of television and film adaptations over the original stories. This story is set in 1916, between the penultimate and final chapters of *The Eldritch New Adventures of Becky Sharp*. Villiers and Clark are also from *The Great God Pan*, who have been hunting Helen since the events of that novella. A band of artists have gathered to avenge the death of Aubrey Beardsley. They also mistakenly attribute Helen Vaughn for the deaths of Dorian Gray and Basil Hallward. The artists are Francis Aytown (a painter cut from the final version of *Dracula*); Randolph

511

(from the film version of *Magnificent Obsession*, directed by Douglas Sirk); Charles Delaware Tate (from *Dark Shadows*; see the main timeline above); and Richard Pickman (from Lovecraft's short story "Pickman's Model").

The Richard Pickman of this timeline is inspired by the version from the episode of the horror TV anthology series *Night Gallery*. In fact, there's a subtle tongue in cheek reference to the show. In this timeline, "Pickman's Model" was set in the 19th century rather than the 1920s. Micah has portrayed Pickman as a ghoul who is unaware of his "condition." He is banished to Leng, where he will become a heroic ghoul, explaining Lovecraft's use of Pickman in two separate stories where he was depicted very differently. Pickman's pal Pierre de Pris is a descendant of Rodin, who painted "The Grim Reaper" from the *Thriller* TV series.

Amongst the Rogues' Gallery is Lord Henry Wotton, the corrupt influence in Dorian Gray's existence. The kidnapped child will grow up to be Ann Darrow (of *King Kong*). The child's father is not the demon as some think but is actually... nope! Go read *Eldritch New Adventures*.

The midget Jacques and his dog are from "Spurs," the short story by Tod Robbins that inspired Tod Browning's notorious pre-Hayes Code film *Freaks*.

Monsieur N, who is hypnotized by Sâr Dubnotal, is an ancestor of the titular character from Stephen King's novella *N.* (to be found in his 2008 collection *Just After Sunset*), implying that the hypnotic suggestion carried down over generations.

THE SCARLET SOUL: STORIES FOR DORIAN GRAY
(anthology featuring short stories from various, edited by Mark
Valentine) --This interesting 2017 release from Britain's Swan
Creek Press features ten short stories (the authors are Reggie Oliver,
Caitriona Lally, Lynda E Rucker, John Howard, DP Watt, Rosanne
Rabinowitz, Avalon Brantley, Timothy J Jarvis, John Gale, and
Derek John) centering on themes inspired by *The Picture of Dorian
Gray,* specifically how a cursed portrait can affect the lives of
various individuals in a variety of time periods and milieus.

None of them feature Dorian himself, but some could possibly
represent parallel universe analogues of the basic series of events
recorded by Oscar Wilde, or even allude to different enchanted
paintings that may potentially connect the tales and the individuals

within – indirectly, of course -- to Dorian's saga and the mystical forces behind his notorious canvas. Each tale would have to be taken on a case-by-case basis to determine possible canonicity in the WHU or CU proper, so for now, the entire tome will be placed in the Alternate Reality section. The anthology certainly deserved at least honorable mention in this timeline.

THE WOLF OF DORIAN GRAY: A WEREWOLF SPAWNED BY THE EVIL OF MAN (novel by **Brian S. Ference**) --On this alternate timeline, Dorian Gray's painting not only confers immorality upon him, but it also brings him the curse of lycanthropy as the result of the artist mixing wolf blood into the enchanted canvas's paint. More interestingly, the characters of Lord Harry Wotton and Basil Hallward are gender-swapped! This thought-provoking 2016 alternative take on the Dorian Gray saga (seemingly connecting him even more to Quentin Collins) was followed up with two other novels by Ference in 2017 -- *Purgatory of the Werewolf* and *Lupari: Werewolf Hunter* -- to form a complete trilogy.

Please note there will doubtless be Dorian Gray appearances, both potentially WHU canonical and from alternate realities (not including comic book adaptations of the novel), that slipped by both authors and the various other contributors from Wild Hunt Press and the Television Crossover Universe Crew to this timeline. There are likely too many for even this motely legion of researchers to catch in their entirety this time around. Indeed, this work had to be amended a few times while in production to accommodate the addition of previously overlooked Dorian Gray appearances. Nevertheless, we sought to include as many as we could find -- which, as you can see, was quite a few! Future updates of this anthology will add sources we may have overlooked for this edition, as well as any post-2017 appearances of Dorian Gray that will eventually appear across various mediums to thrill and chill the venerable character's many fans.

FINI

Thank you for reading! Please do leave reviews on Amazon, BookBub, your personal blog, and wherever else you are so inclined! More reviews, especially of the positive sort, might very well result in more original Dorian Gray prose!

ABOUT THE AUTHORS

MICAH S. HARRIS is the winner of the 2016 Pulp Ark Award in the category of best novel for *Ravenwood, the Stepson of Mystery: Return of the Dugpa*. He is also the author -- with artist Michael Gaydos (Marvel's *Jessica Jones*) – of the graphic novel *Heaven's War*, a historical fantasy pitting the Oxford Inklings against Aleister Crowley.

His most recent publications are the mystery novel *Murder in the Miracle Room* and an in-depth article, published in *Little Shoppe of Horrors*, on the lost sword and sorcery movie of the early 1980s, *Thongor in the Valley of Demons*. His other fiction includes *The Eldritch New Adventures of Becky Sharp*, *The Frequency of Fear*, *Jim Anthony: The Hunters* (with Joshua Reynolds) from Airship 27 Productions, the Image Comic book *Lorna, Relic Wrangler* (with artist Loston Wallace) and his short fiction collection from Minor Profit Press, *Slouching Toward Camulodunum*.

In his day job, he teaches literature, film, and composition at Pitt Community College in Winterville, N.C. Currently, he is working on a fantasy novel, the projected first from the *Memoirs of the 9th Marquis of Cawthorne*, which are a mélange of Hans Christian Anderson, Terrance Fisher's Hammer movies, *The Prisoner of Zenda*, and *The Count of Monte Cristo* – with a dash of *King Solomon's Mines* thrown in.

He is also a regular columnist for 18th Wall Publications official website, where his *Just Like In the Movies* examines the history of screenwriting.

You can find out more about Micah's writing at his Amazon Author's page at

https://www.amazon.com/Micah-S.-Harris/e/B01E2UY78O/ref=sr_tc_2_0?qid=1525134958&sr=1-2-ent

KEVIN THOMAS HEIM was born in Louisville, Kentucky in 1969, and pretty much went downhill from there. He is survived by a son, Jonah Michael Heim, and a daughter, Alexandria Nicole Heim. He is well known in online genre circles as an authority on horror, sci-fi, and pulp adventure fictions. He also happens to have a few published short stories to his name. Kevin is a long-time contributor to the popular Television Crossover Universe blog, where his contributions include a continually updated timeline for his monster-hunting, time-displaced character "Crazy" Ivan Schablotski ("Some People Call Me Crazy: Ivan Schablotski in the TVCU"), one of the most popular timelines ever written for the blog), who is apt to turn up just about anywhere under his various aliases – from Kevin's own short story in *Dorian Gray: Darker Shades* by Wild Hunt Press, to the Kaiju novel *Megadrak: Beast of the Apocalypse* by Severed Press.

PETER RAWLIK is the author of more than fifty short stories, the novels *Reanimators*, *The Weird Company*, and *Reanimatrix*; and *The Peaslee Papers*, a chronicle of the distant past, the present, and the far future. As editor he has produced *The Legacy of the Reanimator* and the forthcoming *Chromatic Court*. His short story "Revenge of the Reanimator" was nominated for a New Pulp Award. He is a regular member of the Lovecraft Ezine Podcast which in 2016 won the This is Horror Non-Fiction Podcast of the Year award. He is a frequent contributor to *The New York Review of Science Fiction*.

DAVID MACDOWELL BLUE, a Sagittarius born in the Year of the Boar (make of that what you will), hails from San Francisco but grew up in the Deep South. After going to school in New York City, and eventually ending up in Los Angeles of all places, he reconnected with live theatre, becoming a fairly well-known critic as well as a published playwright. *Carmilla*, based on the 1872 novella, has seen six productions to date. He now has a surreal (almost) haunted house play looking for a director and is working on a play he describes as "The Little Mermaid meets A Shadow Over Innsmouth." He acts as dramaturg for the Actaeon Players and will soon be directing an original play (not his own) about the "chance" meeting between the direct descendants of the Marquis de Sade and Leopold von Sacher-Masoch.

Projects in the works include adaptations of Bram Stoker's *Dracula* and Arthur Machen's *The Great God Pan*. His writing idols include William Shakespeare, Anton Chekhov, Dennis Potter, Lorraine Hainsberry, Edward Albee, and Tennessee Williams. He is a widower, a former fencer, a sometimes belly dancer (he prefers Middle Eastern Dancer, because that really is more accurate—he specializes in cape and sword), and an original fan of such things as *Star Trek*, *Dark Shadows*, and *Star Wars*.

Blue believes very strongly any society which actively discourages compassion and/or loyalty is doomed to become hell on earth. He dislikes the passive voice very much, adores language, hopes to once again have a cat in his life, misses his beloved Colleen every single day, generally wears greys and blues, identifies with the Eastern Orthodox Church, and designed his personal website himself: www.davidmacdowellblue.cf. He believes that is quite enough to say about himself, not least because given a chance he will tell his entire life story in a series of mostly accurate anecdotes for hours and hours and hours.

Those wishing to conduct legit business with David can contact him at zahir13@gmail.com.

ROBERT E. WRONSKI, JR. is a life-long fan of everything the TV medium has ever had to offer, as well as every corner of fantastic fiction and the fan favorite concept of crossovers, all of which he integrated into the popular *Television Crossover Universe* blog many years ago. It's chock full of his writing and that of the contributors he recruited over the years. His production outfit, Super Entertainment, brought us a memorable run of the popular Television Crossover Universe and Random Fandom podcasts, and he has taken his knowledge into book format with his independently published *Television Crossover Universe: Worlds and Mythology Volume I* and *The Horror Universe Encyclopedia* published by 18thWall Productions.

T. CASEY BRENNAN is a comic book author perhaps best known for his work at Warren Publishing during the late 1960s and 1970s, having contributed well-received scripts for Warren's fondly remembered horror anthologies *Creepy*, *Eerie*, and *Vampirella*. During that time, he had a stint as the writer on Warren's popular Vampirella strip, where he provided an important tweaking of Dracula's origin and character; as well as having scripts published by DC's popular horror anthology *House of Mystery* and Archie's own contribution to that genre *Red Circle Sorcery*. He is also known for his activism, including his successful anti-smoking campaign for comic books in the 1980s. His experiences with the infamous MKULTRA program of the CIA has been well documented among numerous media interviews and references. When not occupied with writing and interviews, he performs as part of the band Frankenhead. T. Casey's most recent published work to date was for *The Creeps* comic magazine, which is an homage to the classic Warren mags.

CHRISTOFER NIGRO is yet another life-long fan of fantastic fiction in all its various sub-genres, and across all mediums. This includes horror, sci-fi, pulp adventure, and crime noir, with a particular fondness for monsters, slasher characters, Kaiju, super-heroes, and pulp heroes. He has done his best to tackle each of these genres and sub-genres as a published author, most recently as the founder and head honcho of the small indie digital publishing label Wild Hunt Press. His short stories have appeared in anthologies published by Black Coat Press, Sirens Call Publications, Pro Se

Press, Grinning Skull Press, Pulp Empire/Metahuman Press, Horrified Press, and Local Hero Press; and his first novels in the Kaiju genre have been published by Severed Press. Chris has also contributed short stories and forwards to independently published anthologies and is now on the path towards self-publication courtesy of Wild Hunt.